GUATEMALA, 1976

A NOVEL BY

FRANK ORR

Copyright © 2018 Frank H. Orr, III.

All rights reserved. No part(s) of this book may be reproduced, distributed or transmitted in any form, or by any means, or stored in a database or retrieval systems without prior expressed written permission of the author of this book.

ISBN: 978-1-5356-1392-7

Published by Woodmont Baptist Church
Nashville, Tennessee
www.woodmontbaptist.com

Cover design by Ellen Parker-Bibb
ellenparkerbibb.com

No characters in this book are intended to resemble any person, living or dead; they are the products of the author's imagination. Any suspected resemblances are purely coincidental.

For Clarke, Sarah, Shirley, and Joe,
and their missionary colleagues,
who introduced us to the wonderful
Land of Eternal Spring.
And for Woodmont Baptist Church,
Which sent us there.

Guatemala, 1976

Chapter One

GUATEMALA

TUESDAY, JANUARY 20, 1976. The man in the narrow cot groaned, not quite audibly, but loud enough to convince himself that he was at least partially awake. . . and fully alive. Utterly confused, though, he didn't know where he was or what day it was or much of anything else. He couldn't see; he turned his head slightly and yelped – or thought he did, not knowing if it was reality or imagination – *that hurt!* In fact, he hurt all over. He tried to move his hands and found them restrained. He didn't, or couldn't, open his eyes; his mind was swamped by thoughts, images, and memories all wrapped up together in a swirl of semi-consciousness. He thought of Melanie – who was she? – and beautiful little Connie, dark red-tinged black hair, curly like her grandmother, then *his* mother, the beautiful half-Hispanic, half-Anglo Consuela; of his father Tom, the ranch, and . . . his mind cleared for a moment and the scene, now vivid, the last thing he remembered. He caught his breath and gasped! . . . Then it was gone; he sunk again into whatever dreams his tortured mind held for him.

Friday, January 16, 1976. The long shadows of late afternoon skewed across the dirt and melon-sized rocks of the mountain road as it descended toward the lake. At 7,000 feet above sea level nestled among the craggy cones of the double Sierra Madre range of volcanoes forming the backbone of Central America; it was cool in late January, more so in the higher elevations. The Tzutujil men, in their gray and white striped knee pants and sun-bleached dirty white blouses were turning toward home in sandals and floppy straw hats, with hoes on shoulders, after spending another long day cultivating the corn fields, some planted on slopes too steep for even sure-footed donkeys to master. Their subsistence level was too low to support both man and beast anyhow, so few, if any, used animal labor, even on flat land. It was Friday, January 16, 1976, the fifth day of the field work for the team from Global Geologics LLC.

The road was flanked by pine trees, becoming denser as the tan Land Rover belonging to Global Geologics approached the lake. When the road reached left bank of Lake Atitlan, the largest and most beautiful of many volcanic lakes in Guatemala, it bent to the right, following the shoreline, the beguiling azure surface intermittently obscured by trees and scrub from any distance of more than fifty yards.

Dennis Reade was in the front passenger seat, daydreaming; he was the team leader, but that wasn't too important; it was a team. Global Geologics of Houston had a contract with the Guatemala government, partially funded by US Aid, to investigate the feasibility of providing electricity through hydro-electric dams in the highlands. Dennis was the leader of the two-man team sent down from Houston. In the noisy, rigidly-sprung vehicle – bone-shaking and constant – talk was difficult and, after four days in the field, all members of the team had drifted off into their own reveries. Bruce Kalchik, the only other American, was driving; in the back were the two young Guatemalans, Pedro and Jesus, assigned as interpreters, and – to be crude – *gofers*.

As usual when he had nothing bearing on his mind, Dennis ruminated on his meaningless and misspent life – on his depressing self-image – and chastised himself for it, for the mess he had made of it back in the States; and how he hoped this job was a way to correct things, to start over and become the kind of man he – until recent years – thought himself to be. He knew he should try to relax and keep from sinking further into self-pity, but there was so much pushing him down.

The road descended at an increasingly steep slope toward the lake bank; at a low point the road swerved dangerously close to the shore, just a few feet above the water line, then it reversed to the left and began a rapid upward climb. As they approached, he was distracted from his self-loathing by the unfolding beauty of the lake and the mountains. He had only seen it from the air and had looked forward to being there; it was, simply put, breath-taking.

Then something else took his breath away; everything exploded; everything was shattered!

Chapter Two

GUATEMALA

TUESDAY. IN HIS BLIND CONFINEMENT, lying inert in his cot, he gradually began to recall things in his, disjointed and largely sad journey to this place, and this predicament. It came in jumbled order. He tried to concentrate on the most recent event . . . but he reached a blank after the explosion by the lake.

Until he woke, he'd been dreaming, nothing that would help him figure out, well, *things*. He was safe he felt, but confused, in a maze of unknown nature. He had dreamed of being chased by something menacing, he knew not what it was, but knew it was after him and meant him harm. The images swirled and shifted continually and sometimes he knew where he was and at other times he didn't. Sometimes there were walls closing in on him and sometimes spaces appeared to be endless; it was all bad, all unsettling, producing creeping anxiety. In his dreams he was frantically seeking a safe haven but found none; open doors loomed ahead only to be closed when he got close enough to reach for the knob. He wanted to urinate but could find no place. He would feel a surge of pain, and then a sweet sense of peace would sweep over him.

Swimming into consciousness again, he began to wonder about his surroundings. What kind of place was this, why he was blindfolded, and why was he tied down? He decided to try to listen for any clues, and to smell anything that would help; he was conscious of these senses. He

Guatemala, 1976

was very quiet for a time, holding is breath. At least I can do that, he thought. I can control my breathing; what else can I control?

It seemed he could not do that very long; when his breath ran out he groaned. A soft female voice replied, in Middle American Spanish, "Senor, please be at ease; you are safe; we are taking care of you."

Startled, it took him over a minute to digest this. Finally he said in raspy Spanish, "Who are you; where am I? . . . What's happened to me?" Then a little surprised that he understood Spanish and could speak it, he repeated the questions.

"You have been badly injured, and Senora Doctore Harris has fixed you up very good," the voice said.

"Where is this?"

"This is our little clinic here in the north part of Guatemala," a different, more mature but still female voice said. "I am Laura Harris, the co-director here."

"You a doctor . . . Senora?"

"Yes I am. My husband Rodney, also an MD, and I run this outpost, and we do our best to serve the needs of these people. We are rather primitive in medical technology, but it's usually enough for the things our friends here need."

She had a nice American-sounding voice. He asked, "You American?"

"Si. We are missionaries from the States."

"I can speak English." Then he proved it, asking, "What's happened to me; why am I tied down? Why are my eyes covered?"

Replying in English she said, "You were found early Sunday morning just outside our gate, badly injured and with a high fever. We had no clue about how you got that way or how you got here. You had no identification on you, only your shirt, pants, and underwear. Not even a belt or shoes. We had no choice but to do what we could for you. Your fever seems to be gone, but you have a pretty ghastly cut on your face. Fortunately before you got here, someone bandaged it with what looks like sterile, modern dressings, and apparently treated it with something antiseptic. The cut missed your eye, also fortunately; we sewed that up, as well as a small tear on your upper left arm. That is why your eyes are covered. The rest of the cuts we just swabbed with antiseptic and dressed them. I think they will all heal well, but I can't imagine what kind of scar you will have on your face."

"Where is this scar, where on my face I mean?"

"It runs from near the left corner of your mouth up to the left end of your eyebrow."

"What else? You haven't said why my arms are tied down."

Laura signed and put a hand on his. He was startled and calmed at the same time. "You have a couple of broken ribs and many small cuts and contusions – bruises. We bound up your chest to help the ribs heal. You may have a concussion but if so it doesn't seem serious. You'll probably have some pretty severe headaches but not any lingering damage, or so we hope. We don't have an x-ray so we can't check other possibilities, but we hope what we have to work with is good enough. We checked your skull and could feel no fractures. You will probably have an impressive scar on your face, but we think we were able to stitch it up, well, nicely." She paused and sighed, then said with a light chuckle, "You may be able to cultivate the myth that you got the scar dueling!" she joked. "The reason," she went on, "we tied your hands is so you wouldn't bump or try to pull the IV out in your unconsciousness."

"I have an IV?"

"Yes. We have had you on antibiotics and something for pain. That will wear off soon and you won't feel very good for a while, but we can give you more when you need it." She was silent for a while. "I think we can untie his hands now, Maria." She paused while his hands were freed and then said, "Please try not to scratch your stitches. Also, you have a catheter in case you haven't noticed." She gave him time to absorb all this; she said, "We'll let you rest now. When you are ready we can talk again. Tomorrow we can change your dressings and uncover your eyes so you can see what we look like, and what *you* look like. Sleep well."

Chapter Three

Guatemala

The two women left, leaving him to wonder about almost everything since he wasn't able to see anything. They must have given him something to put him to sleep, he thought, because he felt drowsiness enveloping him, a fog of peace.

Though he wasn't aware of it, he slept in deep, dreamless abandon for over an hour. Then the dreams returned. Connie, his beautiful two-year-old was calling frantically, sometimes pleading, sometimes as if in stark, hopeless terror, although he couldn't see her. He struggled to pull his feet out of what clung to him like tar. 'Daddy! Daddy!' she mouthed, and he could see only fog at first and then trees and then a brilliant eruption of light, only eye-searing light, in rapid bursts, but no sound. He groaned and found himself fully awake, sweating.

He was alone. His thoughts veered from that dream to his unknown and unnerving situation, and to his life before all this; where he came from and how he came to be here. The flickers of the parade of memories came in disjointed order, some in reverse, some bouncing around, pinballs of scenes, and he slept again.

When he woke it was dawn the next day. Maria had been checking on him for some minutes and called Laura, telling her that their patient was awake. Laura came in immediately. She said, "Time to get you up and ready to meet the world!"

"You sure? I don't feel like doing much."

"Nonsense; any patient, especially one as robust as you, needs to get up and move around soon after surgery. You aren't really on death's doorstep, you know."

He groaned but allowed Maria to help him to his feet. He stood for a couple of minutes but then sat down again..

Laura had left but Maria said, "I heard you wake up and make a sign. Are you hungry? I have some soup for you. I can help you, feed you with a spoon. Will that be alright?"

He slipped unconsciously back into Spanish, "*Gracias*. I am hungry . . . I think."

He began to shift himself back and up but she said, "No! Wait, let me do that for you, Senor." She pulled out his pillow and helped him shift upright and draped a towel over him. That settled, she said, "Open please, Senor. I have the spoon right here."

It was awkward but soon they found their rhythm, and he felt his strength returning. He was hungrier than he'd imagined and took it as quickly as he could, almost choking once or twice until he decided to let her be in charge. "Do you want any more, Senor?" she asked when it was gone. He grunted and nodded, and she brought a refill; he got that down in quick time. She wiped his mouth and chin a final time and sat back. She said, "Do you want to lie back down?"

He said, "No. I think I want to sit up a while. I think I can get back down if I want to by myself, gracias Senorita," assuming by her voice and manner she was unmarried. He was right, not that it mattered.

When she was gone he let his mind spin back to almost the beginning, his growing up on a cattle ranch in extreme south Texas. Thoughts of the ranch led his rattled mind to settle again on Melanie, and then back into a dreamless sleep.

Maria busied herself with checking his vitals; when satisfied that he was doing well, she left. Feeling stronger and filled he drifted off again. Then he woke and Maria returned with a tray with another bowl

Guatemala, 1976

of steaming broth, and a cup of hot tea. It was all very welcome; his appetite surprised him. She watched him eat, spooning it himself, and said, "We have more if you want it." He nodded and realized his head did not hurt, not as much anyhow. She left and came back in less than a minute with the re-filled bowl. He eagerly lit into it, relishing it and how good he was feeling, even with the bandages limiting the use of his mouth. He wanted to get on with the removal of the bandages and see what he looked like. A facial make-over might be just what he needed to create a new identity he had fantasized about.

Dr. Harris came in and slipped on surgical gloves; Maria did the same, and pushed Dennis back into the pillows but not flat. Laura said, "Be very still, this shouldn't hurt and you shouldn't be distressed. Be still and let us do the work." She tilted his head back to an almost painful angle; he grunted but didn't resist. She went to work cutting and peeling back the tape and fabric of the bandages. Maria held his head so he wouldn't move. He wondered what all this looked like from above, from outside his body. In the time alone he'd absentmindedly brushed the hair not bound by the dressings with his hands and realized it, the hair, was a mess, tangled and gritty. He couldn't imagine how he looked; he was not especially vain, but he'd always been aware that he was fairly nice-looking, not bad in fact, but now things would be different, *how* different was the great unknown.

Harris tugged at the tape, and he had to pull back; it came off grudgingly, and it did hurt, but that was only briefly. She said, "That's not all of the tape; we've got more to do." Then she tugged at a different place, and he resisted the same way. There were three more brief episodes of peeling back long-stuck tape, and then that part was over. Laura said, "Now the unveiling," and she slowly and gently pulled the bandages away. She handed the fabric to Maria who tossed it into a pail. She said, "We're not through. Be still. I have to clean you up." She pressed a wet cloth to his face and said, "Don't worry; it's only peroxide, it shouldn't hurt at all. If it doesn't bubble much it means that there is no infection; that's what we want to see."

He waited with what he thought was commendable patience. Harris worked over the stitches with the cloth and signed. She said, "well looks like we are home free." Then she caught herself, realizing she had used English and an American idiom, and said in Spanish, "That means it all looks good, Senor." Maria was busy cleaning the rest of his head and combing his hair. Harris said, "In a few days we'll take out your stitches." He blinked and concentrated on adjusting his eyes to sight again, after almost a week without. " It looks like you'll heal up nicely. In the meantime you can see yourself if you want, and talk and eat solid food. Alright?"

Maria held out a mirror; at first he was hesitant but then took it and faced it. He was not as surprised as he'd imagined, but the lip and the scar running up to near his eye did look, well, rather vicious. Maybe when it healed it would give him a more distinguished look; that caused him to chuckle, and the women smiled back at him. He then turned to the women; both were attractive in their own ethnic ways.

There were a dozen or so of lesser wounds on his fact, three held together by butterfly-shaped strips of adhesive tape. "I know you have a lot of questions but for now just rest. I'll be back in a couple of hours." Then he was left alone again and dozed intermittantly.

Dr. Harris came back. She looked him over and seemed pleased with her patient. She said, "Well, Senor, we are going to see how fit you are. We are going to remove the drip and the catheter and check the stitches in your face once more. She nodded to Maria; both women pulled on surgical gloves again. Maria pulled Dennis's left arm out from the covers and began to untape the IV needle in his arm. That done, she looked back at Dr. Harris who said, "Maria, lay him back flat." Addressing him, she said, " Mr. no-name, this will be a little uncomfortable but it'll be quick, all right?" Maria rearranged his pillows and laid him back. Harris lifted the covers from his feet and legs. She said, "All right, grit your

Guatemala, 1976

teeth, we'll be as quick as we can." Before he could react she jerked the tube out of him, and he gasped but felt no lingering pain. "There now," she said, "that wasn't too bad was it? How do you feel?" Not waiting for an answer, she said, "I'll be back in a little while to take care of your face. Until then just rest, you'll need it." Maria left with the tube and the sloshing plastic bag tinged yellow.

He felt some degree of relief although he couldn't have said exactly how or why. He was alone again; he didn't know for how long, but he began to review again his survival from . . . from what, he could only guess.

Maria returned and said, "Would you like to see yourself again, Senor?" handing him the mirror.

He took the mirror and slowly lifted it. His appearance made him almost gasp but he checked himself without saying anything. He took his time and stared at the image, and assessed the damage and guessed at what changes this was going to make to him. At a minimum, he thought, it might make his transition into a different person easier – an idea that had come to him as a way to put away the self he had come to detest. He lay back down and handed the mirror back to Maria, and sighed.

"Well, what's the verdict?" Laura said.

"Better than I expected. I guess I'll have to just wait it out," Dennis said. He remembered to avoid telling them his name. He had to get used to thinking of himself with a new name and identity.

Laura said, "We'll take the stitches out in a day or so."

Left alone again his mind settled on remembering Melanie. Melanie June Williams, daughter of an oil man of substantial success in Houston, though not quite in the top tier. They met in collage, Texas A&M, he on an Army scholarship, she on the traditional *parental* fellowship. They met at a mixer her sorority organized with the junior class of the vaunted A&M ROTC Corps. She was a year behind him, a sophomore and in full swing in the social life expected of one of her station; her academic energy was much overshadowed by her extracurricular activities. There was an instant spark between Melanie Williams and Cadet Master Sergeant Dennis Reade.

It was the spring of 1971. The rest of that school year they saw each other every time they could manage. Dennis was more serious about school and the military than she was about anything not Dennis, but he made all the time he could to be with her. By the end of the term, they were both convinced they had found *The One*.

His memory skimmed over that entrancing time, reliving one of the most intense and thrilling periods in his then short life. Then he drifted off to sleep again.

He didn't dream this time, but woke feeling stronger and refreshed. He had no idea of the day or time of day or how long he'd slept. Laura Harris had said they found him on a Sunday morning but not how long he'd been there, nor even which Sunday it was. He was beginning to feel uncomfortable in the cot and in some pain; he remembered that Doctor Harris warned him about scratching his wounds. He wanted to call out for something for the pain but decided he had some serious thinking to do while he was lucid. He wanted to think through things before any medicine clouded his mind. Not quite fully reviewing his life in Texas, he knew he had really messed it up, and he had come here to get away and start over. Did he want to pick up where he had been?

He let his mind spin back to almost the beginning, his growing up on a cattle ranch in extreme south Texas. Thoughts of the ranch led his rattled mind to settle again on Melanie.

Chapter Four

TEXAS

MELANIE. AS SUMMER APPROACHED IN 1971 the thought of separation tormented him. He hesitated to bring it up; he was on a shoestring despite his Army scholarship, his father had stretched to send him to school, and he knew he had to help on the ranch as he had every summer. His mother died when he was thirteen.

Melanie knew his circumstances and seemed to understand. On one of their last evenings before the end of the spring term, she said, "Dennis, why don't you come and see me in Houston this summer, stay a week or so. I want you to meet Mama and Daddy, and of course, I want them to meet you."

"Let me see what I can arrange, Melanie; I'll do it if I can," he said. "I have summer camp with the ROTC of course, but there should be a break somewhere. I really want to do that." He did go, only for four days, four glorious and enlightening days they were! "Daddy," Herbert Williams was a traditional oil man and had made a roaring success at it. Her mother, Priscilla, was a social star, and Melanie was expected to follow her mother's pattern in her adult life. Herbert and Priscilla welcomed him warmly if a little warily; he felt no negative vibes, but was on edge the entire time. Melanie expected that her future social life would mimic her mother's as well and made no bones about it. Her college focus, if not her major, was intentionally FAH, *Finding a*

Husband, and to her mind she had. Dennis didn't know how he felt about that but was so dazzled by Melanie's beauty and love, and by her family's wealth that he didn't try to analyze it.

He returned to the ranch for the rest of the summer, except for the weeks-lomg Army camp mandated by ROTC. In the fall their alliance crystallized; both knew what was ahead, marriage and a life together, with at least part of it in the military.

The ranch, *The Reade Ranch*. It wasn't much of a ranch by Texas standards by the time Dennis was a teenager and old enough to see what was what. His father, Tom, a fifth generation descendent of Scots-Irish cattle-raising settlers in the south Texas flatlands, had inherited only a fraction of the original fifteen thousand acres the family had begun with, south and west of Kingsville and the of iconic and larger King Ranch. Succeeding generations of Reades had squandered their assets in overextended debts, spurious oil schemes, ill-advised experiments in cattle breeding, poor management, and general bad behavior. Dennis' grandfather, Amos, had been an alcoholic and left Tom a bare five hundred acres on which to eke out a living. It was doable, but barely. Tom was a good man and hard worker and an adequate manager, but it was always a struggle. Dennis loved the ranch and his life there. He couldn't imagine any other.

There were then only Tom and Dennis. Tom made sure his son learned all about the running of the ranch as well as the lore of the land, care of livestock and garden crops they grew to augment their diet, plus hunting and fishing. Tom hoped Dennis would come back to the ranch after graduation and his Army obligation was over, and take over managing it. He never said as much to Dennis, but both understood that was the plan. Dennis was unsure of that but never challenged his father. He couldn't stand the idea of disappointing Tom and was torn, though he chose to defer any decision until some later time.

A different future had been growing in Dennis' mind. He wanted to see some of the world before he returned to south Texas and dug in as

Guatemala, 1976

a rancher. At A&M, he was attracted to a certain professor of geology, Dr. Patton, and declared geology as his major at the end of his freshman year. In geology, he found a pursuit worthy of his passion, and passion was how he saw it. His grades were near the very top in his geology and in military classes, and acceptable in everything else.

He and Melanie married immediately after graduation, in late May, 1972; full military honors, crossed swords as they left the Chapel and all that. Tom, his aunt, Angelica, and Melanie's parents attended; the only other guests seemed to be Melanie's relatives and fellow Cadets. He had to report for duty as a Second Lieutenant in three weeks. After a brief honeymoon in New Orleans – Melanie understood he could not afford much else – the couple moved into an off-campus married student apartment vacant for the summer, on a short week-to-week lease. Melanie bubbled and glowed as they moved their meager things and arranged it all just so; they were an old married couple, all of one week. Then . . . then his axis was knocked off its center.

Chapter Five

Guatemala

In his cot Dennis slept off and on. He had been given another offering of soup with a little meat, bread and native tea. Maria came in as daylight grew dimmer and checked him over; she checked his pulse and took his temperature. She said goodnight and left, leaving only a kerosene lantern nearby, turned low.

He came fully awake sometime in the night; he had no idea of the time and groped for his wrist. No watch; that somehow didn't surprise him but it did spur him to explore the rest of his condition. Feeling around and peering as best as he could, he discovered that he was dressed only in what passed for a typical hospital gown, though of fabric rougher that he would have expected at home. He'd never been sick enough to go into a hospital, and chuckled to himself, wondering what had happened to his clothes and papers and other things.

He doubted that he was going back to sleep, and resumed his recollections. On the road where his last memories lay, he had been looking forward to seeing Lake Atitlan from the ground. He saw it from the air in the team's flying tour before going into the field, and its stunning beauty overwhelmed him, left him eager for more.

Their host on the plane, Colonel Mendoza, was effusive in his pride in his country, and in his own prestige. The Colonel had tried to present himself as a benevolent guide and protector to the Americans, but was

Guatemala, 1976

unable to establish a real bond; just "too full of himself," his team partner Bruce remarked. He wondered what had happened to Bruce and their Guatemalan colleagues. If he was so badly injured, what about them? Where are they? Are they even alive?

With warm memories of Melanie swirling in his head, and despite his wakefulness, Dennis did drift off to sleep again after a while, but not before flashing back to the enigma of the explosive, blinding lights; what had happened? He had to accept that he might never know, or know all of it. A whisper in his exhausted mind reinforced the idea: why not get rid of his identity and all the things that he had allowed to go wrong? Why not reinvent himself, give himself a totally new persona, name, and background? Why not? The people here seemed not to know who he was; did anybody else know? Was he assumed to be dead? With that idea buzzing around in his head, drowsiness overtook him, and he slipped into a deep abyss of sleep.

Again he dreamed. Flashes of hot light, tumbling, and yet no noise, just confusing images spinning around him and spinning him around. He knew in his dream he had to do something, get out of something bad, but he couldn't figure out what. He twisted around in the narrow bed and groaned. Maria went over and looked but did nothing else. Doctor Harris had told her to expect this and not wake him, just watch him. He was sweating, but that was alright; he would come out of it.

Gradually he did come out of it and was calm, breathing evenly, no sweating, no temperature. Maria watched for several minutes and then left him; he slept quietly for another half hour and then woke, more clear-headed than before. No one was there; he sensed he was alone with his memories. It was still dark. He resumed crafting a fictional new life.

He would have to pick a name. He chewed on this a while. His name, he decided, would be Alonso Mendoza, after the flying tour host, Colonel Mendoza; it was a fairly common Latino name. He would be half-Mexican with an American mother and a stern and distant father in some unnamed, perhaps shady business in the northern Mexican city of Matamoros on the Rio Grande, the border with Texas. The fewer questions the better. He had been there and would, he thought, be able to bluff his way through any questions that might come up. In a way it would be the reverse of his true story. There would be a lot of details to be filled in, but this was a start. He sighed; he had taken a step in his mind but was unsure if he could go through with it. He had already been told he had no identification on him, so what could go wrong? Who knew who he really was and where that other man was? Nowhere, he convinced himself, though he didn't know the reality of what he had only guessed.

No one actually knew where he was, only that he was separated from Bruce, Pedro, and Jesus and the Land Rover they were traveling in, last contact somewhere on the road near Lake Atitlan. Where were the other guys, he wondered.

# # #

Again his mind drifted back to Texas and his life there. Melanie had visited the ranch with him over the Thanksgiving break the fall of 1971 after he visited her parent's home that summer. He had planned it thoroughly, schooling his dad over several phone calls to be nice as he could, and Tom could be nice when he wanted. The house – stuccoed adobe with high ceilings, tile floors, lots of arches, fireplaces in major rooms, and Spanish tile roofs; cool in summer, warm in winter – was clean and flowers sat on every available surface. Even Dennis was impressed. Tom was as gracious as any well-bred gentleman would be welcoming a pretty girl. He did have his manners and his graces, even if life had been hard. He dressed up for the occasion, meaning clean khaki slacks and a white shirt, no tie, though. He even wore black dress shoes, not his usual roach-killer cowboy boots.

Melanie took to Tom as well, embracing him warmly on first sight. The two seemed to begin immediately to conspire to shape Dennis into

Guatemala, 1976

the man they both wanted him to be, a strong, loving husband and provider, and perhaps later on a father. Tom thought he had taught Dennis as well as he could, especially without a mother's tempering hand. It all went pleasingly well, bonds were made and cemented.

Funny, Dennis thought, how memory of one event triggered another in a tangential direction, unbidden and not in any order. Dennis' memory spun away from Melanie's visit to the fact that he wished his mother could have been there. He began to review her life and her meaning to him, and . . . to her death.

# # #

He was thirteen, in school at the county high, not at home. His beautiful half-Latina mother, Consuela Maria Taliaferro Reade, on a bright morning was riding Fernando, a spirited bay she preferred. She had grown up with horses and was fully at home on them. She was roaming along the edge of the herd – only about a hundred head at the time – just observing, alert for anything out of the ordinary, anything needing attention, a regular, needful task she thoroughly enjoyed. Dennis was told that it was thought a rattler spooked her horse, and it reared and threw her. She landed on her neck and must have died instantly. She wasn't found for three hours; when Tom became concerned he asked his man, Cesar, if he knew where Consuela might be. Cesar didn't know; the two rode out to hunt for her and found her less than a quarter mile from the house, led there by circling buzzards. Tom sent Cesar back to the house to call the doctor, and then drive to the school to get Dennis. Tom waited with Consuela, and since he was alone, he allowed himself to cry.

Fernando had to be put down, a loss to Tom, but only economically. He didn't tend to bond with his horses, inured to that sentiment by the hard knocks of his life. But that was nothing compared to his loss of Consuela; it had been a true love match, overcoming the difficulties of a mixed marriage as well as the challenge of hard ranch life.

Then Dennis' memories became painful and confused. At thirteen he was on the cusp of manhood and of understanding what it would mean to be an adult; that awareness shaped his reaction and sense of loss of his mother. He thought he was a rational person, and he knew he had to stand up like a man and bear the loss and pain. Tom needed that in him. Dennis had been close to Consuela; she taught him Spanish and saw that he knew his Latino heritage. Tom was content with that but also made sure Dennis knew of his Celtic lineage and what that meant. Dennis inherited his swarthy complexion and black hair from Consuela and his lanky height – six feet by age thirteen – and blue-black eyes from Tom. He would grow another inch or so by his eighteenth birthday. Consuela was of mixed blood herself; her mother had been the impetuous and sassy, red-headed Lily Walters, daughter of a rival Anglo ranch to the Reades. It was thought by some that Lily married Gustavo Taliaferro out of spite because Amos Reade, Tom's father, didn't fancy her. Consuela inherited from Lily a faint reddish tint in her black hair, visible only in a certain kind of light. Dennis's hair sometimes reflected this.

The Taliaferro clan had moved into south Texas from Mexico in the 1870s – no one paid much attention to borders and immigration back then – and settled on a scrap of land southwest of the Reade ranch. In a drunken episode, Duncan Reade, Dennis' great-grandfather, deeded several hundred acres over to the Hispanic family in lieu of back wages he couldn't pay. Later, similar lapses by Dennis' forbearers shifted more land to the Taliaferros. Now they had a spread almost as big as the Reades and considered themselves fully Americanized and equal socially and economically to Tom's and Dennis' family. In actual fact, they were probably better off, but no one felt like they had to say that. Community harmony was more important, and since Consuela married Tom, they were related. Even after Consuela's death, Tom still tried to keep the ties strong; he attended Baptisms, Confirmations, weddings, and funerals at St. Barnabas Church, established by Padre Joseph, who migrated to America with the original Taliaferros. It was by then pastored by Father

Guatemala, 1976

Borguski, a Pole who served five other tiny, struggling parishes. Unless summoned for a special event, he appeared only every six weeks or so. Tom did nothing to cement a closer faith alliance. He and Dennis might have been called agnostic, but they were not antagonistic toward the church; it was just something "other people" did . . . and they didn't.

After the wedding, he and Melanie settled into as much of a routine as they could with him expecting to be summoned to active duty at any moment. He would go first to Fort Benning for Officer Basic Training for twelve weeks, or that was what he'd been told. In the Army, the only constant was *change*. He had to wait until the good old Army decided if it had room for him; it might be tomorrow, or it might be next month. It would be soon; fighting in Vietnam was still raging, though it seemed to be edging toward some sort of standstill; men were still being called up; some would be killed in combat. Dennis expected to be there within a year.

Melanie had one more year of college; she would stay in College Station after he was called up and go back to university housing until she graduated. Dennis would come home, or to wherever Melanie was living, when he could. Despite the sword of Vietnam hanging over them, life felt idyllic. They were besotted with each other and the life lying before them. Dennis was open to a military career; a good military wife always waiting for him, twenty years or so in, then retirement with a good pension, a job in something to do with the military or geology. He had a family history of military service. Tom and his brother, Amos, Jr., had served in World War II; Amos came home from the Pacific Theater in a casket; Tom saw service in Europe and came home unscathed, visibly at least. Ancestors had fought on both sides in the Civil War.

Tom would want Dennis to take over the ranch at some point but both realized that was less and less likely the longer Dennis stayed in the Army. At some time in the future, they would have to settle that. It was not that the ranch couldn't go on; it might even be absorbed into the Taliaferro holdings. Dennis had thought of that and didn't feel he could object; his Latino cousins were his closest friends growing up; it was all family. As far as he was concerned, his future was all mapped out; he and Melanie never thought or talked about the risk of combat; that was for "other people." He was as well trained for the next step – active duty -- as the Army could make him. He was ready to face the future with confidence, a smile, and firm resolve.

Then that was all blown out of the water.

Chapter Six

Texas

The doctor harrumphed and said, "Reade." He stood on Dennis' left side and had just completed the routine tests for a typical military physical: chest thumping and listening, turning-your-head-and-coughing, temperature, pulse, and blood pressure, poking, peering into the throat, ears, and nose, tracking eye movement, general looking over. Dennis didn't respond so the doctor repeated louder, "Reade!"

This time Dennis did answer, "Sir?"

"You didn't hear me before?"

"Hear you sir? I thought I heard you," he said.

"I had to repeat myself, Reade. Have you ever had difficulty hearing?"

"Not so I've noticed sir."

The doctor, identified only by his white lab coat, was not in the military but was under contract to conduct physicals for graduating ROTC seniors at A&M, all branches. He stood silent, looking at his patient, pondering, clearly uncertain about something.

The exams were being conducted in the armory, in the huge, gloomy all-purpose space, split into semi-private compartments by movable screens. Finally, he said, "Reade, get dressed and let's step over this way for a minute," and turned toward an unoccupied side room. Dennis rushed to get dressed and followed him and sat in the chair the doctor indicated as he closed the door. Dennis had no idea who this doctor was and hadn't been curious, until then. He began to worry. He had seen no other Cadet that day being led aside for anything like this; he sat up, alert.

The doctor said, "Reade, have you ever had an injury to your ears?"

"No sir, I can't recall any."

The doctor pulled a tuning fork out of a pocket and tapped it on the edge of the desk. "Hear this okay?" he asked.

Dennis said, "I hear that just fine."

Moving over to Dennis' left side he struck the tuning fork again and placed it against Dennis' skull, just behind his ear. "How does that sound."

"Okay, I guess."

Then he repeated the test on the right side. When he placed the humming fork against Dennis' skull he winced and pulled away. He yelped, "Yow; that hurt!"

Still on Dennis' right, the doctor clapped his hands. "How's that?" Dennis shrugged. Then he moved back to the left and capped again. "How's that?"

"What?" Dennis said.

The doctor paused again, "Do you have any ringing in your ears?"

"Sorta, I guess; more like a buzzing."

"How long have you had this?"

"I dunno; as long as I can remember."

"It's called tinnitus; that's the Latin name for ringing in the ears. It's not exactly in the ears usually but in the brain. We don't always know what causes it; it could be one of several things. There's nothing we can do for it; maybe some day we can but not yet. No one but you can hear it so we don't even know what it sounds like to you." After a pause he said, "Let me ask you again, ever had any injury of your left side; could be just a very loud noise, anything like that?"

Dennis sat and thought for some time; then he said, "Yeah, when I was ten I think."

Guatemala, 1976

"What happened?"

"Dad and I were on the veranda," he said, reminiscing. "It was about sundown, and we were relaxing after a day moving the cattle to a new area. I was tired, and I'm sure Dad was too. My little cousin, Esmeralda, was playing with her doll in the yard, squatting in the dirt. . . we don't have much grass at the ranch."

"And?"

"And then a big old daddy coyote came slinking across the yard, tongue lolling and teeth showing. Dad didn't say anything, just picked up his over-and-under twenty gauge and blew that sucker into coyote heaven!"

"And you were close?"

"Yeah; I was sitting right by him, on his right side and the gun went off about six inches from my ear."

"Your dad always keep his shotgun handy?"

"Usually. We get vermin a lot around a place like ours. Just makes sense somehow to be ready."

"You haven't noticed any hearing loss related to that?"

"When it happened I couldn't hear much of anything on that side, well on either side for a couple of days I guess." Dennis was beginning to be concerned. "After a while it all seemed to be normal again."

"Probably your right ear has compensated," the doctor said. He turned away and consulted his notes. After what Dennis thought was too long a wait, he said, "Reade, I'm no ENT man, but I'd say you have a rather severe hearing loss in your left ear. In fact, I think if we had more tests we'd find you have only about twenty percent hearing on that side. Compared to eyesight, you'd be legally deaf. Can't have you going off into the jungle and not being able to hear a gook coming up on you from your left side can we?" He chuckled. Dennis was too stunned to say anything; he didn't find anything funny about it. The doctor went on, "You can get some more tests done if you want them, but I'm afraid the Army won't pay for them; you'll have to pay for them on your own."

Dennis sat there dumfounded and afraid of he knew not what. The doctor continued to write and said, "You can go now. I expect you'll be contacted by your unit and told where to turn in any gear you've been issued." He motioned for Dennis to stand and leave. When Dennis didn't respond, he said, "You hear Reade? You okay son?"

Dennis stood and looked around as if just then realizing where he was. He said, "I need some time to think about this, sir. You sure I couldn't get into the Air Force or Navy instead of the Army?"

"Not a chance, son." Dennis noticed that instead of being called, "Reade," it was now "son." The doctor said, "Most young men might be glad they don't have to face going to Nam. You *want* to go?"

"Not really, sir; it's just that I don't have any other plans, no other job or anything!"

"Time to get a Plan B, then."

At their temporary home, a married student apartment vacant for the summer, he walked in briskly, having determined that he would keep a *happy face* on things for the encounter with Melanie. She came out of the kitchen with a huge smile and hugged him and lifted her face for a kiss. When he stiffened and didn't smile, she knew something was wrong but couldn't imagine what it might be. His kiss was perfunctory and brief. She pulled back and anxiously said, "What is it, honey, what is it?"

He couldn't look her in the face; stared off at something unseen. At last he said, "Well, honey, I'm out of a job."

"What do you mean out of a job?"

"I mean that I'm of no use to the Army anymore; they don't want me. I'm 4-F!"

"What?" again.

"I failed the physical; I have severe hearing loss in my left ear and they don't want anybody who can't hear," he said as calmly as he could.

Melanie took her time to absorb this. She said, "Tell me about it."

Guatemala, 1976

"There's nothing else to say; I don't hear well enough for the Army."

"What about the Air Force, the Navy?"

"No dice; no place for a semi-deaf man in any of the services."

She led him to the sofa and pulled him down next to her. She put her arms around him and held him tight and cooed to him, beginning to weep softly. After a moment she pulled back and said, "We'll get by; we'll make it, Dennis. We'll work something out."

"What?" he exploded. "All I have counted on, prepared for the last four years is the Army! It's all I wanted to think about as a career, at least for the next four years. I had even thought I might make the Army a twenty-year career, then I could retire and get a job in some related industry or something."

"But your major is in geology; what about that?"

He pondered that a moment, then said, "That's like a side interest, a hobby, not a career."

"But you could do something with that, couldn't you?"

"Maybe but I wouldn't know how to start. Maybe we could go to the ranch and live there."

Melanie was surprised and a little frightened. She loved Tom and Tia Angelica, Consuela's older sister and Tom's housekeeper, but she never imagined a life on the ranch; she was a city girl and expected an urban life, though maybe unrealistically. Maybe she expected a future just like her socially-driven mother. She sat back, pulling her arms away and said after a long pause, "What if Daddy could help find you a job in the oil industry, Dennis?"

Dennis stood and paced around the small room. He didn't say anything for several minutes. Melanie said, "Dennis, talk to me, look at me; tell me what you are thinking. What do you think you want to do; what do you think you *ought* to do."

"I dunno, Melanie, I just don't know!"

"Please come back and sit down again." He shrugged and complied, sitting next to her. She hugged him again. "What do you *want* to do?"

"If I was a drinking man I'd probably say go out and get drunk! But I'm not and I just don't know what to do or what to think."

Through the afternoon and into the night they thrashed and argued and wept and tried to comfort each other. Finally exhausted, Melanie said, "We ought to eat something, don't you think?"

He said, "I thought we would celebrate tonight, but . . . that's kind of out, isn't it?"

Dennis found his thoughts swirling around, undisciplined. In addition to the pain of losing the future he had planned on, he felt guilty for not going to Nam, certain in the belief that some of his cadet mates would not come home.

She picked up the phone and ordered pizza; they fed themselves on that, with one beer each, walked around the house and said little until, without saying anything more, they got ready for bed. She clung to him and tried to get him aroused but it was useless; he was unable to respond.

As directed, Dennis reported to the ROTC offices and to Master Sergeant Paisley, to turn in his gear and get his decommissioning settled. Paisley was known in the Corps as a hard-nosed combat vet who brooked no nonsense from anyone, especially the Cadets. His first name was Percy but you never dared say in his presence. That was for active Cadets. Dennis was not active and not a commissioned officer; his status was somewhat unsettled, and Paisley was careful with him.

Paisley knew of and encouraged his hard reputation but also saw himself as a compassionate man, looking out for the Cadets and the Corps. When he met a situation like Dennis' he brought out his father-figure image. As he inventoried the gear, he said, "Reade, I know you are disappointed but you might think of yourself as lucky."

"Why is that, Sergeant?" Dennis asked.

"Because, son, well, you are well-trained and passed everything and have absorbed the things you'll need to be a good field officer, better than most, really."

"I hear a *but* in there somewhere, Sarge," Dennis said.

Guatemala, 1976

"Yeah, well, Reade, " Paisley said, "you may not have the *meanness* being in combat needs. You may lack the killer instinct. In Nam you would be chopped up in days; you might show bravery but not survive a week. The non-coms look to you to not only lead but also to protect them; if you don't show that mean spirit they'll turn against you and you'll be on your own."

"You think, Sarge?"

"I *know*, son! I've seen it! Maybe you ought to think about who you really are, who you want to be, and find your way in that direction. I don't believe you know who you are. When you figure that out, you'll have a happy life."

Trouble and uncertainty pressed down on him. First, there was the physical exam that sealed the door to a career in the Army, and then the confusion and despair and he and Melanie thrashing about angrily, trying to make sense of things. When Melanie suggested that her father could help get him a job in the oil industry he flat-out rejected it; she flat-out rejected moving to the ranch. Finally, caring for her too much to cause her any unnecessary pain, he gave in. He would ask her father to help him find a job. Melanie had told her parents about the reversal of their plans the morning after she and Dennis spent the evening agonizing over their calamity. His call to his father-in-law was not unexpected, but was welcomed.

Herbert Williams answered Dennis' call with a hearty, "Hello, son. I hear you're not going into the Army."

"Yessir," Dennis replied, "That seems to be that, the end of that career."

"Well, Dennis," Herbert said, "Try to put the best light on things. Actually, as you can probably guess, I'm kind of glad. Melanie's mother and I would always be afraid you'd leave her a widow, with all that stuff going on in Nam and all." Dennis just grunted to show he was listening. "Why don't you come over to see me here at the office, say this afternoon, about two?"

"That'll be fine sir, and thank you," Dennis replied, trying to put as much enthusiasm into his voice as he could, though it was difficult.

The meeting went well. Dennis was ushered in to Herbert's office – more practical than plush – and offered coffee. He declined and sat back, waiting for Herbert to take the lead.

After a significant pause, Herbert said with a broad smile, "Well, Dennis, you have any ideas about what you and Melanie are going to do?"

Dennis noted that Melanie was included in the question. He said, "Not really, sir. I guess my fall-back choice would be to go live on the ranch, but I know Melanie wouldn't be happy there. I really don't have any clear idea right now."

"You're right. Melanie wouldn't like that at all; she's a city girl. You want her to be happy, don't you?"

Dennis felt a surge of resentment at the thought that he didn't want her to be happy, but pushed that away and said, "Yes, of course, sir, of course."

Then Herbert launched into a long telling of his start and rise in the oil industry; he didn't have a college degree – only two years at a community college – but he bore down on how hard work and good, sound strategies had worked for him and brought him to where he was. He said, "The next step might be, son, that some big outfit will come sniffing around and buy me out; I'll take that money and start a new business. That's what people do, you know, and I'm ready for it!"

"You think that's going to happen, sir, soon?"

"I'd say within the next five years, Dennis, and you could be right there with me. You interested?"

Dennis knew that was exactly what Melanie hoped for, and what he dreaded. He also knew, though, that he'd accept the job; his choices were limited to this and none. Details were thrashed out; he would report to work the next Monday.

In the meantime he and Melanie had to find a more permanent home. Herbert had a friend who rented houses, and they moved in over

Guatemala, 1976

the weekend. In a nice neighborhood; it was clean and more or less up to date. Melanie set about to make it as home-like as she could; she was bubbling with happiness, her mind whirling with plans for their future. Dennis pitched in and tried to appear as happy as Melanie, swallowing his pride for harmony; he began to get into the right mood, reluctantly deciding to enjoy their good fortune.

Chapter Seven

GUATEMALA

When Laura Harris returned, he was awake and had formulated his questions in what he thought was an orderly fashion. He sat up as straight as he could. She asked, "How're you feeling?"

In his identity-shift, he'd decided that if he was allowed to use English, he would add a slight mid-American Spanish lilt to it. That would reinforce his new personhood.

He said, "Where is this? How did I get here?" He had too many questions and was tempted to pile them together, forgetting his vow to proceed systematically.

"You are in our mission clinic," she said. "We are a Christian mission, and we try to minister to the local populace in the needs they have that we are able to address." This sounded almost like a canned speech, one she would give to potential donors.

He said, "But where? Where is this?"

"We are in Guatemala, in the northwest, not far from the border with Belize," she said. "The nearest town or settlement, it really is not a town, is San Miguel, about seven kilos south. It has an old, old Catholic Church but not much else. We are in Quiche Province if that helps you, not too far from Tikal and some other Mayan ruins."

Dennis nodded and said, "Are you the only Americans here?"

Guatemala, 1976

She smiled and said, "Yes." Then, "You are too tall to be a native Guatemalan or even a Mexican, and you have brilliant blue eyes." She said, "I told you my name, Laura Harris and my assistant, the nurse is Maria Alvardo. I am a real doctor. I run this station with my husband, Rodney, also a doctor, who is in the States getting supplies and trying to raise money, as I think I mentioned."

He said, "You hooked up with some church?"

"Not *some* church but a small group of independent churches support us." She looked at him intensely. "Tell me who you are," she said, "you haven't told us your name."

He pulled in a breath and began, "My name is Alonso Mendoza. I am Mexicano; I come from the north near Matamoros." He had pondered where his choice of name came from. "Alonso" was common enough; Mendoza was the name of the Colonel who hosted their flying tour.

"And what are you doing here in Guatemala?"

"I was driving a truck. I was given a contract to deliver a load to Coban, here in Guatemala."

"You drove all that way?"

"No. I rode the bus to Oaxaca and picked up the truck there and drove from there into Guatemala," he said. "The delivery was to be in Coban, but I must have been attacked, or ambushed maybe, before I got there; I don't remember much after I crossed the border. I do know I never got to Coban. How did I get here, to your clinic?" He knew a little about Coban; it was one of the stops where the team had stayed overnight on their flying introduction to the country, so he felt safe talking about it.

"As I told you, you were found on our doorstep Sunday morning unconscious and badly injured. How does your head feel?"

"My head feels okay, a little sore but okay I guess. Do you have my passport and other papers and such?" This worried him; if she had his passport, she would know he was lying about his name and nationality.

"No, you didn't even have shoes, no papers or any ID at all, just a shirt, pants, and underwear; not even a belt, you were stripped dry. They are American by the way, your clothes." She let that drift, wondering if she would get an explanation. He didn't rise to the bait; he knew that she knew if he lived that close to the border, American clothes would not be all that unusual. After a quiet spell, she said, "Where did you get your height and blue eyes?"

"My mother is American. I lived off and on with her in the States, so I'm almost a dual citizen," he paused. "But I'm really Mexicano." He paused to let this sink in. "What do you think happened to me?"

"I'd guess you're right about being ambushed," she said. "The rebels are thick on the ground around here. They like to raid south of here and then retreat back into this area. They may have a more or less permanent camp somewhere nearby, but we don't ask; we just try to be good Christian neighbors and doctors when any of them show up. They leave us alone as long as we treat their illnesses and injuries without questions. But back to your question, they probably took anything you had with you or on you and left you here so we could take care of you." He digested that but was quiet.

"What were you hauling?" she asked; she didn't think he was really a truck driver.

"Don't know." He had anticipated this and plotted his story accordingly. "I wasn't told what it was, just told to go to Oaxaca and pick up the truck and drive it to Coban. The truck was covered, enclosed, and I was told to not open it."

"Have any trouble at the border?"

This was a potential problem; if she or anyone had cared enough to check, it would be revealed that he had not crossed the border, but he'd anticipated that. He said, "I was given an envelope to give to the border guard, to only one individual name . . . I don't think I want to tell you his name, and there was no wait, no problem; I was just waived through. They didn't even ask to look inside the truck."

Guatemala, 1976

"Ever done this before, brought something across the border?"

"No, first time, for me at least."

"How are you supposed to get back home, to Matamoros?"

"I have, uh, *had* a bus ticket." He chuckled, admitting he was now in effect stranded. He smiled, hoping she saw the humor and irony n his situation. She smiled back, apparently understanding, or pretending to. "What day is this?" he asked.

"It's Tuesday, January twentieth."

"So I've been here three days?"

"Almost; three days in the morning."

"And you found me on your doorstep on Sunday?"

"Yes, Sunday morning. We get up and start moving around about six; and there you were, in the dirt in front of our gate, laid out like a drunk if you want to know what we first thought. We have a Chapel service a little later on Sunday mornings; some of the locals show up, sometimes."

"How long has your husband been gone?"

"He left right after Christmas."

"He do this often? How long will he be gone? Is there a set schedule?" Dennis asked, running his questions together again.

"One month or so; could be longer but probably not much. He or I one do this once or twice a year; one of us is always here," she said.

"Doesn't sound like a very good arrangement," thinking but not saying, "*for a good marriage.*" He remembered that there were many factors that drove him and Melanie apart. Who was he to judge? "How do you keep in touch? Radio?"

"Yes, we have a ham radio, and both of us are qualified, but we don't like to use it. Usually, but not always, the telephone can be used; it's not always working, but is often enough, *usually!*" she laughed. "We try to be careful and conserve our fuel, so we don't use the generator any more than we can help." Gesturing, she said, "We rely on these kerosene lamps for lighting most of the time, but we do need the generator for essential medical things like the autoclave, the sterilizer in other words. Our refrigerators work on bottled gas." She was enjoying talking with this proto-American who was apparently well-educated, and too cultured for a mere truck driver. She smiled a lot more than she had earlier.

"Do you have a car or truck?" he asked.

"Yes, we have a jeep, not really that brand but here any light vehicle, no matter what the brand, is called a jeep. Ours is a Toyota I believe," she said. "Rodney drove it to Guatemala City and left it there at a church while he is gone. We also have a pair of mules, closer to donkeys, actually, we use around here." She gave him a wide conspiratorial smile.

"You don't have many beds here; is this the only bed you have?"

"We treat mostly walk-in people who are sick with a fever or a minor injury or something like that. That's why we are called a clinic, not a hospital," she explained. "We keep this bed for the really rare cases like yours; if it had been feasible, we'd have sent you to a hospital in the closest city, but I decided, since you didn't have any identification, the better part of valor would be to keep you here. I hope that's okay with you," she asked.

He ignored her implied question and asked, "And you do all this because . . .?"

"Because that's what the Lord called us to do," she said quietly and rather solemnly. "If you are not a committed Christian, that might be hard for you to understand, but God loves all of us, and Jesus taught us to love others in His name, even our enemies."

She looked at him with a disconcerting intensity for several minutes, then with a sigh said as she stood, "Enough of this for now, Alonso Mendoza. Maria's grandmother, Celesta, our housekeeper, cook and laundress, has washed your clothes," she looked over to a hook on the wall where the clothes hung on a wire hanger; Dennis hadn't noticed them. "When you feel up to it, you can get up and put them on. I think you are strong enough for that, but let us know if you have any trouble, any dizziness or nausea. There is also a pair of sandals there for you.

Guatemala, 1976

There is a bathroom next door if you need it. You can wash up but please avoid a shower for now; we don't want your dressings and stitches to get wet." She smiled at him again and turned and left to give him privacy.

Stiff and still sore, Dennis gingerly pulled the multi-colored cover off and sat on the side of the cot. He stretched and twisted and pushed himself up to his feet; he paused to see if he would be woozy; thankfully he was stable. He took a tentative step toward his clothes and found he was able to walk. He was stiff from inactivity; each step was agony. He brought his clothes back to the bed and put them on, the sandals as well. He wrapped another serape he found on a peg on the wall around his shoulders. The room was rather cool. It was not big and plainly furnished, odds and ends of medical gear around on pegs and on a cupboard of utilitarian nature. One small window let in a modicum of light and told him generally the time of day.

He stepped through the open door into the outdoors, a roofed passageway between buildings. Immediately across he entered another door, not locked for some reason, into what had to be an anteroom for the clinic, a room where daily supplies and the autoclave, and lab and other equipment were kept. A counter ran along one wall with enclosed and locked cabinets above and below, and a refrigerator with its cylinder of gas next to it. A large basket was there apparently for soiled linens and another for trash. There was a sink and in a corner a wood-fired water heater, with a stack of firewood next to it.

Through another door was the clinic itself, a large room with an exam table in the middle on which a dirty-faced child sat; several generations of adults and older children stood around. Laura Harris attended the howling child, probing into his – or her, he couldn't tell – right ear; Maria stood by ready to help. She saw him come in and looked over and smiled at him. He knew he was in the way and went back outside.

The bright sunlight stunned him; he reached up to his shirt pocket expecting to find his sunglasses, momentarily surprised, trying to remember when he'd last worn them. He'd also worn a baseball cap with the Global Geologics logo on it, when whatever happened . . . happened. Then reality returned, and he just squinted and looked around. He took in the clinic compound, mapping it out in his orderly mind; it all seemed familiar to him, similar to what he grew up around. There were no trees in the largish dirt-paved square, but in the near western distance there was a line of trees meandering along, presumably following a stream, and beyond that, spectacular mountains. Around the square, in no discernible pattern, sat other buildings. He would learn that one housed the kitchen and dining shed and the laundry – an open air stone tub, a *Pila*, he had learned in his short time in Guatemala, with a water tap, and a paved surround – and housing for Maria and Celesta and another granddaughter, Malinda – not Maria's sister – and Juan, the handyman, Celesta's husband. No one was washing anything, but he could smell cooking aromas and saw a slight wisp of smoke coming from an open brick fire pit outside, under the same palm-frond shelter over the Pila. Next to that was a small structure from which emanated a rough hum, a generator, he concluded. And next to that was a large wooden water tank on stilts. This answered a question that had not actually occurred to Dennis; where did the water and electricity originate. Then an anomaly emerged; there were electrical cables coming into the compound from somewhere; if they had a power from a utility, then why did they have a generator? He decided he didn't have to know that.

Another building appeared to be a large, open-air workshop, and tool house. Dennis wandered over; Juan was at work honing a scythe on a foot-powered grinding wheel. Dennis spoke to him, introduced himself. Juan grinned, revealing too few teeth to do much damage to anything tough. Juan didn't speak but turned back to his grinding, showing Dennis he preferred to be left to his work.

Dennis strolled back outside, enjoying the freedom of just being out into the air and openness. A well-fed dog of mixed heritage looked up at him but found nothing interesting and lay his head back down on his paws. A few scraggly chickens scratched around aimlessly. Two small

Guatemala, 1976

children played in the dirt in the shade of the work shed, reminding Dennis of his many Hispanic cousins back in Texas. All the enclosed structures were built of heavy, plastered abode walls with clay tile roofs, and everything was adorned with hanging potted flowers and flowering vines. Another building sat a little farther away from the others; this was clearly the residence of the Americans; it had that look of a permanent home. Dennis sighed and found a bench near the children and spoke to them. They giggled and grinned and began to tell him solemnly of their very important work there in the dirt. He smiled back and listened, contented.

He continued his stroll, exploring leisurely his new home, at least for the present. He discovered that a high, masonry wall surrounded the entire site with a wide heavy wood two-leafed gate the only apparent entry. It stood open; he strolled outside. Aside from a small well-tended kitchen garden, there was only the receding dirt road and encroaching vegetation to be seen. He turned around and re-entered the enclosure. The home of the doctors, in its own remote corner, was separated from the other structures by a rail fence, with abundant shrubs and flowers, obviously well-watered. A wide veranda graced the front. The sun was high; he was beginning to tire, and meandered back to his bed.

Chapter Eight

GUATEMALA

Dennis settled into his clinic routine over the next days. Laura and Maria would come in and check his wounds and vital signs. All seemed to be good; Laura invariably declared it so. He ate in a communal dining shed with everyone else. He was now able to chew anything they had to offer, basic peasant fare: refried beans, rice and occasionally a little meat, chicken he suspected but never asked. He never complained. Maria seemed to look at him with more than just a typical nurse's TLC; she smiled and found occasions to touch his arm and stroke his face. One time Dennis gripped her arm and looked intently into her eyes. She surprised him by almost coming to tears; then she pulled away, wiping her eyes. He was interested; he was not immune to female attention. He had never had much trouble attracting them. Was this another possible conquest he mused; then he remembered his disfigured face. That was a new reality he'd have to learn to live with.

Thursday afternoon Maria came in with a basin towels and a jug of water. She put the things down and pulled a stool over to the side of the bed. She said, "Please. Alonso, lie across the bed, with your head hanging over the side. We are going to have a shampoo!"

"What?" Dennis was surprised but pleased. He had not thought about his hair much at all. "Okay I guess," and complied. Maria sat in a side chair and positioned the stool and the basin under his head, poured

Guatemala, 1976

some water over his head and into the basin, and began to scrub his scalp. "Aah! That feels wonderful, Maria!" She poured some more water on him, and soaped his scalp again. He moaned in happiness again.

She stood and picked up the basin, carrying it outside to empty it. In a minute she came back in and put everything back in place and began to rinse his hair, poured water from a large clay jug. She stroked and caressed his head, and he loved it. She said, "Oh, Alonso, your hair was very dirty! It is very beautiful and I will dry it and comb it for you."

"Just dry it; that'll be enough, Maria. I can comb it."

"No problem, Alonso. I enjoy doing it for you." He made no further objection, enjoying the attention, remembering he had no comb.

On Friday, he lay fully dressed on his cot for his exam; Laura sat in the bedside chair and said, "We took your chest dressings off yesterday, and I believe we can take the stitches out on Monday. You have already been up and around. Have you seen the whole clinic grounds?"

"Some; what I have seen impresses me," he said. I guess I have a lot to be thankful for, especially to you and Maria. Gracias; there, I've said it!"

"Da nada," she said.

"If I can get up and move around is there anything I could be doing to earn my keep? he asked.

"I don't believe you are up to chopping wood yet!" she replied with a disarming grin. "Just hold onto that thought; maybe we'll think of something. I have asked Maria to walk around with you when you want to; you need the exercise. You seem strong and agile; I wouldn't want you to get rusty and flabby with all this bed rest! Just stop and rest when you feel like it." He acknowledged this with a nod. "This is Friday as you may remember. I hope you do, remember that is; your concussion doesn't seem to have affected your mental capabilities, as far as I can tell. What do you think?

"I feel like I'm as smart as I've ever been, not that that's a lot!" He grinned; she smiled back, stood and left.

Maria came up to his bed immediately and stood quietly, smiling down at him. She said, "Do you want to walk now? I can go with you if you want?"

He nodded and said softly, "later," and in the afternoon, after a short siesta; she led him out into the sunshine. At first they just ambled along, silent After a few minutes she said, "Please Alonso, tell me about yourself, what was your life like in Mexico?"

"I've told Doctor Harris all I can, all I want to. To tell you too much wouldn't be good."

"Good for you or for me?"

"Both of us, Maria, all of us here." They walked on quietly. Maria pointed out features of the compound he had already discovered for himself. He said, "How long have you been working here, Maria?"

"Since I was sixteen, almost four years."

"And before that?"

"I lived with my parents in our village."

"San Miguel?"

"No, another place, not too far, just a few houses together."

"It has a name?"

"No, just our little village." She seemed rather ashamed and might have been blushing, with her dark complexion it was hard to tell. He knew enough to stop prying about it.

"How did you come to work here at the clinic?" he asked.

"Doctor Harris, Senora Laura," Maria said, "came to our house to see my mother; she was very sick. Doctor Harris tried to make her well, but it was too late. My mother died the next day. Doctor Harris came back to take care of the funeral and those things. She knew it would be hard for the family then, and said to me if I would like to come and work for her. That meant one mouth my father didn't have to feed. So, I did, I came and have been here ever since."

Guatemala, 1976

"And that was four years ago?"

"Almost." She smiled broadly, her eyes sparkling. "I am so glad I did; I have learned a lot that I would not have learned if I did not come. My grandmother and grandfather already worked for the doctors, and Malinda came a little while after me, so they knew our family."

"You learned about nursing and assisting Doctor Harris?"

She nodded vigorously, "Also, she taught me to speak in English!" she proudly exclaimed. "I can speak English with you if you want me to," she said in English expectantly.

Dennis grinned and responded in English, "Good, I'd like that."

After the next day's exam, Laura looked at him with more, it seemed to him, than a physician's interest. He was up and dressed, and they met in the main clinic room. She said after a moment, "Tomorrow is Sunday, you know. You have never talked about religion, but it is very important here. We have a Chapel service here at the clinic; we usually meet in a little glen under the trees near the creek. We have set up an area with some rough seats and a cross and a, well, a lectern, which we call our *Pulpit*. Our services are not Catholic, but we get a few of the people around to come, especially if we have treated them for something." Clearly she was inviting him without saying so outright.

"What time is your service?" he asked.

"Nine o'clock, before it gets too hot. Would you like to come?"

"Okay, I guess. Don't have anything better to do."

"Don't put yourself out, Mister!" she joked.

"If it's not Catholic, then what is it?"

"It is evangelical, sort of generic Protestant, I guess, but we try not to use that word, Protestant." She paused to see if he was following. "Just what *is* your religious background, Alonso?"

"Nothing much," he said, "growing up in a split household made me kind of shy of any religion."

"Split household?"

"Yea, I told you my mother is American," he said, "She and my dad split when I was about eight, I think. She went back to the States. I stayed with my father most of the time, but with her a good bit, too. She's Episcopalian, I think, but she never made much of an issue of it." Reminded of it, he remembered that Melanie's family was Episcopal also. An Episcopal priest officiated at their ROTC Chapel wedding, but he couldn't share that with anyone now.

"And what about your father, what is his religion?"

"About the same as me, nothing much," he signed. "Oh, he tries to keep in good with the Church, but giving them money is about all he ever does."

"What is your father's business?"

"*Business;* that's it." He clammed up. It was obvious he didn't want to say any more. She could make her own judgment about it. He wanted to leave all that in mystery so he didn't have to invent anything that might trip him up. Leave her in uncertainty. Let her think it was something not quite legal.

She seemed to accept that and nodded. She said, "You seem to be well educated. Where did you go to school?"

This he could wing, he thought. "I actually went to high school in the States, mostly, when I was living with my mother." Laura looked askance at him. He added, "In San Antonio, where she was living at the time."

"And college, did you also go to college in the States?"

"No. My father wanted me back home with him. He thought I'd had all the education I would need."

"When did you graduate?"

"I didn't. I went home to Matamores for Christmas that year, my senior year, and just never went back."

She accepted this, stood, and said, "So get up and move around. I hope to see you tomorrow at Chapel." She left him alone.

Guatemala, 1976

He and Maria spent some time together that day, as they seemed to do every day. Maria sought him out and invited him to stroll around. That day she led them through the clinic gate to the outdoor Chapel. They sat and were content with the only sounds from distant birds and the ripple of the creek. Occasionally a voice could be heard from the clinic, but it was always muted and not disturbing. He didn't try to make anything happen or try to force any issue. He knew he'd have to figure out what to do with himself soon but didn't want to think about that then.

Maria wasn't exactly acting coy, but she seemed to be trying hard to keep him interested in her. She smiled at him, it seemed to him, all the time, and said inconsequential things to him, like, "Your hair is very nice, very pretty," and reach up and stroke it ever so lightly. He enjoyed the attention, but it could be a little irritating if he let it. They sat side by side on a log seat; she sat a little closer than he expected but he didn't move. In truth, he wasn't sure himself how he felt about her. She was a pretty, Meso-American Indian girl, and her attention was flattering, and he didn't want to offend her in any way. But he, when he was honest with himself, was more attracted to Laura Harris and had to put the brakes on himself to avoid fantasizing about her. It was easy to forget that his face would not appeal to women in general or probably not to either of the women he was forced into company with here in this confining little compound. Then he remembered Maria's interest.

Since leaving the ranch, going to college, and settling in Houston in an office and in suburban life, he had lost the sensitivity to the distinct and stronger smells of rural and, more to the point, Hispanic, life. Here it had returned, and Maria's presence brought it all back, Laura the same but with less certainty; her personal scent was mixed American and local. He recalled from his Psych 101 class that smell was the most basic and important sense in reinforcing memory and bringing it back. The smells of this place as well as the distinct scent of each person enveloped and claimed him, and it pleased him. He was not sure he wanted to leave it.

It appealed to something intuitive in him, something primary, things he had pushed away for too many years. Perhaps, he thought, all this was returning, and he would find himself again.

Maria reached over and grasped his hand and smiled up at him. He didn't pull away. He said, "Maria, why do you look at me that way. I know with this scar and all I am not handsome; I'm pretty ugly, actually."

"It's what's inside, isn't it, Alonso? Do not you agree?" This was her boldest step yet. He was on alert.

He said, "You are a very pretty girl, Maria; I'll bet there are dozens of boys around here that come courting you. Haven't I seen some of them? Didn't I hear someone playing a guitar and singing the other night? You can't tell me somebody was serenading Celesta or Doctor Harris!" She blushed and turned away, still smiling, though.

He changed the subject. He said, "Maria, you have family and other friends in the, well, outside of here in the clinic. Do you know anything about what happened to me? I, know, we *all*, know, I was in some kind of accident, or possibly in a rebel attack. If you know something, I think I ought to know. What are people saying? What have you heard?"

"I only know what Doctor Harris knows, Alonso," she said. "You appeared at the gate of the clinic, and we brought you in. We don't know how you got here, but it just looks like you were badly injured and somebody found you and brought you to us because they knew we would try to help you."

"And you haven't heard any rumors about it at all?"

"Nothing. We don't ask many questions about things around here, Alonso; it might be dangerous," she said. He understood and decided he would have to be satisfied with that.

He asked, "Maria, do you still think of yourself as a Catholic?'

"Si, of course. What else would I be?"

"Yet you attend the, well, non-Catholic Chapel services here. How do you work that out?"

Guatemala, 1976

"Doctor Laura is so good to all of us that we want to please her and honor her God as best we can." Dennis let it go at that.

As they turned to go back into the clinic grounds, he noticed the gate from the outside. To the left of the gate a large lantern hung; opposite was a big rusty bell, with a cord that frayed-off only a short length below the bell, too high to be reached from the ground. "Maria," he said, "even though I am pretty tall, I could not reach that bell rope. What if someone came at night and needed help? How would they get someone inside to hear them?

"They would just knock or yell until Juan heard them and he would come and open the gate for them."

"Always Juan?"

"Usually. If not Juan then Celesta would. We always hear them and let them in."

"How long has the rope been broken?"

"I do not know, Alonso; it has been this way all the time I have been here."

A large wooden beam spanned across high above the gate opening; carved into it were the words: "CLINICA EVANGELICA DIOS SANA ." Dennis translated to himself: "Evangelical Clinic, God Heals."

In his gradually emerging awareness of his situation, he often wondered about what happened to his team, Bruce and the Guatemalans. He couldn't ask outright and maintain his invented persona and story. But he had become fond of Bruce, the short, stocky, and witty squirt, who would come up with a quip, or more often a pun, on the slimmest of openings. Dennis remembered one time when the team saw field workers toiling along on hillsides so steep it was hard to see how they could keep their balance. Bruce said, "I'll bet their donkeys have legs longer on one side."

Pedro replied, taking this comment literally, "But Senor, they do not have donkeys or any other animals. It would not be possible for the donkeys to stay on the ground so the men do not have them; besides, it costs too much to feed donkeys."

That shut Bruce up for a minute or two, but not long. He said, "Then to go home they have to *hoof* it themselves." Dennis groaned. The Guatemalans may not have understood or appreciated the humor, but that was never a deterrent to a wag like Bruce. After a few minutes, he added, "These guys could make a killing as mountain climber guides: Central American Sherpas!"

Chapter Nine

Guatemala

More out of courtesy than desire, Dennis decided to attend the Chapel Service the next day. He was surprised to find Maria, Celesta, Juan, and Malinda all there, along with a dozen or so other native families. Malinda was a slightly chubby early teen with the smooth tawny skin, and the coarse, bronze-black hair of her heritage. Laura had told him some locals came out of gratitude for the care and treatment they received at the clinic, and they paid with eggs and vegetables and an occasional chicken. The way they smiled at Laura and they way they showed deference toward her told Dennis that they were returning the love she showed to them. He surmised that her love – her *Christian* love – was not only expressed in healing but also in just her loving and affirming nature; he certainly had sensed and received that himself.

Maria had come for him a little after eight. She said, "Please get up, Alonso. We are going to Chapel." There seemed to be no question about his going. He shrugged, got out of bed, and dressed; then he went to the shed for a spare breakfast. It puzzled him that neither female had appeared to check his health that day; then he figured that Sunday was a day-off for the health professionals except for emergencies. Apparently his case was no longer bad enough for that; he was healing right on schedule.

Walking through the central courtyard of the compound with Maria, he noticed that several trestle tables had appeared, loosely arranged. Some had something piled on them, under light-weight cloths. He wondered but said nothing; Maria volunteered nothing.

As they approached the Chapel glen, gentle guitar strumming set a mood of quiet, meditative calm. In front, under the tree, Laura sat facing the log "pews;" two others sat beside her. One was the guitar player, a local youth in a clean, well-worn native costume. The other was dressed in an ill-fitting and obviously old black suit coat and non-matching, and clean, faded black knee-sprung pants. His shirt had originally been white – the collar frayed, the ends turned up – and he wore a narrow tie of an uncertain dark color. He was a rail-thin man of some years revealed by a leathery face and near-white generous mustache, matching his full heard of hair; he sat calmly in his granny glasses, holding a Bible as well-worn as his clothing.

When he and Maria sat down near the front, Laura stood and began humming a tune the guitarist backed. Soon the entire congregation joined in the humming, and after a few phrases, Laura stood and began to sing in Spanish a soft, slow song he had never heard; all the others stood and sang as well. It told a story of Jesus' love to the poor, those with hard lives, and a call to all to return that love, all in slow, uplifting, appealing phrasing. Quiet, smiling open faces reflected the singers' familiarity with the song and its message. It was a time of serene peace and unity, and went on for longer than Dennis thought necessary, but he found it uplifting.

After the singing, the man with the Bible, who apparently needed no introduction, stood and delivered a long, rather impassioned prayer. With his Amen, several in the group answered with, "Amens," and other words of praise as well. He noticed several locals crossing themselves. Maria whispered to him, "That is Pastore Zacharias."

All sat down, and Laura stood again. In the local dialect she said, "Welcome, my good people. We meet again to celebrate our Savior's love

Guatemala, 1976

and to show our love for each other. We have a special guest today, Senor Alonzo Mendoza, from Mexico. As most of you know, he was badly injured, and we are helping him heal." Several welcoming expressions came from the people, and Dennis felt he had to turn around and nod to them, smiling as best he could with his taut face. He hoped he didn't scare the children; no one seemed to be bothered by his disfigurement, all returned his smile with broad, unconditional smiles of their own.

Then Laura said. "We sing our giving song," and began to croon again, joined by the guitar and most of the folk. As they sang a few stood and brought parcels wrapped in paper or cloth to the front and laid them on a low table Alonso had not noticed before.

Maria joined them and laid a small bundle with the others. As she sat back down she whispered to him. "This is our offering; nobody has money to give but they bring what they can, mostly garden crops, sharing."

The gaunt man stood, looking kindly at his meager audience. Zacharias was obviously going to deliver a sermon of a sort. He smiled and began, "Holy is the Lord; praise the Lord!" and the congregation responded with the same words. He went on to exhort over and over in what Alonso thought were repetitive ways the message of the love of God and Jesus. After a short time he concluded and turned to sit down.

Laura and everyone else stood once again and she led in yet another chorus, ending in hearty Amens, and the service was over.

Everyone chattered and began to move back into the compound, laughing and exchanging greetings. Gradually the crowd filtered into the courtyard and toward the tables he had spotted on the way to the service. There were now more piles on the tables, and the covers had been removed. It was food of course, a feast of sorts, an important part of their Sunday routine.

The guitar player from the service was joined by two men with musical instruments, one a bass guitar – typical in the Mexican music he grew up on – and maracas shook vigorously by a third man. As the folks began to file by the tables with plates and bowls and pick up their food, the musicians began to play. Maria took his arm and led him to the tables and insisted he fill a plate; then she handed him a cup of chilled tea. At first leery and puzzled, he soon relaxed and enjoyed it. Many made a special effort to come over and greet him personally. Maria never left his side, and found opportunity to touch his hand and arm. He didn't object; he rather liked it.

Chapter Ten

GUATEMALA

On Monday morning Maria came into his room and said, "Doctora Laura is coming very soon to take out your stitches, Alonso. Sit up, please." Dennis did so; he had already been up and dressed and had eaten his breakfast. The coffee was always good here he mused. He could get used to it.

Laura came in and he stood. "Please lie back down, Alonso. We are going to remove your stitches" He obeyed, dropping back down on the cot and reclining back on the pillow. She sat on the side of the bed and probed his face gently with her fingers. Dennis felt something undefined but pleasant at her touch; he watched her face and searched for eye contact to confirm that her interest could be more than medical, but she showed no awareness of his feelings for her.

She turned to Maria, who handed her a damp cloth; she swabbed his face and spent extra time cleaning his scar and the surrounding area. Then she handed the cloth back to Maria who dropped it into a bucket and picked up a small square of gauze and handed it to Laura. Neither had said a word since Laura began to clean his wound. She sat back and said, "Well, Senor, we now are at the critical stage. This may be uncomfortable but it shouldn't actually hurt. You're a big boy and can handle any pain, can't you?" He grinned and she bent over him again and with small scissors and tweezers began to snip at the stitches and pull them out very gently. He steeled himself and grimaced a little but didn't make an audible sound.

When she finished, she sat back again and looked over her work carefully. "Looks like you are good to go," she said as she swabbed the wound and then stood. "When you feel like it get up and move around and come to lunch. After lunch come back and rest; take a siesta."

After his siesta, Maria came in and said, "Doctora Laura asked me to tell you she would like to see you at her house." He had not been inside but had seen it from the outside; it reminded him of his home on the ranch, though maybe smaller: the same rough-troweled stucco walls, tile roof, arched veranda, and cascading flowers. Laura greeted him at the door and waved him through a small entry hall and into a largish room, obviously a living room combined with functions of their medical practice. Typically, a large arch-topped fireplace with a rough wood mantel stood diagonally in one corner. Colorful pottery and other small local crafts pieces crowded across the mantel, and on other flat surfaces. Almost opposite the fireplace, she and her husband had set up their office area, a huge, clearly antique wood desk of native design and craftsmanship, plus two filing cabinets, and on the walls charts of medical arcana, and a chalk scheduling board. Native fabric wall hangings, paintings and crafts items adorned the walls in neat array; Colonel Mendoza and others involved in the Global Geologics team orientation had stressed how brilliant colors were iconic in Guatemalan culture, especially in fabrics.

Laura led him over to the desk and asked him to sit in a straight-backed wooden chair decorated with bright, typical Guatemalan colors and designs. She sat in a decrepit swivel office chair holding a folder in her lap, and looked at him as if seeing him for the first time. Mixed thoughts ran through her mind.

"Alonso," she said, asking herself if that was his real name, "We have done about all for you we can here. I have removed your stitches and

Guatemala, 1976

patched up the few other injuries you have, and you are about as good as we can make you. Here," she said, handing him a small screw-top jar, "is some balm for your face, to relieve the itch and help it heal. You need to take time to think about what you will do, where you will go."

He picked up on "go," sending through him a tremor of anxiety. "Couldn't I stay here a little longer, maybe earn my keep by helping out some?" he asked.

"You might but it would be only make-work," – Dennis winced at that term – "nothing we really need," she said, "and your food would have to come out of what we have for ourselves here and those we share with. Do you have any plans, any ideas?"

"Not really. I have to be careful; my father has enemies . . ." He let that drift, assuming Laura would come to her own conclusions.

"And?" she asked, rather brusquely.

"And, I guess they'd like to kidnap me or maybe just kill me if they knew where I was."

Laura was quiet a long spell, looking at the papers in her lap, then up at the wall and glancing out a window; she squirmed around some, trying to decide how to proceed; she then settled down, sighed, and said, "Let me think about this and maybe talk to Padre Augustine and see what we can work out, okay?" He nodded and suppressed a smile. "Here," she said, inching her chair closer, "Let me check your temperature and pulse."

"Who is Padre Augustine?"

"He found you at his church and brought you here."

She put her hand on his forehead a moment, and felt his wrist. A shiver of pleasure ran through him at her touch, hoping it didn't show. He was more and more conscious of her allure for him, of her native beauty despite the lack of any makeup or effort to magnify her femininity, and of her scent. Her dark blond hair was always tied back and he wondered how she would look with it down.

She sighed, "You are healthy as a burro!" she joked and grinned. She was well aware of Dennis' attraction to her, and was both pleased and frightened by it. She must do nothing to encourage it. "Let me show you around a little," she said, stood and led the way through the open double doors into the entrance hall. "Here is the dining room," she said, pointing to the opposite paired, open doors. The room was decorated with inexpensive local artifacts and features. The table was draped with a fabric runner in a hallmark Guatemalan color scheme. It showed that someone with taste -- probably Laura -- planned it all. They stepped into the kitchen, Because all cooking was done outside, the room held mostly storage, work surfaces and a small, bottle-gas refrigerator. "The house was built some fifty or so years ago by a Canadian, I was told," she said, "**more** dreamer than farmer; it is said he left after only three years."

He tried to appear to be impressed, but was more impressed by Laura. He uttered the expected appreciative remarks on cue. As he left the house she said, "I'd like you to come to dinner tonight, at seven or so, please." He was pleased and smiled his acceptance.

The dinner would be at her house instead of the little open shed where everyone ate most of the time. He was continuing to improve, and spent more time that afternoon on his feet, exploring the clinic compound. He was back at her house a bit early. Maria let him in; she and Padre Augustine were invited as well. As at the Chapel Service, Laura appeared in tasteful Guatemalan attire; a change from her daily uniform of a white lab coat and comfortable, utilitarian shoes.

The conversation at the table was lively and informative for him. Laura wanted to provide a time and place she thought where Alonso would feel the level of conversation was closer the what he was used to, given his *claimed* background; she still wondered about that. She had to keep giving Maria poorly-veiled hints that she was not a servant there but a guest, equal to the others. Celesta and Melinda cooked and served the meal; it was nothing more than their typical fare, good and nourishing; the atmosphere was congenial. Laura's hair was up but done with perhaps more care, with more decorum than practicality.

Guatemala, 1976

Laura could not miss that Maria was attracted to Alonso, and that he hadn't rebuffed her. She thought it might be a good match for both, and might help shift Alonso's attention away from her. She also recognized that Alonso was sending romantic hints to her, Laura, and that her own feelings of loneliness, and Alonso's good looks and virility pulled at her as well. Pitching Maria and Alonso together might ease that away.

Augustine had called at the clinic the day after Alonso was found at the clinic's gate. He explained how he and one of his parishioners had found Alonso on their doorstep and brought him to the clinic.

"Can you tell me how I came to be at your church, Padre?" Dennis asked.

"I do not know, Senor; I have no way of knowing." Augustine said, "I arose Sunday morning and went open the church doors and there you lay. It was maybe a little before six of the clock, my usual time for the early Mass. Sometimes a few of my people come at that time, sometimes no one, but I always am there if I am needed."

"And you had never seen me before?"

"No, Senor, never. You were a stranger in need. How could I not help you? You were badly injured and I knew our people could not help you, but the good doctors at this place could, so Armando, my good friend and sometimes helper and I brought you here on his burro, and left without awaking any one here."

Laura said, "Well, Padre, we were up and stirring but had not opened our gate; I am sorry our bell is broken. If we had heard you we would have brought him in sooner. But I don't think he suffered any more by waiting another half hour for treatment."

"I am so glad Senora Harris, so glad we could serve the Lord together, again." It was not the first time the clinic and San Miguel Church cooperated in a mission of mercy. Augustine occasionally sent some of his people to the clinic with a cart load of the after-gleanings from a harvest of corn or other crops. Augustine and the Harrises knew and understood that lesson from the Book of Ruth. Laura and Rodney treated anyone needing their help; most were loyal Catholics, communicants of San Miguel, as were Maria and the other indigenous clinic staff.

How Alonso arrived at the church was a great mystery, and would always be for all but two young toughs who didn't know enough to care.

The next day Laura found him sitting outside on a bench in the shade, joking with the two tots, Eliza and Pacco, who seemed to be always there but no one had told him to whom they belonged. He showed them a finger trick that fascinated them, drawing them into a frenzy of screams and gasps, almost hiccups, grabbing at this hand as he appeared to pull a finger away from the rest of his hand.

Laura sat beside him and said, "Let's walk around a little."

He stood with her, saying to the kids, "Tomorrow I'll show you how it's done." The children squealed; the adults chuckled and walked away.

When they had ambled some way she said, "Alonso, Padre Augustine has sent word that he has found you a place and some work. It is with one of the local families, the Fernandezes, people we have known and loved and treated over the years. There are only the two, Josefina and Tomas, good people but growing old, with no children. They will welcome you and treat you as a son." He tried to digest this but said nothing. She went on, "Armando, Augustine's friend, will be here tomorrow to take you to them. Here is some money," she said, handing him a small wad of wrinkled Quetzales, "to give you a head start in a new life." He hesitated but she insisted, saying, "Take it; you will need it. Please," she said, knowing he was embarrassed, but he accepted it and stuffed it in a pocket.

They strolled along in silence for several more minutes. Laura stopped and with a hand on his arm, turned him to face her; again he felt a buzz where she touched him. She said, "Look at me, Alonso. I can only imagine how you feel, well, about everything right now," she wouldn't let him see that she had disturbing feelings herself, "but you know you have to go. I can plainly see that you are lonely and attracted to Maria . . . and possibly to me as well. Please put any feeling for me away, *forever*. When you leave here we can try to keep from ever seeing one another

Guatemala, 1976

again; I hope so. You are a very attractive man, Alonso and I believe will make some lucky girl a good husband, but not me, not me."

He started to speak but she put her hand on his lips and said, "Alonso! Please; it is not God's will or plan that we continue to be close here and always under temptation. Please understand!" She turned away and put her hands over her face, then turned back and stared into space.

She began to walk again, and he followed her over to a shaded bench, well away from any ears. She said, "Alonso," or whatever your name really is, she thought, "We, Rodney and I, came here to serve our God. We gave up a lot but we believe deeply that it is what the Lord wants from us, and we are happy doing it, despite some pretty severe hardships. We have to be separated two or three months a year in total; one of us has to go back home to raise money for us to keep operating and for our survival."

"I see that and I appreciate it," he said. They both were lost in their own thoughts for a long minute or two. "You don't have children?"

Surprised by this shift, she said, "No, it is one of the hardships we have to bear, but we decided that it would be too hard on a child to be here, and distracting to us and our work." She looked away and sighed.

"And you aren't open to any new, different word from God?" he asked, hoping to keep alive the possibility that he could win her love somehow.

"No, Alonso," she emphatically said, then she sighed, "I don't presume to second-guess God, that would be arrogant, but whatever change He has for us it will not be a permanent separation between Rodney and me. He joined us together, and it was, *is,* for life. Please understand that and accept it." Smiling then, she said, "You are a romantic, Alonso," and immature she reminded herself. "And you are apt to think there is a romantic life out there for you, and you look for it everywhere, but my advice is to let God reveal it for you in His time," after a beat, she added, "I know as certainly as that we are sitting here that it, your romantic life, is not here," and certainly not with me she said to herself.

Making sure she had his attention she said, "Are you a Christian Alonso?"

"I think I am but maybe not."

"Why are you not sure?"

"When my folks were together," he said, improvising, "they argued about that and a lot of other things. I didn't get much of a chance to figure out anything much about religion."

"And where did, *does,* that leave you?"

"I was occasionally taken to church, went with my cousins, mostly, in Matamoros, and I went to church school until my mother took me to the States. The Nuns in Mexico were harsh and turned me off anything religious."

"And in the States?"

"I think my mother is an Episcopalian, but she was pretty irregular about going to church," he said. "I went to US high school through the eleventh grade like I told you, I think."

"Did she take you with her to church any?"

"Yes, a few times, and it was so much like a Catholic church that I just tuned it out. She never really insisted."

Laura let that settle in her mind and said, "Do you have a Bible?"

"No. I don't have anything, do I?"

"I should have one to give you but we don't have any right now. Rodney will bring some back with him," she said. "It's important that you have and read the Bible, Alonso; try to find one. The scripture can show us how we are lost and how God's and Jesus' love changes us from being centered on ourselves and what we can do for ourselves to be centered on Him and sharing His love with others, even those who hate and abuse us." She paused and smiled broadly. "That's why Rodney and I are here, showing the Lord's love by helping these people who may not have much in their lives as best we can, but who deserve the respect and the value and the love God has for them." She grinned and spread her hands wide. "Whew!" she said, "I've gone to preachin' as we sometimes

Guatemala, 1976

say back home." Both laughed. She stood and said, "See you in the morning."

Then she turned back and said, "You haven't shaved since you got here." He wondered why this abrupt shift. "We had to shave you a little to clean your face for the stitches, but that was minimal. Think about this: let your whiskers grow a while; it might serve to visually distract from your scars and maybe, well, discourage anyone from recognizing you. Then, after a while you could trim it into a neat mustache and beard, or maybe just shave off part of it or all of it if you want. Think about that, okay?" He grunted but kept quiet. "Another thing before I forget, drop by Celesta's kitchen after dinner; she will have some clothes for you, and a parcel of food for your first days." Before he could answer thanks or anything, she stood and strode away determinedly.

Swamped by these new realities, he was left to ponder it all. He went back to his cot, lay down and began to sort through it all and try to make plans.

Chapter Eleven

GUATEMALA

LYING IN HIS BUNK IN THE CLINIC, he recalled and re-played his last visit home before leaving for Guatemala; he observed how heavy the load was on Tom; he didn't have a hired hand then. Tom had to rely on his Taliaferro kin for help when he really needed it, paying them what he could. His aunt, Angelica, had moved in with Tom after Consuela died; she raised Dennis and he sometimes called her "Little Mother."

On the night before his last day he cornered his father and asked, "Dad, how much longer do you think you can stay here operating the ranch on your own?"

"As long as it takes me to talk you into coming back home, Dennis."

"Dad, you have to know I won't be coming back. This is not my life. I may not even come back to the States for good; we'll just have see how things work out down there. After this project is done, I may come back and keep working for Global but that'd be in Houston or somewhere else, not here."

Tom looked off in the distance and frowned. He said, "You know your mother and I always planned to make this place for you, ready for you when you came home to stay."

Dennis hurt for Tom, he had to. It was brutal but he knew of no way to make it better. He said, "Dad, I'm sorry, but that's just the way it is." There was an extended, strained time between them. "Dad," Dennis said, "Have you thought about selling out to Jorge?" Jorge was his uncle, Consuela's and Angelica's brother, the reigning Taliaferro. They owned the land bordering the Reade ranch, and would be the logical buyers of the Reade land.

"Jorge and I have discussed that, yes." Tom, being closed-mouthed by nature offered nothing more on the subject. Dennis left and there was no decision.

# # #

He and Bruce met at Houston Hobby Field as they prepared for the flight to Guatemala. It was Saturday, January third, 1976. They had met for the first time only the day before, the first work day of the year. Both had been interviewed separately and were hired specifically for the Guatemala project. Global Geologics gave them an intense orientation on Saturday. Now they were on their own. Dennis decided that Bruce was going to be a congenial companion and a competent coworker. He was especially pleased that Bruce would be the radio operator. They had both watched a lot of football and were pumped by it, and about the Bicentennial celebrations, regretting they would miss much of it, but relishing the adventure that lay ahead.

On the trip down he and Bruce got acquainted and at ease with each other. Bruce had graduated in Geological Engineering from Auburn the previous spring and was on his first permanent job, although he had interned full-time every summer he was in college. Both, they discovered, but to neither's surprise, were avid football fans. Auburn had a disappointing 1975 season; A&M's was better; Dennis said, "I'm sure you've heard of the *12th Man.* "

Bruce said, "And a big *War Eagle!* back at you!" After they laughed to avoid sinking into a long brag session on football, he said, "I'm really looking forward to this, Dennis. It's a good way to break into the field. Ha! *Field*, that's good! I've always been a camper. I could tell you some hair-raising things that happened to me and my family and in Scouts. You wouldn't believe: I remember one time . . ."

He was interrupted by a Flight Attendant announcing that they would be arriving in about twenty minutes. "Please have your Immigration Forms filled out and ready, with your Passports and Visas."

At Guatemala City, after going through the bureaucratic immigration routine without a hitch, they were met by Pedro and Jesus, who introduced themselves. Pedro said, "We are your companions, Senores, and your interpreters." He spoke English with a distinct but understandable accent. "We have your vehicle and equipment." Their major baggage, equipment and supplies and the ham radio rig had been sent ahead. "Please come with us, Senores." In the parking lot they were led to the company Land Rover, already packed; they checked over everything and found it in good order. Pedro said, "Come, Senores, we will go to your hotel."

A three-day flying tour began on Tuesday, after a weekend of touring the city with their Guatemalan hosts and a tedious session on Monday with various government representatives; it was more confusing than helpful, but, oh well, that was bureaucracy for you, Dennis thought. Bruce probably felt the same, but didn't say so.

The flying tour itself was pleasant but of limited use the Americans felt. They gained a better understanding of the scope and character of the country but little of the feel of the ground they would be investigating. What stuck in Dennis's mind was the beauty of the terrain – he knew it would be different on the ground – especially this enthralling natural body of water called Lake Atitlan. From the air it sparkled and pulled at him in ways not felt . . . well, ever before. It was almost like the first sight of a beautiful woman he couldn't keep his eyes away from. Approaching it on the ground he almost itched in anticipation, as eager as he ever remembered being, at least since meeting Melanie.

As they approached the evening of the first of three days cruising over the country – their plane was a twin Beechcraft of uncertain years, but it seemed to be satisfactory – their host, Colonel Roberto Mendoza, said, "We are coming into Coban, our first overnight stop." They knew this; they had a big packet of information Pedro gave them at the airport, and it included their itinerary for the flight. The papers also had reams, Dennis thought, of information on Coban and on Quetzaltenango, their second overnight stop. Then they would end the tour on Friday, back in the city.

# # #

He also mulled these intractables over and over in his mind in those early morning hours in the clinic; the more he dwelled on his situation the more frustrated and depressed and mentally exhausted he became. The first timid glow of daylight began to creep in the room; he forced himself to push those things away and try to see what he could do about his future, whatever that might be and however he would be able to shape it. Even though he had revealed his alternate identity to the people at the clinic, he didn't want to totally erase who he really was; but that would be another step in separation from his irreparably damaged past. Even if successful with his new life, he would still find a way to give Connie what she would need from a father, even if she never saw him or heard from him again.

Chapter Twelve

Guatemala

"What do you think of our country so far, Senores?" Colonel Mendoza asked the second day of their flying tour in early January.

"Beautiful! Just beautiful!" Bruce yelled over the airplane's roar. Dennis nodded in agreement. At top volume, Mendoza went on to talk about what a wonderful country it was, something he had been preaching about the entire flight.

As they disembarked at Coban, Mendoza said quietly, "In case you wondered about the plane having civilian markings," they hadn't noticed or thought about it one way or another, "it is because if it was marked as belonging to the Army or the government, it would then be a prime target for the rebels. They probably wouldn't be able to shoot us down, but they might hit the plane. We don't want that to happen, of course." Dennis and Bruce were not reassured. They had been briefed about the rebel threat, but had pushed it away; that was for "other people."

On the ground at both overnight stops they were given lengthy road tours, pointing out too much to retain. Bruce made copious notes. Pedro and Jesus were not along; it was assumed they already knew the territory. The hotel in Coban was clean if old. The food, though, was exemplary, lavish even. They were encouraged to feel like royalty, but were more eager to get on with the project, to get out into the field.

Guatemala, 1976

At Quetzaltenango, after the rather repetitive and jarring road tour, they were escorted to their hotel, Pension Bonifaz, a well-preserved nineteenth century hostelry, originally a baronial home for a nineteenth Spanish immigrant family who had pioneered growing coffee, cane, and pineapple. It was a landmark of considerable local esteem and national renown. The restaurant was more expensive than the general population could afford, but a strong core of the well-heeled locals kept it full and flourishing.

After getting his guests settled in their rooms, Mendoza led them into a small alcove, off the main dining room. Four Guatemalans sat at the single table in the room; several more chairs sat close by in quiet readiness. All were well-dressed and rose as Mendoza led the Americans in, and motioned them to seating places. Before sitting, introductions were made. The official host was the Mayor, Senor Raf de Gorgio, who ran a successful real estate business. Also present were Colonel Ugo Santana, Commandante of the local Army garrison; Senor Silvio Amendaraz, the owner of large land holdings, growing coffee, corn, sugar cane, and various other crops plus cattle; and Senora Doctora Elsa Stiles, Professor of History at a local university, widow of a businessman whose family had migrated from Germany to Guatemala in the nineteen-twenties. She was a tall, striking woman in her mid-forties. The name was pronounced as it would be in America or Germany, not as it would appear to Spanish speakers. Dennis and Bruce remembered no names at that moment, knowing they would do better after spending time with them, especially the woman. It was clear to Dennis and Bruce that all were Ladinos – mixed European blood with indigenous natives -- and that this occasion was designed to have special meaning for them. With Dennis and Bruce and Colonel Mendoza, there were seven at the table, a rather awkward number but manageable. Senora Stiles was seated across from the two Americans. The hosts were anxious that the Americans would have a positive impression of their country and Quetzaltenango specially.

The Mayor rose to toast Guatemala, Quetzaltenango, the United States, the Americanos, and their mission. The drink was *Horchatia*, an exotic, non-alcoholic local favorite. Dennis and his dad and occasionally his Hispanic family would indulge in more spirited liquors, but he didn't much like them and participated only to please others. Dennis sipped and found the drink pleasing, a little tart and not too sweet. Bruce didn't drink at all, although he raised his glass with all the toasts and put the still full glass down; he said nothing. Dennis knew the story; Bruce had a struggling alcoholic younger sister, currently in recovery, but she had been there before. Based on the past the family had scant hope that it would last. No one said anything about it; the Guatemalans were too courteous to mention it. Dennis knew that Bruce just declined any and all exotic drinks out of principle.

Dinner was served, surprising the men with how *American* it seemed to be; perhaps their hosts wanted them to feel at home. A delicious salad came first – avocados, tomatoes and cucumbers, then grilled steak. "This is called *Churrasco*, Senores; the sauce is *Chirmol*," the Mayor declared proudly.

Talk was limited while they ate. Bruce seemed intent on making appreciative smacks and "yum" sounds. The hosts grinned in response. At last a flan came for dessert, and was devoured by all with the usual gusto, with even more eagerness by Bruce. He is having the time of his life, thought Dennis. Coffee was brought out and all accepted.

"Very good, Senores, and Senora, very good!" Bruce exclaimed; Dennis concurred, mumbling his praise.

The Mayor tapped his glass and said, "I am sure the Colonel has given you a good education about our beautiful country, and about Quetzaltenango. Maybe you have some questions Senores, yes?"

The Americans had been expecting something like this. Bruce, who had appointed himself spokesman, said, "Yes, Mayor, we have been bombarded, well," he paused, being unsure that the American vernacular "bombarded" would be understood, and continued, "that is, thoroughly

Guatemala, 1976

enlightened by Colonel Mendoza and others I am sure, and we are looking forward to learning a lot more!"

The Mayor said, looking at his fellow Guatemalans, "Maybe some of you have special things you want our American friends to know about, Yes?"

Senora Stiles pulled herself up and said to them, "Senores, as a professor of Guatemala history I am concerned that our cultural history is protected and understood. Unfortunately many of our young people her have been left in ignorance about what a blessed country Guatemala is. I hope you will not remain in such ignorance while you are here with us." Dennis thought that was a rather harsh way to put things but neither Americans reacted. "Perhaps you have been told much about our history and government, not all of which is flattering, but there it is . . . "

Bruce, thinking a response should be made, said, "This kind of ignorance in not unheard of in America, Senora."

Senora Stiles ignored the interruption, drew in a breath and said, "I hope the work you are doing, Senores, will not lead to dams that will damage our fragile and unique environment."

"Oh, no, Senora!" Bruce was quick to say, "we are very environmentally-conscious!"

She went on undeterred, "There are subtleties in every country's culture, Senores. Perhaps you have seen some of our Mayan ruins?"

"We've not had time yet to see any of those, Senora," Bruce said, "But we look forward to doing so. We have seen some modern images reflecting the Mayan history, in Guatemala City. Very impressive, Senora, including some pretty frightening depictions of the mythical creature, the Quetzalcoatl."

Stiles smiled, then said, "Then perhaps you have heard of the *Resplendent Quetzal*, not the currency but the national bird, yes?"

Bruce jumped it with, "You bet, Senora!" then realizing he himself had been uncultured, recovered with a swallowed, 'harrumph," and said, "Forgive me, Senora, what I had in mind was that we have on our vehicle

69

the image of the Quetzal, in fact two on each side, on each door, four in all."

"But do you know anything about the nature of it, of the Quetzal?" she asked. Neither man responded. She went on, professorially, "The quetzal is a most beautiful bird, brilliant colors, perhaps either reflecting or inspiring the Guatemalan penchant for color in our everyday and cultural life. The male, with his long, curving tail, can reach almost a meter in overall length." She paused and looked to the men for approval and understanding. She was making a noble effort to enlighten them, and wanted some little acknowledgement.

The Americans nodded and tried to appear eager for more. Bruce did in fact find it interesting; he said, "Please, Senora, this is fascinating! Please go on."

The professor smiled her gratitude and said, "He, the quetzal, is very reclusive, very rarely seen if he does not want to be seen. Efforts to breed or raise them in captivity have all failed, although some, shall we say, foolish people keep trying."

"What about his call, Senora?" Bruce asked.

"I am sorry; it is not very pretty, a sort of cawing, but he is mostly quiet, does not use his voice much."

"Maybe that's one of the reasons he isn't seen much, nobody knows he's there." Bruce suggested.

"Perhaps," said Senora Stiles. "His refusal to live in captivity may be seen as his relevance to the Guatemalan ethos, what makes him the easily understood and universally embraced symbol of the *freedom* of our people."

"Freedom," thought Dennis; that's what he needed, freedom from his past.

Later drives between sites when they did get started in the field, on their own, were long and tedious, the roads often not paved and typically rough; he couldn't even doze on these roads and used this idle time to

Guatemala, 1976

reflect on whatever came to mind. What most often came to mind was how truly messed up his life back in the States was, and how he hoped this new venture could be the opportunity for a reset. Earlier on this leg of that last day's trek, he had found it impossible to avoid chewing over his past failures; his marriage and the abrupt rejection from the Army, and his inability to endure the demeaning of working for his father-in-law in a make-work job. He could not yet fully accept personal responsibility for his downfall; it was too easy to blames others. But during those long silent – the road noise ruled out most conversation – rides, he hesitantly began to try to step back and look at things objectively. It wasn't easy, he hurt too much; then there was a child, his and Melanie's daughter, Connie, beautiful little Connie, age almost two; he could not avoid responsibility for her, for the true, unconditional love between them on a level he did not know even with Melanie. He had wanted to name her Consuela after his mother, but Melanie and her family firmly objected to any name even remotely Hispanic in origin or by hint. It was bad enough in the parent's sight that their son-in-law carried any tainted blood, however slight. A compromise was negotiated; Constance, shortened to Connie. Beautiful Connie, now age almost two. Near black arresting, trusting eyes and gently curling hair, black with flashing glints of red, like her father and grandmother. Now he was separated from her, by distance and time; at times he didn't know how he would endure it, but he knew he had to and had to try to rebuild his life without hurting her. It was an intense and constant pain for him, but for the benefit of all of them, separation seemed best. He carried no picture of Melanie; the experience of a gradual, growing abrasion between them due to the conditions imposed on the marriage by her proud and domineering parents eroded any love they had to the point of leaving nothing for the nourishing love a solid marriage needs.

With Connie it was totally different; he *was* responsible for not only the conception that brought her into being but also for her care and protection and for shaping the person she would become. Now his ability to fulfill these responsibilities was next to impossible; he wrestled with this daily and never reached a resolution. He was obligated to give her child support and, so far, had not reneged. He did carry a photograph of Connie, the only others in his wallet were his parents. Now did didn't even have those. The pain of separation from her was the most consuming of his time and feelings, and there was no relief that he could see.

Chapter Thirteen

Guatemala

The guerilla leader, the self-titled Commandante Marco, watched the road after concealing his men in the deep foliage. It was Friday, January sixteenth, almost dusk. They had marched most of the day to arrive at the dip in the road right along the shore of Lake Atitlan, the most beautiful lake in Guatemala, maybe in all of the Americas. At this key spot, the road was only a few yards from the lake edge and a few feet above water level, climbing back up steeply in both directions. It was a place of great vulnerability for a vehicle and an ideal place for his band of some two dozen rag-tag rebels to stage an ambush. He barked at the men – some just boys – to wait until he gave the order and then shoot to stop any vehicle he picked out, any he chose to intercept. If there was an Army convoy, he would probably not shoot; if it was a single Army vehicle or a civilian he would decide on the spot, and to try not to do too much damage because there might be usable salvage. If he thought they could use a vehicle, then capture it or what was inside; passengers injured or dead were just collateral damage. His troop had no vehicles, and capture of one was a high priority. All they had were four mules to carry supplies. If the travelers were not military, he would probably let them pass. His men were well-hidden. The Army patrolled this area frequently; the ragged troop would not expose themselves unless it was safe for them to attack.

Lake Atitlan is a spring-filled volcanic crater and a natural wonder. Long known as a place of great beauty; in 1976 it had just begun to be recognized for its tourism potential, and a few shore-side accommodations and marinas had appeared. The clear, deep blue water plunged to over one thousand feet in depth, and spread over fifty square miles of surface. The shoreline was accessible in only a few places because of the severe mountainous slopes around most of the perimeter.

It was late afternoon, the sun setting slowly in the west of the lake and the road. A few straggling field workers walked by, hoes and other farm implements on their shoulders. A couple of small trucks with workers hanging on bounced by, struggling up the hill, revving engines and grinding gears to regain momentum after hitting the low point. Marco let them pass. After a long spell it was quiet; by then locals would have arrived at their homes and the quiet of the evening settled in; the only sounds were made by insects, night birds, and the occasional monkey hoot. At rare times, the tinkle of laughter from a settlement across the lake broke the silence, but only faintly. There was a little light lingering in the western sky, but that would soon be gone and without a strong moon, total darkness would descend.

The guerillas had lanterns and flashlights but held them unlit until the Commandante gave the command to use them. Marco thought himself wise in the ways of commando operations; in reality he was just a twenty-three year old farm boy but had been fighting since he was seventeen. Although his training in military matters had been mainly in live operations, he had been seasoned under the mentorship and leadership of commanders not much older, many now dead or captured; and he brought to the position the tempering and toughness a hard, deprived peasant and rebel life gave him for authority to lead, at least in the eyes of his men. His immediate superiors allowed it but gave little support..

A minute before the last of the light faded away, the men heard the grumbling of a motor not far to the south approaching. Though in the tropics, much of Guatemala is mountainous, and in the highlands it can

Guatemala, 1976

be cool all year long, and chillingly cold at night. The official motto of the country is: "Pais de la Eterna Primavera," translated: "The Country of Eternal Spring."

The vehicle was a dust-covered tan Land Rover, bouncing along over the roadbed of close packed stones the size of watermelons. It had official-appearing seals on both front doors, double circles with lettering between, and a symbol of some sort in the middle. Had any of the guerillas been able to read either Spanish or English – **they** were fluent in their native Indian language, and Marco could converse in Spanish but could read neither that nor English – they would have known it was not a government vehicle. Between the circles on the top it read: GLOBAL GEOLOGICS LLC, and on the bottom: GUATEMALA PROJECT # 75-027. In the center were the large initials: GG, bracketed by twin, black and white images of, long-tailed Quetzales, the official bird of the Republic. The quetzal is a national symbol and is found on everything official, most notable on the national seal; even the money is named the Quetzal. In 1976, the Quetzal exchanged onefor-one with the American dollar; dollars were accepted almost as universally as Guatemalan bills. The quetzal itself was considered by some to be an endangered species; they lived in tropical forests and were increasingly harder to find. They could not live in captivity.

Marco and his men could be excused for mistaking the vehicle for a government car and, therefore, a viable target. The car paused at the bottom of the dip and Bruce shifted down and revved the engine.

Marco shouted, "Fuego!" and shots rang out, indiscriminately shattering trees, other foliage, the earth, and the car's windshield, nearside windows and front tires. Shots found the men inside as well, and some component of the engine that was necessary for operation; the car was dead, probably destroyed beyond the guerilla's ability to repair it. The noise of the gunfire had been too loud for any groans, yells or other human sounds to be heard.

Marco called a halt to the firing and waited for the dust to clear; no voice was heard from the car. No bird or insect sounds were heard for three or four minutes, then they gradually resumed their nightly serenades. He motioned for his next in command – who might change from day to day – to advance and see what had been done. Oscar, putative Officer-of-the-Day, cautiously advanced to the car, holding his gun ready, and stood for a moment in front. Satisfied, he walked around the passenger side and the rear, inspecting thoroughly. At the driver's side he looked in the window and confirmed that none of the four passengers appears to be alive. He turned back to Marco and reported, "All dead, Commandante."

Marco huffed a satisfactory grunt and motioned for the rest of his troop to advance to the wreck and stand guard. He would plan to spend maybe fifteen minutes to take what they wanted and clear out. The car was beyond worth to them so would have to be abandoned; he regretted that, but it would have been a mixed blessing, only one or two of the men could be trusted to drive cautiously enough to manage it. Oscar poked around inside and reported back that there was a lot of technical equipment in the rear, as well as some luggage; he couldn't tell what the equipment was but it looked expensive, mostly undamaged and perhaps useful. Marco said to get it all out and he would decide if he wanted to cart it with them when they left. They had a quartet of mules for transport, already partially loaded. What he wanted to capture was a large truck he could pack all or most his men into; this would not have sufficed even if drivable.

Oscar shouted, "They all have *pistoles,* Senor."

Marco told him to retrieve them. When Oscar pulled the front passenger over to reach the gun in a right-side holster, the man groaned; he was still alive. He jumped back and yelled, "One is still living, Commandante."

"Check on the rest and make sure they are also dead" Marco commanded, "then bring the guns to me."

Guatemala, 1976

"No, Senor, they are dead, all three," he said. He handed the guns to Marco.

Marco said, "Pull the one still alive out of the car. Lay him on the ground over here by me." Oscar called the nearest man over the help him; they climbed into the car and began to ease the unconscious man out, and, gently, almost reverently, laid him on the ground next to the Commandante.

Marco motioned to the rest of the troop to come up and unload the equipment, stacking it in more or less orderly fashion on the ground. He walked around the stack of square metal cases, bristling with dials and knobs and nothing to show what was what, at least in a language he could understand. If he couldn't understand it he knew no one else there could, so he didn't bother to ask. He said, "Pack up anything not damaged and put it on the mules." He would decide what to do with it later, *manana*. He told two of the men to open and go through the luggage. He said, "Take out any papers and any clothes anybody can use; give me the papers." Now he had to decide what to do with the injured man.

Oscar sidled up to him and said, "Commandante, what do you want to do with the car?"

Marco hadn't thought that far ahead. It blocked the road and would attract more attention than he wanted. No doubt the sound of the attack would have been heard over the lake and around for miles, but civilians were not going to investigate; the Army or Police might if anyone reported it. In the morning people would be passing this spot early, most on foot. He thought about this a long moment, then said, "Put any damaged equipment and the bags back into the truck and push it into the lake. Don't leave anything here on the ground."

"What about the bodies? Oscar asked, thinking it too barbaric for his Catholic upbringing.

"Si, all of them!"

Oscar assumed leadership and commanded the men to come and take care of that. The vehicle was heavy and the front tires were flat; one of them had to go inside – there was some hesitation but the one chosen had to be the least squeamish about the dead he'd have to crawl over – and disengage the gears. That done, the car was slowly edged over to the bank, Oscar himself reaching in to man the steering, and into the deep water. It made almost no sound as it rolled down the increasingly steep incline and into the water, and sank lower; only a small gurgle was heard, and then it was gone. A few bubbles rose to the top but that was all, no more sound, no sign of the vehicle itself although the evidence of gunfire on the environment would linger until the jungle took it back to its natural, primordial state. The men scuffed the matted grass leading down to the water with their feet to disguise the marks of a descent into the lake.

One of the men brought Marco a battered briefcase; it was stuffed full of papers found on the dead and in the luggage, and documents that Marco couldn't read; he had no concept of any value they might have, but accepted them as if he knew everything about them. He didn't open the case.

He sniffed, hitched up his belt and looked down on the prone figure on the ground. The man had a serious gash on his face and had lost a lot of blood; it was slowly clotting. Perhaps there were other injuries not visible. He bent over and began to go through the multiple pockets in the khaki field jacket and pants the man wore. He found a wallet with an American – Texas – driver's license, two credit cards, insurance certificates, an ID from Global Geologies, and eighty-eight American dollars. There were also over two hundred Guatemalan Quetzales in various denominations, all a windfall for Marco. In another pocket was his US Passport and a letter from the Guatemalan government authorizing the project the team was involved in. Marco could read well enough to see that the man's name was Dennis Taliaferro Reade, but that meant nothing to him; the name had appeared on the other documents

Guatemala, 1976

as well, but the US Passport was official, and meant something to him. Marco knew he didn't have much time, and yet he was undecided as to what to do with this man, this Norte Americano. After a period he put everything taken from the pockets out in display; then he took the cash from the wallet and stuffed it in his pockets, and put the rest of the documents identifying the man in the brief case. Lastly he took the field jacket for himself.

He stood and called for Oscar, "We will take this man with us." He didn't offer an explanation. "Bandage up his head." Among the things found in the vehicle was a generously-filled first aid backpack. Dennis's face was cut badly, and his head and left arm bled, but Marco had found no other visible wounds.

"There is no room on the mules, Senor," Oscar said, "how can we carry him?"

"Unload some of the equipment and give it to the men to carry or put it on the other mules. Put the man on the fourth mule propped up, not slung over. He has head wounds and he should sit up straight. Tie him securely!" Oscar turned to take care of these instructions. Yelling at his men, with many grunts and huffs told them how to lash Dennis to the animal. Like the other mules it had a rough plank frame already on it to lash the loads onto. To this they tied pieces upright and crossed and to Dennis, looping under his shoulders. He sat, looking extremely uncomfortable, but erect.

Chapter Fourteen

Guatemala

Marco called, "Pepitto, come here." Pepitto was a boy of short stature and undetermined age; no one in the troop knew his real name. Pepitto was a nickname given him by the rebels because he was small, and always cheerful and full of energy: "Little Pepper." He ran errands and performed other tasks the men gave him; he was a welcome camp follower, not allowed to use weapons . . . at least not yet.

"Si, Comandante," Pepitto appeared at Marco's side, grinning broadly.

Marco handed the boy the valise of documents taken from the car and the wounded man. "Here, he said, "I want you to take these to Supreme Generale Maximilian," an assumed name and title, "and tell him that we have this man here and await the General's pleasure as to what to do with him."

"Where can I find the Supreme Generale, Senor?"

"He has a house and a camp outside San Marcos, several kilos outside, northwest, I believe; you will have to ask, *carefully*, Pepitto, all with care, great care," he cautioned the boy. There were several San Morcoses in Guatemala, usually with a suffix, but Pepitto and all the rebels knew which one Marco meant. It would be in the mountains. "If you hurry, you can probably be there by noon tomorrow. Take some food and water. Tell the Generalissimo where we are now and that we will move north from here. We will advance

Guatemala, 1976

toward *Point Sixteen*. Stay off the roads; go cross-country as much as you can." He paused, thinking things through. "You have all that, Pepitto? Remember *Point Sixteen;* that's very important, *very important."*

Not daring to admit he had any doubts, he nodded his head vigorously and said, "I can do this, Senor, please trust me!" Marco nodded and patted the boy on the head and motioned him away. Pepitto spun around and began to run, in his elation at being given such an important assignment, loping along. In his haste he forgot about food. He was sure of his ability to make his way in the dark, through the night and the next day. He ran along the road; in a second he was invisible and the sound of his foot-fall lingered for only a bit longer; then he was gone.

The troop packed up and left the road, disappearing into the woods.

Late Friday after dark, Paulo, as Pepitto was known to family and friends, began to trot through the brush, skirting open areas and roads, sticking to concealing woods and fields of tall corn or cane. Despite his determination to fulfill the mission given to him, he soon began to tire; the trot became a slow lope, the lope a brisk walk and soon, a stumbling amble. He paused to rest and sat on a rough stone wall, and took his bearings. He knew the territory well, but knew it would take more than two days to reach the encampment. He was without food or water and was smart enough to admit he needed them to go much farther. Marco expected him to get provisions from the poorer folk. Paulo knew that was not realistic, but pushed on valiantly; few locals would openly support the rebel cause. Most of them depended on their rich landlords for employment.

He had to decide what to do. He wanted to be loyal to Marco, but he was bright and realistic; besides he was tired and hungry. He chose to detour to his home to rest and be fed. He arrived at the small adobe, thatched-roofed hovel after midnight. He eased the door open – there was no way to lock it; who would want to steal anything there? – trying to be as quiet as he could. Despite his efforts to not disturb his parents, his mother sensed and knew he had come home and called out, "Paulo! Paulo! You are here!" She came rushing to him, enveloped him in her arms and cried into his shoulder.

She was followed by Jose, his father, whose reaction was not the same as the mother's. He shouted, "Paulo, you ungrateful pig! Where have you been? Your mother has been overcome with fear, thinking you had been killed!" The boy cringed but said nothing. "You have been with the rebels, I know. Don't try to lie to me!" He raised his hand in a mock threat but Paulo knew he would not hit him, he never had, even though his son was typically mischievous. Jose stood there, anger mixed with relief sweeping over his face.

Elena, the mother, said, "You must be hungry, my son, and you are tired. Come have some food, and then go to bed." Exactly what Paulo wanted. He was given the usual fare of beans and rice and as much water as he wanted and, after many hugs and kisses from his mother, and a fatherly slap on the shoulder from Jose, he crawled into his familiar cot and fell asleep almost before pulling the thin blanket up over him.

Jose and Elena got up early, their habit for they had work and responsibilities; they were hard and loyal workers. They intended to let their son sleep a little longer, but before leaving Jose shook him awake. "Paulo! Wake up, wake up!" Paulo sat up and rubbed his eyes. Jose stood over him, holding the satchel his son had with him when he arrived. "What is this?" he asked, shoving the bag toward his son.

Paulo tried to explain what he had been doing during the four days he had been gone. He said, "I was trying to help the rebels, Papa."

"Then what is this, what are these papers?" Jose demanded.

"I do not know, Papa. Commandante Marco ordered me to take them to the rebel headquarters."

"Where is that?"

"San Marcos, north of here."

Guatemala, 1976

"And he thought you could do that? Ridiculous! That is maybe thirtty kilometers!"

"He had faith in me, Papa."

Jose harrumphed and asked again, "What are these papers, Paulo?"

"I do not know, my father. Marco cannot read. He just wanted to send them to someone who can read." None of the family could read either in Spanish or in English.

Jose sat on the side of the cot, paging through the papers. He said, "These are English I think, most of them." He continued to look and mull over the papers; finally saying, "You are not going to deliver these to anybody! You are going to stay here and work with me and your mother!" He stood and put the satchel on a high shelf and said, "Come we will eat and then go to the fields."

Chapter Fifteen

GUATEMALA

THE ATTACK ON THE GLOBAL GEOLOGICS team occurred just before dusk on January sixteenth. As night descended Marco's troop slogged into the dense growth around the lake, angling away to the west, then north. They marched for two hours then stopped for two hours rest, possibly to sleep, then another two hours moving slowly, furtively toward their base. They came to a stop for the second rest period. Marco told Oscar, "We will stop only an hour here. We are only a few kilometers from the base. We will eat here."

Oscar knew how unreliable Marco's estimates of distance or most other measurables were, but passed the word to the men, and they began to find places to sit and put down their packs and weapons. Dennis was left tied to the mule, still not conscious. An hour later the men were alerted to get up and move on.

In the disorderly time as they were shuffling around to be ready when Marco commanded them to move, there was a sudden blast of gunfire. An Army troop had been alerted to their presence, and had tracked them for the last hour, following a parallel path. The Army unit moved ahead when the rebels stopped, and set up an ambush. The attack was launched just as dawn broke and was a complete and utter surprise. None of Marco's thirty or so men was ready; no arms were ready, all either leaning against a tree or half way out of the shoulder slings, none

Guatemala, 1976

cocked — the arms were an unmatched collection of out-dated rifles, plus a few shotguns -- ammunition was not uniform and each man was expected to keep himself provisioned with whatever his weapon used.

It was over in less than three minutes; less than a dozen shots were fired by the rebels. No Army men were hit but all of Marco's died or were severely wounded. A few groaned when the firing stopped but the Army men quickly shot them in place; all was quiet. Birds had stopped singing when the shooting started but gradually, almost timidly, began again. The mules scattered into the brush; three were caught, the fourth, Dennis' transport, was not. It tore through the woods and didn't stop for almost a kilometer. Dennis did not wake up even though he had slid over to the mule's side, still tied securely, still feverish and unconscious.

The Army troop Commander looked over the equipment the rebels were carrying. He recognized that it must be from the Global Geologics project. The team members could be captured or dead -- he assumed dead -- their vehicle commandeered and likely camouflaged. Even though the radio was intact, as far as he could tell, he nor any of his men could operate it. He would report this to his superiors next week. It was Saturday morning and Sunday was a day of rest.

Dennis' mule galloped through the underbrush, frantic and spurred beyond any speed it had ever shown. It panted and ran until fatigue stopped him. He had come to a thin brook, bent his head, and noisily drank his fill. He had never had to find water for himself but nature gave him the motivation and the moves. Finishing, he snorted and looked up and around for something to eat, and began to nibble on some handy leaves, not his usual fare but edible and filling. He snorted and chomped noisily, and every once in a while would whinny and pass gas.

Two scruffy young men, who disliked working in the fields but had to do it anyhow, were out after midnight on a scavenging mission for melons and cantaloupe lying innocently in some farmer's field. They heard the animal.

"Mario," one said, "You hear that?"

"Of course, you *idiote*. I could not miss hearing it. Can you see it?" said Victor, the bolder of the two, and the organizer of the raid.

"No, but there is no other sound but the animal. Let us see if we can find it."

They edged through the brush until they spotted the mule. Without approaching they waited and watched until they were sure there was no one with it.

"Come," said Victor, "There is no one here." They walked up to the mule and saw the bundle slung on the right side of the animal, tied securely. Mario stepped up to look at the bundle and exclaimed, "Holy Mother! It is a man, Victor!"

Victor went over and lifted up Dennis' head and saw the damage; he felt the body and sighed. "He is alive but badly injured; we have to do something for him." He pondered things in his head for some minutes, walking around the mule. After thinking through this surprising discovery and the duty a decent person would have, he said, "We will take him to the church and leave him there; we will not let the Padre or anyone else see us. Padre Augustine will get him the help he needs."

"Can we keep the mule, Victor?"

"Si," Victor said after a moment, "but we will have to be quiet".

Nine a.m., Monday, January nineteenth. American Embassy all-purpose staffer Wilmot Jennings picked up his ringing phone. It was an overseas call; he was designated by the Embassy to take calls from the States *other than* from the State Department. "Yes, Mildred?" he said, not caring to hide his boredom.

"A Kenneth Townsend identifying himself from Global Geologics is calling, from the States," she added unnecessarily.

"Mildred, please dig out the file on Global for me." She grunted that she would.

Guatemala, 1976

Jennings knew the firm name but not the caller. He knew that Global had a team of technicians in Guatemala doing some kind of, well, something for the government, funded by good old Uncle Sam. When Mildred brought the file in to him, he quickly scanned it and then picked up the phone identifying himself. "Mr. Townsend, I am Wilmot Jennings," he said, "what can I do for you?"

"We, Global Geologics, that is, have a team in Guatemala as you probably know," Jennings murmured an affirmation. "We have a daily schedule of radio contact with them; they carry a ham radio rig with them since they are out in the countryside most of the time and a telephone may not be available, and . . ." Townsend stopped for some reason.

Jennings said, "And?"

"Well, we haven't heard from them in three days, and we are concerned that something has happened to them."

"Let me review the file a minute, if that's okay?" Jennings said, humming as he scanned. "I believe they arrived in country on three January, and had a week or so orientation conducted by the government."

"That's right. After the orientation, or as part of it, the Guatemalans took them on a flying tour, identifying some of the sites or areas they were going to investigate, and then they went out on their own in our vehicle." Jennings let him talk. "The plan is for them to make visual inspections from the air, then on the ground, and then go back and take soundings at the most promising places."

This was getting too technical for Jennings. He said, "You said you have a daily radio schedule for reporting in. When did you last hear from them?"

"Three days ago, on Friday, the sixteenth. They over-nighted the fifteenth in Cacales, I believe it's called, and were gong to work their way around the west side of Lake Atitlan…"

"You know, I guess, that the lake and a big area around it is a National Park?"

"Yes, and we know we can't build any dams anywhere near it. It's just that the lake is there and, we are told, worth seeing, and the area might give us some understanding of the geology we need to look for elsewhere in the country."

"I see here that you have two men on that team, plus two nationals, a Dennis Reade and a Bruce Kalchik, and I supposed you would like us to try to find them, right?"

"Yes. Exactly."

"My records show that after their orientation and all they left Guatemala City on Monday, January twelfth.

"That's right," Townsend said, "they are planning to scout along the western slopes of the mountains, those closest to the Pacific, looking for possible sites for hydroelectric dams."

"You do know that they are traveling through rebel country, don't you? Are they armed?"

"Yes, side arms but no rifles or anything like that."

"It might be helpful if we knew where they stayed after leaving the City, and before they, uh, disappeared," Jennings said.

"They checked in by radio late Monday night; next morning they had a day of sightseeing in Antigua and stayed overnight there, Tuesday. Then they went to Escuintla, spent Wednesday night and moved on to the last overnight, like I said, at Cacales."

"Where had they planned to spend Friday night?"

"I'm not sure I'm pronouncing it right, but looks like *Quetzaltenango*," mis-pronouncing it "**Quetzal**" as if in English, not the correct "**Ketzal**," as in Spanish, and locally, "that right?"

"Fine." He wouldn't correct Townsend just then; time enough for this capitalist-exploiter to learn that the Quetzal was an important Guatemalan symbol and should always be treated with respect, like getting the pronunciation correct. "Did you have any back-up plan in case the radio failed to work, lost power, or was damaged or something?"

"Yes, if that happened, as soon as they could reach workable telephone connections they were to telephone you. I guess you haven't heard anything from them?"

Guatemala, 1976

"No, we haven't heard," Jennings said and then was silent, then said "About all I can do, Mr. Townsend is to send out an alert to the civil authorities in the country, and Guatemala is so small that it would be sensible to just include the whole country in the alert to look for these men and any sign of them or their vehicle. The file here says that they are in a Land Rover, tan; I'll include that information; I have the license number. That's about all anybody can do at this stage, sir."

"You'll let us know if . . . and when you find anything?"

"Naturally, Mr. Townsend, naturally. We'll be in touch regularly. Please call us if you hear from them."

Later that day a report came in that the radio and other items from the team had been found by a Guatemalan Army unit, who were scouring the area to find any localized evidence of an attack. At of the end of the day none had been found.

Wilmot placed a call to Townsend. After identifying himself he said, "Mr. Townsend, I'm afraid we have some bad news for you and your company." He waited for Townsend to respond.

"Well, thank you. What is it?"

"It looks like your team was ambushed while on their field work . . ."

"Ambushed? How? Any survivors?"

"Not that we know, Mr. Townsend. Reports are sketchy but it looks like no one survived, at least to be found. The Guatemalan Army recovered some of the team's equipment but there was no sign of the men, any of the four."

"How did they recover it?"

"The Army met a small troop of rebels and defeated them, there were no rebel survivors, but some of the equipment the team had was recovered. That is what makes the identification of the team certain," Wilmot said. "What makes it less certain is that there were none of the men's papers there, among the things recovered. There is also no sign of the vehicle they were in, but there are signs that it might have been pushed in the lake."

"Lake?"

"Yes, Lake Atitlan. The attack apparently happened along a road skirting the lake."

Townsend was quiet for some time. Then he said, "Could you fax us a written report on this? Include as much detail as you can. I have to notify the families of our men, the Americans."

"Certainly. I will get that to you this afternoon."

Chapter Sixteen

Texas

June, 1972, in Houston. Dennis and Melanie began to settle into a typical middle class suburban life for comfortably-situated couples. The fact that their comfort was largely due to Melanie's father's largess grated on Dennis, especially at first, but over time that gradually diminished. He enjoyed the perks and tried to be happy and make Melanie happy. As a part of her parents' wedding gifting, Melanie's allowance from her college days would continue indefinitely. Dennis wasn't especially happy about this but could do nothing about it.

His job at Williams Oil was to maintain the records of the field operations: the contracts, deliveries and follow-ups for more orders. He wasn't required to go into the field but he asked if he could. He wanted to learn all he could about this business if he was going to make a career of it. He had an office of sorts, a corner cubicle with a view; it was better than many others in the big *boiler* room. Tacitly, he had ready access to Herbert, being the boss' son in law, but he never tried to take advantage of it. Usually Herbert called him in, and the discussion was more often personal than business. There might have been resentment among the rest of the staff, but no one had ever shown it.

As he was moving into his office on his first day, Herbert strode in followed by another man, slightly older than Dennis, obviously a veteran in the firm with a rare four-walled office down the hall. Dennis knew who he was of course, Edgar Blaylock, but had never met him. Blaylock was well over two hundred and fifty pounds, Dennis guessed, and something over six feet tall; they could see eye-to-eye. Herbert said, "Edgar knows more about the business than I do. I want you to follow him around for a month or so; he'll teach you the ropes."

Blaylock said without introduction, "Come on. You can put that stuff away anytime; let's go down to the break room and get some coffee." Dennis turned and followed him out the door. "We can do our introductions on the fly, and strode off toward the elevators," Blaylock said, but said no more in the elevator.

In the break room, two floors below Williams' twelfth-floor penthouse suite and one floor below the big pen, Blaylock said, "Grab a table and I'll get the coffee." He headed toward the service counter, then spun around and said, "Whadda you like in it?"

Dennis said, "Just black, please." He thought that "grabbing a table" was an unnecessary request; there was only one other table occupied in the room, among a dozen or so.

Blaylock returned with the mugs; he sat and said, "Okay, my name is Edgar Blaylock. I've been with Herbert for going on ten years, came here right out of college. Everybody here knows who you are and we don't have any problems about a son-in-law coming in if he's qualified. I pretty well figure you are. Herbert asked me to look over your resume, college grades and such. On the surface you *are* qualified. What we don't know is if you have the passion for the work. We'll find out soon."

Dennis figured he ought to say something. "Well, Edgar . . . "

"Just call me Eddie, okay?"

Dennis nodded. "I'll do my best here, Eddie. I didn't exactly plan to go into the private sector right away, but . . . "

"We know about that. Sorry it didn't work out, but maybe this'll be better than Nam."

Dennis felt a flush of anger, wanting no one to think he had benefited by avoiding his military duty, but he pushed that away. He said, "You

Guatemala, 1976

already know just about everything about me; what about you? What's your background for this work?"

If Blaylock resented that, he didn't show it, in fact he grinned. "I figured you were no push-over. Maybe you'll do!" He chuckled and said, "I went to Abilene Christian on a football scholarship, as you might have figured. I majored in Physical Education, shorthand for coaching. Had no interest in science at all. Thought I'd start at a small high school in west Texas and work my way up to college and maybe eventually to a big-time school, Southwest Conference, Big-Ten or SEC, maybe someday head, head coach, that is."

"Sounds like that was *your* passion," Dennis said.

"Was, that is until my wife found out how much high school assistant football coaches are paid, or how little. She pushed me into looking at the big picture as she called it. I asked around and looked into a bunch of things, and the oil business just jumped out at me. I came to Houston looking and after a bunch of no-interests, I found my way to Herbert Williams."

They finished their coffee. Blaylock raised his eyebrows to ask if Dennis wanted more. Dennis shook his head and turned his Styrofoam cup upside down. Blaylock went on, "Herbert hadn't been on his own very long then, but he was expanding and he must have seen something in me. He brought me on and taught me all I needed to know, and we've been a great team ever since." He stood, picked up the soiled cups and dropped them in a bin as he walked back to the elevators; Dennis followed. As they arrived at Dennis' floor, he said, "Get your stuff put away and tomorrow we'll start to get you going. Good to get to know you," and stuck out his hand for a hearty handshake, and left.

The days and weeks flowed by faster than Dennis expected, and he found the work, or rather the oil business, more interesting than he expected. As it evolved, and it had to be that way because neither Herbert not Edgar Blaylock knew in advance how Dennis's job and performance would go; apparently it was going to work out, at least for the present. Dennis was pleased, Herbert and Edgar seemed to be pleased, and Melanie was pleased.

One day early in Dennis' time at Williams Eddie made a stab at calling him, "Denny." That temporarily brought out Dennis' temper, evident only with a scowl and a quick intake of breath. After cooling down Dennis said, "Sorry Eddie, if I flared up. I've never liked "Denny," and prefer not to be called that. Please call me Dennis if that's okay."

"Sure, uh, Dennis," Eddie said;" didn't mean anything; most of us have nicknames around here. Thought . . . well, never mind what I thought. Any particular reason?"

Dennis didn't like to talk about his past, but he figured he owed Eddie an explanation. "In I think the third grade a particular vicious bully tormented me; he was two years ahead of me. At that time I was just getting into my growth spurt and I was very awkward and uncoordinated. I was taller than him but he had maybe a twenty pound edge on me in weight. He taunted me by calling me "Denny." I decided right then I didn't like Denny and refused to answer to it, in class or anywhere else, especially on the playground. He chased me around calling me "Denny, Denny, bean-stick Denny!" he tried to get me to fight him but I wouldn't unless he hit me."

"And if he did?"

"Then I would try to hit him but usually I just couldn't connect. It made me the laughing stock of the playground. Hah!"

"And is there an end of that story?"

"By the fifth grade I shot up and had filled out and my nemesis had been held back a grade so we were on more or less equal terms," Dennis said. "If I saw him on the playground or anywhere else he slunk away; I tried glaring at him but it didn't work; he just turned away and avoided me. End of story."

Eddie said, "Well, Dennis, I know you are here and qualified for the work, but if I were you, I'd try to decide just who I am, who I want to be. Being the boss' son-in-law does not seem to be a formula for a good, long-term career. Think about it."

The third week of Eddie taking Dennis around to the customers' offices, the first stop of that day was to Southwest Explorations Inc. Blaylock strode up to the receptionist and said, "Hello, Fancy, how you been?' Dennis wondered about the name, "Fancy." Was this Eddie's regular way of greeting pretty girls or could it be her actual name?

"Well hello yourself you big flirt!" the girl said. "Who's this?" she said, nodding at Dennis.

"Miss Fancy McGregor, meet Dennis Reade, our newest grunt." Fancy stood and reached over her desk and shook hands with Dennis. Dennis smiled and felt a slight blush. Fancy was a stunning blonde beauty, her grip firm and held a little longer than he thought necessary. "You'll have to cut our boy here a little slack, Fancy," Eddied continued. "He's the boss' son-in-law."

"Really?" Fancy said, sitting back down, "Congratulations! And welcome to our dirty little business." Dennis knew she was citing an inside joke. Everyone knew the oil business in the field was grubby work, maybe not as bad as coal mining but those working in it daily went home expecting to face a hard session of scrubbing away the days' grime.

Blaylock and Dennis were led into an inner office where they met their contact at Southwest Explorations, Billy Long. Introductions were made, the usual chit-chat exchanged; no business of any consequence was discussed. Nothing pressing, just the usual get-acquainted pow-wows, just enough chatting to make sure Dennis was familiar with people and things.

After less than fifteen minutes they left, Dennis nodded to Fancy as the passed her desk. On a whim he said, "Is Fancy your real name?

She chuckled and said, "Everyone asks me that! It's Francine, which I detest! Wouldn't you?" She left it at that. Dennis smiled back, and the visitors left.

Dennis' days were filled with a routine of keeping track of their shipments – most of the equipment they handled was actually leased rather than sold – checking to make sure the products arrived on time, or arrived at all; was it undamaged, was it what the customer ordered?. If there was a question, then his job was to chase it down, and try to make it right. He got out of the office enough to keep him interested, and occasionally wondering when he would get into something involving geology. Although he tried to find fulfillment and a sense that he was doing something useful and important, something about it niggled at his mind; in those early days he couldn't quite bring it up to a conscious level. He tried to push that away and not brood about it, and tried to not take it home with him; his primary driving motivation was to keep Melanie happy. He wouldn't give her anything to worry about if he could possibly help it.

Chapter Seventeen

Texas

After a few months of wedded bliss and a steady job and paycheck Melanie surprised Dennis one night after an especially satisfying time of intimacy by saying, "Dennis, honey . . ."

"Huh?" They were still in bed and he was barely conscious.

"Honey, maybe it's time to think about family . . ."

"Huh?"

"Wake up, dummy!" she punched him on the shoulder. "Dennis, we need to talk about family and, well, we need to get a more permanent home; we need to buy a house." She let that sink in. Likely some maternal instinct led her raise this kind of question when he would be most vulnerable. "I'd like to be more settled and safe, and a house we actually own would help us feel more settled, don't you think?" He didn't respond; he'd drifted off again. "Wake up! Wake up! Did you hear what I just said?"

He rolled over and said, "I guess I heard you. You want to buy a house. Is that it?"

"Yes, Dennis, I do."

"No way," he said, "can't afford it, not now, not yet; maybe after another year or so; we'll just have to wait and see." He rolled back down and deeper into the covers.

Melanie was smart enough to accept that for the time being. She had been coached by her mother, who wanted the new house for her daughter perhaps more than Melanie did herself. She would wait until another time to bring it up again, but wouldn't wait too long.

A few days later at breakfast, she said, "Dennis, honey . . . " He had learned that when she called him "Dennis, honey," it likely was something to be wary of; he braced himself. "Honey," she went on, "about buying a house, can we at least talk about it?"

They were renting a small but comfy three-bedroomer in a stable but not particularly upwardly-mobile neighborhood, a one-story ranch among thousands built for returning GIs after World War II. It had the usual conveniences, but was not as up-to-date as Melanie and her mother would like. Neither Melanie nor Dennis intended to stay there permanently but his nature, honed by his ranch upbringing, was to be cautious and frugal, not obligating himself before he could see how to pay for it. They had taken out a loan to buy a new car, thought necessary for a rising executive in a Houston oil company. It was a Mercury Grand Marquis, better that a mere Ford, but not so showy that he would appear to his co-workers or business contacts to be job-proud. Melanie had her own car, a compact Toyota her folks had given her after her sophomore year at A&M. Dennis cringed each month when making the car payment; rent and utilities were bad enough. He gave Melanie a part of his paycheck to cover groceries and other housekeeping expenses.

Dennis was a conscientious husband and wanted to keep Melanie happy, but he could not see going into more debt. In his analytical mind he concluded that this was not yet he time to take that step. "Melanie," he said after a thoughtful moment, excused he hoped by crunching loudly on a bite of toast, "I just don't see how we can buy a house right now."

"It's the money, isn't it?"

"Of course it's the money," he barked, instantly regretting it. "You know I want us to have our own house some day but it's just not that day yet."

Melanie was prepared. "Daddy could help us, Dennis. I know he will."

Guatemala, 1976

"Could or will?" Dennis asked angrily after a pause to make sure he'd heard correctly. "Have you already asked him?"

Melanie looked away; she knew she couldn't fool Dennis, couldn't lie to him, and didn't want to make him mad. Tears began to puddle in her eyes, seeping out and onto her lids and cheeks.

Dennis' anger ebbed away and his face softened. He said, "I'm sorry, Mel. It's just that we're already obligated to your father for so much that it just doesn't seem right to add to that. Can't you see that, the kind of position it puts me in?"

"Well," Melanie sighed and sniffed, abandoning her campaign for the time being, "what plans do you have for today?" She did see that he was troubled by their reliance on her parents, and didn't want to add to that.

It was Saturday; he rarely had to work on weekends but there had been exceptions. If not a conscientious home owner he was a basically responsible person, and maintenance of his homestead – owned or rented -- had its place in his order of life. He said, "I don't think those gutters have been cleaned since the First World War."

Melanie understood his sarcasm and laughed, "The house wasn't even built then, dummy!"

"I didn't say it was, only that the gutters had that much gunk in them. I think I'll see if that ladder leaning on the wall out back is weight-worthy and make a little progress on them, the gutters, I mean." His breakfast finished, he went on, "First though I think I'll act like a good old businessman on his weekend and read the paper." He stood and went into their living room and plopped down into a sagging and worn easy chair, with the paper. Melanie busied herself with something to do with housework, not necessarily needed, but she needed to be busy and calm her frustration and give him space. They had furnished the house with things she could bring: her bedroom suite she had had from her earliest memory; it had a double bed.

Practical, despite her social climbing nature, Priscilla, had insisted on a bed big enough to accommodate a husband when the time came.

Plus they had acquired a few cast-offs and items they picked up at thrift stores and yard sales. Dennis' chair was one such purchase and it suited him just fine.

Summer came and the Reade's routines seemed fixed and mostly satisfying. One day Dennis came home and found his wife in the virtually empty third bedroom, the smallest; it was tiny, hardly bigger than one of the bathrooms in the Williams' house. She had spread newspapers over the floor and was wielding a paint roller. She had on old sweats and paint spots on her nose a few other places on her person.

With an innocence that astonished even him, he said without thinking, "Melanie, what are you doing?"

"What does it look like I'm doing?" She had expected his reaction and planned to play it with subtle innocence. "I'm painting the room."

"Okay, I'll bite," he said. "Why are you painting this room instead of any other? It seems to me all the rooms here are equally dingy, but this is the one we use least, not at all that I remember."

"I just thought it needed sprucing up," she said smugly. "You have to start somewhere. You can help, you know."

He sighed, knowing he was out-maneuvered. "I'll be right back," he said and turned to go change. At least he knew to put on some grubbies; he'd done plenty of painting at the ranch. He came back and looked at what Melanie had done; it wasn't very orderly. "Mel, you've started the wrong way." Melanie turned away so he couldn't see her smile; she knew enough about husband management to let Dennis think he had his way. "You should have painted around the edges, with a brush, before starting on the walls. Here, I'll take a brush and do that; you do have a brush don't you?" He cast his eyes around and found the brush and set about edging the baseboards and trim.

They worked an hour more. Melanie said, "About time for dinner; you go clean up and I'll put the things away and start dinner."

Picking up the brush, roller and paint tray, he called back to her, "Why did you pick that color?" It was a soft yellow. The existing trim

Guatemala, 1976

was white; the two colors looked good together. "Do you plan to paint the trim, too?"

"Just thought it was a good color; I don't really have to have a reason, you know. If I like it that should be enough, don't you think?"

Out-maneuvered again, Dennis chose to keep quiet about that. He left, going out to the backyard to wash the tools with a garden hose.

At the table a little later Melanie said out of the blue, "Dennis, honey, since you found out about your hearing loss, have you thought about getting hearing aids?" Finding this strange and unexpected, Dennis was unable to respond. He did look up at her, with a face of great puzzlement. She went on, "Sometimes, honey, you seem to not hear me when I ask you something; maybe hearing aids would help."

"No, Mel," he finally said, "I haven't thought about that at all. I've been able to function ever since that shotgun blast when I was a kid. 'If it ain't broke don't fix it!' That's what I think."

"Well, please think about it, honey. I just want you to be the best you can be." It was evident that she wanted him to be the best she *planned* for him to be.

In college Dennis had been in good physical shape, strong, trim and agile, all disciplined by his Army routines and the new-found pride he felt in being in good condition. Not long after joining Williams he felt he was getting flabby and gaining weight. His ideal was around two-hundred, it fit his six foot-two; to his dismay he one day weighed and read "two hundred thirty!" on the dial. He got on the phone and began to look for a workout gym; he found that the local YMCA was a good fit. He joined and began a daily routine there and soon was down to his best weight, and in better over all condition. One day when leaving he met Fancy McGregor coming in. They stopped and chatted a minute, she said when parting, "Come see us sometime; haven't seen you in a while." He only smiled in return, observing again what a gorgeous woman she was.

Chapter Eighteen

TEXAS

THE REST OF THAT YEAR, 1973 and into the next, Melanie – and her mother; Priscilla, seemed to have been at their house every time he came home from work, and, as he thought of it, pursuing *the campaign,* her campaign for a new house.

Melanie began to ask for and then demand a new house, one they would own. He had resisted, driven by his inherent prudence. She had tried more, then began to repaint their rental house, a tactic he found out after too long a time, longer than it should have, indirectly aimed at having the new house, and at a different desire, a baby.

A baby! Of course he wanted to have children some day, but now? he'd asked himself. Reliving that day, the day it dawned on him that Melanie was serious about a baby! He felt confined, penned in, when the idea of a baby for him and Melanie sunk in, became real and certain, and soon! Was he ready to be a father, a Daddy? He didn't think so, not yet.

He didn't know whether Melanie or her mother wanted a child more. He didn't see Priscilla as the grandmother type, but maybe, he recalled thinking at the time, it was what was happening to her friends and contemporaries, and she had to keep up.

He sat down again and, as was his nature, began to systematically review the years in Houston. Some of it surprised him; he hadn't realized that the baby idea was, or could at least, be seen as a continuing strategy to achieve her goals, not only to have a child but also to have a house of their own. He could see now that the room painting was just a beginning. After the first project, the spare room, there had to be another, and another, until all three bedrooms and the bathroom had been painted, the kitchen would be next.

She had become the sexual predator of the pair. He was only human, and responded enthusiastically, and after almost every vigorous and sweat-inducing session, she would hint again at her want for a baby. He would feign sleep or drowsiness, but she was persistent. She attacked, he reasoned now, at his most vulnerable time, exhausted and groggy. Practically every night she rushed him so eagerly, that many times he would forget or forego any birth control.

So it went for the next months. On the twentieth of April, 1973 at dinner, she said, "Dennis, honey," she allowed a little time to slip by, "Honey, maybe we should have been more careful . . ."

"Huh? Careful about what?"

She reached across the table and laid her hand on his. "I went to Doctor Adams today. Dennis, honey, I am pregnant!"

"What?"

"We are going to have a baby, Dennis! Isn't that wonderful?"

"Oh!" he groaned, "I thought . . . " he realized that no matter what he had thought, it was too late, and he had to accept it and face up to the responsibilities of fatherhood. It all came down on him like a load of rocks. "Oh," he groaned again, shaking his head.

"Aren't you happy, Dennis? Please tell me you're happy about the baby, honey, please!"

"Uh, yes, well, I guess I am, but I just wanted to wait a while longer, until we got more, uh, settled."

"You know sometimes these things are taken out of our hands, Dennis," she pled, honey-eyed.

He recalled thinking just then that maybe his name ought to be "Dennishoney!" He said, "Melanie, I'd just like to be alone for a little while now, Okay?" She joyfully complied.

She just had to let him absorb and work through all this. She smiled throughout the evening, and kissed him heartily and eagerly as before at bedtime. Afterward she said, "I am so happy, Dennis, so happy! We'll have to start making plans, won't we?"

Melanie put more and more pressure on him for it, justifying it by making it *for the Baby*. In late September she said, "We need to have the baby's room and everything ready by Christmas, don't you think? It'll be here in January, late January!"

"Yup. Guess so," he said in his best Gary Cooper style. At that point he felt it was his job to just tag along and try to be supportive, and otherwise to stay out of the way. He had by then come to the point of accepting the idea of a child; he decided he wanted a girl, Melanie hadn't yet said anything about gender. They wouldn't know until it arrived, but he was surprised to find himself fantasizing about having a daughter, imagining how she would resemble her grandmother, Consuela, playing with her, crooning to her, rocking her, as his mother had done with him.

Early in Dennis' life Tom had not been much of a hands-on father, but then, after Consuela died, became more of a mentor and almost buddy to Dennis. They were partners at the ranch, and Dennis liked that. He felt like that was a really good growing-up time, and he vowed he would be the same kind of dad, only just after she, his new daughter, grew up a little.

Melanie saw his transformation and rejoiced, but not out loud. He smiled a lot and she smiled at his smiling. She took that as a sign that she – and her mother – should press harder for the new house. Priscilla took the lead; she scoured the market for desirable locations and properties, and led Melanie to open houses and other showings, and had, Dennis knew, the deciding vote on the house they settled on, as Dennis saw it. It was a fiat accompli; Herbert would advance the couple the down payment and the mortgage payments would be what he could manage, not having to pay rent. He also got a small but measurable raise, with a deduction to repay Herbert for the down payment. His take-home was virtually unchanged. He didn't complain.

In late September they closed on a nice house, similar in style to the ranch they were renting but newer and larger and in a better neighborhood. Dennis' daily drive was longer but that gave him more time to think about things during his commute.

The first months of Melanie's pregnancy her sexual appetite seemed undiminished, but by her fourth month she began to withdraw, saying, "We have to think of the baby, honey," when Dennis felt the urge. Sex became less frequent until by December, the eighth month, it was non-existent.

Christmas approached and, as in the previous year, it was largely spent with the Williams. They did go down to the ranch for a weekend in mid-month but for Melanie at least it was just not Christmas, not the way she expected. At the ranch the Latino family dominated with celebrations common to them. It was as foreign to Melanie as a Buddhist festival would have been; she was not comfortable. Dennis tried to ease things for her without offending his cousins. The only thing enjoyable for Melanie was the to-dos made over her by the enthusiastic women, gushing over the coming birth. Dennis was one of them and the next heir would be his child.

Tia Angelica said to Melanie in private, "You will have a girl."

"How do you know, Angelica?" Melanie was truly surprised; her doctor had ventured no guesses.

"Some of us have the gift," Angelica calmly replied, with the smile of one confident in her gift gracing her face. "I have always known. I have never been wrong; you will have a girl. Have you chosen names?"

"Dennis is convinced it will be a girl, but we have talked a little about names in either case. If it does turn out to be a boy Dennis wants to name him after his dad, Tom, or Thomas. We have argued about a girl's name. He wants to name her after his mother, Consuela, but I," and my mother she thought, "would like something more main-stream American, but we haven't settled on anything yet."

When she told Dennis about Angelica's prediction he grinned and said, "Not surprising; she's never been known to be wrong."

But back in Houston when she told Priscilla, her mother was skeptical and almost snorted. The two of them had discussed Dennis' preference for Consuela for a girl's name, and Priscilla was dismissive. "He doesn't know yet that we are an All-American family, even if he does have a smidgen of Mexican blood in him. When the child comes, he'll back off and accept whatever we choose." Seeing the distress on Melanie's face Priscilla softened. She put her hand over her daughter's, she said, "Please don't worry darling; I know Dennis is a good man and the one you want and need; let's give him time. He'll turn out to be a fine father and, well, your father hopes, the perfect successor for the business some day. This was something Melanie had always known instinctively from childhood; the man she married would be expected to take over her dad's business.

Dennis never mentioned to Melanie her father's prediction that sometime in the not too distant future he would sell out.

Herbert, though, was beginning to rethink that premise. Dennis was doing the job well, and as far as he could tell, with dedication and enthusiasm. However he sensed that Dennis was sliding into a going-through-the-motions attitude. Dennis made no bones about his desire to get into a job more related to geology than work at Williams had so far given him. He was beginning to be bored but tried to keep that from showing. He and Herbert never discussed this. They cruised along, Dennis a rising executive in the company; Herbert accepting him. If Herbert knew how bored and disillusioned Dennis was becoming, he chose not to show it, but relations between them were growing distant; both knew it but neither wanted to bring it out into the open.

Chapter Nineteen

TEXAS

A WEEK AFTER THEIR TRIP to the ranch, the rounds of business Christmas parties were erupting. While Dennis was informed he had to attend at least one or two, he could chose which. One of the ones he picked was at Southwest Explorations. He guessed there were over a hundred eager and gradually becoming intoxicated guests and staff in attendance. Dennis was not a regular or excessive drinker, but he was feeling particularly depressed about his situation. It was looking clearer by the day that his job was pretty much make-work, there only because of who he married. In addition he was feeling sexually deprived, although he might not have admitted it. He took one drink; didn't know what it was but it tasted good. When a waiter cruised by with a tray he took another one. And told himself that would be the last. He walked around greeting those he knew and meeting new ones who introduced themselves.

He had spent about all the time at that party he intended to; he'd greeted and thanked the hosts -- done his duty -- and was making his way to the door when he felt a tug at his sleeve. He turned around and looked into the bright hazel eyes of Fancy, looking even more gorgeous than any other time he'd seen her. She said, "Hello, stranger. You can't leave now, the fun is just beginning."

He was a Texas boy and could and maybe should have expected this, but it surprised him nonetheless. He said, "I guess I'd better go, Fancy. It is good to see you, though, but I've got another party to go to tonight. Besides, I don't drink much and if I'm driving I'd better quit now."

"Don't be silly. If you want we can get someone to drive you home, or wherever you need to go. Let me get you another drink." She did and the two of them drifted over to a bench and sat and talked. Fancy told him she was a daughter of an oil man who went bust and drifted away to the west somewhere. She and her mother were left on their own, and she was lucky to have this job.

"How long have you been here, with Southwest I mean?"

She told him three years and she loved being there. "I don't know much about you, Dennis. Tell me something I don't know," she said. Gradually she pried his story out of him, including, after three more drinks, that Melanie was pregnant and he was kind of pushed out of things at home. He didn't realize he was revealing so much of his family and home life, but Fancy was a gifted listener and she wanted to keep company with him.

About nine o'clock he started and said, "Whoa! Look at the time. I've got to be going, Fancy."

"I'm afraid, cowboy, that you're in no condition to drive," she said, stood and said, "let me take you home; you can come back for your car tomorrow."

But the car didn't take him to his home. When it stopped, Fancy got out ahead of him. He struggled to find money to pay the cabbie, wondering why he was having so much trouble getting that done. Fancy pulled him out and said, "This isn't a cab, Cowboy; it's my car!" She led him to her front door. Before he could protest, she said, "You don't want to go home until you sober up a little, do you?" She opened the door and led him. "You can sober up here for a while and then go home."

Guatemala, 1976

"But," he muttered, "what about my car?" Then he collapsed on the sofa in the softly-lit room and decided he didn't care about the answer to that.

Fancy showed up with two drinks and sat down with him, handing one to him. He looked at it and said, "I don't need another drink. I'll never sober up at this rate," and took a deep swig.

Fancy snuggled up to him and slipped her arm through his. "Comfy?" she asked. Dennis looked at her, into her eyes, searching her face. He reached over and pulled her chin up to him and kissed her. She said in feigned surprise, "Wow, Mister! You don't waste any time, do you?" She didn't pull away.

Dennis said, "Fancy, I am just a lonesome man who needs some . . . company, yes, company, that's what I need." He pulled her closer and kissed her again, and again. She responded eagerly. After a while she stood, pulled him up, and led him to her bedroom.

Sometime after two o'clock she shook him awake and said, "Dennis, honey, I think I better get you home." The "honey" didn't register with him just then. Later it did, along with the deep guilt he felt about the whole episode. He struggled into his clothes, and she led him out to her car. As she stopped at his house she said, "Just tell you wife you had to go to a bunch of different parties and you had too much to drink and a friend brought you home." She wasn't sure this had registered with him. He stumbled to his door and let himself in.

Melanie woke up when he got in bed but said nothing. The next day was Saturday and she let him sleep. She suspected he had something on his mind he didn't want to tell her, but vowed not to be the one to bring it up. If she had he might have spilled everything, but it was left festering between them: her suspicions, his guilt, neither bringing it out into the open.

Dennis couldn't forget it; he thought about it constantly. It weighed heavily on him. Around Melanie he tried to appear unchanged but he knew he was changed, it was all different now. How would he ever get things back to where they had always been between them? he agonized to himself. What made it worse was that he and Melanie were to have Sunday dinner with her parents. Pulling himself together he suffered though that and through the rest of the weekend with what he hoped was his old, normal self. If Melanie mentioned her suspicions to her parents they didn't take notice, at least in any obvious way. However, relations with them, particularly with Priscilla, had cooled.

On Monday Dennis fretted all morning. He was schooled enough in the ways of a gentleman that he knew he should do something, call Fancy and apologize, or should he ignore it all? At lunch he went out and sat in his car for he knew not how long. Then with an intake of breath, he started the car and drove to a convenience store and called Fancy from a pay phone. The only number he had was the main number for Southwest Explorations and he wasn't sure she would answer; she didn't, it was answered by another female. He quickly hung up and looked at his watch; it was twelve forty-seven; she would be on her lunch hour. Back in his car he spent several more minutes sweating and mentally squirming. At ten after one, he got out of the car and phoned again. This time she answered. He said, "Fancy, this is Dennis." He waited for her to say something or hang up; she didn't. "I want to apologize for the other night. I've never done anything like that before. I don't know what came over me . . ."

"Shush, sweetie," she said softly. "It's okay. We both were lonely and we comforted each other. Please don't think about it anymore, okay?"

"Well," he stumbled, "I am sorry. I promise it won't happen again."

"It's okay; it's okay," she said. "See you around, Cowboy!" and hung up.

Chapter Twenty

Texas

IN THE FRENZIED RUSH OF about everything running up to Christmas, Dennis was able to push away his guilt and anger at himself most of the time, but not all the time. He went to work, although it was typically a seasonally-relaxed time, and time seemed to be filled with frivolous antics by the staff at Williams. Business for Williams was slow during the holiday season, as with others, especially their customers. At home he tried to be more attentive to Melanie; she mostly responded cheerfully, but the door to intimacy remained shut. This served to frustrate Dennis all the more, and to bring his thoughts back to Fancy.

At home almost all the talk was about the baby. Melanie seemed to be unable to talk about anything else, and about things she wanted for Christmas for the baby. Dennis was also excited about the baby; it was distracting and he tried to concentrate on that, and not on his troubles. In that his success was mixed; the problems with his job, and his growing dependence on Melanie's parents, and of Fancy, pressed on him as often as he let them. As time went on and he had time to brood over things, his attention turned more and more to the bad in his life, despite so much good.

When he thought of the baby, he was filled with a consuming sweep of joy and elation; but that did not last. This was splitting him in two, and adding to his distress. At times he was grouchy with Melanie but would immediately apologize. One time she laughed and said, "I'm the one who's supposed to be grumpy!"

Adding to his gloom, on December 22 he sat at home and watched A&M lose to USC in the Liberty Bowl. Herbert had not attended college but was an avid University of Texas fan. Dennis learned to avoid football gab with his father-in-law; they didn't share watching games. Despite a winning record that year – up till the final game – A&M had lost to Texas the last regular game of the season.

On Christmas Eve at the Williams' neighbors dropped in at odd times to wish everyone good cheer, and to partake in the hosts' eggnog, fruitcake and whatever else they had on offer, and praise the huge, extravagant tree and other decorations; it was a tradition Melanie told him that had been practiced as long as she could remember. Christmas Day was for family only; the only relatives were a sister of Priscilla's and two nieces who had moved to California some years ago. It was just the four of them, plus, in the wings, the *baby*, who got the most presents. Dennis gave Melanie several small gifts, including a bracelet costing more than he would have spent had he not felt so guilty. He received a nice wool tweed sport coat and several other clothing items, things his wife and her mother decided he needed.

He tried to add fuel to his growing excitement about the coming birth, and the object of that birth, his baby girl, He had no doubts about it being a girl, after all, Tia Angelica had never been wrong. He held onto his desire to name her Consuela despite resistance by Melanie and Priscilla.

Thoughts of Fancy plagued him almost daily. Their only contact since their tryst had been on the day before Christmas Eve, the last work day before the holidays. She called him, "Hi, Cowboy," she said, "Just called to wish you a Merry Christmas."

He could think of nothing to say except, "Thank you, Fancy. Same to you." He hung up before it became another irresistible entanglement, but he still thought of her daily. He was constantly tempted to call her,

Guatemala, 1976

but he always steeled himself and never yielded; he thought he'd licked that obsession but it came back over and over and hung over him like dense, formless smog. Two days after Christmas he moved his workout location to another gym to avoid running into her.

Chapter Twenty-One

Texas

As the date for the birth came closer the unresolved choice of name for the baby loomed large among the three principals: Melanie, Priscilla, and, by a distant third, Dennis. The women had no problem with "Tom" for a boy, but remained adamant that a girl would not be named "Consuela," or anything Spanish. One evening as they were getting ready for bed, Melanie said, "Dennis, honey," he cringed. "The doctor thinks the baby will arrive in two weeks or so and Mamma and I want to settle on the baby's name as soon as we can. Mamma just doesn't want Consuela . . ."

"Or any other Spanish sounding name, does she?"

"Well, yes, but honey, can't we find a name the sort of sounds like Spanish but isn't?"

"You have something in mind, or you and your mother?"

"Mamma suggested maybe 'June,' my own middle name, with a second name that might be more like Consuela, but in English."

"Mamma suggested, huh? What middle or second name for instance?" Dennis asked, struggling to keep the sarcasm out of his voice, but not very hard.

"Well, what about 'Constance,' honey?"

Dennis turned away and tried to assess the situation. He had known for some time he would not win this argument, but he had to appear confident of winning to hold on to his dignity. "Let me think about that," he said. That was the end of that night's skirmish; it was not resolved but eventually the issue would be he knew, and not in his favor.

When the pregnancy was in its late months, Priscilla had hired a young Latina girl, Delys, or "Dilly," as the family called her, from Honduras, to help Melanie with the baby, and for general housework; Priscilla believed a young mother needed to be free to tend to things away from the house as much as she could. Also, Priscilla herself had "help," as this was called, and had come from that tradition in her parent's home as well. It was part of the culture of the social class she thought she deserved to be in, and so did her daughter.

Dennis had little to do with Dilly; he related to her in his mind as a part-Latino himself, but had to keep a social distance between them to maintain appearances within the family. Dilly was of course shy and deferential; relations between Dennis and Dilly were always formal. She might not have known about his heritage, but Dennis suspected she did.

Early in the afternoon of the twenty-third of January, 1974 Dennis got a call at work. He knew what it was; Melanie was ten days overdue, but had seemed normal that morning, showing no symptoms. He rushed to the hospital and arrived fifteen minutes after the birth. Priscilla had of course driven Melanie and had been with her through a number of contractions at home before tearing off to the hospital, almost too late. This was her first grandchild and she actually didn't know much of what to do. She was panicky and Melanie was the calm one. It turned out to be a normal birth in every way; a nurse commented that the first was always quick.

When Dennis was let into the room, Melanie was beaming and holding her newborn. She looked wonderful, Dennis felt; he also felt a rush of tumbling emotions he hadn't expected and hadn't prepared for. He could only stare for a moment. Melanie said, "Give the new mother a kiss, Daddy." He leaned over and complied. Then she said, "Would you like to hold her?"

"Her?" he said, more gratified than affirmed.

"Yes, husband of mine, father of my child, a girl! Angelica was right!"

"I never doubted it!"

"Would you like to hold her?"

"Can I? Is it alright?" he asked but held out his arms and took the sleeping beauty from her mother. Like almost every new father he could barely contain the love that seemed to surge though him. He could say nothing, just gazed at the tiny life that was his, a brand new part of him.

Choosing to close the question of a name as quickly as possible, Melanie said, "Dennis, honey, how about naming her Constance Angela Reade?"

At that point he would have agreed to almost anything. He said, "Sure, that's fine."

Melanie had been holding her breath, and let out a big sigh and grinned. She said to the nurse, "Please ask my mother to come in." Priscilla must have been listening at the door; she came rushing in and gushed all the more, although she had been with Melanie right up till the actual birth when she was whisked out of the room. No one was allowed in the labor room except medical personnel during the process and clean up. The Lamaze process had become the rage in some circles of pregnancy and labor care, but not in this hospital; the medical staff was just not ready for that.

Priscilla had been in to greet her grandchild before Dennis arrived; she was sensitive enough to know she should allow the father a little time alone with the mother and child. Some days later Melanie agreed that they would call her baby, "Connie."

From that moment Dennis tried to think of Fancy as only an acquaintance of sorts from a distant past.

Despite the joy Connie brought to their marriage, Dennis and Melanie continued to grow apart. She hounded him again about hearing aids. He said he would look into them, but kept putting it off, and she resented

Guatemala, 1976

that to the degree that it was a constant irritant between them. Melanie never said anything that would make him think she knew about the Fancy episode, but it seemed as though she did. She was as distant and cold as ever. He mother seemed to be there all the time, lurking, looking for something more to criticize Dennis about.

Finally in September Dennis could take it no more, and confronted her. "Melanie," he said one evening after dinner, "We need to talk." Dilly, who came early and stayed late, had prepared dinner and served it, and cleaned the table; she was in the kitchen. The two of them strolled slowly into the den and closed the door. She turned to him, not smiling, not frowning, just giving him her attention, something he seldom saw over the last months. "Mel," he said, "you've got to admit that we aren't living very much like a married couple now. What do think we ought to do about it?"

"I am quite happy, Dennis." She stated flatly. Dennis noted that she hadn't added "honey."

"I guess you are; your mother is here all the time looking after everything, leaving no time for me."

"Please leave my mother out of it, Dennis."

"Glad to but she won't go away! She's always here, managing, running things for you and us. That leaves little for me to do for you."

"I don't see what you have to complain about, Dennis; you have a good job, a nice house and everything we need right now."

"Sure, all courtesy of your parents. I don't feel like I have any control over my life anymore; it's all decided for me, and, well, you have turned away from me . . ."

She started to sputter, "Well, Mr. Reade," she had never called him that, "I like that! When you precious Army career fell apart, you became a different man, not as much of a man I might say!"

"That's because everything that made me who I am was taken away, first my Army career crashed, and then by you and your mother trying to make me something I am not!" The debate was growing more intense and angry, toward the point of outright yelling. He would never hit her but the temptation had risen in his mind. "I feel emasculated!" he paused, trying to regain his composure.

Tears edged out of her eyes. She said, "Well, Dennis, I'm really surprised after all my family has done for you!"

"Done for me?" he almost shouted. "I have a job that's basically make-work; a low-level secretary could do what I do. It doesn't take a full day to keep up. I have to invent things to do to keep looking busy. I'm surprised that the rest of the staff tolerates me; I guess it's only because I happen to be the boss' son-in-law! Nobody at work wants to spend time with me; I'm a pariah!"

Trying to back off, giving time for them both to cool down, he turned away. They had both stood during the argument; now he sat down. Suddenly, instead of sitting, she stomped off, saying, "I'm going to bed!" Calling back after she was in the bedroom, she said, "If you feel that way, why don't you sleep in the spare room?"

"I'll do that, thank you!"

Day after day, night after night it was like that, the only change was the growing distance and barely concealed hostility. He continued to sleep in the spare room; she continued to live her own life. She began to accompany her mother to social gatherings, lunches with female friends, movies and shopping. Dilly's presence had given her more freedom.

The fall holidays loomed and the atmosphere grew worse. By early November Dennis felt he had to force a resolution. After dinner one evening, after Priscilla had left for the day, he confronted his wife; he said, "Melanie, this can't go on. What do you want? Do you *know* what you want?"

Looking him dead in the face she said, "I want things to go on just as they are, Dennis."

"Well, I don't!" he said, "I just live here. I stay just to spend time with Connie, but that has to be scheduled around all the things you and

Guatemala, 1976

Priscilla plan for her. Things cannot just go on for me. I think it'll be better if I move out. What do you think?"

"I think you are ungrateful Dennis Reade; that's what I think!"

"Well, Mrs. Reade, things are not going to just go on just as they are! What *do* you want, separation, divorce, what?"

"Mother and I have been talking about that, Dennis. We feel that maybe a separation would be a good idea."

"Mother and I?" he exploded. "You used to be mine; now it seems you are your mother's and I am nowhere, nobody!" He stomped around the room. He said, "I'll be moving out in the morning. Let m know when I have to see a lawyer!"

She said nothing; she felt a sweep of dismay and sadness run through her, although she knew it was coming. She had known this was coming but didn't understand her feelings or herself in any way. She felt like crying but had no tears.

For Connie's sake Dennis spent Christmas day with the family, at the Williams' house, trying to be the father he felt she needed him to be, and civil with the others. It was a strained time, but he endured it. Finally it was time to leave. He hugged Connie and kissed her for several intense minutes. He was crying and telling her he loved her and wished he could be with her, but he couldn't just then. She cried and would not let go until Melanie came and pulled her away. Dennis hid his tears as best he could. He said quick and cool goodbyes to Melanie and his in-laws and left as quickly as he could.

After months of negotiations the divorce became final in early August of 1975; there was no alimony, just child support. Herbert took over the mortgage and Dennis surrendered any claim on the house. He took a month-to-month lease on a tiny apartment.

Herbert told him he could keep his job for now but to be looking for another place to go. This was more liberating than he imagined. He began looking immediately, taking his time. In October, he made contact with Global Geologics LLC and was hired the next month. He would began working right after Thanksgiving, on December first, learning the job; it would involve some international travel, but he wasn't told where. Strangely, he realized he had had no thoughts of Fancy in months.

A schedule was worked out for his visitation with Connie. They became precious and heart-rending with tears; he knew, though, for the meantime, it had to be endured. He vowed to himself that some day he would have a much better relationship with his daughter, his beloved daughter. His relations with Melanie did not improve.

L

Except for occasional Sunday dinners, Dennis rarely saw Herbert and Priscilla together. Even then the two seemed to grow apart, much like him and Melanie, and he felt more and more distant from the Williams family. He wasn't in the family "loop," as it were. A lot could be happening and he wouldn't know anything about it. It was happening.

Dennis knew Herbert was sensitive to the things that had gone on between him and Melanie and thought he would side with Melanie. If a choice arose, he was generally sympathetic toward Dennis. He might not have been as kindly in thought toward his wife at this point. Dennis wasn't aware of this at the time, but Priscilla had been becoming more than casually friendly with the tennis pro at the country club, the Bright Gulf Club.

Though relatively new, Bright Gulf was generously endowed – mostly by oil people and those in business with oil people – and had not only an eighteen-hole golf course and all the other usual amenities, but also a recently built indoor tennis facility. In the months before Connie's birth Priscilla became bored and had begun to take tennis lessons. The pro, Hadley Parsons, had seen in Priscilla a very attractive woman with a good deal of money, and had turned on the charm. She responded and soon it drifted into a compulsion too deep for either to break off from. It was not known if either wanted to.

Guatemala, 1976

If Herbert knew, he never challenged her. But he was perceptive and realized something was going on; she grew distant and curt with him and their domestics, and was hardly ever at home. He began to rethink his situation. If they divorced, she would get a huge part of his fortune; but he could see that happening; he didn't decide anything at that time, just to be aware of things at home and in their social life.

All that changed. Two days after Christmas Herbert moved out of the house and filed for divorce, citing "alienation of affections with an unnamed person." Priscilla didn't seem to be surprised, and made no outward reactions. Melanie was not surprised either. Dennis seemed to be the only member of the family who hadn't seen it coming.

Then, on New Year's Eve Herbert announced that he had sold the company to Southwest Excavations. The employees were assured that their jobs were safe, at least for the moment. His divorce stance was that any money coming to him from the sale of the firm after the divorce filing had been made, was not part of any settlement between him and Priscilla. The result was yet to be seen.

Herbert called Melanie the next day. "Honey," he said, "I don't want to talk about your mother and me right now. I just want to ask you to do something I think will be good for you, and for your mother, okay?"

"I'm listening, Daddy," Melanie replied coolly.

"I advise you to sell your house and move in with your mom. You will be more secure and, well, your mom needs looking over. She has a hard time making good, uh, choices, and, well, you know the story."

"Yes, Daddy. I know; everybody in town does I think."

"You will think about it, honey?"

"I'll think about it, I promise." She had always been her Daddy's girl and found it hard to break old habits now. She didn't feel like an independent, grown woman, especially since her marriage broke up. She felt like crying but wasn't going to now, with her father listening.

"If you need to get a hold of me, the people at the office will know how to reach me. You know I love you and Connie but this just has to be, you know."

"I love you, too, Daddy."

As they hung up Herbert thought he could have told her that this was not the first time for Priscilla to wander. After reflection he admitted to himself that was true for him as well. Some family! He and Priscilla had not done a very good job as parents.

Two days later Herbert left town, destination unknown for the present. It was not immediately observed that Fancy McGregor left town about the same time; but that became common knowledge in time. By then Dennis had left the firm and was deep in preparation to go the Guatemala with Global Geologics.

Chapter Twenty-Two

Guatemala and Texas

After picking up the clothes that Celesta held for him that evening, Dennis retired to his cot and sunk into an inescapable funk of despair and uncertainty. He knew he had to think through his situation and settle on a definite plan; he didn't want to let his fate be determined by others and to just accept what was handed to him. He didn't want to be a farm hand, if only for a short time. That might be a good short-term idea he thought, at least in the eyes of Laura and Padre Augustine, but they had decided to put him in that box without consulting him, and he wanted to decide for himself.

He was now in the sight of all who knew him, Alonso Mendoza, at least those who knew he was alive. If he invented that new identity, he could keep inventing and make a good life for himself, a life of his own devising. To the best of his knowledge he and the team had been wiped out by an ambush of some sort, probably by the rebels that roamed the countryside and attacked anything that at all resembled a government vehicle or an official. He just didn't know who or what had happened to his colleagues. News here in this remote area was sketchy and no word had made it to the clinic or the folks living close by about an ambush that conflicted with the story he concocted on his own.

Guilt sometimes washed over him, guilt about abandoning his real life and leaving Melanie, Connie and his friends uncertain. "*Connie, oh*

Connie! My adorable little Connie!" he moaned to himself. Her second birthday had been the previous Friday; he'd marked in his mind but not outwardly, and tried to not remember or grieve over the loss of her unconditional love.

Even after the breakup and then the divorce, Connie never turned against him, always ran to him and hugged him tightly; Melanie had turned out to be a good mother and hadn't made Dennis the villain. She explained to Connie that her Mamma and Daddy had decided to live apart for a while, but that he would see her as often as possible. A visitation schedule of every other weekend had been set up. Melanie had not asked for alimony; it seemed ridiculous with her family money. It seemed to be more or less an amicable arrangement.

Arousing from his reverie, lying on his cot in the clinic, Dennis realized he needed to think about his current situation and decide what he was going to do. Typically he had to analyze the matter: he had two choices: one, to to live with the Fernandez family and work in the fields, or two, take control of his life and leave on his own terms. What would it take to do that? He would have to get away; the question then became would he tell Laura and the others here or just sneak away? He looked out the small dusty window in his living space. He supposed it could be called *his room,* but to do so meant that he had invested something of himself in it, and he didn't want that kind of attachment tying him down, if only symbolically.

There was no sign of dawn yet but he knew it would arrive soon. If he was going to leave, especially if he was going to sneak away unseen, he had to do it soon, immediately. He stood and grabbed his things, meager though they were, the food and clothes, including a dingy, plain and crumpled straw hat, that Celesta had given him, and the few bills Laura virtually forced on him. He cracked the door and peered out. There were no lights, nor more than a trace of moonlight, though there was enough starlight to make a cross-country trek barely navigable, if he was careful. Stealthily, he stepped out. He waited a few seconds to let his eyes adjust to the available light and made his way through the campus and across the compound to the gate. No one stirred.

The heavy wooden gate was about sixteen feet wide he guessed, in two equal leaves. It was locked only by a large wood beam resting in brackets on the inside of the doors about shoulder high to him. There was only the inoperative bell and the unlit kerosene lamp on the outside. The gates appeared to be about ten feet high. With its cross bracing and the lock bar it would be an easy climb for him. He tossed his bundle over the gate and dropped down in a squat on the outside, easily and quietly.

Stopping to see if there had been anyone or any animal disturbed by his movements, he stepped away lightly in the direction he knew to be the road; it was unlikely to have anything he might trip over. Growing in confidence, he began to make his way carefully forward in a generally southerly direction, following the road as best he could and keep his heading south. He had learned where nearby workers' houses were and which had dogs or goats or chickens that his movements might rouse, and tried to stay as far away from them as he could. His walk was not easy and occasionally he would trip and curse silently and stop to hear if anyone stirred. He continued on unchallenged until dawn's coral-tinged glow began to seep in from the east. Then he could move with less care; he looked like he belonged, just another field worker on his way to the fields, or on some other errand.

After an hour at a steady walk hunger began to prey on him; he had not eaten since the evening before. The meager rations Celesta had given him would do for only at most two meals. He had to limit himself, curb his appetite. Celesta had given him a small re-filled plastic bottle of water; he would have to ration that, too. He could usually find a well at a worker's hut, but he would go as far from the clinic as he could before stopping for any reason. At a secluded glade he did stop and ate a half loaf of bread, and took a sip of water. In less than ten minutes he was on the move again.

As he passed a house he spotted a much-used hoe leaning against a wall. Checking to make sure no one was about, he stepped over and picked it up and strode away with it on his shoulder. Now I look more like I belong here, he mused. He felt only a slight twinge of guilt.

He kept walking at a steady pace, not too fast, but ambling along as a native would. At what he judged to be about noon, he came upon a small group of field workers taking a break for their lunch; he decided to risk joining them. "Hola," he greeted. "May I join you? I have my own food." No one seemed to object, so he found a place to sit. "I am Alonso," he said. No one replied; no one offered their name in return. They seemed to tolerate him but chose to just ignore this newcomer. It never occurred to him that his disfigured face would make the men wary. Soon he finished his meal and stood. He said, "Gracias," and walked off, on his way. He didn't know precisely where he was going, only to the south; his knowledge of this part of the country was sketchy, only what he learned from studying the maps and data his bosses in Houston and his hosts in Guatemala had given him. He wanted to find a town or city of some size where he could disappear into the crowds, maybe find a menial job and begin to build a new life for himself, with a new identity and a future, away from the disaster he had made of his life as Dennis Reade.

He regretted the pain his father would experience, not to mention the loss of time with Connie, watching her grow up, growing close as father and daughter, molding her character. "Hah! *Character,*" he thought; who was he to mold character, a man who abandoned his family? He missed Melanie, too, but the break with her was already too wide and certain to ever be restored, he convinced himself. At the divorce he had settled on being responsible for child support, a set amount would be paid directly from his Global Geologics salary, but no alimony.

Among all the things he wallowed in guilt for, the worst was abandoning Connie. From this remote distance he knew his life with Melanie was over months before the open breakup, the angry disagreements about almost everything, the quarrels and the combative yelling, finally, the divorce. In his heart he knew he was more to blame than Melanie but he kept telling himself it was not totally his fault. She became obsessed with having the baby well before it arrived, and she gradually withdrew from him until there was basically no love or love-making left. In his mind Melanie let her mother take over her life. Wasn't a girl supposed to give herself totally to her husband, in priority over parents?

Dennis respected his father-in-law, and regretted the way they parted, not only as the result of the breakup of his marriage, but also leaving the job. He didn't regret that because it just did not seem to be a real job, just something Herbert arranged to help his daughter and her husband. He came to hate the job, but not Herbert. After the trouble with Melanie began to develop Dennis sensed that Herbert was more sympathetic to Dennis than certainly Priscilla was. It looked to Dennis like Herbert understood that he had spoiled Melanie and that the best man in the world would have difficulty with her.

Chapter Twenty-Three

Guatemala

Mid-afternoon he approached a small village, with, looking at it from a safe distance, only a few houses, a market square and of course, a church. A few women clustered around a well and chatted; grubby children were nearby, mostly sitting quietly, occasionally one or two would jump up, tearing away on some errand essential to only them. He chose to chance entering the town and seeing what opportunities there might be for work.

He walked up to the well and greeted them, "Hola." Though the women looked up at him, no one replied; they just stared at him, and then went back to their own business. He stood there uncertain of what to do. He needed to rest and thought he could draw some water, but he hesitated to ask. A pretty young woman in her late teens, pulled away from the group and stood in front of Dennis. She said, "Please forgive us, Senor. No one else here speaks Spanish; we all speak only K'iche."

"You are the only one here to speak Spanish, Senorita?" He responded.

"Si, Senor I do. I am the only one except for a few of the men. How may we help you?"

He had concocted a rather involved story, but decided to say as little as possible; he was on unsure ground and didn't know what to expect. He said only, "I am looking for work, Senorita." The girl was not sure how to respond. There was no work that the men of the village were

Guatemala, 1976

not already doing. He said, "My name is Alonso, Senorita. I am a hard worker."

She looked at him, assessing him. He was taller that most of the people at her village, and lighter in skin color. Also his accent was a little strange, not local. She found him strangely attractive, but she was cautious; his scar and his blue eyes scared her. She continued to stare; what kind of devil is this?

To break the stalemate, he said, "How is it that you speak Spanish here, Senorita, and not many others do?"

She wasn't sure how to react to this man, obviously of a more educated class that the people of her village. How did he get that horrible scar on his face? He had several day's beard growth and looked like a *Bandito,* yet he seemed harmless and friendly. How was it that he needed work? On one hand could she trust him or send him away or wait till the men came home and let them take care of it? On the other hand she was attracted to him and wanted to help him. At her age she was just awakening to these feelings, and didn't fully understand them.

After a moment he understood; she was put off by his scar; he rarely thought about it, occasionally rubbing some of Laura's salve on it. He smiled and said, "My scar; it is from an accident with a machete. I had to take time off to heal and lost my job." When there was no response he asked, "Would it be alright if I stayed here until the men came home and talk with them about work?"

She smiled and wanted to say she was sorry and warm to him, but she was by then fearful and unsettled. She turned away and said, "I think it would be best, Senor, if you go; the men are suspicious of strangers and they will not like you here I think."

"Gracias, Senorita, gracias. I will go now but before I go may I draw some water?"

"Si, of course; come I will help you." she said and turned to lead him to the well.

He trudged on, ever southward, still unsure of exactly where he was at any point. The day was growing closer to the end of labor; he met small groups of field hands going home, sometimes trying to mix with them, but soon realized that his height made him stand out and likely to arouse suspicion. So, he kept to himself as much as he could, and tried to keep a steady pace without drawing too much attention to himself.

Occasionally he recalled the story of the Quetzal, the national bird, and how shy and reclusive it was. He too was shy and reclusive but not beautiful like the bird. He knew, he recalled, that he had been considered rather good-looking, but no more; the scar ended that.

The day grew late; he decided he wouldn't stop to eat until it was fully dark. A three-quarter moon rose before dark; that will be good for nighttime travel he thought but at the same time realized he was hungry and tired and needed to take time to rest. He watched the sky begin to glow in a light magenta and then darken, gradually segueing into purple, and then as dark as it would be that night. Dark descended quickly in the tropic highlands. He stopped and sat, leaning against a tree, resting for a few minutes. Although life on the ranch, and for that matter on bivouacs in ROTC, was rugged, he had little experience staying out in the rough for more than a day or two. It was different and, well, *challenging*, he thought. He would have to pace himself and learn as he went. He opened his bundle. Celesta had given him two loaves of homemade bread. He had eaten half a loaf since leaving the clinic; that's all he'd had all day and he was famished, but knew his food was limited and he would have to ration his intake to survive. Taking stock, he saw that he had the rest of the bread, and two bananas. Fortunately, his ROTC training had included tips for living off the land called "Survival Skills." He ate one of the bananas and a pinch of bread, and sipped water.

Also in the pack were a basic change of two shirts and one pair of pants, plus underwear, a bandana and a pair of heavy socks, all worn but clean. To his delight there was also a clean but well-worn serape; at least he wouldn't freeze. He stood looking for a place to lie down

Guatemala, 1976

and sleep; he was sagging and didn't think he could go on without at least an hour or so of sleep. Curling up in the hollow between two rows of cane, with his bundle for a pillow, his hat shielding his eyes and the serape pulled over him, he was asleep in less than a minute.

He awakened much later than he planned; it must be close to six o'clock he reasoned; the sky was already beginning to blush with dawn's light. He clambered to his feet, instantly alert and ready to flee. If he stayed in the rough any more nights he'd have to get something more to keep warm enough; he roughly brushed away the dew from his clothes and the serape. Relaxing, he found there seemed to be no one around. He took stock; there was no reason to rush he felt. Looking around at the surroundings he had only sensed last night, he saw that the cane was over head high. With the blade of the hoe he still carried he sawed off the top two feet of a stalk of cane and peeled back the outer rind of the top end to reveal the core inside. He chewed on that, sucking out the sweet juice, and cleaned his teeth with the fiber at the same time.

Soon workers would be coming but he didn't know if any would be working in that field. He chose not to stay and gathered his things together, and moved away from the field into a glade of pines a few yards away. He relieved himself and used a tiny portion of water to rinse his hands and face. He wanted a bath but knew that would have to wait. Sitting down he ate the other banana, and sipped a little water. He would have to replenish his supplies soon or find a place to work and earn his keep. He stood and began to move off again, using the sun as a compass heading south, as always, but still skirting any signs of humanity. As he went he sometimes saw smoke or occasionally a house; he steered clear of all of them. He wanted to find a reasonably large town where he might fit in easier and maybe find work.

Reminded again of his disturbing face he wished for sunglasses to help hide his memorable features, but that would truly look out of place for a bottom-of-the-scale worker. His beard helped but not enough. He developed the habit of wearing his hat down as low on his face as he could.

Nearing a village he stepped off the road and into the brush to reconnoiter; he was consumed by hunger but had to be careful. He watched a small group of women standing around a rough table preparing vegetables for cooking, predominately beans and rice with lesser piles of corn and peppers hanging on strings on racks. To one side was a small boy was sitting by himself, stacks of husked corn to his side; he held a bowl in his lap and was scraping the kernels off the cobs into the bowl with a crude knife with a five or six inch blade, handmade but functional. Dennis looked on at the abundance of food; his stomach growled out loud, sparking an alert in him. But no one heard or reacted.

One of the women yelled, "Benito, go and bring us more water, my son."

"Si, Mama," the boy said, and jumped up and took off running on his errand. He dropped his knife carelessly on the ground.

Dennis saw an opportunity; he desired food, but the knife would be better to steal. With it he could cut fruit and vegetables directly in the fields; the hoe was only a disguise, practically useless as a tool. The knife was a true tool, and would be handy in multiple ways. As soon as the boy was a few feet away, Dennis strode into the clearing as if he belonged. He got a few glances but no one seemed disturbed. He ambled over to where the boy had been working, and casually kicked the knife several feet to the side, meandered over to it, picked it up, shoved it into a pocket, and moved on. As he passed the back of one of the huts he laid the hoe against the wall without missing a step. He casually grabbed an old blanket off a line as he strode by.

That night he "harvested" four small watermelons and ate two before bedding down to sleep.

In his resolve he doggedly kept on his southward quest for three more days, scavenging for food, drawing water from wells when no one was

Guatemala, 1976

around, sleeping raw as before, avoiding human contact. His path kept to the east of the mountains, on flatter land so the going was not too strenuous. On the fourth day away from the clinic he reasoned he had walked maybe eighty miles in total, putting him close to denser populous areas. Coban should be close he thought. He might be recognized there and would not go into the center, but maybe he could mix in with people at the markets always found around the outer edges of large towns like Coban.

The road began to be filled with people either heading for town or away after completing their errands. He pulled away into a secluded glen and changed clothes. Back on the road he meandered along with the crowd, slumping over as much as he could to minimize his abnormal height, and pulling his hat down to conceal his face. He came to a market area and strolled along the displays of fruit and vegetables and felt his hunger raging. He still had the twenty Quetzales Laura had given him; he was saving that for the last ditch of survival, and now might be that time he thought. He stood there trying to decide whether to buy something to eat, or not when a very unexpected event changed everything for him.

Chapter Twenty-Four

Guatemala

"Ah, Senor," he heard in a strong voice, approaching him; involuntarily he turned and saw a familiar form striding toward him. It was Colonel Mendoza of the flying tour when he and Bruce first came to Guatemala. "I believe I know you, Senor!" Mendoza said, smiling and holding out his hand. The Colonel did not wear a uniform; instead he wore typical casual but upscale Guatemalan attire. Dennis was so startled he could only respond by reaching for the offered handshake. This confused him and he wavered about how to react, when Mendoza said, "Senor Mendoza, I think."

Trapped he felt, Dennis accepted the Colonel's hand and said, "Colonel." After an awkward pause, he said, "Strange that we meet here, Colonel, but even stranger that you called me by, uh, a different name."

"I think we have become cousins, Senor," smiling broadly. "You now call yourself by my family name." the Colonel said, pulling Dennis closer with a firm grip. "Let us walk over here a little where we can renew our friendship, Senor," guiding him over to a vacant shaded nook. "Ah, Senor, let me look at you," inspecting his face. "You have had a very bad accident, Alonso, but the good Doctor Laura at the clinic has done a very good job of sewing you back together. I believe you will heal nicely, but you will have an intimidating scar; useful for getting your way in, let

Guatemala, 1976

us say, certain circles." Dennis generally forgot about his scar, thinking about it only when it itched or when someone remarked on it.

Dennis said, "You obviously know about me, that I survived some kind of attack and was taken to the clinic and fixed up. How have you found me, Colonel and what do you want?"

"I knew what had happened to you almost from the beginning, Senor Mendoza," the Colonel said. "Do you think people I know do not tell me of new, unexpected events they believe I should know about, such as the sudden appearance of a stranger in their territory, one who is badly injured, who is taller than anyone they know, and who speaks Spanish with a strange accent?" He looked away as if to be simply observing the people and the activity. "And who has blue eyes. I know the story you told the good Laura and her people, a story you made up so you could have a new start in your life. What I do not know is why, but that is not important now; you will tell me when it is time." He gripped Dennis' arm and led him away. "We will go now. I think you are hungry; we will get you some food, and later some suitable clothes." Feeling helpless and without a choice, Dennis didn't resist.

Mendoza led him to a small dusty car, and into the back seat, climbing in beside him. Mendoza barked a command to the man behind the wheel; the car pulled away, merging into the light traffic. Nothing was said for some time, the two in back holding in their thoughts. After several minutes, Mendoza said, "Alonso . . . I shall call you Alonso from now on since you have chosen it for yourself. We are going to a safe house, as I believe it is known in American movies. There we can get reacquainted and make our plans, and you can get some rest." He was then quiet for a spell. The car jounced along, more bumpy and jarring than Dennis thought necessary. "Do not drive so fast, Felipe, we do not want to attract attention!" Mendoza said to the driver.

Arriving at a medium-size house on a rather large tree-covered lot, among other houses and lots of similar size and design, Felipe pulled the car around to the back. Dennis was led into the kitchen. The house was modern, very much like what could be found in any American suburb. It was even air-conditioned, with units at the ceiling in the major rooms. They walked from the kitchen, through a small serving space, then a dining room and into a living room. Furnishings were adequate and clean but unremarkable and worn. It reminded Dennis of both his home at the ranch in Texas and Laura's house at the clinic, but perhaps newer and better maintained than either, a generic, Spanish-style ranch house.

Mendoza motioned for him to sit, and walked over to a side table and began to pour himself a drink. He grunted at Dennis, raised his glass and shrugged a question – "would you like one?" Puzzled by everything happening so quickly, Dennis could only shake his head. Mendoza clapped his hands and called, "Inez . . . " After a moment a middle aged woman appeared wiping her hands on an apron , "Please bring our friend here some food, a large lunch of some kind, and some tea."

She said, "I did not hear you come in, Generale. I was cleaning the bathroom. I will get the food. Would our guest like something stronger to drink?"

Mendoza passed the question to Dennis with a quiz on his face. Dennis said, "No. Tea will be fine, gracias."

"Please excuse Inez." Memdoza said when she was gone, "This was her house until her husband, a dear friend of mine, was killed. Then I bought it from her." Then he said, "Excuse me for a moment, Senor," and left the room."

Dennis sat quietly, trying to puzzle things out. Inez came back and said, "Senor, please come into the dining room and have your food." She turned; he rose and followed her. The meal was plentiful, not the usual beans and rice but a large slice of hot braised beef, side dishes of rice pilaf and a vegetable mix, and bread. It all looked delicious. He had not had a meal this sumptuous since the dinner in Quetzaltenango; at the clinic the only meat he had seen was chicken, only at dinner and then rarely. He and Bruce ate well on their route before the ambush but not with such abundance and luxury. It took him only a second to dig in; he had

Guatemala, 1976

forgotten how famished he was. He emptied his tea glass in seconds and Inez stepped up immediately and refilled it. "I believe you have not eaten much lately, Senor," Inez observed. She smiled, the contented hostess.

He grunted "Gracias," between mouthfuls.

As he finished, Mendoza came back in, accompanied by Felipe. "Please stand up, Alonso." Turning to Felipe, he said, "Take a good look at the Senor, Felipe. Here's what I . . . " he grasped Felipe's arm and led him back to the rear of the house, out of Dennis' hearing. He returned in a minute and said to Inez, "Please show Alonso where he can have a bath, Inez, with shaving gear and a robe to put on after the bath." To Dennis, he said, "Please follow Inez and she will show you where it get a shower; please take as long as you need, and feel free to rest after." To Inez again, "Gather his clothes and bring them to me when he has undressed, please." And to Dennis again, "When you shave, Alonso, why not leave yourself a mustache; we will see what it looks like!" He grinned, "Like you would see in Mexico, right?" He twirled his fingers next to his upper lip, grinning and chuckling to himself.

When Dennis had bathed and shaved according to Mendoza's instructions, he pulled on the soft cotton robe Inez left him. He looked at himself, and at the mustache in the mirror. He found it pleased him, especially with the scar. He remembered that Laura had suggested that, too. His appearance was changed from a typical middle-class American to a prosperous Middle American, probably Mexican. While in the shower, Inez had brought in new clothes and laid them on the bed. The clothes, a Guayabera shirt and another long-sleeved shirt, pants, a short jacket and accessories, were well-made but would not draw attention to him in the right settings. Also, a nice new straw hat and an almost new pair of rugged shoes, not showy, just serviceable and unremarkable. He dressed, tried on the shoes – they fit well – then took them off and laid back on the bed. He pulled his serape over him and almost at once dropped off into a deep, dreamless sleep.

No one disturbed him for over an hour. He woke on his own, feeling much better but more uneasy at his good fortune, and over what his future might be with the Colonel; he was sure whatever his fate was it would be with and at the beck and call of Colonel Mendoza. After a few minutes, Inez stuck her had around the door. She said, "You're awake, Senor. Good, the Generale would like you to join him."

In the living room, Mendoza was sitting and motioned Dennis to sit as well. "Please join us, Alonso," he said. There were two other men in the room. "These are my friends, Alonso. It doesn't matter what their names are, for you to know their names, that is. Would you like a drink?" Dennis shook his head and sat. "We will all be working together but not together, if you can understand, Alonso. I hope you do. I want you, Alonso, to be my Aide. I think you will find it not too difficult, not too rigorous. I have every assurance that you are the right man for this job. Do you think you are, Alonso?"

"How do I know until I know what it is, Colonel, and by the way, When I met you before, uh, my accident, you were a "Colonel;" now you are called "Generale." Is that an Army promotion, Senor, or something else?"

"That I will explain later, Alonso," he said and turned to the other men, "You have seen my friend here and seen how bright he is. If you have any questions about our plans ask me later. Please leave us now, gracias." They stood and left. When they had gone, Mendoza said, "Alonso, I know how puzzled you must be. Why don't you ask me what is on your mind."

Dennis sat and stared at the man. Finally he said, "Well, Colonel or Generale or whatever, you explained how you know about my time at the clinic and what name I have chosen to use. You even seem to understand that I wanted to change who I am. My question, my basic question is, what exactly happened to me and my friends on the road at Lake Atitlan? What happened to them, where are they, and are they alright? Please tell me!" He let that hang in the air, but before Mendoza

Guatemala, 1976

could respond, he said, "Then you can tell me who you really are and what you want me to do as your Aide."

Mendoza stood, paced around, lit a small cigar and finally sat again and said, "I am very sorry, Alonso, but your friends are dead. A troop of rebels ambushed them, and you, and after they had stripped the jeep of any usable equipment and of your friend's things, they pushed the vehicle, and their bodies, into the lake. Some of that is just assumption but evidence suggests it. Early the next morning the rebels were ambushed by an Army unit. All the rebels were killed or disappeared, and the gear they had stolen was recovered by the Army. That is how it has been reported in Guatemala City: that two Americans and two Guatemalans are assumed dead."

"How did I get away? Do you know?"

"Not exactly, Alonso. The rebel attack on your team happened on late Friday. Early Sunday morning you were found at the San Miguel Church and the good Padre brought you to the clinic. That's all anyone really knows, but we have to assume that somehow you got away from the rebels in the confusion of the Army attack. You had many injuries but among them were what seemed to be rope burns and bruises that may indicate being tied down to something, maybe a mule, to transport you while you were unconscious. Your face had been bandaged with good quality sterile dressings."

"How do you know the Land Rover was pushed into the lake, and that the bodies were in it?" Dennis asked.

"When the Army cleared out the rebel group there was evidence on the ground at the edge of the lake: signs that some kind of thing had been pushed into the lake. You know the lake sides are steep but the water is very clear and the Army men could see that something was down there, but not exactly what," Mendoza said.

"And . . . " Dennis asked.

"And, preparations will be made to retrieve it, but that is not a high priority, and it may not happen for many months, Alonso."

"So," Dennis drawled, "for all anyone knows I am dead, and I suppose that will be or has been communicated to the US and my company and my family?"

"We suppose so, Alonso, we must assume so." Both men were quiet and reflective for some time. Finally Mendoza stood, walked over to the bar table and said, "Would you like a drink, Alonso? I think we both need one."

Dennis made no reply but accepted the drink when Mendoza placed it in his hand. He sat stony-eyed, staring straight ahead, and at last looked down at the glass; realizing what it was; he raised it and took a healthy swallow. Although it was Jack Daniels with a dash of water his only reaction was to wipe his mouth with the back of his hand.

Mendoza said, "Alonso, I will leave you alone for now. Please enjoy the house and grounds but please do not leave the property. Gracias, Senor, and please accept my sympathy for the loss of your friends," and he left the room.

Dennis' thoughts had been reeling around in his mind, undisciplined and more and more confusing ever since hearing the facts and suppositions about the ambush. Alone his thoughts continued in their undisciplined way, and were making him more muddled by the second. He just couldn't get around it; he had decided to reinvent himself and then, without any action on his part it happened. It dropped right in his lap. One of his greatest burdens was that it happened, and that he had wanted it to happen, and that he got what he thought he wanted, though it cost his friends their lives. "Be careful what you wish for," came crushing through his mind. Guilt grew and made him almost cry.

"What am I going to do?" he asked himself, then remembered that his immediate fate rested with Mendoza. He didn't dislike Mendoza, but did not want to be dependent on him. The Generale was an impressive and imposing man; tall and full-bodied, he had a commanding presence, a "military" presence. Mendoza had spent many months in the US, involved in various Army training programs. He admired America, and

Guatemala, 1976

had studied its history, particularly the examples of Lee and others from the Civil War. He believed the Texans heroic defense at the Alamo, and the subsequent victory and independence was admirable. He had little love of Mexico, nor for the current American support of the Guatemalan government.

During the flying tour Colonel Mendoza was the perfect servant, almost too obsequious with the hosts at the Quetzaltenango dinner, as well as with other local officials, and, of course, with him and Bruce. Now Mendoza was in his element as the leader of men. His behavior toward Dennis could be seen as sympathetic and helpful, but obviously with a longer-term objective; what that might be Dennis had no clear idea but assumed it would not be what Dennis would have chosen for himself. He had no choice but to wait until the Generale was ready to tell him what his role was to be. An Aide to a General? Did Mendoza know of his military training? He knows a lot about me, Dennis realized; maybe Mendoza read about his ROTC stint in the data given to the government when the team was chosen and sent to Guatemala. He could not afford to doubt that Mendoza knew more about him than anybody else in Guatemala. His new life was out of his hands; he'd just have to let it unfold and ride the waves.

After this time of self-examination and chastisement and self-pity, he rose and began to explore the premises. It was early afternoon and he strolled around the house; then he went outside, taking in the ubiquitous flowering trees and shrubs and potted plants, and the almost drowning scents. The environment and the weather perfectly endorsed the national motto: "The Land of Eternal Spring." This had been true for him since arriving in the country; it buoyed him up every day in spirit, and he breathed deeply and he swung his arms and stretched, and felt better than at any time since the ambush. His soreness was gradually ebbing away. That, the "ambush," seemed to be the benchmark event in his recent life; everything revolved around it, the before and the after, the future as well. He was still sore and scarred but felt that the future was brighter than the past, the *immediate* past, that was.

Inez found him to tell him his dinner was ready. He followed her into the house and sat at the table. Mendoza was not there. The meal was similar to the quick lunch he'd enjoyed earlier but there was more of it, and it was just as delicious. He was feeling better all the time.

Chapter Twenty-Five

Guatemala

Dennis finished his dinner and didn't know what to do with himself. He wandered into the living room and looked around for something to read. There was no television, but there was a radio. He started to go over to it and see what he could find, when Mendoza came in. He said, "Ah, Alonso! You are looking very fine. How do you feel?"

"Not too bad. I guess I owe you thanks for rescuing me. Gracias Generale, for the food and clothes. I assume you have something in mind as a way for me to pay you back." Dennis replied, trying to keep the sarcasm out of his voice.

"Well, yes, Alonso, I do. You already know I want you to be my Aide."

"Yes, but not what that means, Colonel-Generale. Why don't you tell me what Army you are in?"

"Why don't we go into my study, Alonso? Mendoza said, dodging the question, and turned to lead him to a room in the back of the house, one that Dennis had not come across. Dennis, knowing he had no choice, followed. The "study" was one of the bedrooms set up as an office-cum-den. The Generale sat at the large impressive desk and motioned for Dennis to sit in a leather sofa opposite. A large weather-beaten attaché case sat on the floor beside it. Mendoza gazed at the younger man for a while and then said, "Alonso, to answer your question, I am still a Colonel in the Guatemalan Army, currently on leave." He let that sink in. "But I am also the head of the rebel corps trying to overthrow the government." Dennis suspected as much; he didn't react at all to this revelation. "I am known to my troops as Supreme Generale Maximillian. It is necessary to have an impressive title to maintain discipline, you'll understand. You have seen them, or a small contingent of them, in action, more directly than most of my countrymen. It was a mistake, the ambush of your team. Marco, the leader of that unit, couldn't read a street sign if his life depended on it! He was an idiot! He thought your jeep," *Land Rover*, Dennis mentally corrected, "was an Army vehicle and just shot it up without verifying anything. Regrettable, very regrettable!" Mendoza looked indignant and angry. "We have not yet established good military order, and that is our next important task, Alonso."

At that moment Mendoza reminded Dennis of Mussolini; he mentally chuckled. So, he thought, the Generale is beset with the disease of vanity, and typically is blinded by it. With that kind of leadership, the revolt would never win. Dennis was fundamentally a patriot and tended to side with established order and legitimate government, though he knew the Guatemalan government was thought to be about as corrupt as any third-world regime. He intended to be neutral, or at lease passive in this struggle, and would remain that way in his mind until he was free of Mendoza's grip. Until then he would bide his time and appear to support Mendoza.

"Just what is it you have in mind for me, Supreme Generale Maximillian? What is your Aide supposed to do?"

"Only, Alonso, be constantly at my side and do whatever I decide you should do to help the rebel cause. I cannot say at the moment what that will always be. Things will reveal themselves," he said. "Tomorrow we will go to Escuintla where I have a secret central headquarters and polish our strategy; you will meet some of my colleagues. You will be introduced as Alonso Mendoza, my nephew, and be given the rank of Captain; of course there will be no uniforms or symbols of rank, but all will know the trust I have in you. Your story will be that you have been

Guatemala, 1976

in the US for advanced military training, and had an accident that has left you scarred."

"Are you sure you can trust me, Generale?"

"Alonso, Alonso! I have knowledge about you that you do not want anyone to know, that you, Dennis Reade, are alive and are trying to remain incognito. That is the reason I am willing to trust you. I think you understand, and will not violate my trust."

"In other words, blackmail."

"If you say so, Alonso, but I would hope you grow to not see it that way. You will be in line for great things when the revolution triumphs. Think of it that way, think of the honors and tribute and celebrity you will enjoy, Alonso. Think of the victorious end!"

"If I live that Long," Dennis said under his breath. Swallowing his bile he went on. "I will do my best, Generale. As long as the revolution succeeds, I will try to prove my trust to you." After a moment he said, "Senor, I don't have any papers, either as Alonso Mendoza or Dennis Reade. Shouldn't I have some, one or the other?"

"Good, Alonso, good! Get a good night's sleep. We leave at dawn tomorrow," Mendoza said, and signaled for Dennis to leave. Again he declined to give Dennis an answer.

Back in his room Dennis found a small valise, some basic toiletries and more clothes. He showered and packed and prepared for bed. He had no idea what time Mendoza considered "dawn" to be, and wanted to be ready.

At peace with himself and secure for the present, he slept well, allowing his body to continue to heal. Apparently "dawn" was a flexible term for his erstwhile leader; Inez knocked on his door at seven-thirty. The sun was well up in the sky. He washed, shaved and dressed, and went out to the dining room where a generous breakfast was laid for him. Evidently being the Generale's Aide didn't mean he ate with him. Inez said, "The

Generale said to be ready to leave in a quarter of an hour, Senor." She nodded and left.

Felipe walked through carrying two large pieces of luggage, and Mendoza followed closely, carrying his impressive briefcase. He paused and said, "Are you ready, Alonso? Please get your things and come out to the car," and continued on out.

In the car, not the same one as the previous day, but a larger, more rugged, dark gray sedan, cleaner than the junker he had been in the day before – Dennis didn't recognize the make, something European, he thought -- they traveled south again. Nothing was said for well over an hour. Felipe apparently knew the way and didn't need instructions. The roads were as good as Guatemala offered, some multi-laned.

About two hours out Mendoza said, "We will have to change to some back roads, Alonso. We are going to by-pass Guatemala City; we do not want to get too close." Felipe turned off to the south and they were on roads that resembled what he had seen on the team's trips, dirt and big round rocks, not too bad but certainly not as good as what they had just left. Another turn and they were on rougher ground, almost a dirt track. They passed villages and lone huts and fields, and a few laborers walking along the dusty paths. At a larger, unnamed village, they turned onto a better, but still unpaved road, and after a few more miles, onto a fine highway. The big car purred along. Once, Mendoza had to caution Felipe to slow down, so as not to attract attention. Felipe seemed to want to prove he was a race driver-in-waiting.

As they sped along, Mendoza said, as if it just occurred to him, "Felipe, when we get to the house I want you to go out and get Alonso a pair of sunglasses, large ones." Felipe nodded to acknowledge.

Approaching Escuintla, Felipe turned into a built-up area not far from the center of town, and to a street lined with cheek-to-jowl two-story buildings. Ground floor windows were protected with wrought iron decorative but effective security grilles. The front door was right on the street, blue, decorated steel with a tiny grille-protected window at

Guatemala, 1976

eye-level. They parked at the curb and got out. Felipe went to the trunk, removed the luggage and carried it to the door; the men followed him inside and upstairs to a large, central room. It seemed to occupy the rear half of the second floor, spanning across the width of the building. Mendoza sighed and said, "Alonso, I own this house," spreading his arms, "The government knows about it; it is totally legitimate and no one bothers me. What I do here, though, is my business."

Dennis looked around. This must be some kind of office, Mendoza's "secret central headquarters," he decided. Four tall windows filled the rear wall, but were covered with shades. The other walls held pinned or taped-up maps, papers and notes, in no discernible order. A chart resembling a chain of command was on display, heavily marked up, showing many revisions. A large table held more papers, and seven of eight chairs sat in disarray around the room. Not knowing what to do, he just stood there, more or less *at ease*, in military jargon. "So much for military orderliness," Dennis mused to himself..

Among the things pinned to the wall was a calendar. It was Sunday, February first, 1976, the second month of the American Bicentennial, a year to be celebrated with great gusto in the US, especially on July Fourth. Dennis felt a twinge of frustrated patriotism and regret, but he knew he had cast his lot here and had to push that lament away and work through it.

Mendoza excused himself. Felipe said, "Your room is right in there," pointing the way, "and the bathroom is along the hall that way." Then he left Dennis on his own. Dennis found his room with his valise on the bed, along with a new pair of sunglasses; he had no idea when Felipe had found time to get them. The room was more luxurious but also more use-worn than the room he had in Coban. The trip had taken a little over five hours. Dennis was hungry and tired and stiff. He needed exercise so he went back out to the large room. Felipe looked up from a magazine and said, "We will eat in an hour I think. The Generale has left but will be back later." Dennis had to accept that.

He began to pace around the room. He asked Felipe, "Can I go outside or am I trapped in here? I need some exercise, Felipe."

Felipe said, "I think not, Senor Alonso. The Generale would not like that I think."

"What about the back yard?" In the HQ Room -- as he had mentally labeled it -- he had pulled a shade aside and glimpsed out. "Could I just go out there and get some fresh air?"

Felipe sighed and said as he stood, "Perhaps, Senor, if I go with you. Come, I will show you the way." The man didn't seem to take much convincing.

Outside, Felipe lit a small cigar. He inhaled deeply and looked at it with an expression of something resembling love. He said, "The Generale does not wish us to smoke in the house, or in the car even."

It was mid-afternoon. Dennis breathed, almost gulped the air, avoiding Felipe's smoke; he had been cooped up, first in the Coban house and then in the car, and he needed the fresh air and the sense of body and mind reinforcement that nature gave him. He had become used to the scents of people at the clinic who did not always have an opportunity to bathe, then in the tight confines of a car with two men whose hygiene habits seemed to be casual; that those two were supposed to be refined men was little improvement.

He said, "Felipe, is this the Generale's home; where his family lives?"

"No, Senor, he has a villa, a farm, in the hills to the north. He does not let anyone go there for the rebel work, the fighting. It is where the Army thinks he stays when he is not on duty."

"Where do you live, then?"

"I live right here, Senor, with my wife. I am the caretaker, as well as the Generale's driver and helper when he is, uh, not here." After a moment, he said, "I am also the Generale's cousin."

Dennis considered that bit of information; he knew "cousin" was a loose term in Latin America. He let his thoughts roam. Felipe appeared to be in his late twenties; he was of average Guatemalan height and

Guatemala, 1976

coloring, but perhaps in better condition than most of his countrymen. He said, "I haven't seen your wife, Felipe. Is she away?"

"No, Senor, she is here, preparing our dinner. You will meet her soon."

As if on cue, a pretty young woman, perhaps a little younger than Felipe, appeared at the door and called, "Felipe, please bring our friend in to eat," and turned back into the house. Felipe smiled broadly and said, "That is Adriana, my wife, Senor." Dennis saw a girl tall for a Guatemalan, and slim; she reminded him of Consuela, his mother. She seemed to be poised and full of restrained energy.

"Pretty name, Felipe, pretty wife as well," Dennis said. "You are a most fortunate man." Felipe smiled in agreement.

Chapter Twenty-Six

GUATEMALA

THE KITCHEN AND DINING ROOM were on the ground floor of the house, occupying one side; Felipe's and Adriana's living quarters on the other side, he found out later. Access to the back yard was a hallway from the front door, straight through the house to a matching back door. Adriana was placing the finishing touches, the drinks, on the table. Felipe said, "Adriana, this is Senor Alonso, our cousin. He is going to be the Generale's Aide, and will be living here for a while."

Dennis bowed and said, "I am pleased to meet you, Senora. Your table is inviting." She smiled and sat with them. During the meal they tried to talk, always about things unrelated to the rebels; it was strained and a little difficult to sustain. Adriana shared with him that her family was from this area, as was Felipe's. Her husband had little to say; Adriana, though, tried to keep the conversation going. Dennis tried to keep up his end, but struggled, mostly complimenting her on the food.

They had finished the meal, and about worn out any conversation when Mendoza came striding into the room. He wore a full dress Guatemalan Army uniform, rank: Colonel. He greeted all, took off his visored hat, sighed, and plopped down in a convenient chair. He said, "Something to drink, Adriana, gracias." She jumped up and hurried off, returning in a minute with a bottle and a tall glass. Mendoza poured a half-glass and took a deep swallow. He turned to Dennis and said, "Ah,

Guatemala, 1976

Alonso, my friend! I have been checking in with my Army people. I am still on leave but it never hurts to appear without warning to check on one's troops, and to maintain contact with people who you might need for support some day, or who might be in a position to cause you hurt, some day."

He drank, motioning with a lifted glass an offer for Dennis to join him. Dennis declined. Mendoza finished his drink, stood and said, "Alonso, we will go into the office and talk now." Dennis followed a step behind the Generale up the stairs. In the room Mendoza sat at the head of the long table and bid Dennis to sit to his left. He seemed at a loss of where to begin. "Alonso," he finally said, "During this next week I am going on a long tour, reviewing our men and the facilities and try to tighten up the organizations, see to training, that kind of thing. You will accompany me. I believe you have experience in training men for combat; am I right?"

"Yes, Generale, some, although I have seen no actual combat." As you no doubt know, he thought to himself. He would call Mendoza "Generale," if that kept the peace, but he was damned if he would call him "Maximillion!"

"Yes, but you have had extensive training, in the ROTC at your college, Texas A&M, is it not?" Dennis nodded. "And in your summer camps, too I believe. This is why, Alonso, I have chosen you for this important position. In addition to being my Aide, you will be my Training Officer. At the encampments we will visit you will review the training procedures in place and order any improvements you think necessary." He looked at Dennis, trying to see if the younger man had any reservations or problems with the assignment, or questions about it. Dennis did not react in any way.

He went on, "We will leave here Wednesday morning, early. In the meantime I have some other things I have to take care of. Until then, please make yourself at home." He stood and started toward the stairs, then spun around, "Oh, Alonso, I forgot; here are some papers, not the best I am afraid, but should be acceptable, especially if you are with me. Also some money," he handed Dennis the identification papers and the cash. The passport had a photo copied from his American Passport. He vowed to never underestimate the powers of Mendoza. Dennis didn't bother to count the money. "And, oh yes, here is a letter for you, from your friend Maria at the clinic. Good Padre Augustine keeps me in touch with the people there, and he told Maria she could contact you through me." He handed the letter to Dennis, who was both flattered and confused. The way people here led intertwined lives was beyond trying to untangle.

Dennis went to his room to read the letter and to try to digest what lay ahead.

The letter read:

Dear Alonso,

We miss you very much. Dr. Laura is angry with you for leaving and for not going to live with the Fernandezes. They are disappointed, too. I am missing you very much and hope to see you again soon. Padre Augustine told me that Generale Maximillian had found you and was looking after you. Be careful, Alonso. I do not know what the Generale is doing but it may not be good for you.

I want you to know I will be in Guatemala City on Monday, the Second of February, to attend the wedding of my cousin, Elenza, on Wednesday. I will stay at Elenza's father's house. I do not know the address but I will send word to the Generale by Padre Augustine where I will be. I hope I can see you, wherever you are.

Love, Maria

Then he noticed on the back of the envelope, in a different hand, an address In Guatemala City; there was no signature.

Guatemala, 1976

Dennis was surprised and glad to hear from Maria, although in his heart he would rather have a note from Laura; he knew that attraction was doomed and still he yearned. He mulled over the idea of trying to see Maria while she was close, and decided to put that off. He found Maria attractive, if young and naïve, and of a different culture, but he wasn't immune to the lure of a liaison with a pretty female when the chance presented itself. Chastising himself, ruefully remembering Fancy. He pulled his thoughts away from romance and back to the immediate future with Mendoza and whatever that held for him.

It was late and he was tired. He went to bed.

Chapter Twenty-Seven

Guatemala

Adriana woke him at seven. Again Mendoza had been up long before and was not around. She set breakfast for him and Felipe, who said as they sat, "The Generale left word for you to look around Escuintla today and locate the main streets and buildings, get familiar with them."

Dennis nodded and considered this. It was likely that the General had plans that included military operations here in this city or close around. His Global Geologics team had visited Escuintla on their orientation before beginning their work, but it was a quick overnight and he didn't remember much of anything about it. Data on Escuintla had been included in the packet given them. It was near the Pacific, on a lower elevation and in a more tropic and humid area that the highlands where the work of the team was to occur. It was just an orientation stop; they hadn't included it on their work itinerary.

Felipe said, "He also said that there will be a meeting this evening after dinner, you are to attend, in the big room upstairs."

"I'll be there, Felipe; will you?"

"No, Senor, I will not be asked to be there, I have other things I must do."

"Felipe," Dennis said with sympathy for Felipe's awkward position, "Please call me Alonso, alright?"

Dennis left soon after breakfast and strolled along the street. From the traffic and general indications he found the direction to the center

Guatemala, 1976

of town. There were modern buildings and other urban amenities like any progressive city, but the covered sidewalks he discovered were the same as found in every Middle American settlement of any size, as well as the same sights, sounds and scents, and people. Small shops ran along jammed together. He walked along what seemed to be the main street until he ran out of densely built-up areas and into a looser mix, residential seeping in to the retail, and growing more so. Then he doubled back and explored crossing and parallel streets. He found an almost abandoned railroad station and stopped a passer-by and asked, "Por favor, Senor, Are there any trains to Guatemala City today?"

"Ha!" the stranger barked. "Senor, you must be from somewhere else! No trains for passengers have been here for many years. Freight sometimes but who knows when! If you want to go to Guatemala City, you can try the bus."

"Gracias, Senor. Can you tell me, where is the bus station?"

The man simply pointed across the street. Dennis looked and after a quick scan saw what seemed to be just another row of stores, but with a bus logo sign hanging over the curb; a few people loitered on the walk, waiting for the next bus. Dennis crossed the street and stepped up on the walk. He asked one of the men waiting, "Por favor, Senor. When is the next bus to Guatemala City?"

"In fifteen minutes, Senor, or maybe an hour; who knows?"

Dennis thanked him and wandered off. He had no intention of getting on a bus at that time, but wanted to build up his knowledge of things like that; later on he might decide to flee and wanted to collect and sort his options. He strolled away and watched and mulled the choices and how he might take control back from Mendoza. So far, the Colonel held all the cards, but maybe Dennis could break loose.

Then he remembered that he had already decided to break with his past, his true life. To go back to being Dennis Reade with his ex-wife and his child and his father dependent on him and how he had messed it all up so bad would be next to impossible He had burned his bridges, or

155

rather they had been burned out from under him. To return as Dennis Reade now would have opened up so many wounds and require so much groveling and struggling to rebuild his life . . . he just wasn't ready to face that. And he wasn't sure he could do it.

He wanted to get away from Mendoza and yet the alternative was no better, for now, probably worse. If he fled, Mendoza would either chase him down or expose him. He'd have to wait till he had more leverage, if ever.

He counted his money before leaving the house; Mendoza had given him two hundred Quetzales, and he still had most of the twenty Laura had given him. He could buy some different clothes, but his height meant that would not help much; he could be recognized instantly by anybody looking for him. A different hat might help some, but then he would have to return to the house before taking off and the people there would likely know, see his purchases.

He realized he was tiring and hungry and not thinking straight. He found a sidewalk stand selling snacks, bought a taco and a Coca-Cola, and ambled off to find a place to sit and think. He sat on a bench in a pleasant park, and ate and watched the flow of people go by. No one seemed to be in a hurry. Traffic drifted by without a break, tending to mesmerize him as he relaxed, bringing on drowsiness. He felt he was stronger for his days in the rough, fleeing the clinic and the specter of being bound to farm life. Yet he was not as strong as he wished to be, as he was back in the States. He had to conserve his strength and grow stronger, and to learn more of the country before he would try to break away. He mulled over the options for another new identity, and could come up with no easy answers.

He stood and walked some more, covering some of the same territory he had already seen, and exploring new streets. He wanted to know as much as he could about this town and the area. He bought a newspaper and another coke and sat again to read. He tried to read every word, even the ads and commodity prices and the like; world news was scant and not particularly helpful. He learned that not only had the railroads in

Guatemala, 1976

Guatemala almost disappeared—taken over by superior U.S.-financed roadways—but also much small industry had withered away. In the briefing data the Global Geologics team had received, Escuintla was shown to have had a sizable percentage of the manufacturing activity in Guatemala, but apparently that had diminished in recent years, not only in Escuintla but across the nation. The population of Escuintla was about fifty thousand and growing, but mostly because of peasants moving in from farms because that work was growing scarcer; not because of a better overall economy.

The middle of the afternoon he made his way back to Mendoza's house and napped, a siesta, for over an hour. He woke up just in time, he thought, for dinner, cleaned himself up and wandered down to the dining room. It was empty but he heard noises in the kitchen, and went in. Adriana was busy with dinner preparations. When he wandered in, she looked up and smiled, and he, knowing he shouldn't, felt a shiver of attraction. He admitted to himself that he was prone to do that, feel drawn to beautiful women, even those off limits, such as Laura and now Adriana, and who were pretty. To curb that he said, "Hello, what's for dinner tonight?"

Adriana didn't reply immediately. She also was assessing the stirrings she felt and that he was having for her; it couldn't be denied. Yet she was a loyal and loving wife and would no sooner think of being unfaithful to Felipe than to deny her birth-branded Catholic faith. Distantly she said, "Hello, Senor Alonso," putting up a shield of defense, setting boundaries. "We are having the usual chicken with beans and rice, nothing fancy, and fresh bread and tea, fruit for dessert. We cannot afford to be luxurious here."

"I understand; I know it will all be delicious. Can I help, Senora?"

She handed him a stack of plates and flatware, and said, "You can put these on the table, Senor." She quickly turned back to her cooking; Dennis took the things to the dining room and began to place them. Cloth napkins in decorative rings stayed on the table between meals.

Before he finished, Felipe came in and greeted him. He said, "Did you have a good day in town, Alonso, see a lot of the city?"

"Yes, quite a lot," Dennis said. "I just walked around and watched people mostly. It is a most pleasant place. You are fortunate to live here."

"Yes, it is, but working for the Generale I don't get to stay here for very long."

Dennis could sense resentment in his voice. It was obvious that Felipe and Adriana were dependent on Mendoza. He wished he could do something about that, but that was a whole new problem, and not his to solve.

Around eight he was summoned to what he had come to think of as the "HQ Room." He found not only Mendoza there but also two men he had not before met. They were typically short, roughly-dressed and steely-eyed, and obviously Mendoza's lieutenants. The Generale introduced them as John, Frank, and George; Dennis was quick to grasp that the use of English names was to hide their identities, not only from him, but from the world. Mendoza explained to them that Alonso had until recently been in America studying with the US Army, and had an accident that made his scar. Mendoza said, "Please sit, Señores. I have a new vision of strategy to review with you tonight. First," going to a large map on the wall, "we will muster each of our armies at these points . . ."

Dennis soon lost interest and let his mind wander. Mendoza was more of an idiot than Marco that the Generale had so demeaned with that word, "idiot." He must think of himself more a MacArthur than a Lee, Dennis thought. What had he found himself stuck in, stuck with? *Armies*, indeed! More like scraggly mobs! They couldn't win much of anything on their own, less with Mendoza at the helm. They could only harass and make life difficult for the populace and the economy.

Mendoza droned on for over an hour, finally winding down, leaving Dennis more confused than when the meeting began; he couldn't speak

Guatemala, 1976

for John, Frank, and George, but he had his doubts about them as well. As the meeting broke up Mendoza pulled Dennis aside and said, "Don't forget, we leave early Wednesday, Alonso." Dennis nodded and left as quickly as reasonable.

Chapter Twenty-Eight

GUATEMALA

DENNIS SPENT MOST OF THE next morning alone in the HQ Room, apparently studying the maps and notes left from the previous night's session. In truth, he was concentrating on a detailed map of the area, and another of the entire country, absorbing as much as he could so that any escape he launched would be girded with the best possible chance of success. In his excursion the day before, he'd bought a small notebook and a pen and began to plot an escape plan, or start an outline for it. He'd also bought a small, loose cloth satchel that he rolled up and hid among his clothes.

At breakfast, he and Adriana ate alone. "Where is Felipe?" he asked.

She sighed and said, "Last night the Generale received a message from one of his Commandantes in Chimaltenango. I do not know what he was told, but he and Felipe left before dawn to go there."

"Where is Chimaltenango, Señora?"

"It is not very far I think, a little to the west of Guatemala City." Dennis knew from his briefings that it was likely maybe an hour's drive from the capital city, two hours from Escuintla.

"Did the Generale say whether or not he would be back in time to begin the trip to Guatemala City in the morning?"

"No. Maybe yes, maybe no. He did not tell me anything about that."

Guatemala, 1976

"It must be important to send them so far on such short notice," Dennis said. "Does this happen often?"

"Sometimes, Alonso, too often for me," she said, unable to hide her unhappiness. Dennis wished he could comfort her but held back, for reasons he wasn't sure he understood. He understood that something in him seemed to compel him to be drawn to pretty women who were out of reach. A surge of guilt swept through him. He quickly finished his meal and excused himself.

Shortly after lunch he left the house, nodding to Adriana as he passed the kitchen door, holding his now full satchel behind him so she would not see it. He was taking his essentials—his new identification, a change of clothes, and toiletries—with him. He left a note in his room for Mendoza:

"Generale, I met some new friends yesterday and they invited me to spend the day with them. They will show me some of the lesser-known places in Escuintla, and we'll probably have dinner afterward. I will return late tonight and be ready to leave tomorrow morning as planned. Alonso."

His decision to leave was not permanent; he fully intended to return and stay with Mendoza as planned, but he wanted to see the capital city again – he and Bruce had seen some of it when they first arrived in Guatemala – and to find possible pathways to escape if he ever felt he could take that risk. Also, he would seek out and find Maria. She liked him and he was not immune to her kind of attention. Surprised at himself, he acknowledged that he'd missed her.

He had to check himself from hurrying; to walk too fast would certainly not be the norm here, and his goal was to accomplish his mission without attracting any undue attention. So he walked with an unnatural casualness for him. He had been able to keep the serape Celesta had given him and draped it over his shoulder in the native fashion

When he came to the block with the bus stop he slowed to an amble, and casually gazed around like he'd done the day before. The bus stop was on the opposite side of the street. He loitered around, watching the crowd gather, and waited until he saw movement. The people soon stood and began to move toward the curb and shuffle around, trying to get a place closer to the bus door when it stopped. Dennis had decided to get on this bus even if it was not going to Guatemala City. If it was going somewhere else, he would get off at the next stop and try again for the right one.

He crossed the street and muscled his way through the crowd and onto the bus. He asked the driver, "How much to Guatemala City?"

"Three Quetzales, "the driver replied gruffly, sensing that this stranger would not know that the standard fare was one-third of that. Dennis paid the fare without protest – he did not want to cause any kind of commotion and call attention to himself -- and moved back into the bus with the mass of travelers. There were no unoccupied seats so he stood stoically along with most of the passengers. It would be short in miles but a lengthy journey in time, but he was going to be patient and accept the irritations of the trip. Had he known he could have hired a taxi for the same amount, but he would not have taken that option; he wanted to remain one of a large group of locals.

The bus stopped a dozen or more times before reaching Guatemala City. At each stop some got off and others got on. Practically all carried bundles of some kind, including a few with chickens in hand-made coops. No one seemed to be interested in the luggage bins under the bus. At least, Dennis told himself, no one rode on the roof as he had seen in pictures of many third world countries. If there was any change in load as they progressed it was that more arrived at the end than had been on the bus when they left Escuintla.

The bus stopped twice in Guatemala City before arriving at the main station in the city center. Dennis had intuited this, and stayed on until the environment appeared as urban as he could expect. He stepped off and gazed around to take in all he could. One of the first things on his agenda was to find a news stand and buy a newspaper, and a city map, if there was such in existence. Fortunately, there was. On his arrival in

Guatemala, 1976

Guatemala to begin their work, he and Bruce had been able to take a little time to look around the city. Its modernism surprised him. Tall contemporary buildings, wide, landscaped avenues, plazas and parks abounded. He particularly remembered the Torre del Reformador, an open steel work structure resembling a miniature Eiffel Tower, sitting in the middle of a broad grand avenue they drove down as they entered the city. It would not be until today that he would discover the lesser developed areas consisting of slums and deep poverty.

Now he cruised around on foot and found an available park bench. It was after three o'clock and he was tired and famished, but he wanted to get his bearings before he ate and began exploring. He put the newspaper aside and spread out the map, looking for Maria's address.

Chapter Twenty-Nine

GUATEMALA

Dennis wandered around for a couple of hours getting to know the center city, but found no sign of the street, nor any other sign of the address. He had asked several people he met; the answers he received didn't seem to help. He was no nearer to finding Maria than when he arrived. One of his last inquiries was at a large, modern hotel. The clerk said, "Your best bet, Senor, may be to get a taxi. A good driver would probably take you right there."

It must be near five or six, he thought; he was getting hungry. It would not be a polite time to drop into Maria's cousin's house unannounced at dinnertime. He decided he needed a watch and found one for ten Quetzales. Deciding to treat himself, he found a small café close in and took his time eating and watching the other patrons. By the time he finished, it was near eight o'clock and growing dark. He found a taxi stand, got in one and gave the driver the address.

The driver said, "That is not a very good area, Senor."

"That's all right, Senor; it's where I need to go," he said, "Please find it for me, Gracias."

It was a nice car, large, modern and clean, a Chrysler. He knew the fare was likely to be rather high, but that was acceptable to him. He was on his way to see a pretty girl.

Guatemala, 1976

The driver pulled away from the curb and pointed the car into a more or less northwesterly route. Soon he recognized Calzada Roosevelt, a major boulevard. At some point the car turned right and into a more densely populated district. Houses were built side by side like Mendoza's house in Escuintla. The sounds and street activity reminded him of a number of other places in the environs of his life close to the Hispanic settlements near the ranch. The driver seemed uncertain; he turned several times, looking for the street name or some sign that they were near. So many streets looked the same and were not always identified prominently if at all.

After perhaps forty minutes, he stopped the car, turned and said, "Senor, I believe we are here."

Dennis paid and got out. Looking around, first across the street and then at the front of the house, trying to assure himself he had the right place, he finally approached the open door of what he hoped was the right house, and stepped inside, calling, "Hola!" loudly because of the music and clamorous chatter. No one replied so he moved ahead a few steps and stopped again. The room was about as full as possible and everyone was almost yelling; most held a drink and were nibbling on something, and gesturing wildly. He didn't recognize anyone but after scanning the room for a long spell, he spotted Maria and felt an involuntary twinge in his heart. It was only then he hung his hat and satchel on a peg near the door. Maria stood next to a girl of similar age, coloring and costume. Soon he realized this must be the bride. Other girls clustered around them, all trying to be heard; all faces were beaming; all seeming to want to touch the bride. Older women grouped around them in the next circle. Dennis didn't want to approach Maria when she was engaged with this cluster; he would wait.

Across the room there was an equal crowd of younger males, with the obvious groom in the center. Finally someone noticed him and shoved a drink in his hand, and turned away. Then an older man stepped up to him and said, "Senor, we are honored to have you here. Are you a relative of the groom? I do not believe I know you."

"No, Senor. I am Alonso Mendoza, a friend of Maria Alvardo, from the north. I heard she was here in the city and I thought I would try to see her."

"Let me introduce myself, Senor. I am Hector Alvardo, father of the bride, Elenza, and also a cousin to Maria." They shook hands formally. "Pardon my manners, Senor. Let me introduce you around and then you can visit with Maria." Following tradition he first led Dennis to his wife, the bride's mother, Senora Pilar Alvardo, where the formalities were observed. Dennis said the right words of blessings and well wishes. Then Hector led him to the groom's group and introduced them all. Dennis said all the appropriate words of greeting, and knew he would remember only the groom's name, Nicolas.

A band of two guitars, a rather elaborate drum set, and a marimba filled the room with traditional music mixed with what was considered the latest rock, and occasionally a romantic ballad. It made it all the more hard to hear conversation, so everyone yelled louder. Very little of substance was understood, but perhaps that was not the point.

Dennis tried to circulate, nodding politely to everyone whose eyes he met. Most indicated a mild interest until they decided they didn't know him and then resumed their intense dialogs with their friends.

He and Maria spotted each other after several minutes. She smiled at him and nodded at the bride; she tilted her head to say, I will come to you in a minute. He waited. He was not uncomfortable; he had been in similar situations many times. He was able to chat amiably with others; even with his strange accent, ugly scar and blue eyes no one seemed to notice. He did want to see her, though, alone if possible. They had some serious catching up to do.

Maria's catching up seemed to be more serious than his. After making the rounds of giving the females, especially the next older generation, last greeting and hugs, she went to Dennis, eyes sparkling. She stood before

Guatemala, 1976

him, beaming. Neither had words for a moment. She said, "Alonso, oh Alonso! I am so glad to see you. Doctor Laura and everyone at the clinic worried about you! We are so glad that Colonel Mendoza found you and took care of you. Padre Augustine told us that you were starving and alone and . . . in great need when the Colonel found you. And now you are his helper! How wonderful! You look wonderful!" She realized she was running on and stopped.

"You look good, too, Maria; I am very glad to see you."

Suddenly Maria grabbed him by the arms and pulled him down and planted her lips on his, put her arms around his neck and held them there, holding the kiss as well. Dennis was astounded but did not pull away. Strangely, the numbness of the scar near his mouth didn't seem to affect the impact of an unexpected and spirited kiss. She eventually broke off and smiled, tears beginning to puddle in her eyes. While he enormously enjoyed the kiss and appreciated her ardor, he knew he couldn't reciprocate to the same degree. He said, "Maria, is there somewhere we could just sit and talk?"

She grabbed his hand and led him to the rear door of the house and out into the back yard. She sat down on a rough wood settee and pulled him down beside her. She wiped away her tears and said, "What do you want to talk about, Alonso?"

"Maria, I have to be with Colonel Mendoza tomorrow morning and I must go back to Esquintla tonight." Before she could respond he went on. "How are you, how is Doctor Laura, and Celesta and the others? I guess Padre Augustine has told you what happened to me. It is good, I think, for now, but I owe Colonel Mendoza much and have to stay with him. That means I do not have much time to see you or the others at the clinic."

"I know, Alonso," Maria said. She grasped his hand harder and leaned against his shoulder. "We are all well. Doctor Rodney is expected back soon, maybe tomorrow. If he stays here in the city until Sunday -- the wedding is Saturday -- I will ride back to the clinic with him, Doctor

Laura has told me this. She has told him about you as well, Alonso." Suddenly she said, "I like your mustache, Alonso. It tickles when we kiss!"

Knowing this was an invitation for a repeat, he bent down to her and obliged. They held this for more than a brotherly kiss, and held each other tightly. He knew this was wrong but had the same impulses he'd had with Fancy; this time, though, he was not drunk. He didn't know what to think; he was unsure of his feelings and responsibilities. With Fancy he simply let go of his restraints; here he hadn't and was pulled two ways, desiring what Maria was offering, and feeling his own moral underpinnings, pulling him back. He desired her but knew he didn't love her.

The answer was taken away by the mother of the bride coming to the door and calling Maria back into the house, saying, "Maria, the guests are leaving; you'll have to say goodnight to your young man. You must come in and attend Elanza; you are the Maid Of Honor, you know."

Maria sighed and stood. She said, "Alonso, it is late, you cannot go back to Escuintla tonight. Let me find a place for you to stay. You can go back early tomorrow." Back in the house, most of the guests had left. She spotted Nicolas and went up to him, dragging Dennis with her. "Nicolas," she said, "My friend Alonso came here from Escuintla and needs a place to stay tonight. Do you know of a place he could stay?"

Nicolas, feeling especially mellow, said, "Of course, Maria. He can stay at my house with me and my family. It is only a few blocks from here. Come along, Alonso. Any friend of the family is my friend, too. It will soon enough be my family, too." Dennis grabbed his hat and satchel from the peg, and followed Nicolas out of the door.

Nicolas reeled down the street, accompanied by six or seven of his friends, with Dennis following. At his house the friends made a great joking and joshing to do over his impending loss of freedom. Risking disturbing the neighbors, Nicolas tried to shush them, but they continued on for many minutes more, finally breaking up like a receding tide and drifting away. Nicolas turned to Dennis and said, "My good friend,

Guatemala, 1976

Alonso, here we are. Come in and I'll find you a bed. The bedroom for you is on the first floor, up the stairs. My room will be directly across the hall."

In a strange bed, although he had not slept in an *un*-strange bed for many nights, Dennis found it hard to unwind and fall asleep. In his tumbling mind he thought about Maria, and her hinted promises, and then, despite his knowing it was wrong and not to be, of Laura, and, to his surprise, of Adriana. Then his mind wove back to Melanie and, more importantly, to Connie. His heart broke whenever he remembered her; he didn't know whether he missed Melanie or not. He knew he was more at fault for their break-up than she was, but she did share in the blame, and he couldn't forget that nor forgive it, maybe someday, but not yet. He also didn't know whether or not he cared if she forgave him.

A little after midnight, he finally fell asleep.

Chapter Thirty

GUATEMALA

He had been asleep for less than three hours when a great crashing noise and a series of violent shudders tossed him out of bed and onto a floor that had partially collapsed into the floor below. He groped for something to hold onto, raking his hands around, terrified. There were street lights shining through openings that had not been there when he went to bed, He found his shirt, pants and shoes and pulled them on; he had kept his watch on his wrist; he put his wallet with his fake papers in his pants pockets. It was 3:00 a.m., 3:03 to be exact, although at the time that precision did not register. Then the street lights went out and there was only a little moonlight. Being a geologist Dennis knew exactly what had happened: *Earthquake!*

In the background information he was given before coming to Guatemala, and his orientation in country, the earthquake potential was underscored. In Houston he and Bruce met with the senior engineers and geologists at Global, and thoroughly explored the feasibility of dams at all, and the danger of a dam failure – and failure because of an earthquake was a real possibility – causing devastating flooding in addition to all the other damage severe seismic events cause.

Dennis came away convinced that hydroelectric dams, or dams of any kind, were unlikely to be viable for Guatemala. The Global contract was likely to end with that recommendation.

Guatemala, 1976

Guatemala had experienced many serious earthquakes over the centuries. One of the most significant was in 1773 in Antigua, the original capital. The damage was so severe that the capitol was moved to the present capital site, Guatemala City, whisch had been hit many times since over the centuries, often with severe damage. The country has rebuilt each time, strengthening the building regulations so that with every event new structures were required to be better able to resist the shocks. But not all buildings were helped; many dated from before the last episode and were not improved.

He called out, "Nicolas! Nicolas! Are you all right my friend?" There was no sensible answer, but he heard moans in several voices, coming from different directions, some from inside the house, some outside. He wished for a flashlight, or a lantern or even a candle, not that they would do any good if he didn't have a match or lighter; he didn't.

Finding a stable handhold, he groped for a means to get out of the house; it seemed to be on the verge of collapsing even more. His room was near the back of the house, and the front seemed to have suffered most. He found the door to the hall, clawed his way there without incident, and opened it. Nicolas's room was across the hall, and the door stood open. Dennis went over to it – the floor slanted, so it wasn't easy – "Nicolas! Nicolas, are you all right?"

"I am here, my friend," came a voice from inside the room.

Dennis entered, holding on to the door jambs and the swinging door. "Do you need any help?"

"I do not believe I am injured but I am trapped under the bed and some of the plaster."

"I'll see what I can do!" He worked his way to the pile of collapsed ceiling, bed, and other debris under it. He began to lift off pieces he could grasp. One-by-one, pieces were removed; he tossed them aside and braced his left leg against a chest lying on its side. A pants leg could be seen. It looked like Nicolas had been tossed out of the bed, which then flipped over on top of him. Dennis pinched the leg to be sure it was Nicolas; a yelp confirmed it. He said, "Nicolas, please be patient with me. If I pull out something too soon or without being sure it needs to come out, a bunch of stuff may come down; you will be buried even deeper."

A large section of ceiling plaster had to be taken out next. Gingerly, Dennis gripped the slab in two places where he thought it would give him the best leverage. He eased it up and out in reluctant inches. As it came out from the pile revealing more of Nicolas' legs and torso, the slab of plaster began to split and crack up. Dennis shifted his stance and grip, trying to stabilize the mass. It kept splitting, the rough wood lath exposed and splintering. Dust was everywhere, choking him and obscuring what little vision he had. Dennis stuck his right knee under the largest piece and things stopped moving, for the moment.

Dennis looked around for something he could use to help him. If he could reach the chest of drawers his leg was braced against, maybe he could pull out a drawer and use it to brace the plaster while he moved his leg and buoyed up the load. He talked to himself and to Nicolas while huffing, pushing, pulling, and maneuvering the load. At last he got a small drawer loose and wedged it under a corner of the plaster slab.

He had to balance the load in a stable position and keep trying to lift it enough to get Nicolas out. While he struggled he asked, "Nicolas, who else is in the house?"

"My parents and my sister, Delores. They are in rooms right under us here. I have heard them calling to each other. Please hurry and get me out so I can check on them!"

"Right, Nicolas. I think we are about to spring you free." With another noisy heave, he lifted a big part of the plaster and braced it up with the iron bedstead, and Nicolas twisted and broke free.

Nicolas sprang up, dusted himself off and ran to the hall, and then stopped. Dennis said, "Is there a back stairway? There's no way we can get out the front."

Guatemala, 1976

"No. There is the window at the back. There is one on the floor just below it!" They rushed over to the window, and jerked it open. The window was metal-famed, a two-sash casement, with a stout mullion between, opening to the inside. It was closed.

Dennis had to tug to open it; bending over and looking out he judged the distance to the ground to be over twenty feet, and to the window sill below about twelve. "It's too far to jump or drop, Do you have a rope or anything like that?"

"No. Maybe. I do not know!"

"Maybe we can tie some sheets together like in the movies!"

"Anything! Let us try!" Nicolas cried.

"We can't get back to the bedrooms to get any sheets!" Dennis exclaimed. "Look!" he said, "I'll take my belt off and buckle it to the window here." He pulled his belt off . "If I hang out on my belt and you hang on to my feet you can probably kick in the window down there."

"I do not know if I can do that, Senor." Nicolas was visibly scared. He was not athletic and rather smallish, slender and thin. He was nervous and hesitant. At the Alvardo house Dennis had been told that Nicolas was a student, training to becamae an accountant, a very desirable profession for the husband of a favorite daughter.

"Do you want to hang onto the window and let me hang onto you?" Dennis asked a little sarcastically.

"No, no! Senor!" Nicolas said. "I will try. I will try!"

Dennis buckled the belt around the window mullion, gripped it as tightly as he could, and stepped over the sill, one foot in and one in. He said, "Nicolas, I am going to hang down from here. When I am ready I will tell you and then please climb over me down as far as my feet and hang on. You should be able to reach the window below with your feet."

So, with much huffing, puffing, and other audible exertions, the two managed to get themselves out and hanging from the upper floor window, grasping and finding balance mostly by feel. Nicolas grappled with and clung to Dennis's clothes, almost choking him as he hung from

173

his shirt; when Nicolas held onto his pants Dennis feared they would come off since he had no belt on. He thought it would be comical had it not been so serious. Once stable in his position, Nicolas timidly kicked at the window, wildly for he could see almost nothing. His feet flailed and hit nothing. Dennis watched and reached a conclusion. He said, "Nicolas, is the window open?"

After a moment, Nicolas said, "Si. I think so, compadre. Ah, it is so. I will see if I can let myself inside." There was a "plump" as Nicolas dropped into the house.

"Are you alright, Nicolas?" Dennis said.

"Si, Senor Alonso. Gracias. Gracias, Senor."

"Well, Nicolas, I've got to get down from here someway; I can't get back up into the upper floor," Dennis said. "I'll manage though; go on and see about your folks." Grabbing the side of the window, he gingerly monkeyed his way down and dropped through the same window. He headed toward the front of the house, which appeared to be lying flat in the street, shattered in pieces. Dust continued to float around in the air and pieces of the house shifted slightly every so often As he left he said, "Nicolas, you take care of your people and I will go see about Maria and Elenza and her family."

"Ah, si. Si! Gracias, Senor! Please do that; I will come as soon as I find my parents and sister and know they are alright!"

Chapter Thirty-One

Guatemala

Moving as fast as he felt was safe, Dennis rushed along the street outside. It was not easy; debris lay in disheveled and threatening heaps and clumps all over, strewn into and over the street; it was barely discernible as a street. The houses on Nicolas' side of the street were damaged much like his but those opposite seemed to have suffered far worse; they looked more damaged front to back, more thoroughly destroyed. This was the side of the street the Alvardo house was on, two blocks away and one over, and panic shot through him. Recovering quickly, though, he sped on, leaping over piles of debris and furniture and every sort of household item – crockery, clothing, kitchen and bathroom fixtures -- that the quake had flung out of the houses. Some piles were still trembling and at risk of collapsing at any moment.

Cries for help, moans and gasping, and heart-wrenching sobs filled the air; many people were standing out in the street stunned, unable to focus on what to do or on what could be done. Dennis realized that shock and chaos consumed them and that some sort of authority was needed to pull them out of their stupor. He was drawn toward where he thought the Alvardo house was, and to find Maria and Elenza and their family, but the need right where he stood was just as great, and he choose to do what he could then and there for the moment. Some had fashioned crude torches out of oil-soaked rags tied to splintered timbers.

A few oil lamps shown, and one Coleman lantern, giving the scene an almost festive glow.

His military training tickled his subconscious; he scanned what he could see and counted probably fifteen men, all scrambling among the debris, working a cross purposes, getting in each others' way. He yelled, "Men! Muchachos! Please listen to me! We need to organize if we want to save as many people as we can. Please gather around me! For a minute, please!" No one seemed to hear him. He yelled again, "Men! Please let us try to help each other and save the people who are trapped in the houses! Please let us come together and plan what to do!"

An older man stepped over to him and said, "Senor, I am Diego Alvardo. I saw you at Hector's house last night; I am his brother. Thank you for trying to help. Maybe we need your help. What can I do?"

"Good to meet you, Senor. I am Alonso Mendoza. You can help by getting these men to come together and talk about how best to help the people still in the houses."

Diego turned and called with authority, "Men, please come here over to Senor Mendoza and let us see if we need to work together and not each on his own. Please, muchas gracias!" Soon one and then two men came over, then more. In less than a minute, most of the men in the street were standing there in front of Dennis, and slowly, others drifted over. Soon over twenty had assembled

He said, "Men, I am Alonso Mendoza, visiting friends here. If we organize into small teams working together I believe we can get more done than each one working by himself can do." He paused to let them absorb this. "If we organize into teams of four or five men each, with each team working on one house more people will be rescued. Please, let us try this! Gracias."

Diego stepped forward and began to sort the men out by name and assigning them to which a group and a house to assist. Soon work was moving a little more smoothly and with intense concentration. Dennis worked with the men; he asked anybody who had rope to bring it. He

Guatemala, 1976

taught them to tie off large pieces of rope to hold them up while victims were dug out, and to position ropes so that more than one could pull together and move more than one man by himself. "Please find timbers we can use to prop up the large pieces!" he yelled. Men grunted and told each other to do this or that, and before long, systematic removal of debris was progressing more efficiently than before; the trapped and injured were being found and released, lives were being saved. People were being removed from under terrific loads. The injured were gingerly lifted out and laid on cleared ground. Women began to appear with blankets and other wrappings and to attend the injured, cooing and whispering comfort, amid their own sobs and moans.

Sadly, a few were found without any signs of life, some with injuries so severe that recovery seemed unlikely. The street was filling up with the injured and the dead lined up in military rows on blankets, some with faces covered.

Dennis scanned the scene and decided it was time to find Maria and her family. He bid adios to Diego and sped off in the direction he thought was correct. Nothing was recognizable; parts of houses stood naked and shattered; furniture and household items, and in some cases, plumbing fixtures contents hung precariously from pipes in cracked eggshells of gaping half-rooms.

The primary fault line did not follow the street grid; it seemed to go from near the street back at Nicolas's house, across the street, cutting through the house fronts and then through the centers and then toward the backs. That traverse was not apparent from just one spot, but Dennis, relying on his geology training, could discern a likely pattern.

He worked his way toward the Alvardo's house and before he got more than a few dozen meters, he was accosted by men who had heard of what he had done where he just left and also wanted his help. Again, he called out and repeated his plea for a coordinated effort. After the same initial confusion, it seemed to work again and when he saw the results in progress he moved on. He was stopped twice more and did what he could, always urging himself to keep moving on and find his friends. After uncounted time consumed by the work that had fallen to him, he thought he was close. It was almost dawn, near six o'clock.

He felt a shudder and knew it was an *aftershock!* He yelled, "Cuidado, my friends! Aftershock!" A few wails were heard; everyone stood still until the tremors ceased, then went back to work.

He was sure he was near the Alvardo house and rushed ahead until he found a large group of men and a few women clamoring over and through the trash and ruin where the house he thought the Alvardo's had stood. Again he yelled and tried to get the people to better organize their efforts. No one seemed to pay him any attention; all were obsessed with digging out any survivors. He tried again; none even looked up. Then he noticed a man, obviously not a Guatemalan, looked like American, at least Caucasian, laboring alongside the others. Among other clues, his clothing was not local: dress shirt, although without tie, and sleeves rolled up. As Dennis watched; the man directed two others to gently lift a victim out of the dusty rubble and carry them – with all the dust and rubbish he was not able to tell the gender – to a large dining table that had been brought out to the street and lay them down. The table was draped with a sheet of some sort and it was already blood-stained. He had the give-away stethoscope hung around his neck, and began to clean the wounds and apply what healing balms he had. A small black bag sat on the ground next to him, gaping open. He bound up the person's wounds as best he could and motioned for his helpers to take the victim away and bring on the next one.. Someone grabbed this man's attention and pointed to Dennis. He turned and looked intensely at Dennis. He then turned away from the patient, pulled out a bandana, wiping his hands and clearing his glasses, and made his way through the rubble toward Dennis. He stuck out his hand. Questioning, in decidedly American-accented Spanish, he said, "Are you Alonso?"

Guatemala, 1976

Dennis was a little surprised but knew word of his presence traveled fast through the neighborhoods. He grabbed his hand and said, "Yes, I am, Senor. I am Alonso."

"I am Rodney Harris, Alonso. Laura has told me about you. She has been worried about you. I am glad to see you looking so healthy." He grinned and held onto Dennis' hand and scanned the scar Laura had so skillfully sewn; satisfactory, he mused. Harris was not a large man, slim a few inched shorter than Dennis, he had gray-sprinkled dark hair and a generous mustache.

"I am glad to see you, Doctor," Dennis said. Then, "Why are you here, or how did you get here?"

"I came in from the States last night and checked into a pensione near the church where I'd left the car when I left. I talked with Laura yesterday before I left the States – the phone lines through Mexico and Flores were intact then, they often aren't and I have no hope they are now -- she told me Maria was here and suggested that I drop by and see if she wanted to ride back to the clinic with me. She had told me about you earlier and how you left them; she is worried about you." He looked around stunned and dumbstruck. "Now this," he sighed, waving his arms around the scene. "Now this!"

Just then Nicolas came loping up. Spotting him, Hector Alvardo rushed over to him; they hugged and greeted each other like the kin they soon would be, maybe. Nicolas asked urgently, "Is Elenza alright Senor?"

"Si, Nico. She and Maria are alright. They were in the front bedroom on the ground floor and it was not much damaged. They have been helping Doctor Harris and have gone with some others to find water if they can. Both are fine, uninjured."

"Oh, good, so good, Senor. I am so grateful! What about Senora Pilar, Senor? What about the rest of the family?"

Hector turned away a moment and took out a bandana and wiped his face. He turned back. "She is badly injured, Nico. She has been taken away to the hospital if one can be found. Carlos and Jaime," his sons, "carried her in their arms. I have not heard, I have not heard," he sighed and wiped his face again.

"And others, Senor?" Nicolas asked after a pause for Hector to recover himself.

Hector said, more calmly than before, "Some have injuries, a few broken bones, cuts and bruises, but the good doctor and others have treated them and they will be all right I believe."

"I was lucky," said Harris, "I always carry basic supplies, including surgical thread and needles in my bag."

Dennis wandered away from the others and began to pitch in and do what he could. He looked around for Maria but did not find her. Soon he was so engrossed in the recovery tasks he pushed aside any thoughts about finding her; he knew she was okay, and that was enough. He surmised that word of his organizing efforts had preceded him; the men seemed to be working efficiently in teams, like the other places when Dennis left them.

It was almost dawn. This brought glimmers of pink light beginning to glow in the east, though sooty from the dust in the air.

A stir resonated through the air. An Army vehicle pulled up and stopped. Four soldiers got out and approached the obvious leaders, Hector and Harris. One of the men said with forced authority, "Who is in charge here?"

"No one is in charge, Sergeant," Hector said with as much dignity as he could muster. The Army was not to be altogether trusted among the locals. "I am Hector Alvardo, owner of the house behind us. These are my friends, and this," he motioned to Harris, "is Doctor Harris, who has come to help us. Are you here to help us, Sergeant?"

"We are here to see that everything is done as well as it can be. Is there anything you need, Senor?"

"Of course! We need all the medical help we can get! What do you think?" He paused to let his anger subside. "Doctor Harris is from the north, from a medical clinic in a rural area and happened to be here. He

Guatemala, 1976

has been an enormous help but he can only do so much. What do you think we need, Doctor?" he asked Harris.

"We need transport to a hospital or clinic where there will be more help, and more supplies here," Harris said. "By the way, Sergeant, How did you get here? The streets seem to be blocked as far as we can see."

"A large truck and a crew of men on foot have been clearing a path in the streets back there," motioning over his shoulder, "and our driver is very skilled. Other men are going in different directions to other neighborhoods." The other three soldiers wandered among the workers but did not offer to help; probably not their duty as they saw it.

Hector said, "What is the damage, Senor, I mean where else has been damaged?"

"Very much everywhere, Senor, as far as we have been told" the soldier said. "Communications are down; no way to find out much. Electricity is down in much of the city and roads that are clear are clogged with cars trying to get, well, *somewhere*. Most probably don't know where to go. It is not good, Senor, not good!"

After a pause he said to Harris, "Where is your clinic, Doctor?"

"It is in the north, between Flores and Belize. It is near the San Miguel church, about six kilos."

The soldier chuckled, "Doctor, do you have any idea how many San Miguels there are in Guatemala?"

"No, I don't. The priest there is Padre Augustine if that helps."

The soldier asked, "What is the name of you clinic, Doctor?"

"It is known as *Clinica Evangelica Dios Sana*, Sergeant."

The soldier wrote that down in his notebook, folded it into his pocket, shrugged and turned away, dismissing the doctor and his rural ways.

At last Maria and Elenza returned. Dennis spotted them, pushing a rough cart with four full jerry cans in it. He rushed to them and took one can in each hand from the cart. Maria squealed and jumped up wrapping her arms around his nexk. He had to put the water down.

Maria kissed his face and neck and cried, "Oh, Alonso! I was so worried! I am so glad you are safe!"

Meanwhile Elenza and Nicolas found each other and held tight, sobbing with relief.

The Sergeant called one of his men over. He said, "Corporal, take the names of the homeowner here, Senor Alvardo, and the doctor. And any others that look like they are in charge. Report by radio, especially the needs here, medical and supplies and such."

Harris said, "Sergeant, in addition to medical supplies these people here need food and shelter. Please report that as well." The soldier nodded and turned back to his men.

Chapter Thirty-Two

GUATEMALA

A CAR PULLED UP BESIDE the Army vehicle and two men got out, one with a camera. The other rushed over to Hector and Harris, and said, "Senores, we are with *Prensa Libre.*" – in truth they weren't employees of the newspaper, they were stringers, hoping to sell their stories to the paper -- "we have been told that a soldier is here who got men to cooperate in clearing the rubble and saving lives. Do you know who that is?" Both Hector and Harris looked over to Dennis, wrapped up with a team levering a large slab of plaster from over a cavity where it was thought one or more people could be trapped. No cries had been heard from there for a while so any survivors found might be dead, but maybe just unconscious; they had to keep searching.

Hector replied, "I did not think the man was a soldier. He does not wear a uniform, Senor."

"Well, who is he?"

Hector called out to Dennis who overheard and had not planned for this. For a moment he pretended to not hear, but Hector called again, "Alonso, these men would like to talk with you."

Dennis ambled over to the men, and stood there; he wasn't going to make it easy for them.

"Senor," the notebook man said . . .

The cameraman pulled his camera up and began to point it at Dennis' face. Dennis reacted immediately; he put his hand up over the lens and said with dead seriousness, "No pictures, Senores. No pictures. Understand?" Cameraman pulled back on the device, but Dennis held on. When it looked like the newsman was not deterred and intent on getting a photograph, Dennis twisted it out of his hand. He studied it, turned it over and opened the back and removed the film, letting it spool down in a long spiral, pulling it out of the cassette to the end.. Then he handed the camera back, and crunched the film in his pocket.

The man sputtered, "You can't do that!"

"I just did," Dennis replied. Then he grabbed the kit bag from the photographer's shoulder, dug into it and extracted three more cassettes of film, and stuffed them into his pocket.

The man jerked the bag back and fumed, but realized he would not win this battle.

The other man identified himself as Rodrigo Monte, and said, "We understand, Senor. Please accept our apology. But would you please answer a few questions?" The cameraman rushed back to their car and dug around in the trunk, perhaps looking for more film. Dennis didn't reply but he stood there. "Could we have your name, Senor?"

Dennis wasn't inclined to tell them anything he didn't have to, but he knew the local men knew his name and would think it odd if he played dumb. "I am Alonso Mendoza," he said.

"Do you live in Guatemala City, Senor Mendoza?"

"No."

"Where is your home then?"

"Elsewhere."

"Then why are you here, Senor? If this is not your home, why are you here, on this street, at this house?"

"I am visiting friends."

"Senor Alvardo?" Rodrigo kept digging, also he kept making notes in a small note pad.

Guatemala, 1976

"And his family."

"Are you Guatemalan, Senor?"

"No. Mexicano."

"Where in Mexico, Senor Mendoza?"

"The north, near the border with America, near Matamores."

"Near? Not *in* Matamores?"

"No. Near, not in."

"What is your vocation, Senor?" Rodrigo asked, "Are you in the Army in Mexico? You seem to have impressed these people with your military, uh, bearing and skills; you appear to them to be used to taking command. That's what we have heard about you."

"I believe I have said all I want to, Senores. If you don't mind I should get back to helping my friends," Dennis said, and turned away.

Rodrigo called out to him but Dennis ignored him and kept walking. Rodrigo and his film-less companion conferred and nodded to the others and started toward them, but, as a man, they turned their backs to them, signaling that no more was to be gotten from them. They respected Dennis' privacy and his desire to be left alone.

Among other measures taken to provide light, and in this case, warmth, a trash fire had been lit in a steel barrel. After the encounter with the so called press, he realized that his identity would sooner or later be requested. He had a legitimate excuse for not having any papers. He strolled over to the barrel, and dropped in the fake passport and driver's license and other papers Mendoza had given him, as well as the confiscated film. Now he could claim his papers had been lost in the attack.

As the day brightened and more could be seen, it became clearer how devastating the damage was; no house within sight of Dennis and any of the others was undamaged; very few walls stood whole in this neighborhood, not as far as they could see. Trash and debris lay everywhere and in no order other than crushed walls laid flat and shattered next to their original footings. All the people's spirits were crushed; when it was still dark everything had an eerie glow from the few lanterns and fires that gave the scene only enough light to depict an alien landscape dimly seen. Now, in daylight, their world was glaringly revealed as totally crushed, destroyed, not to be reclaimed in any scenario they were able to imagine.

Work to find and recover survivors continued but most known to be in and around the Alvardo home site had been found and recovered. Men who had been working there wandered to adjacent neighborhoods, looking for more places to help. Those remaining looked around, surveying, and adjusting, wondering what to do next.

After a period of quiet and inactivity, Elenza gripped her father's sleeve, "Papa, where is Cassie?"

Hector looked around, puzzled and even more distraught.

Maria said, "Cassie? Is she the little girl helping in the kitchen?"

"Yes!" Elenza said, "She is my cousin, Mamma's niece. She came to live with us just a few months ago."

Dennis stepped up and said, "Senor Alvardo, is there someone else who would have been in the house?"

"Si!" Hector said."Poor little Cassandra! She is Pilar's niece from the country." Anguish swept across his face; clearly he had not remembered her. She had made only a background impression on him, just another servant, like old Ramona, the cook and laundress, who did not live in the house. "We must find her and bring her out!" He rushed over to the ruins and began digging with his hands. "She is just a child!" he cried.

"How old is she?" Dennis asked.

Elenza answered "Twelve or thirteen, I think. Big enough to help in the kitchen and cleaning . . . and the washing," she added as an afterthought.

"She is just a little thing, you hardly noticed her," Maria added. "Very quiet all the time."

"She just wanted to be *good*, she told me," Elenza said, "she wants to be a good person and help the family."

Guatemala, 1976

"Oh, Mother of God!" Hector cried, "we have forgotten about her and now may she still be alive!" He kept digging.

Dennis joined him and said, "Senor, please let us go at this with some system. Let me help you but I think we will do better if we stop and try to see if we can hear her before we dig any more."

He and Hector stopped and listened. Hector cried to the crowd, "Listen my friends, please let us be quiet so perhaps we can find Cassandra, my niece. Please just stand still and listen. Muchas gracias." All were instantly quiet although noise could be heard from nearby places.

"Where in the house would she be, Senor?" Dennis asked.

"Near the back," Hector said.

"I can show you where I would think she is, Senor Alonso," Elenza said, and trotted toward a particular part of the ruins. She reached the edge of the rubble and began to climb over it. Dennis followed her and clawed at the timbers and plaster and whatever they met for a couple of minutes. Then he stopped, waved his arms out for quiet, and yelled, "Cassandra, Cassandra! Can you hear us? Please call back if you hear us!" Immediately all were still and intent on hearing anything to be heard . . . and, nothing. Nothing. Dennis and Hector began digging again in the direction Elenza had shown them.

Hector called as well, and soon a dozen voices were calling the missing girl. Dennis yelled, "Please be quiet so we can hear her, my friends. Gracias!" Digging resumed, and then Dennis again signaled for a time to listen. No noise was heard and all were reaching for the next piece to pull away, when a small voice emerged; could be a cat or other small animal, but a voice nonetheless. Everyone stood still. Hector called, "Cassandra! Cassandra! This is Tio Hector. Are you there? Are you able to hear us? Please keep talking, keep calling to us and we will find you!" Dennis signaled for quiet again and nothing could be heard for a long moment. Then a baby cried nearby but everyone knew it was from an infant in her mother's arms, rescued earlier. All were silent again.

Then, then! A cry! Were they mistaken? No! It was a human voice! Almost everyone there called out to the voice, but Dennis hushed them again, and nodded to Elenza to be the voice of the rescuers. Elenza called out, "Cassie! Cassie! We are here to help you! It is Elenza, your cousin! Please tell us how you are if you can! Please, Cassie!"

"Help!" came the faint voice, and again, "Help!"

"That's good, Cassie. This is Alonso, Maria's friend," Dennis called in his strongest commander's voice. The others allowed him to take over.

Harris had come up beside Dennis and said to him, "Ask her if she is injured."

Dennis called, "Are you hurt, Cassie? Are you injured?

"Si, I think so, Senor!"

Harris again whispered in Dennis' ear. Dennis said, "Cassie, are you in any pain?"

"Si, Senor, very much pain! I hurt very much!"

"Can you move your arms and legs?"

"A little; not much. I can move my fingers and toes a little but not my arms and legs very much. There are boards holding me down I think!"

"Cassie, don't try to move too much," Dennis said. "We are coming to get you out and get you the help need. You are a brave girl and we are proud of you!"

Elenza called, "Cassie, keep calling out so we can find you!"

"Si! I will!" came the small voice, followed by another series of, "Help!" And then she began to recite the Novena in a voice much louder than usual. Several in the group sniffled in quiet sobs, astonished and gladdened by such bravery and spirit.

Dennis resumed the digging, assisted by Hector and Harris. Elenza kept calling to Cassandra and encouraging her. Cassandra kept up her calls as well.

Chapter Thirty-Three

GUATEMALA

DENNIS STOOD AND SURVEYED the scene, visualizing the structural maze hidden underneath, and where Cassandra was likely to be. She would be pinned down—under *what,* and how *deep*? He said, "Senor Hector, please let us stop for a minute and decide how to go from here." He kept his gaze scanning the ruins. After a moment he said, "I think we should try to go that way," pointing toward a particular gap, with larger timbers laying together and askew in what he thought was a promising pattern.

Hector began to call for help, but Dennis said, "Senor, I think we two are all we need, plus maybe two more strong men, and of course the Doctor who will tell us how to go when we can see Cassandra and how she is, how she is pinned down, and how to remove the things pinning her down without injuring her more," he said. "Please bring lights," he said to the crowd.

Nicolas stepped forward but Dennis put a hand on his shoulder and said gently, "No, Nico, for this we need the strongest men." Nicolas nodded and turned away, sighing.

Hector nodded and called to two of the brawniest neighbors, Raul and Bruno. He nodded to Dennis, who addressed them, "Muchachos, we have to be very careful when we take out the rubble so that when we find the girl we do not hurt her even more. Please do as I tell you! Can you do that?" They nodded as one. Dennis then turned to the pile and began to assign grasping points for each man. As they moved and eased they soon began to understand how the mass fit together and how it could be disassembled.

Work proceeded slowly, carefully, and one-by-one, large timbers came loose and were removed. Dust rose up as each piece in the puzzle was moved and each time, the pile was shaken; the men ignored this except for pausing occasionally to wipe their faces.

After more than an hour they reached a point where Cassandra's feet could be seen. Dennis stopped the work and called, "Cassie, Can you see us? We can see your feet."

Harris called, "Cassie, this is Doctor Harris; I am also a friend of Maria. Please move your toes for us." The toes twitched! "That's very good, Cassie! Very good!" Cassie kept making calls.

"We are close enough that you don't need to talk any more, Cassie," Dennis said. "We are very near and we will get you out very soon."

They could see that two large beams held her down, one crossing over the other. They eased the smaller things away carefully until both beams were more or less isolated. There were still large timbers and slabs of plaster overhead but they seemed to be stable, braced against each other. Dennis surmised that if they could lift the two big members enough so they could slide her out, they wouldn't have to move the rest.

Dennis pointed to the beam on top of the other one and said, "Let us see if we can brace that one from this side," indicating the left side, "and then the other one." One of the men brought up a short timber and held it as the rest gingerly pushed up. The brace was forced into place, bearing at the bottom on a questionable pile of mixed debris. They let it settle. It seemed to hold. Dennis sighed nervously but kept looking at the maze. He said, "Gracias, men. Look, see that long piece back behind us?" pointing to a rather slender board they had pulled away from the pile earlier. "Please bring it over here." He took it and maneuvered it into a slim slot between the remaining overhead beam, and to a gap in the debris beyond, where he jammed it repeatedly until it would not move any more.

"Here," he said, swinging it over to bear at the most advantageous point, "Please together push up gently and I will go in to Cassandra and try to free her. Alright?" They all nodded and as close as they could gripped and began to push up the pole. It creaked and bowed but seemed to hold. Up it came. Dennis said, "Please hold it as high as you can while I try to brace it in place. He had spotted another short piece he thought would fit and hold up the beams. He reached for the piece and could not reach it with his hand, Then he stuck out his right foot and tried to drag it closer, all the while his team was straining. Finally, he nudged it close enough to grasp it with his hands and pulled it in place, thumping it in securely with the heel of his hand. He indicated the men that they could ease off, and they did, very slowly. Again the temporary bracing seemed to hold.

He turned to Hector and said, "Please grip her feet and be ready to help pull her out. I am going in to lift her shoulders. When I give the word, please begin to pull, alright?" Hector nodded and grasped the girl's feet.

Harris said, "One of you be ready to lift her by the hips as the feet and shoulders are pulled out." Raul signaled that he would do that.

Then Dennis said, "Cassie, I am going to crawl over you," the lower beam was only a few inches above her chest, "and then we will pull you out. Are you ready to be taken out, Cassie?"

"Si! Si! Senor! I am ready!"

"All right. I am coming in," he said. Inching into the tight opening, Dennis said, "Cassie, I am going to be very close, so do not become frightened!"

As he moved he reached forward and grasped her shoulders and gently began to rock them back and forth. It was clear that she was wedged more tightly than he had guessed; her body would not move enough to break loose. He said, "Careful Hector; it is not time yet." He realized he would have to go farther into the gap to clear what was holding her from behind, where he couldn't see. Perhaps it was only something snagging her clothes, but he could not see from when he lay. "Please be patient, Cassie, we are going to get you out, please believe it!"

Cassie said, "I know, Senor, I know. I have faith in you and in the Holy Mother! I know you will get me out!"

"How are you feeling, Cassie?"

"I am fine, Senor. I am fine now that you are here."

Dennis was touched by her calmness. "Brave girl!" he said. He edged forward, farther into the gap, until his chest was directly over hers. He turned and looked her directly into the eyes for the first time. He smiled at her and she returned the smile. Her face was covered with dust and he imagined his was as well. He said, "Here we go, Cassie. Please just relax. I think we are about ready to get you free!" He began to run his hands around and under her shoulders and around her back and tried to free anything snagged on her clothes that he could find. A few places seemed to be caught and he freed them as best he could, breathing heavily all the time. He said, "Okay Cassie, here we come!"

He nodded to Hector to at his signal to begin to pull and to Raul to lift her hips, and then croaked "Stop!" He heard a creak, and paused; then, they began again to edge Cassie out. He heard the creak again, this time louder. He yelled, "It is falling, men! Get ready!" Things stabilized again and they all waited. Dennis could not see much of anything but he glanced at the bottom of the first brace and it seemed to be slipping off its footing. It was moving! He yelled, "It is slipping, men!" And he jumped farther into the gap, put his hands and feet on what he hoped were firm footings, and arched his back above the child's slight body, up enough to hold it before it collapsed and crushed the two of them. The whole load was bearing down on him!

He pushed up as hard as he could, gasping and straining, then called, "Men, hurry and get the brace back in place and I will hold it as long as I can!" Sweat poured from his forehead! He could feel his cracked ribs break again and every place Laura had stitched and bandaged pull apart!

Guatemala, 1976

Had he not tried to keep in shape in Houston he couldn't have done this. He thanked God, and hoped He had heard him.

He held on, arching up in transcendent agony. Quickly the men replaced the brace and relieved him. He was not finished. He still had to get Cassie out, so he resumed that struggle and very gradually got her free. He gave a signal and he and Hector and Raul gently edged her out and into the arms of Doctor Harris, who brushed away the dust and particles of plaster, felt for broken bones, and tried to comfort her with soothing words and healing hands. Then he lifted her up in his arms and began to back out and away from the ruins. In the lull in activity, Maria on her own initiative had already replaced the bloody sheet on Harris' work table with a cleaner one. He laid Cassandra gently down on it and continued his examination.

Dennis crabbed his way out, backward. When clear he tried to stand and collapsed to the ground. Harris yelled, "Don't touch him! I'll be there in a minute and take care of him!" Then he said, "Maria," but Maria had rushed to Dennis, sunk down on the ground and held his head in her lap, crying over him, so Harris said to Elenza, "Please try to clean Cassandra up and find a blanket to put over her. Gracias!" Then he joined Maria and Alonso, as he was known to all there.

Maria cried, "Alonso! Please be all right!"

Harris examined Dennis as he lay, sprawled ungracefully on the ground. He could find no fractures, so he carefully rolled him over onto his back. "Are you all right, Alonso?" he asked, "how do you feel?"

Dennis groaned, tried to raise a hand and then let it drop. He was breathing with labor but steadily. Harris pulled up his eyelids and found no signs of severe trauma. He felt for a pulse and listened to Dennis's heartbeat. Dennis said, "Please just let me lie here a while, Doc."

Harris said to Maria, "Please clean his face and see if he can take any water, Maria. Gracias." To Dennis he said, "Lie there as long as you like. You seem to be just suffering from strain. But I can't tell with you lying here. You need to be x-rayed and cleaned up for a full-body exam, but . . ."

Dennis grinned. He said, "The Harris family has sure come in handy for me, eh, Doc? I guess Laura did a pretty good job on me, didn't she?" After a pause, "and Maria."

"Yes, she did a superb job on you. You are quite fit, were all along, and that helps. You should be grateful for that as well."

Chapter Thirty-Four

GUATEMALA

IT WAS MID-MORNING, DENNIS THOUGHT. He hadn't eaten since the night before and his stomach growled; his wasn't the only one. Hector had sent a couple of the men out to find food, and find out what was the situation elsewhere. They had been gone over an hour and there was no sign of them. He had dug into the rubble and retrieved three small loaves of bread. That was all anyone had. Dennis was offered a tiny piece but he brushed it away, saying only, "No, gracias." Hector meted out the meager sustenance to the most needy and it was soon gone. There were still occasional cries, but from distant sites; all the injured there were generally quiet and calm even though some were in pain, some were unconscious. Occasionally a sob or groan could be heard, but the spirit of self-reliance typical of the people of Guatemala prevailed stoically.

Presently, Dennis got to his feet, brushing himself off. Leaning on Maria, he stumbled over to Harris's work table, where the doctor was attending Cassandra. "I believe," he said to Dennis and Maria when he sensed them standing there, "she has a fractured femur and maybe, *probably*, other broken bones. I can't really be sure. I can't say anything about internal injuries of course, but she's breathing regularly, her heartbeat and pulse are strong and her color is good. We can hope she does well, but we just have to get her to a place where better care is available." Then he cast his eyes on the others lying around on the ground and said, "And those as well."

A car or van of some kind pulled up into the clearing. Two men got, one wearing a white lab coat. He spoke urgently, "Who is in charge here?"

Hector answered, "I am Hector Alvardo, Senor. This is my house here behind us," gesturing at the pile of ruins. Who are you, Senor?"

"I am Doctor Lopez from the Central Medical Office. I am trying to find out who needs immediate medical help!"

"Perhaps I can help you, Doctor," Harris said, introducing himself. "You can see the people on the ground. The girl on the table needs to be examined at a hospital; she has just been recovered from under a huge pile of debris. Can't tell if anything else is wrong, but I believe she has a fractured left femur. There could be internal injuries. You are free, of course, to examine her yourself."

"No, Doctor. I trust your diagnosis," Lopez said, "I am glad I found you. Your name was given to us by an Army unit which was here this morning. We need you to come with us now and help in the clinic that has been set up in the Central High School Gymnasium."

Harris said, "Of course. I have my car and can follow you." He looked around and remembered his car was not there.

"Where is your car, Doctor?" Lopez asked.

"I don't know exactly. I had to leave it some blocks away. Streets were blocked and I could not go any farther. I came the rest of the way on foot."

"What kind of car is it?"

"It is a Toyota Land Cruiser, old and beaten, originally tan, but who knows what color you would call it today," and he recited the license number, which Lopez wrote down.

"Please give me the keys and we will retrieve it for you, Doctor." Lopez said, holding out his hand, "Now please come with us."

Guatemala, 1976

Harris gave him the keys and said, "I would like this girl," nodding at Maria, "to come with me. She is a nurse in my clinic in the north and will be a great help at the clinic." Lopez nodded and turned toward his vehicle. "Can you take any of these patients? Do you have a litter or stretcher?"

"No, but we will send someone for them as soon as we can." His partner had been taking down the names of the injured while Lopez, Harris and Hector talked.

Maria pleaded, "Please Doctor, let us take Alonso with us. He is big and strong and can help also." Harris nodded his second to this request. Lopez just tilted his head for them to follow and led the way to the van. Hector watched all of them get in and drive away.

Chapter Thirty-Five

GUATEMALA

THOSE LEFT AT HECTOR'S NEIGHBORHOOD and the hundreds of other neighborhoods in and around the Guatemala City quake site were stunned and terrified and confused in the hours and days after the eruption. They dug into what was left of their homes, pulling out anything they could use for shelter or food. Many were afraid to sleep in their houses and slept on the ground; some erected make-shift tents of bed linen draped over bedsteads and brooms or anything that might work. Survivors had to fend for themselves and had to attend as best they could to the injured family members and neighbors.

In the following days and weeks relief and aid began to trickle in, meagerly at first and then in substance, much from the government but even more from the Red Cross, other private agencies, religious-affiliated and otherwise. Volunteers arrived from America and other countries, some with no clear agenda or supplies, just the desire to help; unfortunately, some were more obtrusive than helpful. Food and water came in trucks; hospitals and temporary clinics began to function again. Several hundred tents arrived from Baptists in America. Electricity was slowly restored where it had been lost, but much of the city didn't benefit because it had not had power before. Debris was first just pushed out of the way but then began to be picked up and hauled away.

Guatemala, 1976

Rebuilding did not follow immediately; first, surveys had to be taken to assess the status and determine which buildings could be saved and restored and which had to be razed. At least one small church found enough of their front wall standing that they didn't have to tear it down to meet the revised building code. There was much confusion over rebuilding, and it took several months before any significant reconstruction got underway.

Despite the destruction of large areas of Guatemala City and other places, there were extensive swaths throughout the country that was not affected in major ways. Downtown Guatemala City seemed almost normal except for the fact that the people stayed away until they felt free to move about. Power was not cut except in places most affected by the quake; other services were generally intact.

More immediately and with greater personal impact, however, was the unwanted attention falling on Dennis. At the temporary clinic where he, Harris, and Maria were taken, the story of his leadership and bravery—the danger and sheer guts he faced just rescuing Cassandra—preceded him. In the Alvardo neighborhood and nearby areas, he was hailed as a hero. News of the rescue of Cassandra traveled through the stricken areas faster than water in a sudden rainstorm, growing with each retelling. He was described as a very tall, powerful Atlas! He grew to gigantic proportions in common belief, almost seven feet tall and strong as a bull! His being taller than most Guatemalans made that easier to believe. A story with a photograph of him appeared in the first *Prensa Libre* published after the quake, describing him as a tall Mexican with a glamorous mustache and a prominent scar on his face. Unfortunately, he had lost his hat and sunglasses, which might have helped with camouflage. He could not escape notoriety, and that was what he dreaded most.

At the American Embassy, Wilmot Jennings picked up the *Prensa Libre* and read every story; that was part of his job, to be able to report to his higher-ups the essence of the daily local news. He paused at the story of Dennis' rescue of little Cassie. The paper's dubbing of him "EL HEROE DE MIXCO," *THE HERO of MIXCO*, and more so, the quarter-page photograph, held his attention. In the picture, Dennis was not looking at the camera; his face was dirty and his hair disheveled. The picture was taken from the right side so the scar was noticeable only if you looked for it. However, it was an electrifying story, one that could galvanize a people, challenge them, energize them, and it cheered him personally. Jennings paged on through the paper, making notes every so often, and moved on. He laid the paper down and picked up another paper, opened it and began to read. The stories of the quake and the destruction and recovery efforts might have been more sensationally handled but were not in any particular in conflict with the *Prensa Libre* story. It hailed Alonso's efforts but declined to copy the "HERO" designation its rival publication coined. After a minute, a something tickled Jennings' mind. He retrieved the *Prensa Libre* and found the story on the tall Mexican again, re-read it slowly and gazed at the photograph. He pondered this for several seconds and then called his secretary, "Mildred, please bring me the file on the Global Geologics team that disappeared. Thanks."

Chapter Thirty-Six

GUATEMALA

An aggressive television reporter cornered Dennis at the temporary clinic where he, Maria, and Harris had been taken, asking for his side of the story that was tearing through the media. He was as reticent and reserved as he was with the reporters who were at the Alvadro house, while trying to be respectful. He claimed he just happened to be there and did what he could, just as any man would do.

"Why did you happen to be there, Senor Mendoza, so far from your home in Mexico?" he was asked.

"I was visiting a friend, that's all."

"All the way from Mexico?"

"Yes. Si."

"Not very talkative, are you, Senor?"

"As you say."

Maria, standing nearby, turned to the man and said, "Please stop bothering Senor Mendoza! I'll tell you why he came all the way from --- "

Dennis stepped over right in her face and interrupted her, "Maria, please do not get into this. I can tell my own story." Surprised and a little chagrined, she stood aside.

This made the reporter even more curious. He said, "Senor Mendoza, what then is your story? How do you know Senorita Maria?"

Dennis stood silent for a strained moment while he organized his thoughts. At last he said, "I was attacked by some outlaws and left for dead. I was unconscious and taken to the clinic where Senoitra Maria works, and she and the doctor there cared for me and restored me."

"Is that why you are so scarred, the attack?"

"That is what they tell me. Now, Senor, please let me be with my friends," and he turned away.

The reporter did not give up. He said, "Who is the doctor who treated you at this clinic, Senor, and where is this clinic?"

Rodney Harris, standing nearby, overheard this and stepped up, "The clinic is known as The Clinica Evangelica Dios Sana. It is in the north." Harris did not want the clinic to be overrun with the press, so he kept talking to keep from having to reveal its locaton. "My wife and I run it. She was in charge of Senor Mendoza's care while I was out of the country buying supplies."

"And you are, Senor? And what qualifications do you and your wife have for medical care?"

"My name is Rodney Harris. We both are qualified Doctors of Medicine here and in the U.S. Her name is Laura Harris." Before the reporter could think of another question, he went on, "We have operated in Guatemala for twelve years and have very good relations with the government and the locals in our area. In fact, one of our very best friends is the local priest." He decided he had said enough and added, "I think that's about all I wish to tell you, Senor. Let's go, Alonso and Maria," he said, leading the two away. The reporter concentrated on his notes and let them go.

Harris, whose car had been delivered to the clinic, took Dennis and Maria to the pensione where he had stayed the night before and several times before, and found rooms for them. It was late the sixth of February, and they were all tired and hungry. The house had not been damaged, but power and water had been cut off. Senora Chavez, the hostess, welcomed them, offering to share the little food she had in house with them. After

Guatemala, 1976

introductions, she looked them over and said, pointedly to Dennis, "Senor, you look like you could use a bath! You are welcome to use the pila if you want." The pila was an outdoor stone or concrete washing tub, used mostly for laundry and dishes, but occasionally for bathing; water for it was from a well. Privacy was usually provided by word being passed to just keep away to avoid the bather's embarrassment. Dennis was only too eager to remove the dirt and grime and the reminder of his recent episode to pass up this blessing, and to endure the possible exposure, even in unheated water. "When you are through, Senor," she said, "I will give you something clean to wear and then I will wash your own clothes."

"Gracias, Senora, muchas gracias!"

"By then I will have a meal on the table for you!"

When he returned to the dining room Harris and Maria were seated, waiting for the meal to be laid out for them. They cleaned up as best they could in basins in their rooms. Senora Chavez was proudly taking time to make this meal the best she could. He found a seat next to Maria and across from the doctor. He said to Harris, "Doctor, why do you do this?"

"You mean minister to the victims of this disaster, or why do I labor in one of the poorest rural areas in the Americas?"

"Yes to both. Why are not you and Laura in a profitable medical practice back in the U.S.?" He stared at Harris, and went on, "Why do you drag a beautiful and capable woman like your wife down here in the hardest kind of life? It doesn't seem like the thing a kind man like you would do for his wife, and for the people who helped him get one of the most intense and expensive educations a man can have."

Harris looked at him; slowly a timid smile crept across his face, as if a new insight had found a home in his brain. He said, "Alonso, Laura made the same choice as I did, to serve our Lord and Savior in whatever way and wherever he led us. It is not a burden but a joy to see the gratitude in the eyes of the people, our friends, we help in the clinic. It is our life and we will keep doing it until God gives us new directions."

"Could he, could God, change his mind about what you are supposed to do with your lives?"

"Of course he could; he is sovereign and can do what he wants. It would not be surprising if he sent us somewhere else tomorrow or never. It is our calling and we will try our best to obey. It is not easy, and many days we are tired and discouraged, but it is our fulfillment and blessing. We will be at work for him. That's what we do!"

The food arrived just then, interrupting the discussion. All three looked up eagerly at Senora Chavez. Harris said, "Alonso, I would like to talk with you again about these things. I hope we can." Then he added, "Alonso, you seem to me to not know exactly who you are, who you are supposed to be; maybe you will meet someone who will be able to help you. We know other missionaries, some who are trained in counseling. I can put you in touch with them if you wish. Think about that and let me know."

In addition to what rice and beans Senora Chavez chose to share, some were available in some of the markets, fruit and vegetables. It was a filling and welcome feast for the trio. As he finished, Harris rose and said, "I am expected to go back to the clinic. I do not know how long I will be, so please rest and try to sleep, and get your strength back, Alonso. Maria, maybe you could return with me."

She was clearly torn, wanting to be with Alonso as much as possible and look after him, but she knew her duty, and left with the Doctor.

Chapter Thirty-Seven

Guatemala

Dennis rose in late morning the next day, feeling sore but thoroughly rested and full of energy. His newly washed clothes were laid out for him; he dressed and wandered down to the central room of the house. Senora Chavez brightened up when she saw him and rushed over to him. She said, "Senor Mendoza, I hope you rested well. Please sit down and I will give you something to eat, please!"

He sat at the large communal table and she brought out generous helpings of fruit and bread and a large pot of coffee and a cup. He ate eagerly and at his fill stood and said, "Gracias, Senora. Gracias!" and asked, "How can I get to the clinic where the Doctor and Maria are?"

"Oh, Senor, Maria came home this morning, late, and is in bed, but the doctor is still at the clinic. While you were asleep a man from a newspaper came to see you. I did not let him stay to bother you, of course!" she said proudly.

"Gracias, Senora. I do not want to talk with anybody, especially newspaper men – or women! But I believe I am needed and could be helpful at the clinic." He paused in thought, and then said, "How long has Maria been asleep?"

"Only a few hours, Senor."

"Then I will not bother her," Dennis said. "I will find something to do."

"Oh, Senor, you will have to stay inside, I think. There are many people standing outside wanting to speak with you. You are a hero, and people want to see you, touch you, talk with you, and maybe just watch you. We have not had many heroes around here, not one so tall and handsome!"

Dennis felt himself blushing, and was at a total loss. He said, "Do you have a television, Senora?"

She shook her head and said, "The electricity is not available now, but I have a radio that works on batteries, Senor. You could listen in the living room. No one will bother you there."

"Do you have a newspaper?"

"No Senor, but I could send out Carmelita to get one." She turned and called the househild's child-girl, and gave her instructions and a few coins. Both left Dennis to wait; he did not turn on the radio. He strolled around the public rooms, ending up in the kitchen. He gazed out the open rear door and started to go outside, but Senora Chavez said quickly, "Please stay inside, Senor. Our yard can be seen from other houses and I do not want you to be seen. Doctor Harris did not want that."

Surprisingly soon, Carmelita returned and handed Dennis the newspaper. He leafed through it, finding the story naming him as: "THE HERO of MIXCO." He was mortified! The last thing he needed was notoriety; if anything he was living on borrowed time, using a fake name and life story. Soon he would be found out and then . . what? He read on, looking for he knew not what, but settled on the lead article, an update on the quake and the known dead and injured. One subordinate article read, "There was extensive damage and many deaths in Chimaltenango." It went on to describe the damage to local landmarks Dennis would not have recognized, but when it came to, "Prominent among the dead in Chimaltenango are Colonel Roberto Mendoza of the National Army and his Aide and cousin, Felipe Mendoza," he perked up. Many varied thoughts and emotions running through his mind, some pleasing, some disturbing. Foremost, he was free from Mendoza's grip.

Guatemala, 1976

Second, Adriana was free from her marriage and he was free to see her and spend time with her; she was now available if she was interested. He had decided he would be happy to stay in Guatemala more or less permanently; she would be a suitable wife and companion. Not only was she pretty, she was more cultured and poised than some in her situation would be. He was, of course, not at all sure she would be interested but now he was free to ask. He would, he declared to himself, ask her as soon as he could. As soon as possible!

It was exhilarating and energizing to be free, free like the Quetzal, free and untamed! And yet sad at the deaths of three men he had come to like.

Chapter Thirty-Eight

Guatemala

Dennis was at loose ends that day, a prisoner in the house with nothing pressing to do. He watched as slowly the crowd around the house dribbled away but a few lingered and stood watch for a glimpse of their hero. Mulling for a good part of the day over things life had left on his doorstep, he began once again to craft a plan to escape. This time he knew exactly where he was going, to Escuintla to find Adriana.

He had noticed a worn straw hat on a peg beside the back door of the house. In his room he found writing paper and wrote a note:

Dear Senora Chavez,

Thank you, gracias, for your hospitality. I must go. Please tell Doctor Harris and Maria that I have gone, and thank them for all they have done for me. I will try to let them know where I am and what I am doing. Please accept this as payment for the room and food and the hat I took from your wall. I have a place where I must go and find something I feel I must have. I wish you and your house the best.

Sincerely, Alonso

Folded in the paper he put twenty U.S. Dollars he had kept, thinking that dollars would be just as useful to Senora Chavez as Quetzales, but

Guatemala, 1976

where he was going he would probably need the Quetzales more. He laid it on the table in the large room, taking the hat and a banana as he left the house, a little before five in the morning.

He slipped out of the house through the back door, climbed over the wall around the back yard, and set off striding vigorously, heading south. No one was around except police and soldiers. He kept alert and tried to avoid them as much as possible. They would want to know who he was and why he was out on the streets. He walked steadily, always south, keeping away from major streets. As it became lighter, he began to look for a taxi, but knew they would not be operating for some time to come. His physical conditioning stood him well. He was not tiring or breathing heavily. His legs seemed to move automatically, and progress was regular and measurably good.

Around seven he began to see life in the streets. He switched over to a major thoroughfare and looked for a taxi. After some minutes he came to a curbside where three taxis were parked. The drivers leaned on the fender of one. Dennis went up to the car appearing to be in the best condition and asked if it was available. The driver opened the door and said, "Where do you want to go, Senor?"

"Just drive south, please," Dennis said, "I will give you the address after we get started," and got in.

The driver pulled away from the curb and slowly drove down the street the way the car had been parked. They moved along sedately for a long spell. Every now and then the driver would glance back in the mirror at Dennis, but he was observing the passing landscape and said nothing. They drove perhaps five miles and were leaving the built-up parts of town. Dennis looked at the driver and said, "How much to go to Escuintla, Senor?"

"Escuintla?"

"Si, Amigo, Escuintla. How much?"

"I do not know, Senor. We could meet damaged or blocked roads and other things that get in the way."

209

"There is no damage from the earthquake in Escuintla, not on the road there either, Amigo, so the newspapers say. The road will be clear." Dennis tried to remain calm but was not averse to asserting his commanding voice. 'Please, Senor, how much?"

"Twenty Quetzales, Senor, twenty."

"How about ten American Dollars, Amigo?"

The driver made a pretense of considering this, but agreed and sped up; soon they were flying along smoothly and rapidly, impeded only by an increasing number of private cars and other vehicles fleeing the city. The drive was about forty miles. The road was well-kept, and despite the growing volume of traffic, they arrived in less than two hours. Dennis was dropped off near the bus station he left from three days ago. He set out walking briskly.

In ten minutes, he was at Mendoza's house. He knocked and heard no response, and tried again with the same result. He tried to look in the ground floor windows but they were all fully curtained. There was no way he could get into the backyard without climbing the fence, and he didn't know what he would do there if he could. A few people were on the street. He tried to stop a woman with a large bundle but was brushed off. She appeared frightened, perhaps of his scar he realized afterward. He remembered a small market tucked into a row of stores a block or so away, and headed that way.

Inside, he said to the woman at the counter, "Hola, Senora. I am a friend of the Mendozas who live in this neighborhood. I heard that the Colonel and his cousin were killed in the earthquake and I wish to pay my respects. The family seems to not be at home. Perhaps they have moved elsewhere. Would you happen to know where they might be found?"

The woman stared at him, seemingly overcome by his height and his scarred face. She shook her head vigorously. He asked again, with no better response. He glanced around the room looking for another person he could ask. Everyone in the store seemed to be looking intently at something not in Dennis' direction. Finally Dennis announced in

Guatemala, 1976

his most commanding voice, "I am looking for the Mendoza family who live near here. Is there anyone here who knows where they may be found? I wish to pay my respects to the family for the loss of the Colonel and Felipe."

With that, evidence that Dennis knew the names, a man stepped up and said, "Senor, I am Fulgencio Arguello, uncle to Adriana Mendoza. Maybe I can help you. Your name, Senor?"

"Gracias, Senor. I am Alonso Mendoza, a distant relative, from Mexico," Dennis said. "I was here in Escuintla staying in the Colonel's house a few days ago. I left to go to Guatemala City and was trapped in town by the earthquake. When I heard that the Colonel and Felipe had died in Chimaltenango, I knew I had to come and offer my condolences to the family. Can you help me find them, Senor?"

"Perhaps I could, Senor, but why should I?" Fulgencio asked with dignity. "I do not know you. I never heard of you, and I believe if you truly are a relative, I would have heard of you."

"I stayed in the Colonel's house here for three days recently, Senor. I knew Felipe briefly before I came here, and of course the Colonel. Adriana and I met and I suppose she is the only one left in that family who knows me. I would like to offer my condolences to her and the Colonel's family. Adriana could speak for me and would, I think."

Fulgencio took a minute to digest this. Then he said, "I will talk with her by telephone, Senor, and with others of the family and we will see if you will be welcome. Please go have some lunch or something and meet me back here in an hour, and I may have an answer for you."

"Gracias, Senor Arguello. I will be here." Realizing he was expected to leave the market, he drifted out and down the street. Finding himself in the middle of town, he decided he did not want to eat anything; instead he could think of nothing other than Adriana and the prospect of seeing her. How would she react? Would she welcome him in this hour of distress? What about meeting the Colonel's family? How awkward would that be? Questions, questions! Then his conscious crept back and reminded him that great loss had descended on the whole country, and more immediately on the people he was hoping to see. Guilt swept over him; he reminded himself that the families of Bruce and their Guatemalan helpers deserved just as much consolation. He must some how send his condolences to Bruce's family, some day. Then he remembered that his father and Melanie believed he was dead, also. Grief and guilt fell on him suddenly with a force so heavy, so relentless and so draining that he almost collapsed as he stood on the sidewalk, amid the thick foot traffic swirling around him. He found a bench and sat with his head in his hands, hoping to not cry, hoping others around him would ignore him and let him have this time of heartache and anguish to cleanse his soul. No one bothered him although a few stared at him as they passed by.

After a while he thought it must be time to return to the market and see if Senor Aguello had an answer for him. He checked his watch, stood and headed back.

Arguello was waiting for him; he said, "Adriana says she will see you. She is at Roberto's compound west of here. I will take you there."

"Adriana told me once that the Colonel's farm was north of here, Senor."

Arguello smiled, "Like many women, Adriana is a little vague in the matter of directions, Senor." He chuckled at his own witticism. He led Dennis out and around the block to his car, a mid-size imported model Dennis did not recognize; some automobiles were available in Guatemala and other third-world countries that could not be seen in America. They got in and Arguello started it and they left. After several miles, Dennis said, "Please tell me about the family, Senor."

Arguello pondered this for an extended time, finally answering, "Roberto, the Colonel, is . . . *was* the oldest male in a large family. They own a large farm, I do not know how many hectares it is, with many diversified things being done, such as growing cane and corn and raising cattle. They aslo have many other things they do there; they raise melons and grapes, and make wine. It is a very prosperous family, Senor."

Guatemala, 1976

"Is there a next generation male ready to succeed the Colonel?" Dennis asked, then added, "Please call me Alonso if you would, Senor."

Arguello ignored this request; he was not ready to be that familiar. He said, "I think so, Senor, but I am not sure he will be accepted. Luis, the son, has not been a very good son."

"How so, Senor, if you care to tell me."

"Luis went off to university and fell in with some bad people and some bad habits. More than once Roberto has had to bribe someone to have Luis freed from jail. It is a sad story, Senor, very sad."

Dennis sensed that Luis was a sensitive subject and not to be pursued. He said, "Who then, will take over running the farm?"

"I do not know that, Senor."

They drove on quietly for a while, each man in his own head and thoughts, wondering and speculating. In his mind, Dennis returned to his thoughts of grief and regret he had experienced earlier in Escuintla. He had to get word to his father at least, and to Melanie and Connie. He did not intend to abandon his child, and longed to see her and hold her and hug and kiss her, and tell her that he loves her. He was undecided, ambivalent, about Melanie; he wasn't sure how he felt about her.

Dennis asked, "Just where is the farm. Senor? How far is it from Escuitla?"

"I do not know the total kilometers, Senor," -- the formality continued, Dennis noted -- "but it is past Santa Lucia and then north a few more kilos."

"What can you tell me about Adriana's and I suppose your family, Senor?"

"We are a poor family, Senor. It is sad. Adriana's father, my brother, was a gifted man, educated, a teacher in university in Guatemala City. He left our farm as a young man and did very well. He married a girl from there, and they lived and raised Adriana there."

"She seemed to me to be well-educated."

"She is, and Felipe, then a young man, found her and they married. He did not live on Roberto's farm but his father had a small holding next to it, and Roberto became Felipe's patron. If Felipe had lived he would probably be the one to take over the running of the farm. The two of them, Felipe and Adriana, did not marry until she was . . . Her family fell on hard times and she had to return to Escuintla." He seemed reluctant to go on.

Cautiously, Dennis asked, "And why did she end up in Escuintla, if I may ask, Senor?"

"It is very sad, Senor, very sad. Hernando, Adriana's father, found himself on the wrong side of politics. And one night was taken away from his home and not found for several months. He was murdered. Luisa, her mother, just faded away in grief, and Adriana had no home, so Roberto, he brought her back to live in his house in Escuintla. Felipe had known her distantly, and persuaded her to marry him; a very convenient arrangement for both of them. That is how it happened, Senor. As I said, very sad."

"What about Senora Mendoza, the Colonel's widow? Could she take over the management of the farm?"

"Yes, I believe she could. She is a strong woman, Teresa, used to running the household, but whether she will or not has not been decided yet, Senor."

"Do the Senora and Adriana get along?" Dennis asked.

"I think so, Senor, I think. I believe they do. They are much alike in many ways and seem to like each other."

Dennis pondered this for a while. "Is Luisa still living?" he asked.

"Yes. She lives at the farm, but is reclusive and never says anything and seems to not recognize anyone, not even Adriana." He was quiet, then, "Roberto became her patron, as well; he has been a patron to many of us, Senor."

Dennis understood the "us," but did not remark on it, did not pry further.

"We are nearing the farm, Senor; it is not very far now, maybe ten minutes." Arguello said.

Chapter Thirty-Nine

GUATEMALA

The farm was not immediately impressive, similar to others Dennis had seen in Guatemala and Mexico. There was a fence or wall, three or so meters high, stuccoed, probably topped with embedded bits of glass. The gate was flanked by tall pillars; the leaves heavy wooden planks akin to those found on the clinic gate in the north but more decorative. There was only a small sign reading "MENDOZA." Like at the clinic, a large cast iron bell hung on a bracket on the right hand pillar, this time with an intact pull rope. Arguello drove in through the open gates.

As they pulled up to the house, Dennis' heart spasmed in his chest because Adriana was standing on the veranda, up seven steps from the ground. All in black, she held her hands together at her waist and had a faint smile on her face, perhaps making what she thought would be a proper welcome.

He got out of the car on the house side and looked up at her expectantly, his own smile matching hers. She said, "Welcome, Alonso. It is good of you to come. Please come inside."

He had to restrain himself from running up the steps. Holding her hand firmly, never letting his eyes leave hers, he said, "It is good to see you, Adriana, but a bad time for it, I am afraid. I am so sorry for your loss. Felipe was a good man and a good friend. He will be missed." Adriana leaned forward for a double-cheek kiss. She wasn't crying, and showed no tears, but he noticed that in her clasped hands she kneaded a handkerchief over and over. Whatever her grief, nervousness troubled her as much or more. Perhaps she was unsure of her future, he thought, of what she was facing in life. He had to tread carefully just now; he would like to take her in his arms and comfort her, but that could be misunderstood and make matters worse. He held her hand longer than she expected but she didn't withdraw it. She stood aside to add a body gesture to the spoken welcome, and nodded for him to enter the house. Arguello followed, exchanging cheek kisses with Adriana, wrapping his arm around her shoulders as they entered the house.

Inside she led them into a formal parlor. A composed and lovely woman of middle years, also clad in black, sat in a large chair in a position of honor, surrounded by a clutch of other women and children; several men stood in a group to one side. A wine carafe sat on a side table; a couple of the men held glasses. Adriana led Dennis up to the regal lady and said, "Mother Teresa, may I present Senor Alonso Mendoza, a distant cousin from Mexico. He and Colonel Mendoza and Felipe were friends."

Dennis walked up to her, took her hand and bent over to give it a mimic kiss. He had been through similar experiences in the Taliaferro household. He said, "Senora, the Colonel found and rescued me from a dire circumstance a short time ago and I will forever be in his, and now your, debt. I will miss him. Please accept my respects and my grief for your loss." On the trip to the farm he had rehearsed this in his mind; his nervousness seemed to be unfounded, it came out well.

Teresa said, smiling, "You are welcome, Cousin Alonso. Please feel at home; you are to think of this house as your home while you are here." That said, she went on, "We have not received the remains of our kin yet; when we do we will hold the services and burials. We hope you will be able to attend, Senor."

"Gracias, Senora. I feel at home here already." The familiar phrase, 'Mi casa, su casa,' came to mind but he kept it to himself. It was a warm welcome; he was pleased, and at ease. He had dreaded this, and it could have not have been better. Despite the Colonel's rebellious plans, this was a refined and loving household. Although grief flowed through the gathering, the Latino culture of hospitality prevailed.

Teresa turned to Arguello and said, "Welcome Fulgencio. He approached her, gripped her hand and bent over for exchanged cheek kisses. He muttered something to her unheard by the others. She smiled and whispered a reply.

The Colonel had many sides not apparent until now, Dennis thought. He had shown an unexpected dimension in his choice of a wife. She was a treasure, cultured and poised, like Adriana. This was a refined and important family fate had led him to.

At the Embassy, Wilmot Jennings placed a call to the U.S., to Kenneth Thompson at Global Geologics. "Mr. Thompson," he began, "We have some intriguing, well, *indicators* about your team members; maybe not conclusive, but kind of curious. I would like to talk with you about this. Would it be possible for you to come down here and help us sort it out? The airline flights are back on schedule, I believe."

"Could you tell me anything more right now, sir?"

"I can tell you only that there is a possibility that at least one of the team is alive. We don't think we can prove that unless you or someone else from Global comes down and helps us. Could you do that?"

"I'll talk to my bosses and let you know, but I'll push it with them."

Chapter Forty

Guatemala

A distinguished man walked over and introduced himself to Dennis. He said, "Senor, Mendoza, my name is Rodolfo Salazar, a close friend of the family. Teresa has asked me to take over the general management of the farm, on an interim basis of course, until a permanent manager is selected."

"Happy to meet you, Senor." Dennis replied. They shook hands warmly.

"I have a somewhat larger farm a short distance to the west. Roberto and I sometimes cooperated in marketing our products. He was a good friend and an excellent manager despite his Army duties taking so much of his time. He will be missed."

"I did not know him long, Senor, but I found him to be a good friend and a warm person. I am sure he was a successful farmer as well."

"Si, he was," Salazar replied, "I wonder if you would like to tour the farm, Senor."

"Certainly I would, and gracias."

"Do you have any experience in farming, Senor?"

"As a matter of fact, I do. I was raised on a cattle ranch in . . ." He almost said Texas but caught himself and continued with only a slight bobble, "northern Mexico, near the American border."

Salazar walked over to Teresa and said, 'Senora, I am going to show Senor Alonso around the farm."

Guatemala, 1976

"I believe that will be good, Rodolfo," she replied.

Dennis said to her, "Gracias again, Senora. I am sorry to meet at such a sad time, but your hospitality is very warming." He began to wonder if her was laying it on too thick.

Salazar said, "Fulgencio, would you like to accompany us?" Arguello nodded and the three of them left.

The farm tour took a little over an hour. Dennis was impressed. It was a diverse and apparently well-managed spread. They began at the barns, which were much like those at his family ranch, but more extensive and better maintained. The crop fields were well-cared for and took up by far the largest part of the land. Dennis was most impressed with the cattle operation. Unlike those in the arid lands of south Texas, this one thrived. The beasts were sleek and beautiful to Dennis. The herd consisted of Hereford and Santa Gertrudis in approximate even numbers.

After an even warmer goodbye to Teresa and Adriana, he and Arguello left to return to Escuintla. His host invited him to stay with his family; Dennis readily accepted.

Two days later, Wilmot Jennings welcomed Kenneth Thompson into his office at the Embassy. "Thank you for coming down, Thompson," Jennings said, "Have a seat. Would you like a coffee or something?" The offer declined, the two went through the usual and expected small talk. Then Jennings said, "The indication we have is the appearance of a tall Mexican named Alonso Mendoza, or at least that's what he calls himself. He showed up immediately after the earthquake, making headlines by rescuing a young girl in heroic fashion. That attracted the press and we have this photograph," he said, handing the other a slick, developed copy of the picture in the *Presna Libre*, eight by ten. Then he handed him an enlargement of Dennis' passport photo.

Thompson studied them, looking from one to the other, back and forth many times. "You got me down here to look at these?" he asked sarcastically. "You could have just sent a fax of this! Is that all you have?"

"Not exactly. I know the pictures were not taken in the same light or at the same angle, but our people think the bone structure is similar. If you can add the scar and the mustache to the original the resemblance becomes more apparent; see," and he handed Thompson another enlarged print of the passport photo with a scar and mustache penciled in. Indeed, the resemblance jumped out. He also handed Thompson a copy of the data page from the passport. "Notice the match of the height in the news report. Also, although the picture is in black and white, the paper says that Mendoza has bright blue eyes."

Thompson said, "Then where is he?"

"I'm afraid we don't know," Jennings said, "Shortly after the hoopla over his heroics -- by the way, the *Prensa Libre* dubbed him THE HERO of MIXCO -- he just disappeared, just vanished. Mixco is a district of the city, west of the center. He had been in the company of an American missionary doctor who has a clinic in the north and who happened to be in then city when the quake occured. He, Mendoza, was left at a pensione by the doctor to rest and while the doctor was back out, ministering to the injured, Mendoza disappeared, walked away from the pensione, in the early morning of the sixth. We have sent out some discrete inquiries on him but so far no sightings have been reported."

Thompson was quiet for several moments. Then he said, "Looks like he doesn't want to be found."

"Could be. Here is a copy -- I presume you've seen it -- of our report on the disappearance of your team. Some of their gear was found by the Guatemalan Army, and indications of more of it, including the bodies and the vehicle, we think are in the waters of Lake Atitlan, near where we think the team was attacked. The conclusion is that a rebel unit ambushed them, killed all the members, took what they wanted and pushed the jeep and the bodies into the lake. The recovery of the evidence we have was made after the Army, well, wiped out a rebel unit. It's unfortunate that there were no rebel survivors to be interrogated."

Thompson read the report, flipping the pages back and forth. He had seen it but paid little attention to the details; it had told him enough to conclude the Americans were dead, and to notify the next of kin. He turned back to the doctored photo, he said, "This certainly looks enough like Reade to look further. What can we do?"

"We can put out a general notice to please report any sightings; that might drive him farther undercover, or we can notify a few trusted government people to quietly help us."

"Have you interviewed the doctor and the pensione owner?"

"Yes. They don't seem to know any more than I have told you." Jennings said, sighing. "There is one more avenue to pursue, though; we could go up to the doctor's clinic in the north, I'm not sure exactly where it is, but I'm sure we can find it, and ask the folks there. The doctor, Harris is his name, said Mendoza appeared on the clinic doorstep Sunday, January sixteenth, badly injured and unconscious. His wife, also a doctor, and her assistant cared for him, stitching up his face and tending to his other injuries. He seemed to be healing nicely and, on the twenty-seventh just walked away, just like he did in the city. We have no idea how he got to Guatemala City. Harris and the assistant, who was in town for the wedding of a cousin, have gone back to their clinic. Then, if this is our man, and he is still going by the name Mendoza, unfortunately one of the most common names in Latin America, he might be found by looking at Mendozas, but that seems like a long shot."

"Global will pay for a trip to that clinic," Thompson said, "When can we get started?"

"I've already made tentative arrangements. We can leave in the morning."

Chapter Forty-One

GUATEMALA

By nine o'clock the next morning they were on the road north, in a black Embassy-owned Suburban, with two armed soldiers, and Ed Jason, another Embassy man, their translator and driver. Even though they had to skirt some of the more devastated areas, they seemed to make good time. Thompson was surprised at the quality of the roads and commented on that. They were paved and well-maintained for the first several miles. As they went farther north the road switched to gravel, and shortly after to a rural track of the same dirt and melon-sized rock surface Dennis and his team were on shortly before they were attacked. The road was flanked on the left by steep hillsides being worked by the same men in gray and white stripe pants, and on the other equally steep drop-offs. Near the lake the road improved, but still was not paved.

Thompson said, "I can see why everyone thinks the lake is so beautiful; it is stunning!" Jennings only nodded; the vehicle and the rough road made too much noise for casual conversation.

They kept going on around the west side of the lake, and then back more toward more north. After another hour they came to the Church of San Miguel, and stopped. Jennings said, "The Padre, Father Augustine, first found our man -- he was unconscious you recall -- and took him to the clinic. He expects us, and has lunch for us."

Guatemala, 1976

They found Augustine standing in front of his church, in his rusty black cassock, hatless, his white hair falling almost to his eyes. He raised his arms in greeting and said, "Welcome. You are here, Senores! Come back to my humble rooms and let us eat a little -- I know you must be hungry – and I will tell you what I know about our friend, Alonso."

They followed him around the church to a side entrance near the rear; he ushered them in and to an ancient table, laid out with food of the region – melons, rice, beans, and pork. "Please sit down, Senores." After introductions and a brief blessing, they sat and began to talk. A native woman of uncertain years hustled around to serve them, and they began to eat.

"Padre," Jennings said, "Thank you for your hospitality. We are anxious of course to hear what you can tell us about Alonso Mendoza."

"Senores, Alonso came to us early the Sunday morning of January sixteenth. He was lying on the ground in front of the church when I opened the door. He was hurt very badly; I knew I could not care for him so I called my good friend, Armando, to help me. He brought his burro and we carried poor Alonso to the clinic. They are good people there and I knew they would give him good care."

"He was still unconscious then?" Thompson asked.

"Si. At first I thought he was drunk; sadly I see much of that. But when I saw how badly he was injured I knew we had to get him to the Clinica Dios Sana." Only Jennings noticed that the Padre omitted the word "Evangelica" from the title; he said nothing about it.

"Did you go in with him and explain to the doctor, well, anything about the patient you could tell them?"

"No, Senor. It was still very early and the bell on their gate has a rope too short to reach, so Armando and I left him on the ground in front of the gate. We knew he would be found. I needed to get back to the church; Mass would be starting before I could get back and I did not want anyone to have to wait. Also, I did not know him, only what

I could see." Jennings thought that Augustine was a little reserved, not wanting to get deeper involved.

"So the doctor at the clinic just found him like you did, Padre. Did you not check on him later after they found him?"

"Si. I did, Senor. I came back that afternoon but he was still unconscious and the doctor could not tell me anything about him except that he had some broken ribs and other injuries. I already knew about the cut on his face; I saw that when I found him, although there were dirty bandages on his face."

The group talked more but learned little. Thanking him profusely when they finished eating, they stood and asked to see the Church. Augustine led them through and apologized for its crude simplicity. Despite this, the men voiced their compliments. Thompson, a Catholic, knelt and crossed himself. As he passed the offering box he dropped in a five dollar bill. They got in the car and left, having gotten directions to the clinic.

Harris himself greeted them at his gate; he was the only one there who had talked with anyone from the Embassy about Alonso. He knew they were coming and led them to his and Laura's residence. The soldiers stayed outside, alert for anything alarming. They had no idea of what to expect out there, in what they considered "the bush."

Laura was there, and was introduced by Rodney; she had glasses of chilled tea for them. She introduced Maria and said, "Maria is my nurse and assistant; she was in Guatemala City when the earthquake happened, and my husband was also there and intended to go to where Maria was staying to see if she was ready to come back here." Rodney excused himself to go to the clinic where patients waited. She asked them to sit, and said with a smile, "You know neither she nor Rodney was not able to return just then."

Then she began to tell them in more detail about what she and Maria had done for Alonso. Jason took notes, and questions followed; soon her information and knowledge was exhausted. Jennings said, "Could we see your facilities, Doctor?"

"Certainly, although there is little to see." She stood and led them all out into the open-dirt plaza. She pointed out the various buildings and explained their functions and importance. She declined to take them inside the medical rooms. "I am sorry, Senores, but medical care is going on and it would be better to avoid interfering with it.

Thompson complimented her on the facility and on their work. He said, "I wonder if we could talk with Maria, Senora. It seems she spent more time with Alonso that anyone else, here and in Guatemala City."

"I am sure you could, Senor, but she is helping my husband just now. Give me a minute and I'll see if he can spare her. She turned and entered the door to the exam room. In a moment she and Maria returned.

"Senorita," Thompson said, "are you able to speak English?"

"Si. I can, Senor. Ask me anything!" she said proudly.

"I just want to see if you can tell us anything that might help us find your friend. In the time you spent with him did he say anything that might help lead us to him; did he mention any place he might go, or anyone he might try to see?"

Maria pondered this for a rather long spell. Then she said, "When I met him at Elenza's house, when he surprised me there, he told me he had been in Escuintla, with Colonel Mendoza, who had found Alonso in Coban after he left here. I do not know how he got to Coban; it is a long way."

"We didn't know about this, Senorita, about him being in Coban and being connected with Colonel Mendoza," Jennings was quick to say. "Is that Colonel Roberto Mendoza who was killed at Chimaltenango?"

"Si, I believe so, Senor."

"How did you learn of this, Maria?"

"Padre Augustine heard and told us."

"I don't suppose you know how the Padre came to know, do you?"

"No, I do not. He told me and Doctor Laura as well."

Thompson interrupted and said, "Looks like we have a conspiracy to protect our boy, Jennings." Jennings nodded, and motioned for them to leave.

They said their goodbyes and thanks then left. In the car Jennings said, "Jason, please call in on the radio and ask them to get busy seeing what they can find out about Colonel Mendoza, especially in or near Escuintla."

Two hours later they were still an hour from home. There was a squawk from the dash. After radio protocol was taken care of, the voice said, "We have found out that the Colonel was killed in Chimaltenango, and owned a house in Escuintla and a large farm to the west of there. He has a large family, many of whom live there and run the farm. Anything else you want to know?"

Jennings replied, "Just directions to that farm, please."

"Will do. We'll have that for you when you get back."

Jennings said to those in the car, "Tomorrow we will go down to Escuintla and check this all out. If our boy is still in the area, we may be able to find him."

Thompson asked what kind of place Escuintla was, and Jennings and Jason filled him in with what they knew as they continued to drive on toward the city.

Chapter Forty-Two

GUATEMALA

As the Suburban lumbered south toward Guatemala City, Fulgencio Arguello received a call in Escuintla from Rodolfo Salazar. After the expected courtesies, he said, "Fulgencio, Teresa has asked that you and Senor Alonso come to the house tomorrow, at nine o'clock, after Mass. Will that be possible?"

"Certainly, Rodolfo. We will be there. Please thank her, Gracias. Adios."

Dennis had spent the day largely in stress. He had no idea of what he would do with himself. He knew why he was there, to see Adriana and try to begin, well, whatever she allowed him to do. He went out and walked around the town. Naturally, things were not normal; even though Escuintla was undamaged by the earthquake, everything and everyone was shaken by the event. He talked with some of the people he met in the street; everyone seemed to need to talk and be reassured that all would be well. Some had relatives living in the quake areas, or they hoped were still living. News was fragmentary, and shot through the village with rumor and speculation. Dennis could have shed some light on conditions in Guatemala City, but declined; he wanted to remain as anonymous as he could. So far, no one had recognized him as *The Hero of Mixco*. Periodically, his imagination led him to think of the Quetzal, and how his invented identity gave him a sense of freedom that mimicked the national bird.

As the Embassy group loaded up for the trip to Escuintla and the Mendoza farm, Dennis and Arguello were being ushered into the parlor at the farm to meet with Teresa, still dressed in black, but as gracious as ever. She was with Salazar and with a young man new to Dennis, though he was sure he was the son, Luis. After the greetings, Teresa said to Dennis, "Senor Mendoza -- I think I will call you Alonso," she declared, "I would like for you to meet my son, Luis."

Dennis stepped forward with his hand out. He said, "I am very pleased to meet you, Luis."

Luis stood rigidly, slow to accept the hand, but after a calculated pause reluctantly completed the handshake. Dennis was taken aback; he had been warned of Luis' history, but here in his own house it was an unexpected snub, a violation of cultural courtesy. Teresa said, "Please excuse my ill-mannered son, Alonso. He has not matured, as you can see."

Luis tilted his chin up and tried to look down on Dennis, which was not quite possible, due to Dennis's six-foot-two stature; Luis was a shade under six feet. He sniffed and said, "Why should I be courteous with this interloper, this fraudulent impostor, Mother? Where did he get those blue eyes?"

Dennis was amused by his redundancy of words; an effort to intimidate, or belittle? It had not worked and Dennis chuckled to himself. Luis bore some of his father's looks, though not as tall or as robust. Dennis saw nothing of his mother in Luis. It remained to be seen if his character matched the parents'. The more he learned about the Colonel, Dennis found more to admire; in the short time he had known her, Teresa had greatly impressed him in every way.

After an awkward silence, Dennis turned his attention to Teresa. He said, "I believe you have other children, Senora, daughters perhaps?"

"Si, Alonso, two, which you will meet now. Adriana is with them." She turned to a servant standing and waiting and said, "Antonia, por favor ask the girls to come in, gracias." Antonia left through a nearby door and was back in less than two seconds. The girls must have been

Guatemala, 1976

listening at the door. They looked to be about eleven and eight; Adriana trailed them in. Dennis smiled at her rather than the daughters, openly, almost staring; when he realized this, he turned away, back to the young girls. Adriana's expression was neutral and unreadable. Teresa said, "My daughters, may I present Senor Alonso Mendoza, a distant cousin from Mexico. Alonso, please meet my daughters Cristina . . . "

The older one bobbed and strode confidently to Dennis with her hand held out to him. He took it and began to reply but was interrupted.

"And Consuela." The younger bobbed as well and beamed up at him.

Dennis drew in a sharp breath. He almost blurted out that his mother was named Consuela, but remembered in time that his concocted story that gave him an American mother. He shook hands with Consuela and said, "I am most pleased to meet you both, Senoritas." Turning to Teresa he said, "They are beautiful, Senora, just like their mother; pretty names, pretty girls." He recalled ruefully that he had said something similar to Felipe, about his wife, Adriana.

Everyone in the room chuckled, acknowledging his tact and amiability -- except Luis perhaps.

Realizing the attention of the group had left him, Luis, who seemed to never be without a drink in his hand, pulled himself up and said loudly, "Just why did you call us all together today, mother, to humiliate us before this so-called *cousin?*"

Salazar took it on himself to reply, "Luis, please mind your manners. Alonso has been accepted by your mother as who he claims to be, and you should as well." Regret and guilt swelled through Dennis. Only the Colonel had known his real identity, his true story; and now he was silent. He hated to deceive these good people, but he was in a trap he set for himself, and had to live with it.

Luis simply turned away, lit a cigarette, and began to make moves to leave, perhaps hoping his mother would say something to reinstate him as the presumptive heir. She made no such remark. Unease settled down on the room. Salazar said, "Perhaps we should go into lunch. Do you think it is ready, Antonia?"

"Si. I think so, Senor. This way, please." She motioned to the door she had used earlier. All began to stand, and waited for Teresa to go first.

Dennis would remember the meal as a feast. The atmosphere was as light-hearted as could be considering the tragedy that brought them together, and Luis's scowls. Adriana sat across from Dennis. He was encouraged by her attention, but maybe it was just good manners, he thought; maybe, maybe not, maybe something more. Maybe it was only his hope. He had a hard time concentrating on the conversation. She has a lovely smile, he mused.

Teresa was speaking, primarily to Luis, "Luis," she said, "I wanted you and your sisters to meet Alonso. That is the reason we are here today." Dennis thought she could dissemble along with the best; good for her! "He is a cultured man and a credit to the family. You should all get better acquainted." And get along, Dennis added mentally. Hopes look dim for that he thought, especially with Luis.

After lunch the females retired for their siestas, the girls objecting but obeyed, urged along by Antonia. Salazar led Dennis and Luis into the parlor; he made sure the doors were closed. He said, "Alonso, Luis, please sit down." They both found comfortable seats. "Alonso, we have found you a very delightful young man, full of good character and apparent leadership abilities. We like you and wish you to be a family member in every way possible. The family here thinks of me as an uncle. Please be assured I am speaking for Teresa and her family even though we are not actually kin." There was meaningful pause. "But we have only your word of who you claim to be, and Adriana's word; she has Roberto's introduction to go on. Please tell us your story, and, please let us see your papers."

Dennis had been led into complacency. He cleared is mind, took a deep breath and began, "Senores, I have no papers. I was ambushed by some rebels while driving a truck in northern Guatemala; I was left injured -- the scar on my face is testimony to that -- and unconscious. I was found by someone – no one knows who -- who took me to Padre Augustine, who took me to the clinic where I was treated and, well, I think I am healed as well as I can ever be."

"Where is this clinic, Alonso? What it the name?" Salazar asked.

"Who, for heaven's sake, is this Padre Augustine?" Luis chortled.

"Padre Augustine is Pastor of a small church, San Miguel, in the north. I cannot be any more accurate than that." Dennis replied. "The clinic is close by; it is named Clinica Evangelica Dios Sana."

"An *Evangelical* clinic, eh?" Luis snorted.

"It is a very good and valuable ministry, *Cousin!*" Dennis almost barked. He was getting tired of Luis and his sniping.

"Please be quiet, Luis," Salazar said calmly. Please go on, Alonso. Why were you driving a truck in Guatemala when you claim to be Mexican?"

"I was transporting something for my father, Senor."

"And what was that; what business is your father in, Alonso?"

"Senor, it would be better if I did not answer that. He is in a sensitive business and it may be dangerous to dig too deeply into it."

"What did I tell you, Uncle? He is a fraud!" Luis exploded. Salazar just gazed him into silence, and nodded for Dennis to go on.

"The reason I do not have any papers is that they were lost in the attack, Senor." He paused and thought about how he would explain his false identity without making a mistake. "When I felt I was healed enough, I thought it was time to leave, so I walked away one morning. I walked south for four days . . . "

Salazar interrupted him, "Cross country, Alonso? That seems unlikely!"

"I was afraid, Senor. I had been attacked and did not know by whom, or for what reason. That gave me strength and, well, I lived off the land. I avoided large farms and cities and towns, I only stopped at a couple of villages. I had had some experience doing that, living off the land."

"Then what?" Salazar asked after a pause.

"By then I knew I had to find a more civilized place I could disappear into. Then on the outskirts of Coban, Colonel Mendoza found me and gave me food and clothes and asked me to go with him back to Escuintla, where he promised to find me work." Dennis was filling in some details he had not had to concoct before. So far so good, he hoped. "It was a coincidence that he and I had the same name, He decided that we were related; it was a matter of convenience for him I suppose."

"He was a compassionate man," Salazar said.

"Too easily fooled!" Luis blurted, went over to the drinks table and poured himself another. Salazar gave him a stern stare, then turned back to Dennis.

"I took a day of sightseeing in Escuinla and the next day went into Guatemala City. I had heard that Maria, a nurse at the clinic, was in the city for a wedding and I decided to see if I could find her; then, as you know we were all caught by the . . . "

He felt tears gathering in his eyes. "Please excuse me, Senores." The weight of his deceit and guilt had caught up with him. He put his head in his hands and began to quietly sob. The others seemed to understand and allowed him time to get himself under control. After several minutes he looked up and said, "Please forgive me, Senores. I have been living a lie. Luis has been right, I am not Alonso Mendoza." The others gaped. Luis drew in a breath and began to rale against Dennis, but Salazar stooped him with a glare. When he caught his breath Dennis said, "Luis, you are right, I am an impostor; I owe you and your family deep, deep apologies, more than I can ever tell you!"

Luis began to stand but Salazar motioned his to sit and be quiet. "Please go on, Senor."

Dennis wiped his eyes and began again. "My name is Dennis Taliaferro Reade. I am American but one quarter Latino; my mother was half Mexican. My middle name is her family name. I have many relatives in Texas named Taliaferro where I lived, and many cousins, my main playmates growing up."

Guatemala, 1976

Without interruption he continued to unroll his story, his college, his military training, his marriage, divorce, and his beloved daughter, Connie, whom he missed so deeply and ached for her. He explained how he came to Guatemala and how his team was actually attacked and, for whatever reason, he was spared. Often he had to stop, sob and sniffle, and wipe his eyes. He came to a stop, and seemed to be lost in memory.

Outside they heard the sound of a vehicle arriving at the front of the house; doors slammed and a voice, Antonia, saying, "Good afternoon Senores. What can we do for you?"

An American voice speaking Spanish said, "Good afternoon, Senora. We are . . . ."

Dennis was immediately on his feet and rushing to the front door. He ran headlong into Jason and those following him. All stared at each other and stuttered. Salazar came up and said, "I think we are owed an explanation, Senores. Please tell us who you are and why you are here. Let us go into the parlor and sit quietly, please. Then we can see if we can be of help to you." He led them, Jason, followed by Jennings and Thompson, into the room and indicated that they were to sit. Dennis stayed on his feet until Salazar's gaze told him to sit as well.

"Now, gentlemen, my name is Rodolfo Salazar, please tell us." Salazar said. "We will speak English if that would help," he added.

Jennings straightened up and said in English, "Senores, my name is Wilmot Jennings; my associate Ed Jason and I are here with the American Embassy in Guatemala City. With us is Kenneth Thompson, who will explain further."

He turned to Thompson, who said, "I represent the American firm, Global Geologics. My company has a contract with the Guatemalan government to survey possible sites for hydroelectric dams. A team was sent here in January and began the work. Unfortunately, contact with the team was lost on Friday, January sixteenth. Up till now we have assumed that all four, two Americans and two Guatemalans, were killed in some kind of attack that day, possibly by rebels. Now though we have

233

reason to believe that one team member, Dennis Reade, survived and has been living here under the name, Alonso Mendoza. Do you have any information on this man, sir?" Jennings and Thompson knew of course that Dennis Reade sat right there in front of them, but they wanted to see how things would unfold.

There was period of uncomfortable silence. Finally, Dennis said, "Gentlemen, I am Dennis Reade. I have just been telling my story to these gentlemen. I would prefer to not repeat it just now. I am exhausted, and ashamed of my deceit. And I wish for a few minutes to recover myself, please."

Thompson perked up and almost said something, but Jennings shushed him.

Salazar said, "Gentlemen, let us relax a little and be civil. Would you like some coffee or perhaps something stronger? For me, I think a brandy would be welcome." He stood and walked to the drinks table and began to pour all of them short glasses of brandy, and hand them around.

Luis stood in a daze, not knowing how to do anything, or what. He said nothing. Salazar began to chat with the Americans about this and that. Dennis sat with his head in his hands as before.

After a time of get-acquainted small talk between Salazar and the Americans, the talk migrated to the earthquake and any news from the city. Luis sat rigid, as if in a trance; he said nothing.

Dennis had been quiet; he suddenly stood and said, "Please, Senores, I will go with these gentlemen, but first I would like to say my goodbyes and offer my apologies to the Senora," and after a moment, "and to Adriana."

Salazar rose and said, "Gentlemen, let us give Senor Reade and the women a time alone. We will retire to the veranda and continue our visit there if you do not mind." He ushered them out. As he passed through the hall he spoke to Antonia, "Ask the Senora and Adriana to come to the parlor, por favor."

Guatemala, 1976

In a minute Dennis heard the women come in and stood. He said, grief distorting his face, "Senora, Adriana, please forgive me. I have deceived you and made a good thing bad. You extended the embrace of your family to me and I have dishonored your family, in a shameful way. Please sit down and I will try to tell you how it happened, and why."

Chapter Forty-Three

Guatemala

In the second time in less than an hour, Dennis was going to tell his story. The women sat and composed themselves, showing no sign of surprise or irritation at Dennis' request to see them. He began his story with his real name, then his early life on the ranch, what his family was, about his mother and her death when he was just beginning to grow up. He said, "Senora, since her death and since I have been in Guatemala, you have been the closest one I have had for a mother. I will miss knowing you and will ever be ashamed for deceiving you. I hope over time you will be able to forgive me." She did not react.

He continued from there, his college and ROTC years, his marriage to Melanie, his loss of the ROTC commission and working for Melanie's father instead, and the birth of Connie. He had to stop there and gather his emotions in. "My situation was so filled with stress and despair, in a make-work job and having to cow-tow to Melanie's parents and their society ideas and activities. I was ashamed and depressed. Melanie and I divorced in August 1975, and I soon found the work that brought me here, to Guatemala." He consciously omitted mention of his one-night-stand with the alluring Fancy.

He described how this had worked out and how it seemed a blessing. "I was feeling guilty and probably sorry for myself. My life had become so unbearable in Texas that a new beginning sounded like an opportunity

Guatemala, 1976

to start over. It was a good job and I was looking forward to it." He took a break and wiped his eyes and face.

"Senora, the Colonel knew of my deception early on. He was our government host the first few days of our time here in your beautiful country. He was a fine man, and I will miss him."

He picked up the story where he, Bruce, and their helpers left on their own. Then, with great anguish, he told them what he knew and what he had learned later of the attack, and waking up in the clinic. "The people there, Doctor Laura Harris and Maria, her nurse and assistant, are loving people, caring for the very poorest without wanting anything back. Love is returned, though. It is easy to see it in their eyes and the way they try to help them. Anyhow, they fixed me up, leaving me with this scar and everything else pretty well healed. While recovering I decided to invent a new identity, to make my break with what I felt was my unbearable situation. Maybe, I thought, a new life was what I needed, and maybe I could just leave the old life behind. She, Laura, told me the scar would become less noticeable over time, but might never disappear entirely. It was she who suggested I grow a mustache." His narrative was becoming looser and less structured, almost casual. "Then, when I was well enough, I just left; I sneaked out early one morning, determined to seek my way, with my new name. I did not have papers under either name."

He told them about his four-day trek south, and in Coban, where Colonel Mendoza found him. "As I said, the Colonel knew my name, and I found out, he knew about the attack and that I was assumed to be dead. I was – *am* – deeply moved and distressed by the deaths of my friends. Colonel Mendoza convinced me to remain Alonso Mendoza and he would try to help me."

Dennis was not telling untruths, just not telling all of the truth. Most of the time he gazed in the eyes of Teresa, but more often than he wished, his eyes drifted involuntarily to Adriana. Teresa peered directly back at him, but Adriana stared down at the floor, no readable expression on her face.

237

"At the time he found me," Dennis continued, "I was wearing old, worn out clothes and was starving and filthy. He gave me food and clothes, and allowed me to bathe, and took me to Escuintla. As Adriana knows, I stayed at his house there for two days and then went to Guatemala City to try to find Maria; I had been told she was there for a wedding. I did find her the evening of the third, and was caught in the earthquake early the next morning. You may know what happened after that."

"Yes, Alonso – I shall continue to call you by that name despite everything– we have heard the news about that time and your part of it." Teresa said quietly. "You have earned our name and earned our love, no matter what has led to what you did."

"I will always treasure this time with you and the Mendoza family, Senora. I hope someday you can forgive me."

"Forgiveness is already here, Alonso. There is no reason for us to hold any of this against you. You need not ask for forgiveness; you have it. All of us have done things and made decisions that seemed right at the time but later proved to be wrong and maybe harmful." Dennis, and perhaps she and Adriana, were all thinking of the Colonel's rebellious activities. "Now, Alonso," she said, standing and opening her arms to him. He filled them and absorbed the hug with so much gratitude he found it hard to breathe. "I will say adios now, sweet Alonso, and allow you and Adriana have your private time." She turned and left the room. How well she read people, he mused.

Dennis was surprised again at Teresa's perception and tact. He walked over to Adriana, who remained seated. He looked down at her and said, "Adriana, I am so ashamed, not only for my deception but also for wanting you for my own when you belonged to another man. It was unspeakable, and I believe a sin. Please try to forgive me."

He reached out his hand to her. After an aching pause, she took it and stood. She stared into his eyes and said, "Alonso, I will never be able to call you anything else. In Escuintla you perceived that I was unhappy. I told you it was because Felipe was away so much; it was that – I did

Guatemala, 1976

love him, in a way -- but also because I was in a situation because of the death of my father that left me afraid and unsure of the future." She let go of his hand and turned away, and taking a couple of steps away, then turned back to face him. "My life was not what I had envisioned in my youth, and it scared me. I was vulnerable to your approach. Oh yes, I could tell how you felt, and I did not know what to make of it, but it was not unwelcome."

"I do not want to *not* see you again, Adriana," he said, "I do not know what will happen to me now. Perhaps I will have to back to the States and face some sort of reckoning. Maybe I could stay here in Guatemala. Would it be possible for me to see you again, Adriana; would you, *could* you accept that?"

Adriana returned to her chair and sat and gazed into space pensively. Finally she looked up at him and said, "If you can, Alonso, come and see me in six months. That is all I can say."

He longed to reach her and embrace her but remembered his social manners and only said, "I will do that, Adriana; I swear I will be here in six months, no matter what! Adios, sweet Senora." At that, he left.

Chapter Forty-Four

GUATEMALA

THAT NIGHT DENNIS WAS PUT up in a mid-range hotel, thanks to Global Geologics, complete with clean clothes, pajamas and toiletries. He insisted on paying for his meals, though, dinner and breakfast, eaten alone in the hotel restaurant.

The next morning, at the comfortably late hour of ten, he was seated in a small conference room in the Embassy. Jennings, Thompson and a secretary were with him. Coffee was offered and distributed. Jennings began, "Well, Dennis, please repeat for the record your story from beginning to the end." There was a tape recorder on the table; the secretary turned it on and took up her pad to record it all in writing.

Dennis started over, using virtually the same language he had in telling Salazar and Luis, but in English. He was uninterrupted but after he finished, many questions arose; he answered as best he could, until they seemed to be satisfied and talk wound down to zero.

They took a break. Then Thompson said, "Well, Dennis," he and Dennis had not met in Houston, "here we are. What are we going to do?"

"The question seems to me to be," Jennings said, "is what does Mr. Reade *want* to do? He has violated no Guatemalan laws, as far as we know. In our view, he is free to go, free to do whatever he chooses." If Dennis was surprised, he hid it well; he sat immobile.

Guatemala, 1976

"He has a contract with Global Geologics still in effect I believe." Thompson said, "and he is obligated to fulfill it. Global intends to honor our contract with the government, even though the conclusions will be different due to recent events."

"You mean the earthquake, don't you?" Jennings asked.

"Yes, of course. But we still have not written our final recommendations. That is why we would like Reade to stay here long enough to wrap that up for us."

They talked like Dennis was not there, but he perked up and said, "You mean I can stay here?"

"That's exactly what we mean."

"Well, I'd like that. I always want to finish a job; it's in my nature to not leave things dangling." He was almost giddy in relief, grinning, puzzling the others. He looked around to see if he had not made a mistake, a misinterpretation. "But, I will need a new passport of course." Then, "and of course, I would like to go home to the States for a short time; maybe a couple of weeks."

"That's no problem," Thompson said, "Take as long as you want."

Jennings said. "We can take care of the passport right here, today probably." He looked at his notes and went on, "There is also the matter of notifying your relatives that you are indeed alive, Dennis. Had you forgotten?"

"I guess I had. There is my father, my ex-wife, and my daughter Connie, of course, but I have no other close relatives except the Taliaferros, who live close by our ranch; my father can tell them." He was gleeful at the way things were unfolding.

"That has already been taken care of, Dennis," Thompson said, "Your father has been notified."

He and Dennis chatted a while about the aborted project and how to restart it, new equipment supplied, and a base to work from. At a pause, Dennis asked, "I wonder, Mr. Thompson, if I could have and advance in my pay? I am almost down to my last Quetzal, and very few dollars."

"You haven't kept track, Dennis. We owe you at least a month's back pay. A check will be here in the morning." Thompson said. "Also, here is a credit card for immediate expenses."

"What's the limit?"

"I'm not sure, ten thousand, I suppose. Don't spend it all at once, all in one place!"

A few other details were disposed of, and Dennis asked some questions about his family and what was going on in the States. After what seemed to be an exhausting morning, they separated. Dennis went in search of his new passport, which he would need to get a hotel room. He might want to rent a car, but that would require a driver license. He should have asked for that as well. After some thought, he decided that he could request a replacement when he got back to Texas.

As everyone stood to conclude, Dennis said to Jennings, "Could I call my father from here?"

"Certainly, just follow Simpson she will show you where to find a phone." Simpson was the secretary attending the meeting.

That evening he placed a call from his hotel room to Fulgencio Arguello. "Hola, Amigo!" he said when Arguello answered, "It is Alonso!"

Arguello was surprised and delighted by the call. He said, "Alonso! Mi Amigo! It is good to hear from you!" They spent several minutes catching up although it had only been less than a day.

Dennis said, "I am not sure how much you have been told of my story, and my deception of all of you. I am deeply sorry and seek fervently for your forgiveness."

"It is not necessary, Amigo. Rodolfo Salazar has told me of your hardship, and what you have gone through. The family understands and forgives you. Teresa asked me to send her love if I heard from you."

"She is a great lady, Fulgencio, a great lady," Dennis said. "I have been blessed to know her . . . and you and Senor Salazar and all the others at the farm. Please tell them all I miss them, and wish things might have turned out differently." An awkward break intervened, as often it does in conversations between friends of short acquaintance. "Fulgencio, please tell Senors Mendoza and especially Adriana that I am going back to the States for a short time, maybe two or three weeks, but I will be back. It's likely, though, that I will not be here for the funerals, and that I send my regrets and condolences. Can you do that for me, Amigo?"

"Si, si, Alonso, of course. I am sure they will understand."

"I will let you know when I am back here. I will trust you to notify the others, por favor."

"Even Luis, Amigo?" Arguello chuckled.

"Especially Luis! I really would like to be his friend. I think he needs friends, don't you, Fulgencio?"

"I do indeed, Alonso, and I believe you would be the kind of friend he needs."

Dennis had decided that he didn't want to go to the funerals; he didn't want to put any added stress on Adriana at such a time.

Perhaps only Jennings anticipated it, but the news of his reemergence and the full story of his time as Alonso Mendoza and the revelation of his true identity as Dennis Reade was unmasked by the press, and reported in great and often exaggerated detail. Despite the apparent deception, he was hailed over again as the HERO OF MIXCO, and the conqueror of myriad dragons of streaming media imaginations! He held the attention of the nation for weeks. This was reported as well in the States, in proud detail. Dennis was overwhelmed and embarrassed and tried to be modest about it all, but the people of Guatemala would not let him.

Chapter Forty-Five

GUATEMALA

THE CALL TO THE RANCH had been disappointing and alarming. He reached Tia Angelica, not Tom. "Dennis," she gushed, "We are so thrilled to find that you live, you are alive! God bless you, God bless us all! Gracias, Holy Mother of God!" Switching to English then, "Thank you, Lord God, thank you! How are you mi hijito?"

Dennis held back his sobs and said, "I am fine, just fine, Angelica. I am well and," he took to breath to get himself under control and wipe his eyes. "I am coming home in a day or so, maybe tomorrow. I will send word. How is Dad? Can he come to the phone?"

"I am sorry, Dennis. Your father was so crushed by the news of your death . . . that he has not been able to do much. He cannot take care of himself; we have to make him eat and get some sleep. He just sits on the veranda all day, holding his shotgun, gazing out at the land."

"How is he since he learned that I am alive?"

"He is pleased of course but sort of numb, still won't do much. He smiles and tries to hide it, but sometimes I see tears in his eyes."

"That's sad, Angelica, I am so sorry you all have been told that I had died. I wasn't able to let you know. I'll tell you why when I get home; it's complicated, but I am all right now. You can see when I get home, although there are a few changes. I now have a mustache; what do you think of that?" He decided to not mention the scar; it would worry her.

Guatemala, 1976

"I'll have to think about that, you young scoundrel!" she chuckled. "Senor Thompson called and told us about what had happened." The joy of regaining a favorite son flowed through her voice. He was like a son to her since Consuela died and she moved to the ranch to help. "Your cousin Miguel has moved here with us to help with the ranch and help me." Miguel was maybe eighteen, Dennis thought; he would be helpful, but couldn't do everything Tom did. They had not had a hired hand for a couple of years now; Tom tried to do it all. Dennis pitched in when he was there. One of the cousins came to help from time to time. Running a cattle ranch was a toilsome and unrelenting job, and usually unprofitable, as Dennis well knew.

Chapter Forty-Six

TEXAS

HE ARRIVED IN HOUSTON THE next morning before eight; his connecting flight to Corpus Cristi left an hour or so later – these schedules were not to be taken as gospel – but this one was not late. He was met by Miguel at the Corpus Cristi airport, and driven to the ranch in the ranch pickup, a drive of almost two hours. He could have flown on to Kingsville, but it would have meant another layover and a last leg in a small Beechcraft; the overall time in transit would have been about the same. Dennis wanted to have the time to talk with Miguel and catch up on conditions at the ranch as well as on family news.

Miguel held Dennis in awe, a relative not too much older who had accomplished so much, gone to college, had been in the military, and so on. Dennis's adventure in Guatemala fascinated him, and he kept firing questions at his cousin the whole trip.

"Well, Miguel," Dennis said when he had an opening, "what are your plans, now that you've finished high school?"

Miguel was unsure; he wanted to go to college, but was unsure where. He was smart and could go to any one of several places, maybe one of the major universities or maybe to a community college close by, maybe in Kingsville. He wouldn't go far, not out of Texas; he would want to stay close to his family. They talked about this for some time; Miguel wanted to hear what Dennis advised. Dennis cautioned him not to take

Guatemala, 1976

his clues from him; rather, look instead to his teachers and family and contemporaries for guidance.

As they neared home, the road became less smooth, and eventually turned into dirt, still well graded and not too rough. Dennis breathed the dry plains' air, and to take in the flat, endless land of his young life. He rejoiced, realizing how much he missed this, knowing at the same time, he would never live here permanently. By contrast, the mountains and eternal spring of Guatemala held its growing appeal, and might be more so, not for the terrain alone; Adriana had a totally different kind of magnetism for him. He could neither deny nor forget that; six months, six months!

It was mid-afternoon when they drove up to the rambling and familiar and welcoming house; a huge feast awaited them. He had grabbed a Danish and coffee for breakfast at the Houston airport, and had nothing since, but hunger did not trouble him. He jumped out of the truck and ran up the steps. Before he reached to top, he was swarmed over by hugs and back slaps and hearty greetings, and many tears. Hellos and salutes washed over the time and space in both languages. The joy and noise draped over him like a blanket and moved with him as he gently worked his way into the house.

Tom and Angelica had not gone outside to welcome him, but stood back just inside the double doors. The crowd sensed that the three of them deserved a special, separate time of welcome and love to restore them and meld them into a family again. Tom stood with tears streaming from his eyes, unable to speak. Angelica hugged him tightly, then leaned back and surveyed his face. She stroked his scar with a finger, then pulled him to her and seemed unable to let go. Tears and sobs flowed from all three, and from many of the others as well.

They broke and turned to the group. Dennis was expected to say something. He began, "Dear ones, I am so glad to be home with all of you. You cannot know how glad I am, how much I have missed you. I do not want . . ."

A small but loud voice rang out, "Daddy! Daddy!" and a tiny bundle of energy tore out of the crowd and ran into his arms.

He scooped her up, saying, "Connie! Connie! Oh, honey! I've missed you so! I love you! I love you, honey! It is so good to see you, so good!" He returned her tight hugs and smothered her with kisses. He had not expected to see her here, but had made certain he would see her in Houston with Melanie while he was in the States. He would spend all the time he could with Connie, and would make plans to see her as often as he could after that. While this reunion went on, the crowd migrated into the living room where there was more space. Holding her tightly with tears in his eyes, he scanned the room for Melanie, and spotted her standing against a wall across the room.

He walked over to his former wife, the mother of his child. Connie yelled, "Mommie! Mommie! Look, Mommie, here is Daddy! My Daddy!"

As he closed on her, she held out her arms and Connie went into them without letting go of Dennis, and pulled them together. He kissed Connie and snuggled in her neck. She giggled in delight. All three held each other tightly, then Melanie let go and stepped back. In his arms Dennis marveled at how Connie seemed to have grown in less than two months, and how much she reminded him of Consuela, particularly by her huge near-black eyes, and the red glints in her curly black hair. The child leaned back and studied her father's face. She locked on to his scar, tentatively reaching out a hand and then pulling back. She said solemnly, "Daddy's got a boo-boo!" Then she touched it and said, "Does it hurt, Daddy?"

"Not any more, sweetheart. I am fine now."

"You have hair on your face, Daddy!" she giggled, "It tickles!" He grinned and rejoiced in this time of unfettered intimacy with his precious girl..

"Mel," he said to her, "thank you for coming and bringing Connie."

"Angelica suggested it, and I am glad to be here." They air-kissed and tried to look pleased. "When we have a little time, we need to talk."

Guatemala, 1976

"Of course, I want to make arrangements to see Connie." He said. She nodded.

Then he noticed the decorations seeming to be everywhere, and the feast laid out on the dining table across the hall. A big banner hung from the ceiling spanning the hall, saying "Welcome! Bienvenido! Our Hero, Dennis!" He wondered if they had heard of the title *Prensa Libre* gave him: *The Hero of Mixco*.

"It is time to eat!" announced one of his smaller cousins, "Please come!" And they did. Dennis found he was hungry after all and allowed himself to be lavished with helpings of every kind on the table, as well as a never-empty mug of sweet and slightly alcoholic drink. He dug in eagerly, Connie still in his lap, picking morsels from his plate. He looked around, smiling at all his loved ones individually. He was blessed and loved; he was almost moved to tears when he thought about it. It was a party, a celebration in his honor, and he wondered if it would ever be better than this, but he hoped for a different kind of better..

When everyone seemed to be through eating, a gaudily-dressed band of three guitars—one a huge bass, a cornet, and a vigorous maracas player—came in and began to stroll around and serenade them all with what passed for Mariachi music, focusing with pointed attention toward Dennis, still holding Connie on his lap. Those so disposed began to dance. Clapping and shouts encouraged them, and the joy of the occasion filled the house and extended on into the evening. Dennis turned to Connie, "Honey, lets go out on the veranda where we can talk, okay?" In a big rocking chair, still holding his daughter, he said, "Well, little girl, tell me what's going on with you these days." Before she could think of how to start, he remembered and said, "I am sorry I missed your birthday, honey. Daddy was away and couldn't get home in time."

She said somberly, "That's alright, Daddy. Mommie told me you were away and would be home soon."

"What did you get for your birthday?" He had not forgotten and had a present from Guatemala for her in his bag, which he couldn't get to just then.

"Papa," Dennis assumed this was Herbert, "gave me a big doll house. You have to see it, Daddy! It is HUGE!" Connie was a precocious two-year-old, very articulate, Dennis proudly realized.

"And what did Mommie give you?"

Mommie gave me a doll, and a set of blocks and a tea set and some clothes, and . . . " She seemed to run out of words and breath at the same time.

"Anybody else give you anything?"

"Well," she drew it out, "Nana Prescilla gave me a pretty sweater."

"Have you worn it yet?"

"Yes, but it scratches and I have to wear it when she is with us, but not other times." Dennis smiled at the honesty of this little one. She perked up and said, "Dilly gave me a box of handkerchiefs. They are real pretty, and Norman . . . "

Melanie came out on the veranda with Angelica behind, and said, "Connie, please go with Aunt Angelica." Connie recognized Angelica as someone who loved her and whom she also loved, so hopped down from Dennis's lap and took her great aunt's hand and skipped inside. Melanie sat beside Dennis and said, "Dennis, I have some news that mustn't wait. You need to hear it from me and not someone else." He waited, saying nothing; he still held a faint fondness for her, but could not call it love. About the best he could say was that she was the mother of his child. "I am getting married in April," she announced.

"Anyone I know?" He hesitantly asked.

"No, I don't think so; in fact, I know not; he is an engineer with NASA."

"Name, if you don't mind? I'd like to know who will be raising my child."

"His name is Norman Dooley. He has been transferred to Cape Canaveral, is already living there. That's where we will live."

Guatemala, 1976

Dennis let this sink in. Connie's mention of "Norman," was explained. He peered off into the gloom of the night, unable to say anything. He had envisioned something like this, like Melanie getting remarried, but not moving away with his daughter, all the way to Florida!

She respectfully kept quiet, giving him time to sort this out in his mind. Finally, he said, "What can we do so I can see Connie sometime?"

"I don't know, Dennis, but I'm sure we can work something out."

Angelica called to him, "Dennis, please come and tell us all about what happened to you." She led him by the hand back to a chair placed near the center of the room. As he sat she began to tell what she knew, "Mr. Thompson of the company Dennis worked for in Guatemala told me some things about your time there, Dennis, in Guatemala . . ." She seemed to be on the verge of telling the story herself; this amused Dennis so he just let her go on. "Our poor Dennis was attacked and his face was cut bad; you can see that yourselves. In a hospital in a place away from people his face was sewn up and he was fixed up real good. Let's see, what came next? Jorge," her brother, Dennis' uncle, "help me, please."

"I only know what you told me, Ange." She was older and gave him a look of command, so he picked up the story as far as he knew it. "While he was in this hospital, Dennis realized he was in danger so. . . am I getting this right, Dennis?"

"You're doing fine, Tio,"

"So he decided to give himself a new name, a Guatemalan name . . ."

"What is the name?" came a voice from the crowd. Jorge gave Dennis a questioning expression.

"Alonso Mendoza," Dennis said simply and said no more, wanting the others to tell it.

"Alonso, that's right," Jorge went on. "And then he left and wandered in the countryside for many days . . ."

"How many days?" from the audience.

Dennis held up four fingers. Jorge continued, "Then he was found and was helped by a good man who gave him food and clothes and a place to stay . . ."

"A real Good Samaritan!" Angelica said.

"And he went into Guatemala City the night before the big earthquake and the next day rescued a girl and became a national hero!" He stopped and looked at Dennis and said, "I got it right, Hero?"

"Close enough!"

"Who was the girl you rescued?" a youth asked.

"Her name is Cassandra, or Cassie."

"She your girlfriend?" a young female voice.

"No, she's only about fourteen, Chiquita, younger than you!" He recognized the teen, his cousin, and winked at her. "I'm waiting for you!" Some hooted and all laughed.

He sat smiling and silent, then morphed into a pensive expression. He said, "You and Angelica have it about right, Tio, but let's not forget that many thousands of people were killed in the earthquake." After a solemn delay, he went on, "and I lost my colleague, Bruce Kalchik and two Guatemalan team members in the attack. I have to go see Bruce's, parents in Mobile before I go back to Guatemala."

"You are going back?" Miguel asked.

"Yes, in a week or so. I have to finish the work we were doing there . . . but let's have fun while we can!" The party atmosphere resumed, although quieter. The music was less boisterous and more tranquil and romantic.

Angelica sidled over to him and said, "Dennis, let us go out on the veranda and talk, please?"

"Fine, mi estimada Tia," he chuckled. He was slightly tipsy and tired and welcomed a chance to get away from the mob inside. She sat down and patted the seat next to her. He said, "Well, Chiquita, what's on your mind?"

"Dennis," she said, "well, I guess we could call you Alonso, but I can't, not yet. I am happy for you; you have a good job and you seem to

Guatemala, 1976

have found yourself in Guatemala, but have you really? Are you sure this is what you really want to do with your life? You have so much potential and I don't want you to waste it. I am always concerned about you. I love you so much . . . " She stopped to take a breath, almost a gasp. "Everybody likes you, Dennis; everybody here loves you and I expect there are others who love you. That's the kind of boy you are, but you have yet to settle down to the life I believe the good Lord meant for you. You don't seem to know who you are or who you want to be, Dennis."

Dennis froze in his heart. There was that phrase again: "You don't seem to know who you are or who you want to be." He knew that people who cared for him had told him, but he was still unsettled as when he first heard it, from Sergeant Paisley back in College Station. Would he ever know? He was still seeking, and had a pathway in his mind, but too much of it depended on others. Maybe he was too ready to just go along with others told him or expected of him. It bothered him, a lot, more as time passed.

He and Angelica embraced and said soothing words before returning to the party.

Chapter Forty-Seven

The United States

Melanie and Connie stayed for two more days, but not at the ranch; Jorge and his wife, Carlota, welcomed them. Dennis stayed on another week and spent much of the time visiting around his various cousins, aunts and uncles and their friends and the other friends he had grown up with. He pitched in and helped Miguel in ranch chores feeling good about it. Before they left, he gave Connie the large Guatemalan doll, with the traditional brilliantly colored fabrics the nation is known for, that he had brought for her birthday. She was ecstatic and insisting on holding it constantly.

The goodbyes to Tom and Angelica were separate and difficult. He pledged to return as early as he could. He longed to tell them about Adriana, but could not. His claim on her was tentative at best, and his hope was stretched to his limit; he ached when he gave the situation too much thought. Being unsure of anything was not in his nature; he had trouble understanding and enduring it, but he tried to not let his angst show to his most beloved kin, Tom, Angelica, and Connie.

He left the next morning, February 13, flying to Mobile. The Kalchiks, Will and Sue Ann, met him at the airport. They drove him to their home and tried to give him a warm southern Mobile welcome.

Guatemala, 1976

It was awkward at first. After they had offered Dennis something to drink; he chose iced tea, as they did. Sue Ann said, "Bruce told us so much about you. He admired you so much, and said it was good you two had landed on the same team; you got along so well together."

Dennis did not know what to say or how to begin, but knew he had to try. He cleared his throat and said, "Bruce was an ideal partner. We did get along; we had personalities that were different, but we worked well together, complementary. He was so funny! We joked about almost everything, especially football. I'm sure you know he was a die-hard Auburn fan, almost as obnoxious as I am a Texas A&M fan," he chuckled; they joined in. "It gave us a lot to talk about, especially football!" He stopped; he had said about all he had thought of in advance.

Will said, "We *are* an Auburn family, back many generations. Bruce told us a lot about the work in Guatemala; he said he loved it."

"And he was good at it. In addition to the geological work, he was our radio operator; he kept us in touch with Houston, and he always seemed to have a joke. I will miss him," Dennis said, "I really will."

Sue Ann sniffled into a handkerchief she had been kneading in her hands and said, "He was fond of you, too, Dennis."

"I am sorry I could not be here for his memorial," Bruce's body had yet to be recovered but a service had been held in his memory. "I know it would have been good. He often told me what a wide bunch of friends he had, from the community here and from other Auburn people."

Sue Ann said, "Yes; it was very nice; everybody was so kind and loving."

"You are going back to Guatemala soon?" Will said.

"I'm on my way now, but only for a short time," Dennis replied, "just to wrap up the report. It shouldn't take more than a few days."

"Then what will you do?"

"I'm not sure. There's been talk of staying with Global Geologics in Houston, but nothing's decided yet."

There didn't seem to much more to say. Dennis stood and said, "I must be going. My plane leaves in about two hours. If you'll let me use your phone, I'll call a taxi."

"Nothing doing, young man!" Will said, "We'll take you back," and they all moved awkwardly to the car outside. At the airport they said their goodbyes at the gate. Sue Ann hugged him and sobbed a moment; she said, "Please keep in touch; let us know how you are. Please give our regards to your family." She considered it impolite to mention his divorce and his single-parent child. Always thoughtful, these cultured Mobilians, Dennis mused.

Will shook his hands, pulled him close and said in a whisper, "War Eagle!" and winked. They hugged, Dennis thinking, what a way to say goodbye with a good feeling!

Dennis said, "Bruce was my *Twelfth Man*!" He blinked tears away, so did Will.

Chapter Forty-Eight

GUATEMALA

Back in Latin American again, he quickly reabsorbed the laid-back milieu and work attitudes of the place, and re-adapted to the lessons learned in the recent past. He found that he had missed it. Monday morning he located his new office, and a comely native all-skills helper, Mariela, who Thompson had hired in his absence. She said when they met, "Please, Senor, call me Mary."

"That'll make it easy, Mary. Gracias! We will speak English most of the time, if you don't mind.

"Of course not, Senor."

"Just a minute, Mary," Dennis said. "Please don't call me Senor, just call me Dennis, or if you prefer, Alonso. That's what some of my friends down here call me. Okay?" If this puzzled her, she didn't show it. They began dig into the work Thompson had organized and left for them before he went back to Houston.

On the flight back from the States, he concentrated on the work left for him. All the field notes and logs had been lost of course, so he would have to rely on memory and whatever Global had recorded from the radio reports. That is, when he was not thinking about Adriana; it was difficult not to.

The new office was on the second story of a five-year-old plain vanilla combination building, retail on the ground floor, offices above. It was

Spartan, but he didn't expect spend much time there. It had not been damaged by the earthquake, and still had its essential services intact: telephone, electricity, and water, though he would have also appreciated having air conditioning. The three-room suite came with a large electric fan in each room; but with the eternal spring of this blessed country it was hardly missed. The glass jalousie window slats were kept open, closed only at the end of the business day. Dennis busied himself arranging the accessories on the cheap desk Thompson had judged appropriate, and commissioned Mariela to purchase a large combination desk calendar and writing surface, telephone, a pencil cup, and a few other odds and ends. He knew he was supposed to think he was ready for serious work, and he tried to push distractions away in order to concentrate on the job. Instead, he was edgy and unable to focus. He stood and said, "Mary, I think I need to go out and walk around a bit. I should be back in ten or fifteen minutes, okay?" The plans he made on the plane seemed to evaporate; he was in no way an office man, much more a field man. He had to force himself to get down to what he had to do. There would be field work, of course, but getting everything organized came first and he couldn't seem to get over that hurdle.

On the street he bought coffee in a paper cup and found a bench, sat and talked silently to himself. "Dennis, or Alonso, pull yourself together and do the job you're supposed to, the way you're supposed to." He had never relied on any kind of religious faith but kind of knew it, sort of. At that moment he tried to pray as Rodney and Laura urged him, but soon gave up. He recalled the faith the Harrises exhibited and practiced; he had been inspired that these dedicated, well-educated, and skilled people could sink themselves in their work, with the only reward being the aid they could give to people whose lives could never reach much higher than what they were born with. An epiphany came to him: *The best most of these people here could ever hope for was not as good as the worst he could expect in life.*

Guatemala, 1976

With this revelation, he abruptly stood, pulled in a deep breath and strode back to the office, a renewed vigor and resolve propelling him.

Back in the office, Mary greeted him with a smile and said, "Alonso, Senor Thompson left this for you," handing him a folder holding several typed pages. She seemed to sense that he had needed a break to pull himself together and had succeeded, and was ready to buckle down. "It is an outline of the way your report should be done. I have been over it and I have begun a draft; it is in the file, as well." Dennis thanked her and took the file and sat down to digest it. It outlined the format Global wanted him to use and a mock draft of a typical field report. Also included were copies of the daily radio reports the team had sent; from these he could re-plot the actual sites where they took their measurements and made tentative evaluations. There had been eight sites before being attacked, stopping the project, and he hoped the notes from those reports would be enough to reconstruct reasonably accurate reports. Thompson instructed him to re-visit these eight sites and only by visual observation, see if he felt there was anything else to be said about them, and record that.

After that, he would draft a final recommendation report. Everyone knew what that would say, but it had to be done to fulfill the contract requirements and fully cover the technical data and reasoning leading to the conclusions. He and Global estimated that all this would take no more than two weeks, but there were no absolute deadlines; there were always unforeseen complications, and contingency allowances should always be provided.

He made numerous notes and figured he had done all he could before going out into the field. He called to Mary. She came in and stood ready with her note pad, and said, "Yes, uh, Alonso?"

"Is there an escort or driver or someone who is supposed to go with me in the field?" he asked.

"Yes, Alonso." She said, "He came in just now, while you were working, and is waiting in the other room. His name is Eduardo Gonzales. Senor Thompson hired him when he hired me."

"How did he find *you*, Mary, and him?"

"Senor Jennings at the American Embassy found me through and agency I am listed with. I do not know how Eduardo was found."

"You realize I guess that the job will only last a few weeks?"

"Yes, Alonso," she seemed to enjoy playing with his Guatemalan name. "It is all right with me. The agency will find something else for me to do."

"Well, I'm glad they did, glad they found you, Mary. Please ask Eduardo to come in, Gracias."

Mary turned to the door and called. Eduardo came in and Mary started to leave. "Please stay, Mary. Gracias." Dennis said. Then standing, he addressed the man in Spanish, "Eduardo, my name is Reade, but please call me Alonso," and stuck out his hand. Obviously not used to shaking hands with superiors, Eduardo stood rigid for a moment then reached for the hand and shook it. "Please sit down, Eduardo." Both sat and so did Mary, in a side chair.

"Eduardo, please tell me a little about yourself," Dennis said. The young man gave him the short version of the biography on the sheet Dennis found in the folder. Dennis asked a few questions for the sake of form, and then said, "I don't know how much you have been told about this job, Eduardo, but I'll assume not much; here is what we will be doing . . ." and went on to describe the schedule and duties. "We will leave in the morning and go to two sites per day, and find a place, a hotel, pensione or some such, to spend the night. There I will telephone Mary back here," nodding to the girl, "and dictate a short report which she will call in to our base in Houston, Texas. She will also type a report for the file." He hoped Eduardo understood enough of this to function well; most of it wasn't necessary for him to know, but a little overkill was often a good thing.

Guatemala, 1976

He switched topics. He said, "Did the boss ask you to carry a gun or a side arm, Eduardo? Are you qualified in using a gun?"

"Si, Senor Alonso. I spent eight years in the National Guard. I learned good! And yes, Senor Thompson told me about what we would be doing and that there could be danger. I have a Smith and Wesson thirty-eight caliber and a box of ammunition, Senor, that I will have with me on our trip."

"Good. Mary," he said turning to her, "We do, don't we, have a vehicle?"

"Yes, Alonso. The keys are in the desk drawer there. Eduardo knows where it is parked."

"Seems we are all set then," he said, standing. "I will see you right here in the morning."

"What time, Senor?" Eduardo asked.

"Let's make it nine, okay?" he replied. He would have to work on Eduardo to train him to call him something other than Senor, Dennis decided.

Some three weeks later, the field work was done and the recommendations were finished. There had been no incidents; no rebel attacks or interruptions of any kind. He tried to remain anonymous and was mostly successful. A few of the accommodations hosts had recognized him as the hero of fleeting fame; they were respectful and made little of it, but as soon as he left word of his stop spread, giving the hosts much to brag about. He was ready to go back to the States, at least for the time being. Coming back in August remained firm in his plans, but what happened until then was as certain as possible. He would work for Global Geologics for now, at least until August; after that it would be open to how it all went.

The night before he left, he called Fulgencio. "How are you, old friend?"

"We are good, Amigo. It is good to hear from you. Everything is the same; nothing much changes around here."

"Fulgencio,: Dennis said, "I need to tell you that I am leaving in the morning to go back to the U.S. I promise to come back when I can, and see you and the others here. I will miss all of you. Please keep in touch and call me if anything comes up I can help with, okay?"

"Surely, Alonso, of course, of course!"

"And, Fulgencio, please look out for Adriana for me; can you do that? Do not bother her, just try to make sure she is safe and is okay with her in-laws, please. Gracias, Amigo!"

After assurances of continuing and constant care, they closed the call.

"Adios, Alonso. Take care of yourself." Arguello said.

"And you, old friend." Dennis replied.

Chapter Forty-Nine

TEXAS

The time until August went swiftly and well for Dennis at Global Geologics. He enjoyed the work; it was more in line with his college major and his expectations as a career. He talked with Melanie often and with Connie, aching to see her and hold her. He told no one of his intention of going back to Guatemala and seeking the affections of Adriana, but she was seldom out of his mind.

In one conversation he said, "Mel, I would like for Connie to be with me as much as possible."

"Certainly, Dennis," she said. She and Norman had married in April and she had moved to Florida with Connie.

"I know, but I want her to not forget about me and my people; I want her to learn the language." Melanie was silent. She knew what he meant: Spanish. "Maybe she could stay with me in the summers. We don't have to decide anything right now, but please promise me you'll think about it, okay?"

"I promise I'll think about it, Dennis," she said, "but I doubt if Mother will be happy about it, and especially about learning Spanish."

"What does your mother have to do with it? Tell me that!" This irritated him, opening old wounds; he wondered if it was deliberate.

"That's all I can say, Dennis. You know the situation. It's the way it has to be; please live with it."

He was so angry he had to hang up to avoid a shouting match. The matter was left there for the time being. It dragged on, always permeating and poisoning their relationship.

In July, he flew to Florida and spent five strained days with Connie. They enjoyed time at Disney and other nearby attractions. He felt and hoped their bond was growing stronger, and that she would never forget him, although he might not be able to see her often.

One day he and Connie sat out on a bench looking at the ocean. "I have to go away again sweetheart, but I will come back as often as I can."

"Where are you going, Daddy?"

"Back to where I was before. It is a small but beautiful place called Guatemamala."

"What-a-mada?" Connie mimicked.

"That's right, sweetheart; What-a-mada!"

The separation when he left was heart-breaking for both, with many tears and hugs and pleas by Connie for him to not go away, and to come back soon. Dennis was wrung out as he boarded the plane. He spent the entire flight mentally replaying the separation and the cruelty of life, feeling sorry for himself, and feeling guilty for feeling sorry.

He and Tom talked often; he visited the ranch shortly after returning. Tom was still adamant about not talking about selling the ranch; Dennis brought it up on occasion, but tried not to push it too much, too often. He knew, though, a decision would have to be made sooner or later; there didn't seem to be any option. He didn't want the property to go to anyone other than the Taliaferros, and if someone else came in with a better offer than Jorge could meet, Dennis was concerned that Tom might feel pressured to sell it to them. That, he did not want and did not intend to accept!

Guatemala, 1976

On his last visit to the ranch before going back to Guatemala, Angelica cornered him. "Dennis, please take care of yourself. You are so dear to me, and to Tom as well of course. We were sick in our hearts when we didn't know what had happened to you, and then even more when we thought you were dead; that was what we were told by your company . . ."

"Global Geologics," Dennis filled in.

"Yes. But now you have left them and are going back down there without a job or anything to make sure you will be able to make a living down there. We want you up here where we can see that you are all right. I have asked you why you think you need to go back, and all you tell me is that it is something you must do."

"I have to go back, Little Mother, I have to settle something. If it turns out to be what I hope for, I'll stay, probably, but if it is not, I'll come back and try to settle down so you won't worry so much."

"You worry me all the time, mi hittijo, no matter what. A mother hen always worries about her chicks. But there is more, Dennis, all your life you have been a good boy, but maybe too trusting. You let people take advantage of you; you are so likable and trusting. I wonder if you know what you want to be. You do not seem to be able to chose the kind of life you want for yourself and those who love you. You seem to have found something you can be positive and passionate about. I am glad. Please try to settle down, and be strong for yourself and for your family, please?"

There it was again, "You don't know what you want to be." So many different people: Friends, family and just folks he met and spent a little time with, all telling him to "get a life!" in one form or the other. He knew he should but in his own time, at his own pace. He embraced his aunt like a dutiful son, and tried to assure her he loved her and always would, and that he knew what he was doing, and for the time being he knew what he wanted to happen. With many tears and kisses, he left, Miguel driving him back to Corpus Cristi, and then on to Houston.

Chapter Fifty

GUATEMALA

Before returning to Guatemala, he visited Connie and her mother again. He had met Norman on his previous trip. They tended to be courteous toward each other and avoid as much contact as possible. In Dennis's judgment, Norman was as good a partner as Melanie could hope for. He was an engineer and of course, analytical, decisive, and well-reasoned in most things. Apparently he had sized up Priscilla and her influence over Melanie, and chose to go along, but still manage to keep the family on as balanced a footing as he could, a very good way to do what Dennis could not manage to do. Moving to another state seemed like a good move, Dennis thought. Priscilla did not live practically in their pockets as she had in Houston. Norman clearly loved Melanie and was devoted to Connie, and she accepted his love without giving up her primary allegiance to her father. He was amazed at and proud of the perception and wisdom his daughter showed at two-and-a-half years of age.

He had arranged to stay with Fulgencio and his family on his return. Fulgencio's son, Matias, met him at the airport and drove them to Escuintla. "Please call me Matt," the boy had told Dennis when they first met months ago. He felt almost a part of the Arguello family; Fulgencio, his wife, Rosa, and Matt, their only child, had embraced him warmly when they absorbed the revelation of his true identity, and chose to accept him as simply a good man.

Guatemala, 1976

Matt was a senior in high school and – no surprise – a fervent soccer fan and skilled player. He could talk of little else on the drive. Dennis reasoned that he kept his talk of girls, standard for any late teenage boy, limited to time with his contemporaries. No doubt Matt thought Dennis too old for any of that. Of course the family called him Alonso even though they knew his Anglo name.

"Playing hooky to pick me up, Matt?" he asked the boy when there was a pause in the soccer talk; he forgot that it was August and school would not be in session.

"What is hooky? What does that mean?"

"It means skipping school . . ." he realized that "skipping school" was as foreign as "hooky" to Matt. "It means missing a day of school for a reason that the teachers do not approve of. That make sense?"

"Si! Yes, I am skipping school! I am playing hooky!" he laughed, proud of learning two new American slang terms. "But we are not in school yet, Alonso. It is August. School begins next month." It sounded like he thought his gringo friend was too old to remember that.

Before leaving the States, he had asked Fulgencio to tell Adriana that he would be there and wanted to meet with her, mentioning a date, Saturday, the seventh. Fulgencio reported that she had agreed, and requested that he meet first with Teresa, at ten in the morning. He chose to dress up a little more for the meeting, though that would be defined as only a bit more than daily casual. He wore khaki pants and a plain cotton shirt, with a tan western-style suit jacket, his nod to formality. Cowboy boots and an over-sized brass belt buckle had been his daily wear since childhood.

He left his low-crowned plantation hat on the side table in the entry hall when Antonia led him into the parlor. No one was there; he was a quarter-hour early; too eager, he chastised himself, but so what? While waiting, he looked around the room. He had been there before but had not taken it in. It was a large room, gracefully proportioned and warmly decorated in a rustic Hispanic manner, similar to the Harris's tasteful and comfortable house at the clinic, but with more costly selections: Books in Spanish and English in ceiling-high antique cases, well-loved crushed leather seating, striking native art, and carpets. All the wooden pieces were old, hand-made and beautiful in design. It all was reminiscent of his own Texas ranch house, but not as rustic or as ready for rugged daily ranch living. The room was elegant in every way; it pleased him.

While the house reminded him of his childhood home and the Harris's house at their clinic, it stood on a plane of its own. It had the same thick walls – maybe adobe, maybe something else – which kept the summer temperature at bay, and the winter heat contained. The high ceilings and Spanish tile roof, was less Spanish colonial than Grandee swagger. It exuded the assurance of money and position. The front hall proclaimed this with oil portraits of Teresa, Roberto and a few other Mendoza notables, furnishings costly and placed to impress. He *was* impressed.

Teresa and Adriana entered. Adriana wore a simple blouse and a longish skirt; he was instantly warmed. She stood back but Teresa strode directly to him, reached out to him and embraced him. "Alonso, it is so good to see you again, *mi hijo!*" she said. "Welcome back to our home!" She kissed him on both cheeks.

He had not expected this warm a welcome and had difficulty knowing how to respond. He said simply, "Senora, I thank you. I have always felt at home here, and longed to return. Gracias."

Teresa could not be more than mid-forties, he thought. She was rather tall and slim---elegant. He knew that she rode, and had upon Roberto's death summoned the inner strength to assume the home and farm management, and do it well. Her costume was tan culottes -- wide, flaring legs, almost a skirt -- and a marching shirt, and boots, very much the patrician matriarch of her realm. She was also beautiful he realized, not for the first time, but with renewed confirmation. The black mourning she wore when he last saw her was gone; she was now

Guatemala, 1976

her own self in every way. It was no surprise that she commanded the ship of running the farm enterprise so well.

She said, "Please, we can sit, Alonso." He had not dared to look at Adriana since she came in, but now he glanced in her direction. He caught her eyes, seeming to be locked on his. They shyly smiled at each other, but both quickly looked away back to Teresa. "Well, Alonso, please tell us what you have been doing."

He told her, covering his work at Global Geologics and his ranch and Tom. "I may not have told you, Senora, but I was married back in the United States, and am now divorced; I have a child, a daughter, two and a half years old. Her name is Constance, but we call her Connie. Her middle name is Angela," he rushed on, realizing he wanted unconsciously to keep going, at least until he got all that out, and he hoped, out of the way.

"And what are your plans now?" Teresa asked, apparently unfazed by this news if it was indeed news, but how could that be? He had told no one here in Guatemala. "Do you intend to return back to the States?" Her ignoring his revelations surprised him; it once again demonstrated her steel command of herself and her ability to absorb any turbulence without letting it veer her away from her plotted course..

"Not immediately, Senora. I am undecided."

"Let's give up this formality, Alonso. No more Senora; please call me Teresa if you please."

"Of course . . " He almost said "Ma'am," but caught himself and said, "Teresa."

"Before lunch, Alonso," she said, "I wonder if you would take a ride with me," clearly meaning horseback, and now.

"Surely," Dennis said, standing.

"Adriana, would you care to go with us?" Teresa asked.

"No, gracias; I am not dressed for that."

"Ramon has the horses ready, Alonso," Teresa said as she led him out.

On a well-kept gravel lane, leading away from the house and barns, she led them at a slow and quiet pace for several minutes. Shortly she said, "Alonso, I understand you were raised on a cattle ranch in Texas; I would think you would be something of an expert in that subject, running a cattle operation. May I assume that?"

"Well, Teresa, I lived on the ranch only until I left for college, but until then I did about everything that our ranch needed, that I was big enough to do—herded the cattle, fed them, raked out the horse stalls, all that."

"Milked?"

"No, we had only beef cattle."

"Alonso, I would like for you to look over our operations here and give as many observations or as much advice that you might have for me. Would you do that, por favor?"

"Glad to, Teresa; I'd be honored to." They rode on for quite a while, making small talk, mostly details about the farm. They toured enough to see some of all the different enterprises, cattle of course but also cash crops: fruit, beans, potatoes, cane, cotton, corn and a few small melon patches, not to mention the horses kept for pleasure and patrolling the land. He kept his eyes open and occasionally asked a question, but didn't offer any comments.

They retuned and Teresa offered him a time to wash up. Adriana and Salazar were waiting in the dining room. Teresa said, "I have asked Rodolfo to join us for lunch, Alonso."

The two men greeted each other warmly, embracing like two old comrades. "I am glad to see you, Alonso," Salazar said.

"Good to see you as well, Rodolfo."

Talk at the table was light and neutral, concentrating on daily news, especially recovery efforts from the earthquake, a subject Dennis sincerely cared about. When the meal was over, and most would head for a siesta, Teresa said, "Well, Alonso, now that you have seen our operations, do you have any comments for us? Any advice?"

Dennis was thoughtful for a while, then said, "Teresa, and Rodolfo too, of course, yes I do. You have a large and growing family, Senora,"

Guatemala, 1976

he resorted to the formal address, "and a limited land area, some five hundred hectares I believe. Is that correct?"

"Approximately," Salazar said. "Five hundred and eighteen is a little more accurate."

"Well, Teresa," Dennis began, "I believe you have too many relatives you are or will be responsible for to take care of on the land you have. You will probably have to provide a separate home for Luis, and maybe for one or both of your daughters when they marry. You will not want to live anywhere else and you have many years left in your own life." He let that sink in. The others sat silent attentively and waited for the next observation.

"Secondly," he went on, "it looks to me that you are trying to grow and manage too many different crops and livestock operations for the land and the manpower you have available."

"Exactly!" Salazar said, "I have been telling Roberto that for many years. Now you and I will tell Teresa!" He slapped the table for emphasis.

Dennis continued, "You should in my opinion, either buy more land or phase out some of the crops. Also, you could sell off *some* of the land and phase out more of the crops, especially those that are land-intensive, like cattle and cotton. Or," he went on, "you could rent out some of the land to share-crop contractors and keep enough for you and your family to live on comfortably. That's about all I can say for the present. Of course I haven't seen any of your financials; they might tell me more. For example, which crops are profitable and which are less so."

"What do you think, Rodolfo?" Teresa asked.

"I agree with Alonso completely, Teresa," Salazar said. "As you know you, have my standing offer to buy any of your land you want to sell, or I will be happy to broker the sale of land to others if you wish."

Dennis added, "On our ranch in Texas, we concentrate on only one operation, cattle; we grow kitchen crops for our own needs, our own consumption. We share what we don't need with our family and neighbors who live close by, of course. But we don't sell any of it," he

271

could see why Salazar had been invited to this meeting, and it also made him cautious, understanding that Salazar was not just a friend but in some respects a competitor to the Mendozas. Teresa wanted to have his insight, but more importantly, to let him know what she was facing and what measures she would consider.

She apparently already knew what the farm faced. She said, "Roberto was a wonderful husband and father, but not so much a farmer. He was too involved in the Army." She doesn't know the half of it, Dennis realized; she doesn't know of his rebel involvement, or if she does, she didn't want to admit it.

A suspension of talk descended on the group; talk ceased, each one wrapped up in their own thoughts. Dennis looked at Adriana, wondering how she fit into all this. She looked back, and smiled; then a shadow of sadness edged across her face. Then she looked away. She, too, he realized, is uncertain of her future; she is here at the suffrage of Teresa's kindness, and is waiting to see how that will play out. Dennis longed to say to her that he would take care of her, no matter what, but not now, not here, not yet.

Chapter Fifty-One

GUATEMALA

It was clearly time to leave; he'd hoped Matt had stayed to drive him back, but hadn't given much thought to the idea of how to get back to Escuintla. He walked out to the veranda and looked around, waiting. Soon he became aware of someone standing next to him, and turned to find Adriana at his side. "Hello, Adriana," he said warily. She perhaps should not be alone with him, though he dearly wanted to be with her.

"It is all right, Alonso; Teresa knows you want to see me and does not object; in fact, she encouraged it. Why don't we sit down?"

"Does she read minds, too?"

"Sometimes I think she can!" Both laughed, gently pushing the tension away. They sat next to each other on a rustic settee, looking out over the seemingly unending sylvan vista of the holdings of the Mendozas. Like in most of the Guatemalan highlands, the land was nourished by the daily showers in the warm months. Gentle swells and vales were dotted with mature trees, gracing it all with an Edenic allure; Dennis found it hypnotic.

Breaking out of his spell, Dennis sighed and spoke, "Do you know why I want to see you, Adriana?"

"Of course; I can read minds, too." She grinned as she spoke. He grinned in return.

"And? It's been six months and I have been patient, haven't I?."

"Yes, you have. And, there are things we have to talk about, Alonso."

"Please tell me; that's why I am here and why we are sitting out here with all the privacy we could ask for just now. I am waiting, not too patiently, Adriana."

She laid a hand on his arm. *What an encouraging sign, he thought*. She said, "Alonso, we may be meant to be together, to marry even. I am sure it is what we both want, but . . ."

"But?"

"There are questions we cannot answer just now, Alonso." She removed her hand. He wanted to ask her what those questions were, but waited for her to go on at her own pace. She seemed to pull herself together. "What will you do here, Alonso? What job can you have that we would live off?"

"I believe Teresa is going to offer me a job managing the farm."

"Then what? We marry and live here in a house she makes available to us? Is that what you want, Alonso?"

This called for a serious round of pondering; he looked into her eyes and then off into the distance. He had not thought things through to quite this point. He had assumed that some kind of arrangement like this would be offered, but had forgotten the similar gradual suffocation in his life with Melanie, her parents' constant presence and oversight, and how that had ended. He might adjust; he liked Teresa, but what would this mean for Adriana?

It dawned on him. "You would not like that would you, living here still at the pleasure of a family-by-marriage only, a marriage that no longer even exists?"

"I am not related to anyone here, Alonso," she said. "I am an outsider and, even if I am made to feel welcome, resentment will come, I know. Luis resents me, and at the same time wants me. He wants to marry me. He has not said it, but I know; the way he looks at me makes me think he will marry me, by his right, not by my choice. I try to push him away.

Guatemala, 1976

He can be very forward sometimes. It is difficult for me, Alonso. I would not like to live here with him so close."

This reverie was broken by the abrupt appearance of the man himself, Luis, bursting out of the door onto the veranda. He puffed and gulped air and, in a near shout, said, "Look here, Reade or whatever you name is, just go home, wherever that is! You are not wanted here!" It was clear he had been emboldened by how much he had to drink. "My mother tells me she is going to offer you the job of manager of the farm, I will not have it!"

Dennis sprang up, ready to fight if it came to that, almost ready to put his fists up. "Just a minute, Luis, no one has offered me anything, and if it is offered, I will speak to your mother before I talk with you about it!" The two panted and stared at each other. Dennis took a moment for appraisal, and stood firm but without threat, hoping the steam would dissipate. Luis was still breathing heavily but seemed to loosen up a bit. Dennis said, "Let's just relax, Luis. I am sure nothing is fixed in stone yet. Let's just talk about it calmly, okay? Shall we sit down?"

"I am not in the mood to sit, gracias!" Luis replied. He began to pace. He said, "I am the one to manage the farm; I am the male heir and it is mine to do. The family demands it, that I take over the farm and all that, uh . . . means." He seemed to have to search for the right word.

"I am sure you will in time, Luis, but you are still in school, in college, aren't you?" Dennis asked. Adriana was silent, but clearly troubled; she knew Luis was not qualified in the least to manage anything. He was an alcoholic and had slipped into the habits of the young and undisciplined, keeping bad company who fed off his assumed wealth.

"Yes," Luis said, "I am getting an education but my forefathers never had an education, except my father of course, and I am ready; I am ready!" He strutted around, still on his feet. "Besides, Adriana and I will marry; she will someday be the, uh, mother of the house!"

At this she stiffened, sprung to her feet and said, "Never, Luis! That is just a dream of yours! You cannot just assume any woman would come crying to you to marry her. That will not happen, at least with me! You are still a boy with a man's body but the mind and morals of a demented ten-year-old! Please leave me alone and do not mention this again. Gracias!"

Dennis abandoned the idea of defending her; she was doing a perfectly fine job herself.

Luis said, "We will see about that. My mother will have a say about that!"

"Fine," Adriana said. "Let's ask her; let's go into the house right now and find out what she thinks!"

She stepped toward the door, but Dennis stepped into her path and put his arm out and held her back. He said softly, "May we all put this anger aside for a little while and be adults about it?"

"I'll be adult, but I fail to see Luis being an adult about anything. As far as I am concerned, there is nothing more to say. Luis," she said, showing that she had much more to say, "I will avoid you as much as I can; I will appreciate it if you do the same." With that, she stormed through the door, into the house.

Luis stood there, weaving a little, blinking, maybe a little more sober than a few minutes before. He quickly turned and followed Adriana into the house. Dennis had no doubt that they would not meet. He was left alone, and went back in himself. In the hall he met Antonia, and asked her, "Is Matt still here? I need a ride."

"He is here, Senor," she replied. "He is with the kitchen help, eating more than anyone but a teenager ever could; the cooks are piling it on him and he is entertaining them with his stories! I will bring him out to you. I believe he has eaten enough!"

"Gracias, Senorita. Please tell Senora Adriana I am leaving and goodbye for me. And ask her if I may call on her again, soon, Teresa as well of course."

She turned toward the back of the house; soon she appeared with Matt, still wiping his hands on a napkin, who went looking for the car.

Guatemala, 1976

Antonia said, "Adriana said that she will be happy to receive you any time, Senor." He smiled as Matt drove up, engine idling. He got in and they left.

Chapter Fifty-Two

GUATEMALA

Dennis said to Matt as they drove toward Escuintla, "Get enough to eat, Matt?"

"Yeah!" Matt exclaimed. "The best meal I have had in a long time; I mean my mother is a great cook, but those people know how to fill you up, I mean I had lamb and creamed potatoes and gravy and . . . I don't know what else!"

"Did you leave enough for the family to have?"

"Oh yeah; there was plenty left. They kept shoving stuff at me; I couldn't eat it fast enough!"

Dennis was enjoying this, remembering how he had seemed to always be hungry when he was this age. His father had said he must have a hollow leg. "Any dessert?" He was in a good mood, buoyed by Adriana's willingness to see him again.

"Oh yeah; they had flan and cake and . . . well a lot of other stuff. I don't think I can eat another thing for a week!"

I'll bet, Dennis thought. At that age he will be hungry again well before dinner time.

At breakfast the next morning, Dennis said to his hosts, "Old friends, I have imposed on your kindness and hospitality long enough. I am forever grateful. Gracias and gracias!" Before they could voice their objections, he went on, "Fulgencio, is there a place I could rent a car here in Escuintla?"

Fulgencio was the chief mechanic at one of the large car dealerships, selling any and all GM products. He said, "You can use the car Matt has been driving. It belongs to Pacco, my cousin, and he lets us keep it if we pay for gas and I keep it running in good shape."

"But what would Matt drive?" Dennis asked. "Surely he has places to go that you cannot take him to. He is a big boy and believes he is too old to arrive at a ball game or something in a car driven by his father!"

"We can take care of that, Alonso."

Dennis liked being called by his adopted Hispanic name. He said, "I would rather be able to take myself places without dependence on you; you have been too kind for too long."

Fulgencio said, "Pacco has other cars he could rent you, Alonso."

"Does he have a car a little newer than Matt's?" he intentionally named Pacco's car as Matt's.

"I will call him and ask him to come here and take you to his lot."

"Not today, maybe tomorrow," Dennis said. "I want to go back to the Mendoza farm today; Matt can take me if he is available, but this will be the last time. I'm not sure I will stay after today."

"I believe our son will be happy to take you, Amigo!" Fulgencio said, chuckling. "If he can be fed like he was yesterday, he may want to move in with them!" Dennis laughed with him.

At the farm he was met at the door by Adriana. Before he could say more than hello, she said, "Ramon has horses for us today," and turned toward the barns, reaching for his hand. She was dressed for riding, Dennis noticed and was pleased. He followed, glad for the time alone with her. On a well-worn trail they were silent for many minutes, each trying to think of what to say, letting the animals set the pace and wander where they would. Adriana broke the spell and said, "Alonso, dear Alonso, there are more reasons why we cannot marry."

He was surprised but waited for her to go on, but she seemed to be stalled. He said, "I know what you told me yesterday; what else is there?"

"For one thing, Alonso, you are divorced. The Church will not marry us."

He had not considered that; he began to try to think of a counter-argument. He was not any kind of churchman, although if he had to declare he would have to say he was a Christian. He couldn't quite explain why, though. He had no reply; but would try to think of one.

"You don't really know me, Alonso. My life before I came here, or to Escuintla, and married Felipe was quite different." She looked away, gathering her thoughts and choosing how to proceed. "Did you know, for example, that I was educated in the United States?"

"That is a real surprise, Adriana! I knew, I *know*, you are a poised and educated woman, here in a situation obviously below your station. Where did you go to college in the States?"

Almost embarrassed but proudly, she said, "A tiny college for women in Macon, Georgia, Wesleyan College." He waited for more. She went on, "It is very small, only a few hundred students; it is owned by the Methodists."

"I think I've heard of it," Dennis said. "Supposed to be a good school. I've heard of Macon, too. Did you go all four years there?"

"No. My father wanted me to go to a college in the U.S. but my mother wanted me to go to an all-girl's school, and this was the compromise they worked out. I just went there two years . . . then my father was murdered and I came home. You know the rest I think." She turned away to hide the gathering tears.

Dennis sensed her discomfort and was sympathetic; he remembered Consuela's death and his anguish over it. To pull her away from her pain said, "What else do you want to tell me about it, about being in the States?"

Guatemala, 1976

"My roommate. Her name was Sallie Tillotson, *Sarah* to be correct, I think," she smiled, "She was from Tennessee and we could hardly understand each other at first," she laughed. "But she was sweet and we became the best of friends," she smiled.

"Do you keep in touch?"

"No. I am sorry we do not. We just drifted apart, I guess. She had a rich family and expected to go back to a, well, a life her parents had laid out for her when she graduated. She had a boyfriend back in Nashville, in a very rich area called Belle Meade, I think."

"What else, Adriana; what else can you tell me about yourself that I do not know?"

"Not now, Alonso; maybe later."

They rode on for some time. It was a fine day, mild enough to be outside and yet not exactly cold, just brisk and comfortable. Dennis had always worn gloves to ride, and he did today, furnished by Ramon with the tack. A quick breeze whipped by and he was glad he wore a coat. Adriana was wrapped in a heavy hip-length coat, hat and riding breeches and boots. She sits a horse well, Dennis observed, and admired. He said, "To be a city girl you seem to be at home on a horse."

"Oh," she said, snapping out of her reverie, "I always had a horse available, even when I was little and we lived in town. We belonged to a livery club where riding was taught and horses were kept for us, to rent, that is. We never owned them but Mamma always insisted that I would be well-rounded in my experience, dancing, music and that kind of thing. She came from a prominent family."

They were not paying attention to where they were or where they were heading, or to their surroundings. Suddenly right in front of them, Luis appeared facing them, blocking their way, on his own horse. They pulled up; the horses shied away to the side. Luis bellowed, "Alonso or whatever your name is, leave this farm! You are not welcome!"

Understanding the nature of a threat from an unstable and drunk youth, Dennis quietly turned to Adriana and in not much above a whisper, said, "Adriana, go back to the house. Luis and I need to talk."

"He's right, Adriana. You do not need to hear this" Luis demanded. "You are a female and should not be involved in this kind of thing!"

"You silly boy!" she said, stinging him more than he was prepared to hear. "I am not just a female, Luis! I am a woman who is in charge of her own life and . . . "

"Adriana," Dennis interrupted, "Please go back, please."

After some very expressive visible and audible snorting and fuming, she tuned the horse and trotted off. She didn't go far, though; she stopped just out of sight and waited. Dennis watched her go.

"Now, Senor!" Luis barked, "Now I will chase you off of my property!" He reared his horse in western movie fashion and slurred the classic Spanish curse, "Que vaya al Diablo!" or in English, "Go to hell!"

Dennis had not noticed that Luis held a bull whip behind his back, and he realized it late. The whip cracked and slashed down on his back, stinging and splitting his coat, grazing his skin. He pulled his horse up and twisted away, and goaded him to run. The horse -- named Pronto, but he had forgotten -- responded and galloped off; the chase was on.

Pronto leaped ahead, Dennis hanging on, barely in control. Luis may have been energized and psyched up for a fight, but he was slow to chase. In seconds there were some ten yards or more between the riders. The whip cracked behind Dennis but was too short to reach him again. He yelled back at Luis, "Luis! Stop this madness! You will not solve anything this way!"

Luis paid no attention; he continued to lash the whip around and occasionally managed to hit Pronto which made him jump ahead with greater fear and urgency. Luis was not the horseman nor the whip-wielder he must have thought he was; he was mostly angering Pronto and scaring Dennis. This is almost comical, Dennis thought. The chase was in rather close woods; the horses were dodging between trees and swerving around

Guatemala, 1976

branches. If someone was filming this it might be salable to a movie studio! He called back, "You idiot! Who do you think you are, John Wayne?" If Luis heard him, it did nothing to quell his anger and resolve; on he rode, whip slinging and hitting nothing but tree branches.

Dennis mused that if they were not on horseback the fight would be over quickly. Luis was slim and half a foot shorter than his six-two. Luis was only twenty, Dennis thought, and in poor shape due to his dissolute life in the city, nominally as a student. It was likely that was only a pretense, an excuse for how he believed he was entitled to live. Also, he drank too much.

Pronto finally had had enough; he began to slow. Luis' whip found its mark on the horse's flank and he lurched again, lost his footing and flipped Dennis off. Dennis rolled away and jumped up. Pronto stumbled but did not fall, and fled. Luis cracked the whip again, but Dennis dodged, jumping behind a tree. Luis rode around it, still swinging the whip. Dennis kept edging away between trees, jumping from one to the next. Luis drove at him; he grabbed the halter but Luis beat his hands and head with the butt of the whip and he had to let go. Luis pulled far enough away to swing the whip again but Dennis grabbed it in his gloved hand and jerked it, *hard*.

Luis' horse stumbled. Luis tried to hold on but lost hold of both the whip and the reins. The horse galloped off, swerving from side to side, Luis gripping to the pommel, gasping, trying to calm the mount, to no effect. The horse found a more or less straight pathway and increased his speed to his maximum. Luis yelled something undecipherable, over and over again. He was out of Dennis' sight when an ominous *thud* was heard. Dennis rushed ahead and found Luis on the ground with a bloody head, unconscious. Apparently Luis' head had collided with an overhanging limb. The horse had not stopped.

Whipping out a bandana he tried to stem the blood and administer what aid he could. He knelt down and held the boy's head up and wiped his face and gash. The wound did not look severe, but he knew he was no expert. He had first-aid training in ROTC but had no supplies with him. He managed to stem the bleeding, but the boy did not wake up. Dennis was alone and several miles from the house with a wounded man in his care. Luis obviously needed professional medical attention, probably in a hospital. He stood and looked around, hoping one of the horses would wander back, neither had. He whistled as loudly as he could. Nothing. He tried again; he heard a meek whimper, then he whistled again and Pronto meandered up, hanging his head low. Dennis marveled at how humanlike a horse could behave. In a minute the other horse came up, warily. Dennis checked Luis' neck carefully to see if there might be a spinal fracture, tortured because he couldn't be sure. He sighed and heaved Luis up onto his horse and propped him upright. Awkwardly holding Luis that way, he mounted Pronto, holding Luis up with one hand and urged the horses back to the house.

Chapter Fifty-Three

GUATEMALA

FIFTY YARDS ALONG AS DENNIS gingerly led the horses back toward the house, Adriana rode toward him. "What happened, Alonso? Are you all right? I was afraid, but I . . ."

"I am all right, Adriana, but Luis is injured; I don't know how bad, but we need to get him medical help as soon as we can!"

"What happened?" she repeated.

Dennis was winded and didn't want to get into a long explanation since he would have to repeat it at the house, and probably again to medical personnel, and maybe to police. He said simply, "Luis decided he had to get rid of me for good, and started chasing me on his horse." He chose not to mention the whip; that would come out later, if at all. He didn't want to make Luis look worse than he did already, worse as a man; he was injured bad enough and that should be what Teresa had to deal with. "Luis ran into a limb and knocked himself out." He paused to catch his breath, "Adriana, go on ahead to the house and tell them we are on our way, por favor."

"No, Alonso. I will stay with you and help you hold Luis on his horse."

Stubborn woman! his inner voice observed. Out loud he said, "Well, okay." He was still panting slightly. "I guess that would be better. I could slip and let him fall. I surely don't want that to happen!" She looked at him sternly, then broke into a grin. He smiled back, then turned away, pretending he had been serious. Both of them chuckled, shaking their heads side to side.

They remembered simultaneously that Luis was seriously hurt; they gave their attention to the precarious ride back to the house. I was likely still over a mile and their pace was slow; it might take an hour. It was awkward to talk as if Luis was not there, but Dennis had to keep talking with Adriana, if only to settle their future as much as they could. "Adriana," he said, "I think I can get a job in town, in Guatemala City. We can live there. That would suit you, wouldn't it?"

"Yes, it might; it would depend on a lot of other things, things we don't know about now."

"Such as?"

"Such as what kind of a job you could get as an outsider, not a citizen of Guatemala; would you be happy in it? Could we afford to live on what you would be paid, could we afford to live in a place we would be happy in? That kind of thing, Alonso."

"I can be happy anywhere I could be with you, Adriana."

"That's beside the point and you know it!" she declared. "We have to be realistic, Alonso."

He recalled that Angelica thought just like that, always practical. Melanie, on the other hand, was *not* the practical one in their marriage. "I know, *mi quierida*," he said, "we have to think of you just as much as me, what will make *you* happy, what will give you a full life, a life you could be glad and proud of. I can adjust maybe easier than you can, but we can work anything out." He knew he sounded pompous, but said it anyhow.

"You are sweet, *quierido,* I know you think of me, I do."

"What would you say to living in America?"

"I might like it. I have no family here, except Fulgencio and Rosa, and Matt of course."

"No other aunts and uncles, or cousins?"

Guatemala, 1976

"Oh, I am sure there are many of those, but I am not close with any of them." They rode on silently for some time, allowing each other to mull over what they had on their minds.

"We are almost there, Alonso," she said.

"Yes, I know. Please ride ahead now and tell them." Adriana rode on, and as Dennis first spotted the house between the trees, the three women came running toward him. Ramon was in tow, as well as two other men, farm hands Dennis had not met. "Do you have a stretcher or something we can put him on and take him inside?" he asked, "We don't want to shift him around any more than we have to."

"No stretcher, Senor," Ramon said, "but we can lay him on this blanket and pick him up very gently."

"Very carefully, Ramon. His neck could be broken and any movement would make it worse!"

"I have called the doctor!" Antonia said.

"He should be here in a few minutes!" Teresa added.

Matt appeared and said, "I will take care of the horses."

Ramon nodded and said "Gracias, Mathias."

Matt had to be curious, but was smart enough to know to stay out of the way, Dennis realized.

Dennis and the other men gently lifted Luis off his horse and laid him on the blanket on the ground. The four of them gripped the blanket by the edges and picked him up and very carefully walked up the steps and into the house. They were just laying him down on a sofa when the doctor burst in, shooing the others away, and knelt down beside his patient.

Teresa and Antonia stood rigidly nearby, hands gripped at their waists. Adriana stood aside, quieter, more serene. Dennis came over to stand beside her and watched. She said, "He is Oscar Mendoza, the doctor." Another cousin? Dennis asked himself; probably.

Doctor Mendoza placed a scuffed iconic black leather bag on the floor and began to go through the usual checks: pulse, breathing, fractures, and so on. He spent longer on pulling back Luis' eyelids and checking the pupils. He reached into his bag and pulled out a stethoscope and listened to the heart. Luis groaned once and then was quiet.

Luis face had darkened since the impact to look like one big bruise radiating out from the eyes, purple-black edged with a sickly gold. There was a growing, wicked-looking bulge in the center of his forehead. The doctor stood, pondering the still-unconscious youth. After a sensible pause he said to Teresa, "He has a serious concussion, but I believe that is all. He will recover in time, but he needs rest and quiet. He should be in a dark room and not be disturbed."

"Please move him to his room, Ramon," Teresa said, more command than request. All four men stepped up and as before lifted Luis up and moved toward the stairs, up to Luis's room. Oscar and the women followed. As they moved, Oscar said, "Teresa, you know I am sure that he is an alcoholic, and desperately needs to be helped; he needs to go into what in America is called rehab, or rehabilitation. It is a process of drying out and re-orienting his mind. There are several places, mostly in the U.S., that have excellent rehab programs. Does he speak English?"

"Yes, of course, Oscar. Could you find such a place for me, for him?"

"Certainly, Teresa, certainly," he replied. "Let me make a few phone calls. I should know something later today or tomorrow."

Dennis and Adriana went back downstairs and out onto the veranda, and sat silently. Then he said, "Where does this leave us, Adiana?"

She took her time before answering. "Nothing has changed, Alonso. Luis cannot take over the farm, so you could do that until he is well and back home. Teresa could still ask you to manage the farm."

"But what when he does come back? I couldn't just wait and see how things might be then. I have to get my life, and yours, settled once and for all." They were silent again, for a long while. She reached over and took his hand but said no more.

The doctor came out, and seeing Dennis, stopped and offered his hand, "I know you are the famed Alonso. I am Oscar Mendoza, Roberto's cousin. I am happy to meet you, Senor."

Guatemala, 1976

"And you, doctor?" Dennis asked, getting to his feet. "Thank you for your quick response and care of Luis. I am distressed at this happening. I feel some responsibility for it."

"Teresa told me a little of the story, Senor. I have known young Luis since he was born and I have treated him all his life. He has not always behaved very sensibly, and has let alcohol lead him astray, I am afraid. I have instructed Teresa and Antonia to keep him away from any alcohol. It will not be easy, but it is essential. With his concussion, any spirits could kill him. He has to be watched carefully for several days." He paused and continued, "Adriana. Please help to see to that. Gracias." Then he sped off down the steps to his car and left.

Dennis and Adriana stood watching the car leave, scattering gravel and leaving a dust plume; they said nothing for a long spell, thoughts tumbling over and over in each mind. "I must go," he said finally, "I have to decide some things I can only do for myself. I will probably go back to the States now, but I will see you again before I go. I will come back for you, Adriana, please do not doubt that, but there are some things I have to sort out at home." He snorted, "I said *home*, but I'm not sure where home is. All I know is that home is where you are, *querida*. We will make a home where it is best for both of us." They turned toward each other, and awkwardly if naturally, embraced and kissed. Then he tore himself away and called for Matt.

Chapter Fifty-Four

Texas

Back at the ranch, trying to relax and mull over his life and the decisions he faced, Dennis tried to immerse himself in work; it was dull and tedious, but exhausting and mind-numbing hard work, distracting work. Inside his mind was churning and trying to sort things out and come to decisions. He had to have Adriana; that was primary, and she was willing to have him, but how? That was the burr in his saddle.

For a week after he got back, he pushed everything away, refusing to think about them. Then he allowed himself to look at things sensibly and in an orderly way. He had to have stable employment, either here in the States or in Guatemala. In his heart here, the U.S., would be better in a practical way, but he could not deny that his heart was south, in Guatemala. The dilemma was how would that work? He was not a Guatemalan citizen, and he knew of no jobs he could be considered for there. His qualifications were impressive but limited in application. Few would want to hire a field geologist with only a few weeks of actual field experience. He knew he had to settle the questions that kept cropping up: Who did he want to be? What did he want his life to be dedicated to? What would *define* him?

After churning this over in his mind for more time than he should have, he accepted that he needed the counsel of others. He began with Tom, after dinner one night. "Dad," he said, "I am at a crossroad. I'm

Guatemala, 1976

sure you know this. I don't feel I am supposed to come back and work the ranch, but I can't seem to settle on what I *should* do. What do you think?"

Tom carefully folded his napkin and threaded it through the carved wood napkin ring, stalling, he knew. He said, "Dennis, you have one of the best educations money can buy. My advice is to find someplace you can use it." Always close with words, Tom sat and waited for a response. He had said all he thought he needed to.

Dennis knew this, and was not angry with his father. It was good advice, as good as any, and just what should have been expected from Tom. "Dad, I have the time with Melanie's father's company as experience. Even though it was for the most part just make-work, I still learned a lot about the oil business. That's one option, I guess." Tom just nodded, said nothing. "I could probably get a job in that field, but I don't believe I would feel it was what I am supposed to do with my life. I am twenty-six and most people, most men, are settled into the life they will have, or the work they will do, for the rest of their lives. I am not there yet, and I need to be."

Tom studied his son, squinted his eyes, and said, "Son, what is it you're not telling me?"

"I have a girlfriend, more a fiancée in fact, in Guatemala. We want to get married, but before I lock her in that kind of commitment, I want to have a good job and earn enough to support us. She will come to the States with me if I ask, but I feel like I could live in Guatemala and both of us would be happier. I have some bad memories here and I'd like to just get away from them and all the things, the baggage, that comes with them."

"What about you daughter? What about Connie, Dennis?"

"I know! I know! I can't just go away and leave her. I have asked Melanie if she could spend her summers with me. She hasn't said yes, but not no, either."

Tom said, "Son, take as long as it takes. You know you can stay here and I won't run you off. Angelica would like that, too, as well as all your cousins next door. We would like you to be here, but we also want you to be happy and to have the life you need to. Just take your time and let it work itself out."

It was then he remembered Rodney Harris telling him, "Alonso, the best counselor for any of us is God. Seek him in daily prayer. You won't get better advice." He had tried that without any result he recognized. Rodney also said, "You have to let yourself trust, Alonso, trust in God. That's what we call the leap of faith."

Another evening, this time with Angelica present, Tom asked, "Tell me about this girl in Guatemala, son."

This brought a wide grin to Dennis's face. He said, "I know you will like her, both of you. She is not from some peon family, she is beautiful and poised and elegant and . . . "

"Dennis," Angelica said, "we can see that, even if you are so besotted you can't see anything else. Just tell us what she is like, her family, all that."

So Dennis told them all he could in a logical fashion: her tragedies, her U.S. education, Her family background, everything factual he could think of. "You will love her, Dad, and Angelica. I know you will."

"You keep saying *will*, Dennis, meaning I suppose that you know we will meet her sometime. When would that be, *mi hijo?*"

"I don't know but I have to decide soon, very soon or I will bust!"

Chapter Fifty-Five

Texas

Oscar Mendoza arranged for Luis to be accepted into the *La Hacienda Treatment Center* in San Antonio. Teresa, Antonia, and Oscar accompanied Luis to the center. He was entered for a twenty-eight day program. The women rented an apartment nearby, since family participation was encouraged. Oscar returned to Guatemala.

It was a month after Dennis came home to the ranch. The Guatemalan government issued an RFP, a *Request For Proposals* for a new contract to manage their natural resources, especially to advise it on measures to prepare for earthquakes and recommend measures to contain the damage from them and prepare for quick recovery. Among the qualifications required was that the respondent have on staff one or more employees with first-hand experience in Guatemala in that field. One of the quickest responses was from Global Geologics LLC of Houston, Texas. Among their submittal was the naming of Dennis Reade as the proposed Guatemala-based representative.

Technically, Dennis was still on Global's payroll, but he knew nothing about the RFP. He was oblivious about it all; if he thought about Global at all, it was that he needed to check in with them, sometime; maybe later.

Dennis had returned to the ranch and stewed in his inactivity and the uncertainty of the future. One evening, he found Tom alone and pulled him aside to talk things over. "Dad," he said, "I'm still not settled in my mind about Adriana and what we will do. I could just go down there and marry her and see how it goes. I can ask the Harrises to recommend a Protestant preacher who would marry us, since the Catholic Church won't. She would probably do it, but it just wouldn't be fair to her." Tom didn't reply; he seemed to be wrestling with some issue of his own. They were quiet for a long spell. Dennis got up and poked at the fire in the big fireplace, adding another couple of logs. He sat down again and, appearing to have reached a decision, said, "Dad, why don't you sell the ranch to Jorge?"

"As a matter of fact, I was meaning to talk with you about that," Tom said in his laconic way. "Jorge has made me a definite offer, not a bad one. He will allow me to stay here after the sale."

"I think that's called a *Life Tenancy*, Dad."

"Yeah, that's what the lawyer said."

They let that set in, then Dennis asked, "Well, Dad?"

"Well, what do you think, son?"

"I have been hoping you would do something like this for a long time, Dad. I think it's a great idea!" He grinned; a faint smile flew across Tom's face. "You wouldn't have to stay here, would you, Dad? You could live anywhere you wanted, couldn't you?"

"Yeah, I suppose I could, but I don't have any place I want to go to."

Dennis grinned again and said, "Dad, why don't you and Angelica get married?"

"As a matter of fact, we've been talking about that, too."

"Really? That's wonderful, Dad!" He jumped out of his chair. "Do it! Do it! That's the best news I've heard in, uh, I can't say how long! It's terrific! When will it be; any date set?"

Guatemala, 1976

"Whoa, son! All I said is that we talked about it."

"Why wait, Dad? Why fool around? It will be the best thing to happen for both of you, why put it off?" He looked expectantly for an answer. "She has said yes, hasn't she?"

"Actually, she's the one who brought it up. I'd been thinking about it a while, but I guess she decided that I'd never get around to it if she didn't push me a little."

"That's wonderful, Dad!" He turned immediately and ran to find Angelica and hug her. He couldn't wait.

Two days later Dennis received a phone call from Ken Thompson of Global Geologics. "Dennis, get ready to go back to Guatemala!"

"What?"

"You are going back to your old stomping grounds, Dennis!" He let that sink in. "Global's proposal in response to the RFP had been accepted, providing that Dennis Reade heads up the Guatemalan office and lead the whole shebang!"

"What RFP?"

Thompson started to explain, going over the raw details. He said, "You still work for us, you know. Come into the office tomorrow and we'll go over everything then."

"Can we make it the day after tomorrow? Getting there takes a little planning."

"Sure; see you about ten, day after tomorrow, Dennis. By the way, the Guatemalan contact said that you being on the team was what made the difference; having the *Hero of Mixco* living and working there would be a blessing to the whole country. Think about that!"

Dennis ran to tell Tom and Angelica, then he sat back and thought through the things he would have to do, always trying to be a careful planner. After about ten minutes making lists, he picked up the phone and asked for a call to be put through to Guatemala, to the Mendoza house, where Adriana was staying. It took another twenty minutes to make the connection. He was so excited he could barely get it out fast

295

enough, "Adriana," he finally got out, "I am coming home!" he blurted, surprised that he intuitively said *home*. They talked for over an hour, and made plans they might or might not follow, but they would be married and he had a job in Guatemala. It looked like the job would last at least five years. Closing, he said again, "I am coming home!"

Everything would work out; he had faith it would, even if after five years the job ran out and they had to do something else. Connie would summer with them in Guatemala, Melanie could not do anything to prevent that. Faith in her basic goodness told him she would not object. Connie would learn the language and get to know her cousins and fall in love with that enchanting country, *his* country!

One more thing Dennis, AKA Alonso, had to do as the educated and well-mannered man he had been schooled to do was to write to his saviors, the Harrises, and Maria. He began with a heart-felt thank you, plus the news of his new job in Guatemala, his and Adriana's betrothal, and a request that they attend when the date was set. Then he wrote:

I cannot tell you how much I owe you, not only for saving my life and patching me up and for giving me shelter, food and comfort, but even more important for leading me to examine my aimless life, to lose my self-pity, and to challenge me to face my responsibility to choose what I would do and be in this life your God gave me. Your selfless Christian faith and witness is exemplary and my model. I am not yet the committed Christian you two are, nor am I quite ready to take the "leap of faith," Rodney told me about, but I am working on it. Adriana and I will be married in an evangelical church, because the Catholic Church won't marry us since I have been divorced. Your presence will bless our marriage in ways no other friends could.

I will keep in touch, no matter. I am in the Land of Eternal Spring. Good friends are to be treasured!

Gracias, Amigos,

Alonso"

Guatemala, 1976

The figure of the Quetzal flashed thought his mind he was now in, in an ephemeral but striking way. I am free like the bird but I am not hiding any more, he told himself over and over.

I am *going home*! I know who I am and what I want to be make of my life . . . at last. I have found my home; I am going *home!*

THE END

Author's Notes

The Guatemala earthquake of February 4, 1976, is a real event, and was devastating. My attempt to describe it is grossly inadequate. In all, there were some 23,000 deaths and untold injuries, not to mention millions of dollars in damages. Proportionately, those deaths out of a population of approximately six million would compare to almost five hundred thousand American deaths today. I visited Guatemala in 1978 and again in 1982, on mission trips sponsored by Woodmont Baptist Church. Even in 1982 the recovery was not complete, though clean up and disposal of debris had generally been accomplished.

In writing this book I have had to keep reminding myself -- and the reader should also remember -- that the event around which the story is built happened over forty years ago, and of how much the world has changed since. I have tried to avoid using any idioms of recent invention. In 1976, there were no cell phones, no Internet or GPS available to the public, no Facebook or other social media. Personal video recording was in its infancy and most homes could bring in less than a dozen TV channels. Although there were smaller and more efficient cars available, the standard American sedan was around eighteen feet long and got about twelve miles to the gallon. Due to the OPEC boycott, gasoline was up thirty cents from 1974, hovering around sixty-five cents a gallon..

On my 1982 visit, I was told of an ambush by rebels on civilians near Lake Atitlan, similar in some respects to the attack described in my story, but the details and events following are all my inventions. The larger cities mentioned in this story are real places; the small towns like San Miguel, though, were invented. However, none of the characters are real people,

Guatemala, 1976

nor are they fashioned after any real persons; all are fictitious. I confess that the earthquake and the rebel attack were inspirations for this story. Given that framework, I hope the result has been successful and entertaining.

Acknowledgments

Mucho Gracias to the Scanlons, Clark and Sarah, retired Baptist missionaries in Guatemala before, during and after the earthquake, for their hospitality and encouragement. In particular, I thank Clark for his book, *Hope in the Ruins,* which records his personal experiences of the event of the earthquake, and the weeks and months of recovery afterward. His book is full of details immensely helpful in the crafting of my book. Likewise, thanks go to Joe Bruce and his late wife, Shirley, now retired missionaries who arrived in Guatemala shortly after the quake, and to Yvonne Helton Bruce, another missionary who experienced the earthquake first hand. Others deserving gratitude include the army of medical volunteer medical missionaries serving in Guatemala and to many other places too numerous to list, and not to be missed, Woodmont Baptist Church in Nashville, which is still sending volunteer missionaries there to help with whatever needs there be. Also, for those I have met who were generous in sharing their insight into the workings of remotely located and shoestring-funded Christian mission clinics and hospitals. In the mid-1980s, along with a dozen or so others, I worked as a volunteer in a multi-year project on the campus of a mission hospital in remote Sierra Leone, observing first-hand the crushing difficulty of the work there, and the dedication of the staff. Finally, thank you to the volunteer missionary friends from my church who eagerly responded to the call in Guatemala, and worked valiantly in that recovery effort.

About the Author

Author, architect, and struggling Christian, Frank Orr has written widely for daily newspapers and other periodicals. He is a veteran of the Air Force and of many voluntary mission trips and advisory efforts. Widowed, he lives in Nashville, Tennessee, with close family nearby.

Made in the USA
Columbia, SC
03 August 2018